THE BAD GIRL

Mario Vargas Llosa was born in Peru in 1936. His internationally acclaimed works of fiction and non-fiction include *Conversation in the Cathedral* (1969), *Aunt Julia and the Scriptwriter* (1977), *The War of the End of the World* (1981), *The Feast of the Goat* (2000) and *The Bad Girl* (2008). In 2010, he was awarded the Nobel Prize in Literature.

MARIO VARGAS LLOSA

The Bad Girl

Translated from the Spanish by
Edith Grossman

faber and faber

First published in the UK in 2007
by Faber and Faber Limited
Bloomsbury House, 74–77 Great Russell Street,
London WC1B 3DA

This open market edition first published in 2008

Typeset by RefineCatch Ltd, Bungay, Suffolk
Printed and bound by CPI Group (UK) Ltd, Croydon, CR0 4YY

The right of Mario Vargas Llosa to be identified as author of this
work has been asserted in accordance with Section 77 of the
Copyright, Designs and Patents Act 1988

The right of Edith Grossman to be identified as translator of this
work has been asserted in accordance with Section 77 of the
Copyright, Designs and Patents Act 1988

A CIP record for this book
is available from the British Library

978-0-571-23931-3

6 8 10 9 7 5

To X, in memory of heroic times

The Chilean Girls

That was a fabulous summer. Pérez Prado and his twelve-professor orchestra came to liven up the Carnival dances at the Club Terrazas of Miraflores and the Lawn Tennis of Lima; a national mambo championship was organized in Plaza de Acho, which was a great success in spite of the threat by Cardinal Juan Gualberto Guevara, Archbishop of Lima, to excommunicate all the couples who took part; and my neighborhood, the Barrio Alegre of the Miraflores streets Diego Ferré, Juan Fanning, and Colón, competed in some Olympic games of mini-soccer, cycling, athletics, and swimming with the neighborhood of Calle San Martín, which, of course, we won.

Extraordinary things happened during that summer of 1950. For the first time Cojinoba Lañas fell for a girl—the redhead Seminauel—and she, to the surprise of all of Miraflores, said yes. Cojinoba forgot about his limp and from then on walked around the streets thrusting out his chest like Charles Atlas. Tico Tiravante broke up with Ilse and fell for Laurita, Víctor Ojeda fell for Ilse and broke up with Inge, Juan Barreto fell for Inge and broke up with Ilse. There was so much sentimental restructuring in the neighborhood that we were in a daze, people kept falling in and out of love, and when they left the Saturday night parties the couples weren't always the same as when they came in. "How indecent!" said my scandalized aunt Alberta, with whom I had lived since the death of my parents.

The waves at the Miraflores beaches broke twice, the first time in the distance, two hundred meters from shore, and that's where those of us who were brave went to ride them in without a board, and they carried us a hundred meters to the spot where they died only to re-form into huge, elegant waves and break again in a second explosion that carried bodysurfers smoothly to the pebbles on the beach.

During that extraordinary summer, at the parties in Miraflores, everybody stopped dancing waltzes, corridos, blues, boleros, and huarachas because the mambo had demolished them. The mambo, an earthquake that had all the couples—children, adolescents, and grown-ups—at the neighborhood parties moving, jumping, leaping, and cutting a figure. And certainly the same thing was happening outside Miraflores, beyond our world and our life, in Lince, Breña, Chorrillos, or the even more exotic neighborhoods of La Victoria, downtown Lima, Rímac, and El Porvenir, where we, the Miraflorans, had never set foot and didn't ever plan to set foot.

And just as we had moved on from waltzes and huarachas, sambas and polkas, to the mambo, we also moved on from skates and scooters to bicycles, and some, Tato Monje and Tony Espejo, for example, to motor scooters, and even one or two to cars, like Luchín, the overgrown kid in the neighborhood, who sometimes stole his father's Chevrolet convertible and took us for a ride along the seawalls, from Terrazas to the stream at Armendáriz, at a hundred miles an hour.

But the most notable event of that summer was the arrival in Miraflores, all the way from Chile, their distant country, of two sisters whose flamboyant appearance and unmistakable way of speaking, very fast, swallowing the last syllables of words and ending their sentences with an aspirated exclamation that sounded like *pué*, threw all of us Miraflores boys, who had just traded our short pants for long trousers, for a loop. And me more than the rest.

The younger one seemed like the older one, and vice versa. The older one was named Lily and was a little shorter than Lucy, who was a year younger. Lily couldn't have been more than fourteen or fifteen years old, and Lucy no more than thirteen or fourteen. The adjective "flamboyant" seemed invented just for them, but though Lucy was flamboyant it wasn't to the same degree as her sister, not only because her hair was shorter and not as blond as Lily's, and because she dressed more soberly, but also because she was quieter, and when it was time to dance, though she also cut a figure and moved her waist with a boldness no Miraflores girl dared attempt, she seemed like a modest, inhibited, almost colorless girl compared to that spinning top, that flame in the wind, that will-o'-the-wisp that Lily became when the records were all stacked on the automatic changer, the mambo exploded, and we started to dance.

Lily danced with a delicious rhythm and a good deal of grace, smiling and softly singing the words to the song, raising her arms, showing her knees, and moving her waist and shoulders so that her entire body, to which

3

her skirts and blouses clung so perversely and with so many curves, seemed to shake, vibrate, and take part in the dance from the ends of her hair down to her feet. Whoever danced the mambo with her always had a hard time, because how could anyone go on and not be ensnared by the demonic whirlwind of those madly leaping legs and feet? Impossible! You were left behind from the beginning, very conscious of the fact that the eyes of all the couples were focused on Lily's mambistic feats. "What a girl!" said my aunt Alberta indignantly. "She dances like Tongolele, like a *rumbera* in a Mexican movie. Well, let's not forget she's Chilean," she'd say in response to herself, "and virtue isn't the strong point of women in that country."

I fell in love with Lily like a calf, which is the most romantic way to fall in love—it was also called heating up to a hundred degrees—and during that unforgettable summer, I fell three times. The first, in the upper balcony of the Ricardo Palma, the movie theater in Parque Central in Miraflores, during the Sunday matinee, and she told me no, she was still very young to have a boyfriend. The second time, at the skating rink that opened that summer at the foot of Parque Salazar, and she told me no, she had to think about it, because though she liked me a little, her parents had asked her not to have a boyfriend until she finished the fourth year and she was still in the third. And the last time, a few days before the trouble, in the Cream Rica on Avenida Larco, while we were having a vanilla milk shake, and of course, again she said no, why would she say yes if we seemed to be going steady just the way we were? Weren't we always together at Marta's when we played truth or dare? Didn't we sit together on the Miraflores beach? Didn't she dance with me more than anybody else at parties? Then why would she give me a formal yes if all of Miraflores already thought we were going steady? With her model's looks, her dark mischievous eyes, and her small mouth with full lips, Lily was the incarnation of coquettishness.

"I like everything about you," I would tell her. "But what I like best is the way you talk." It was funny and original because of its intonation and musicality, so different from that of Peruvian girls, and also because of certain expressions, words, and sayings that left the boys in the neighborhood in the dark, trying to guess what they meant and if they contained a hidden joke. Lily spent her time saying things with double meanings, asking riddles, or telling jokes so risqué they made the girls in the neighborhood blush. "Those Chilean girls are *terrible*," my aunt Alberta declared, taking off and putting on her eyeglasses with the air of a high-school teacher concerned that those two strangers would cause the disintegration of Miraflores morality.

In the early years of the 1950s there were still no tall buildings in Miraflores, a neighborhood of one-story houses—two at the most—and gardens with their inevitable geraniums, poincianas, laurels, bougain-villeas, and lawns and verandas along which honey-suckle or ivy climbed, with rocking chairs where neighbors waited for nightfall, gossiping or inhaling the scent of the jasmine. In some parks there were ceibo trees thorny with red and pink flowers, and the straight, clean sidewalks were lined with frangipani, jacaranda, and mulberry trees, a note of color along with the flowers in the gardens and the little yellow D'Onofrio ice-cream trucks—the drivers dressed in their uniforms of white smocks and little black caps—that drove up and down the streets day and night, announcing their presence with a Klaxon whose slow ululation had the effect on me of a primitive horn, a prehistoric reminiscence. You could still hear birds singing in that Miraflores, where families cut a pine branch when their girls reached marriageable age, because if they didn't, the poor things would become old maids like my aunt Alberta.

Lily never said yes, but the fact is that except for that formality, in everything else we seemed to be going steady. We'd hold hands at matinees in the Ricardo Palma, the Leuro, the Montecarlo, and the Colina, and though it couldn't be said that in the darkness of the balcony we were making out like other, older couples—making out was a formula that included everything from anodyne kisses to the tongue-sucking and wicked touching that had to be confessed to the priest on first Fridays as mortal sins—Lily let me kiss her on the cheek, the edge of her ears, the corner of her mouth, and sometimes, for just a second, she'd touch her lips to mine and move them away with a melodramatic expression: "No, no, absolutely not that, Slim." My friends from the neighborhood made fun of me: "You're like a calf, Slim, you're turning blue, Slim, that crush is melting you, Slim." They never called me by my real name—Ricardo Somocurcio—but always by my nickname. They weren't exaggerating at all: I was so hot for Lily I was burning up.

That summer, because of her, I had a fistfight with Luquen, one of my best friends. During one of those get-togethers the girls and boys of the neighborhood would have at the corner of Colón and Diego Ferré, in the garden of the Chacaltanas, Luquen, trying to be smart, suddenly said the Chilean girls were cheap because they were bleached blondes, not real ones, and in Miraflores, behind my back, people had started to call them the Camp Followers. I aimed one straight at his chin, which he ducked, and we went to settle our differences in a fight at the corner of the Reserva seawall, next to the cliffs. We didn't speak to each other for an entire week until, at the next get-together, the girls and boys of the neighborhood made us be friends again.

Every afternoon Lily liked to go to a corner of Parque Salazar overgrown with palm trees, floripondios, and bellflowers, and from the red-brick wall we would contemplate all of Lima bay like the captain of a ship contemplating the sea from the bridge. If the sky was clear—and I'd swear the sky was cloudless all that summer and the sun shone on Miraflores every single day—in the background, on the ocean's horizon, you could see the red disk in flames, taking its leave with blazing beams and fiery lights as it sank into the waters of the Pacific. Lily's face focused with the same fervor she brought to taking communion at twelve o'clock Mass at the Parque Central church, her gaze fixed on the incandescent ball, waiting for the moment when the sea swallowed up the last beam to formulate the wish that the great star, or God, would grant. I had a wish too, only half believing it would come true. Always the same one, of course: that she would finally say yes, that we'd go steady, make out, love each other, become engaged, and marry and end up in Paris, rich and happy.

From the time I reached the age of reason I had dreamed of living in Paris. My papa was probably to blame, and those books by Paul Féval, Jules Verne, Alexandre Dumas, and so many others he made me read before he died in the accident that left me an orphan. Those novels filled my head with adventures and convinced me that in France life was richer, happier, more beautiful, more everything than anywhere else. That was why, in addition to my English classes at the Instituto Peruano Norteamericano, I persuaded my aunt Alberta to enroll me at the Alliance Française on Avenida Wilson, where I'd go three times a week to learn the language of the Frenchies. Though I liked to have a good time with my pals from the neighborhood, I was a real bookworm, got good grades, and loved languages.

When my funds allowed, I'd invite Lily to have tea—to say *lonche* hadn't become fashionable yet—at the Tiendecita Blanca, with its snow-white façade, its little tables and umbrellas on the sidewalk, its pastries out of the *Arabian Nights*—iced ladyfingers! almond-and-honey cakes filled with blancmange! cream puffs!—bounded by Avenida Larco, Avenida Arequipa, and the Alameda Ricardo Palma shaded by exceedingly tall Ficus trees.

Going to the Tiendecita Blanca with Lily for ice cream and a piece of pastry was a joy almost always clouded by the presence of Lucy, her sister, whom I also had to drag along every time we went out. She was not at all uncomfortable being the third wheel, interfering with my making out, preventing me from talking alone with Lily and telling her all the pretty things I dreamed of murmuring into her ear. But even though our conversation had to avoid certain subjects because Lucy was nearby, it was priceless to be with her, to see how her curls danced whenever she moved her head, the mischievousness in her eyes the color of dark honey, to hear that way she had of talking, and at certain careless moments, at the low-cut neckline of her close-fitting blouse, to catch a glimpse of the tops of those round little breasts that were already pointing out, tender buds undoubtedly as firm and soft as young fruits.

"I don't know what I'm doing here like a third wheel with you two," Lucy would sometimes say apologetically. I lied to her: "What an idea, we're happy to have your company, aren't we, Lily?" Lily would laugh with a mocking demon in her eyes and that exclamation: "Sure, *puuuuu . . .*"

Taking a stroll along Avenida Pardo under the alameda of Ficus trees invaded by songbirds, between the houses on both sides of the street where little boys and girls, watched over by nannies in starched white uniforms, ran around gardens and verandas, was a ritual of that summer. Since Lucy's presence made it difficult for me to talk to Lily about the things I would have liked to talk about, I steered our conversation toward insipid subjects: plans for the future, for example, like going to Paris to fill a diplomatic post when I had my law degree—because there, in Paris, living was living, France was the country of culture—or perhaps going into politics to help our poor Peru become great and prosperous again, which would mean I'd have to postpone traveling to Europe for a little while. And what about them, what would they like to be, to do, when they grew up? Sensible Lucy had very precise objectives: "First of all, finish school. Then, get a good job, maybe in a record store, that must be a lot of fun." Lily was thinking of a travel agency or being a stewardess for an airline, if she could convince her parents, that way she'd travel free all around the world. Or maybe a movie star, but she'd never let them take a picture of her in a bikini. Traveling, traveling, seeing every country was what she'd like the most. "Well, at least you've already seen two, Chile and Peru, what else do you want?" I'd say. "Compare that to me, I've never even left Miraflores."

The things Lily recounted about Santiago were for me a foretaste of Parisian heaven. I listened to her with so much envy! In that city, unlike here, there were no poor people or beggars in the streets, parents allowed boys and girls to stay at parties until dawn and dance cheek to cheek, and unlike here, you never saw old people like mothers and aunts spying on young people when they danced just to scold them if they went too far. In Chile boys and girls were allowed to see adult movies and, from the time they were fifteen, smoke without hiding. Life was more fun there than in Lima because there were more movies, circuses, theaters, shows, and parties with live orchestras, and iceskating shows and ballet companies and musicals were always coming to Santiago from the United States, and no matter what job they had, Chileans earned two or three times more than Peruvians did.

But if all this was true, why had the parents of the Chilean girls left that marvelous country and come to Peru? Because at first glance they weren't rich but very poor. For the moment they didn't live the way we did, the girls and boys of Barrio Alegre, in houses with butlers, cooks, maids, and gardeners, but in a little apartment in a narrow, three-story building on Calle Esperanza, near the Gambrinus restaurant. And in the Miraflores of those years, in contrast to what would happen sometime later when tall buildings began to spring up and the little houses disappeared, the only people who lived in apartments were the poor, that diminished species of human to which—ah, how sad— the Chilean girls seemed to belong.

I never saw their parents. They never took me or any neighborhood girl or boy home. They never celebrated a birthday or gave a party or invited us to have tea and play, as if they were ashamed to let us see the modesty of the place where they lived. The fact that they were poor and embarrassed by everything they didn't have filled me with compassion, increased my love for the Chilean girl, and inspired me with altruistic plans: "When Lily and I get married, we'll bring her whole family to live with us."

But my Miraflores friends, especially the girls, were suspicious about Lucy and Lily never opening their doors to us. "Are they so hungry they can't even organize a party?" they asked. "Maybe it's not because they're poor, maybe they're just stingy," said Tico Tiravante, trying to make things better and only making them worse.

The kids in the neighborhood suddenly began to speak badly of the Chilean girls because of their makeup and the clothes they wore, making fun of their scant wardrobe—we all knew by heart those skirts, blouses, and sandals that they combined in every possible way to hide the fact they had so little—and filled with righteous indignation, I'd defend them saying that this talk was just envy, green envy, poisonous envy, because at parties the Chilean girls never sat out a dance, all the boys lined up to dance with them — "They let them rub up, of course they don't sit out a dance," replied Laura — or because, at the get-togethers in the neighborhood, at games, at the beach, or in Parque Salazar, they were always the center of attention and all the boys crowded around them, while the rest of the girls . . . "They're show-offs and brazen and with them you boys dare to tell the dirty jokes we wouldn't let you tell us!" Teresita counterattacked. And, finally, because the Chilean girls were great-looking, modern, smart, while the Barrio Alegre girls were prudish, backward, old-fashioned, narrow-minded, and bigoted. "And proud of it!" said Ilse, mocking us.

But even though they gossiped about them, the girls from Barrio Alegre kept inviting the Chilean girls to parties and going with them in a group to the Miraflores beaches, to twelve o'clock Mass on Sundays, to matinees, and to take the obligatory stroll around Parque Salazar from dusk until the first stars came out, which twinkled in the Lima sky that summer from January to March without, I'm certain, being hidden for a single day by clouds, something that happens four-fifths of the year in this city. They did this because we boys asked them to, and because, at heart, the girls of Miraflores were as fascinated by the Chileans as the bird is by the cobra that hypnotizes it before swallowing it, as the saint is by the sinner, the angel by the devil. They envied in these foreigners from the remote land of Chile the freedom they didn't have to go everywhere, to stay out walking or dancing until very late without asking permission for just a little while longer, and without their papa, their mama, their older sister or aunt coming to spy through the windows at a party to see with whom they were dancing and how, or to take them home because it was already midnight, a time when decent girls weren't dancing or talking on the street with men—that's what show-offs, cheap girls, and mixed breeds did—but were in their own houses and their own beds, dreaming of the angels. They envied the fact that the Chilean girls were so free and easy and danced so boldly, not caring if they showed their knees, and moving their shoulders, their small breasts, their bottoms, as no Miraflores girl did, and probably allowing the boys liberties the girls didn't even dare to imagine. But, if they were so free, why didn't either Lily or Lucy want a steady boyfriend? Why did they turn down all of us who fell for them? Lily hadn't said no only to me; she also turned down Lalo Molfino and Lucho Claux, and Lucy had turned down Loyer, Pepe Cánepa, and the early-maturing Julio Bienvenida, the first Miraflores boy whose parents, even before he finished school, gave him a Volkswagen for his fifteenth birthday. Why didn't the Chilean girls, who were so free, want boyfriends?

That and other mysteries related to Lily and Lucy were unexpectedly clarified on March 30, 1950, the last day of that memorable summer, at the party given by Marirosa Álvarez-Calderón, the fat little pig. A party that would define an era and remain forever in the memories of everyone who was there. The Álvarez-Calderón house, at the corner of 28 de Julio and La Paz, was the prettiest in Miraflores, and perhaps in Peru, with its gardens of tall trees, yellow *tipa* flowers, liana vines, rosebushes, and its blue-tiled pool. Marirosa's parties always had a band and a swarm of waiters serving pastries, canapés, sandwiches, juice, and different kinds of nonalcoholic drinks all night, parties for which the guests prepared as if we were ascending to heaven. Everything was going wonderfully until, with the lights turned down, a crowd of girls and boys surrounded Marirosa and sang "Happy Birthday," and she blew out the fifteen candles on the cake and we got in line to give her the required embrace.

When it was the turn of Lily and Lucy to give her a hug, Marirosa, a happy little pig whose rolls of fat overflowed her pink dress with the bow in the back, kissed them on the cheek and opened her eyes wide.

"You're Chileans, right? I'm going to introduce you to my aunt Adriana. She's Chilean too, she just arrived from Santiago. Come on, come on."

She took them by the hand and led them inside the house, shouting, "Aunt Adriana, Aunt Adriana, I have a surprise for you."

Through the glass of the long picture window, an illuminated rectangle that framed a large living room with a fireplace, walls with landscapes and oil portraits, easy chairs, sofas, carpets, and a dozen ladies and gentlemen holding glasses, I saw Marirosa burst in a few seconds later with the Chilean girls, and I also saw, pale and fleeting, the silhouette of a very tall, very well-dressed, very beautiful woman with a cigarette in a long holder, coming forward to greet her young compatriots with a condescending smile.

I went to drink some mango juice and sneak a

Viceroy between the cabanas at the pool. There I ran into Juan Barreto, my friend and classmate at the Colegio Champagnat, who had also come to hide in these abandoned places to have a smoke. He asked me point-blank, "Would you care if I asked Lily, Slim?"

He knew that even though it looked as if we were going steady, we weren't, and he also knew—like everybody else, he pointed out—that I had asked her three times and three times she had turned me down. I replied that I cared a lot, because even though Lily had turned me down this wasn't a game she was playing—it's the way girls were in Chile—but in fact she liked me, it was as if we were going steady, and besides, that night I'd begun to ask her again for the fourth and definitive time, and she was about to say yes when the cake with the fifteen candles for the fat little pig interrupted us. But now, when she came out after talking to Marirosa's aunt, I'd go on asking her and she'd say yes and after tonight she would be my absolutely genuine girlfriend.

"Well, then, I'll have to ask Lucy," said Juan Barreto with resignation. "The lousy thing is, compadre, the one I really like is Lily."

I encouraged him to ask Lucy and I promised to put in a good word for him so she'd say yes. He and Lucy and Lily and I would be a sensational foursome.

Talking with Juan Barreto next to the pool and watching the couples on the dance floor as they moved to the beat of the Ormeño Brothers Orchestra—they might not have been Pérez Prado but they were very good, what trumpets, what drums—we smoked a couple of Viceroys. Why had it occurred to Marirosa to introduce her aunt to Lucy and Lily just at that moment?

What were they babbling about for so long? They were ruining my plan, damn it. Because it was true, when they announced the cake with the fifteen candles I had begun my fourth—and successful this time, I was sure—declaration of love to Lily after convincing the band to play "I Like You," the best bolero for proposing to girls.

They took forever to come back. And they came back transformed: Lucy very pale, with dark circles under her eyes, as if she'd seen a ghost and was recovering from the strong effects of the next world, and Lily in a rage, an embittered expression on her face, her eyes flashing, as if there in the house those fashionable ladies and gentlemen had given her a very hard time. Right then I asked her to dance, one of those mambos that was her specialty—"Mambo No. 5"—and I couldn't believe it, Lily couldn't do anything right, she lost the beat, became distracted, made mistakes, stumbled, and her little sailor's hat slipped, making her look fairly ridiculous. She didn't even bother to straighten it. What had happened?

I'm sure that by the time "Mambo No. 5" was over, the entire party knew because the fat little pig made it her responsibility to tell everyone. What pleasure that gossip must have felt as she told everything in detail, coloring and exaggerating the story while she opened her eyes wide, wider, with curiosity and horror and joy! What unhealthy happiness—what satisfaction and revenge—all the girls from the neighborhood must have felt, the ones who so envied the Chilean girls who came to Miraflores to revolutionize the customs of the children graduating into adolescence that summer!

I was the last to find out, when Lily and Lucy had already mysteriously disappeared, without saying good-bye to Marirosa or anybody else—"Champing at the bit with embarrassment," my aunt Alberta would declare—and when the awesome rumor had spread all over the dance floor and cleared away the boys and girls who forgot about the band, their boyfriends and girlfriends, and making out, and went off to whisper, repeat, be alarmed, be exalted, and open wide their eyes brimming over with malice: "You know? You found out? You heard? What do you think? Can you believe it? Can you imagine? Imagine! They're not Chileans! No, no they weren't! Nothing but a story! They're not Chileans, they don't know a thing about Chile! They lied! They fooled us! They invented everything! Marirosa's aunt found them out! What a pair of bandits, what bandits!"

They were Peruvians, that's all they were. Poor things! Poor things! Aunt Adriana, who'd just arrived from Santiago, must have had the surprise of her life when she heard them speak with the accent that had fooled us but which she identified immediately as fake. How bad the Chilean girls must have felt when the fat little pig's aunt, suspecting the farce, began to ask about their family in Santiago, the neighborhood where they lived in Santiago, the school they attended in Santiago, about the relatives and friends of their family in Santiago, making Lucy and Lily swallow the bitterest pill of their short lives, becoming crueler and crueler until she hounded them from the living room and they were in ruins, spiritually and physically demolished, and she could proclaim to her relatives and friends and the stupefied Marirosa: "In a pig's eye they're Chileans! Those girls never set foot in Santiago, and if they're Chileans, I'm Tibetan!"

That last day of the summer of 1950—I had just turned fifteen too—was the beginning of real life for me, the life that separates castles in the air, illusions, and fables from harsh reality.

I never knew with any certainty the complete story of the false Chileans, and neither did anyone else except the two girls, but I did hear conjectures, gossip, fantasies, and supposed revelations that, like a wake of rumors, followed the counterfeit Chileans for a long time even after they ceased to exist—in a manner of speaking— because they were never again invited to parties, or games, or teas, or neighborhood get-togethers. Malicious gossips said that even though the decent girls from Barrio Alegre and Miraflores no longer had any-thing to do with them and looked away if they passed them on the street, the boys, the fellows, the men did go after them, in secret, the way they went after cheap girls—and what else were Lily and Lucy but two cheap girls from some neighborhood like Breña or El Porvenir who, to conceal their origins, had passed themselves off as foreigners and slipped in among the decent people of Miraflores?—to make out with them, to do those things that only half-breeds and cheap girls let men do.

Later on, I imagine, they began to forget about Lily and Lucy, because other people, other matters eventually replaced that adventure of the last summer of our child-hood. But I didn't. I didn't forget them, especially not Lily. And even though so many years have gone by, and Miraflores has changed so much, as have our customs, and barriers and prejudices have been obscured that once had been flaunted with insolence and now are disguised, I keep her in my memory, and evoke her again at times, and hear the mischievous laugh and see the mocking glance of her eyes the color of dark honey, and watch her swaying like a reed to the rhythms of the mambo. And still think that, in spite of my having lived for so many summers, that one was the most fabulous of all.

2

The Guerrilla Fighter

The México Lindo was on the corner of Rue des Canettes and Rue Guisard, near Place Saint-Sulpice, and during my first year in Paris, when money was very tight, on many nights I'd station myself at the restaurant's back door and wait for Paúl to appear with a little package of tamales, tortillas, carnitas, or enchiladas that I would take to my garret in the Hôtel du Sénat to eat before they got cold. Paúl had started out at the México Lindo as a kitchen boy, and in a short time, thanks to his culinary skills, he was promoted to chef's assistant, and by the time he left it all to dedicate himself body and soul to the revolution, he was the restaurant's regular cook.

In those early days of the 1960s, Paris was experiencing the fever of the Cuban Revolution and teeming with young people from the five continents who, like Paúl, dreamed of repeating in their own countries the exploits of Fidel Castro and his bearded ones, and prepared for that, in earnest or in jest, in café conspiracies. In addition to earning his living at the México Lindo, when I met him a few days after my arrival in Paris, Paúl was taking biology courses at the Sorbonne, which he also abandoned for the sake of the revolution.

21

We became friends at a little café in the Latin Quarter where a group of South Americans would meet, the kind Sebastián Salazar Bondy wrote about in *Poor People of Paris*, a book of short stories. When he learned of my financial difficulties, Paúl offered to give me a hand as far as food was concerned because there was more than enough at the México Lindo. If I came to the back door at about ten at night, he would offer me a "free, hot banquet," something he had already done for other compatriots in need.

He couldn't have been more than twenty-four or twenty-five years old, and he was very, very fat—a barrel with legs—and good-hearted, friendly, and talkative. He always had a big smile on his face, which inflated his plump cheeks even more. In Peru he had studied medicine for several years and served some time in prison for being one of the organizers of the famous strike at the University of San Marcos in 1952, during the dictatorship of General Manuel Odría. Before coming to Paris he spent a couple of years in Madrid, where he married a girl from Burgos. They'd just had a baby.

He lived in the Marais, which in those days, before André Malraux, General de Gaulle's minister of culture, undertook his great cleanup and restoration of old, dilapidated mansions covered by the grime of the seventeenth and eighteenth centuries, was a neighborhood of poor artisans, cabinetmakers, cobblers, tailors, Jews, and a large number of indigent students and artists. In addition to those rapid encounters at the service entrance of the México Lindo, we would also get together at midday at La Petite Source on the Carrefour de l'Odéon or on the terrace of Le Cluny, at the corner of

Saint-Michel and Saint-Germain, to drink coffee and recount our adventures. Mine consisted exclusively of multiple efforts to find a job, something that was not at all easy since no one in Paris was impressed by my law degree from a Peruvian university or by my being fairly fluent in English and French. His had to do with preparations for the revolution that would make Peru the second Socialist Republic of Latin America. One day he suddenly asked if I'd be interested in going to Cuba on a scholarship to receive military training, and I told Paúl that even though I felt all the sympathy in the world for him, I had absolutely no interest in politics; in fact, I despised politics, and all my dreams were focused— excuse my petit bourgeois mediocrity, compadre—on getting a nice steady job that would let me spend, in the most ordinary way, the rest of my days in Paris. I also told him not to tell me anything about his conspiracies, I didn't want to live with the anxiety of accidentally revealing some information that might harm him and his associates.

"Don't worry. I trust you, Ricardo."

He did, in fact, to the extent that he ignored what I'd said. He told me everything he was doing and even the most intimate complications of their revolutionary preparations. Paúl belonged to the Movement of the Revolutionary Left, or MIR, founded by Luis de la Puente Uceda, who had repudiated the center-left American Popular Revolutionary Alliance, or APRA. The Cuban government had given MIR a hundred scholarships for young Peruvians to receive guerrilla training. These were the years of the confrontation between Beijing and Moscow, and at that moment it seemed as if

Cuba was leaning toward the Maoist line, though later, for practical reasons, she eventually allied with the Soviets. The scholarship recipients, because of the strict blockade imposed on the island by the United States, had to pass through Paris on the way to their destination, and Paúl was hard-pressed to find them places to stay during their Parisian stopover.

I gave him a hand with these logistical chores, helping him reserve rooms in miserable little hotels — "for Arabs," Paúl would say — where we crowded the future guerrilla fighters by twos, and sometimes even by threes, in a small, squalid room or in the *chambre de bonne* of some Latin American or Frenchman disposed to adding his grain of sand to the cause of world revolution. In my garret in the Hôtel du Sénat, on Rue Saint-Sulpice, I sometimes put up one of the scholarship recipients behind the back of Madame Auclair, the manager.

They constituted an extremely diverse collection of fauna. Many were students of literature, law, economics, science, and education at San Marcos, who had joined the Young Communists or other leftist organizations, and in addition to Limenians there were kids from the provinces, and even some peasants, Indians from Puno, Cuzco, and Ayacucho, bewildered by the leap from their Andean villages and communities, where they had some-how been recruited, to Paris. They looked at everything in bewilderment. From the few words I exchanged with them on the way from Orly to their hotels, they some-times gave the impression of not being too sure what kind of scholarship they were going to enjoy and not really understanding what kind of training they would receive. Not all of them had been given their scholarships in Peru. Some had received them in Paris, chosen from the variegated mass of Peruvians—students, artists, adventurers, bohemians—who prowled the Latin Quarter. Among them, the most original was my friend Alfonso the Spiritualist, sent to France by a theosophical sect in Lima to pursue studies in parapsychology and theosophy, but Paúl's eloquence swept away the spirits and installed him in the world of the revolution. He was a pale, timid boy who barely opened his mouth, and there was something emaciated and distracted in him, a precocious kind of spirit. In our midday conversations at Le Cluny or La Petite Source, I suggested to Paúl that many of the scholarship recipients the MIR was sending to Cuba, and sometimes to North Korea or the People's Republic of China, were simply taking advantage of the chance to do a little tourism and would never climb the Andes or go down into Amazonia with rifles on their shoulders and packs on their backs.

"It's all been calculated, *mon vieux*," Paúl replied, sitting like a magistrate who has the laws of history on his side. "If half of them respond to us, the revolution is a sure thing."

True, the MIR was doing things a little quickly, but how could they enjoy the luxury of sleeping? History, after moving for so many years like a tortoise, had suddenly become a meteor, thanks to Cuba. It was necessary to act, learn, stumble, get up again. This wasn't the time to recruit young guerrillas by making them submit to examinations of their knowledge, to physical trials or psychological tests. The important thing was to take advantage of those one hundred scholarships before

Cuba offered them to other groups—the Communist Party, the Liberation Front, the Trotskyists—who were competing to be the first to set the Peruvian revolution in motion.

Most of the scholarship recipients I picked up at Orly to take to the hotels and boardinghouses where they would spend their time in Paris were male and very young, some of them adolescents. One day I discovered there were also women among them.

"Pick them up and take them to this little hotel on Rue Gay Lussac," Paúl said. "Comrade Ana, Comrade Arlette, and Comrade Eufrasia. Be nice to them."

One rule the scholarship recipients had been carefully taught was not to disclose their real names. Even among themselves they used only their nicknames or noms de guerre. As soon as the three girls showed up, I had the impression I'd seen Comrade Arlette somewhere before.

Comrade Ana was a dark-skinned girl with lively gestures, a little older than the others, and from the things I heard her say that morning and the two or three other times I saw her, she must have been the head of a teachers' union. Comrade Eufrasia, a little Chinese girl with delicate bones, looked like a fifteen-year-old. She was exhausted because on the long flight she hadn't slept a wink and had vomited a few times because of turbulence. Comrade Arlette had an attractive shape, a slim waist, pale skin, and though she dressed, like the others, with great simplicity—coarse skirts and sweaters, percale blouses, flat shoes, and the kind of hairpins sold in markets—there was something very feminine in her manner of walking and moving and, above all, in the way she pursed her full lips as she asked about the streets the taxi was driving along. In her dark, expressive eyes, something eager was twinkling as she contemplated the tree-lined boulevards, the symmetrical buildings, the crowd of young people of both sexes carrying bags, books, and notebooks as they prowled the streets and *bistrots* in the area around the Sorbonne, while we approached the little hotel on Rue Gay Lussac. They were given a room with no bath and no windows, and two beds for the three of them. When I left, I repeated Paúl's instructions: they weren't to move from here until he came to see them, sometime in the afternoon, and explained the plan for their work in Paris.

I was in the doorway of the hotel, lighting a cigarette before I walked away, when somebody touched my shoulder.

"That room gives me claustrophobia," Comrade Arlette said with a smile. "And besides, a person doesn't come to Paris every day, *caramba*."

Then I recognized her. She had changed a great deal, of course, especially in the way she spoke, but the mischievousness I remembered so well still poured out of her, something bold, spontaneous, provocative, that was revealed in her defiant posture, her small breasts and face thrust forward, one foot set slightly back, her ass high, and a mocking glance that left her interlocutor not knowing if she was speaking seriously or joking. She was short, with small feet and hands, and her hair, black now instead of light, and tied back with a ribbon, fell to her shoulders. And she had that dark honey in her eyes.

I let her know that what we were going to do was categorically forbidden and for that reason Comrade Jean (Paúl) would be angry with us, then I took her for a walk

27

past the Panthéon, the Sorbonne, the Odéon, the Luxembourg Gardens, and finally—far too expensive for my budget!—to have lunch at L'Acropole, a little Greek restaurant on Rue de l'Ancienne Comédie. In those three hours of conversation she told me, in violation of all the rules regarding revolutionary secrecy, that she had studied letters and law at Catholic University, had been a member of the clandestine Young Communists for years, and, like other comrades, had moved to the MIR because it was a real revolutionary movement as opposed to the YC, a sclerotic and anachronistic party in the present day. She told me these things somewhat mechanically, without too much conviction. I recounted my ongoing efforts to find work so I could stay in Paris and told her that now I had all my hopes focused on an examination for Spanish translators, sponsored by UNESCO, that would be given the following day.

"Cross your fingers and knock the table three times, like this, so you'll pass," Comrade Arlette said, very seriously, as she stared at me.

To provoke her, I asked if these kinds of superstition were compatible with the scientific doctrine of Marxism-Leninism.

"To get what you want, anything goes," she replied immediately, very resolute. But then she shrugged and said with a smile, "I'll also say a rosary for you to pass, even though I'm not a believer. Will you denounce me to the party for being superstitious? I don't think so. You look like a nice guy . . ."

She gave a little laugh, and when she did, the same dimples she'd had as a girl formed on her cheeks. I walked her back to the hotel. If she agreed, I'd ask

Comrade Jean's permission to take her to see other places in Paris before she continued her revolutionary journey. "Terrific," she replied, giving me a languid hand that she did not withdraw from mine right away. This was one very pretty, very flirtatious guerrilla fighter.

The next morning I passed the exam for translators at UNESCO with about twenty other applicants. We were given half a dozen fairly easy texts in English and French to translate. I hesitated over the phrase "*art roman*," which I first translated as "Roman art" but then, in the revision, I realized it referred to "Romanesque art." At midday I went with Paúl to eat sausage and fried potatoes at La Petite Source, and with no preambles asked his permission to take out Comrade Arlette while she was in Paris. He gave me a sly look and pretended to reprimand me.

"It is categorically forbidden to fuck female comrades. In Cuba and the People's Republic of China, during the revolution, screwing a comrade could mean the firing squad. Why do you want to take her out? Do you like the girl?"

"I suppose I do," I confessed, somewhat embarrassed. "But if it's going to make problems for you . . ."

"Then you'd control your lust?" Paúl laughed. "Don't be a hypocrite, Ricardo! Take her out, and don't let me know about it. Afterward, though, you'll tell me everything. And most important, use a condom."

That same afternoon I went to pick up Comrade Arlette at her little hotel on Rue Gay Lussac and took her to eat steak frites at La Petite Hostellerie, on Rue de la Harpe. And then to L'Escale, a small boîte de nuit on

Rue Monsieur le Prince, where in those days Carmencita, a Spanish girl dressed all in black like Juliette Gréco, accompanied herself on guitar and sang, or, I should say, recited old poems and republican songs from the Spanish Civil War. We had rum and Coca-Cola, a drink that was already being called a cuba libre. The club was small, dark, smoky, and hot, the songs epic or melancholy, not many people were there yet, and before we finished our drinks and after I told her that thanks to her magical arts and her rosary I'd done well on the UNESCO exam, I grasped her hand and, interlacing my fingers with hers, asked if she realized I'd been in love with her for ten years.

She burst into laughter.

"In love with me without knowing me? Do you mean that for ten years you've been hoping that one day a girl like me would turn up in your life?"

"We know each other very well, it's just that you don't remember," I replied, very slowly, watching her reaction. "Back then, your name was Lily and you were passing yourself off as Chilean."

I thought that surprise would make her pull back her hand or clench it convulsively in a nervous movement, but nothing like that happened. She left her hand lying quietly in mine, not agitated in the least.

"What are you saying?" she murmured. In the half-light, she leaned forward and her face came so close to mine that I could feel her breath. Her eyes scrutinized me, trying to read my mind.

"Can you still imitate the Chilean singsong so well?" I asked, as I kissed her hand. "Don't tell me you don't know what I'm talking about. Don't you remember I

30

asked you to go steady three times and you always turned me down flat?"

"Ricardo, Ricardito, Richard Somocurcio!" she exclaimed, amused, and now I did feel the pressure of her hand. "The skinny kid! That well-behaved snot-nose who was so proper he seemed to have taken Holy Communion the night before. Ha-ha! That was you. Oh, how funny! Even back then you had a sanctimonious look."

Still, a moment later, when I asked her how and why it had occurred to her and her sister, Lucy, to pass themselves off as Chileans when they moved to Calle Esperanza, in Miraflores, she absolutely denied knowing what I was talking about. How could I have made up a thing like that? I was thinking about somebody else. She never had been named Lily, and didn't have a sister, and never had lived in that neighborhood of rich snobs. That would be her attitude from then on: denying the story of the Chilean girls, though sometimes, for instance that night at L'Escale, when she said she recognized in me the idiotic little snot-nose from ten years back, she let something slip—an image, an allusion—that revealed she was in fact the false Chilean girl of our adolescence.

We stayed at L'Escale until three in the morning, and though she let me kiss and caress her, she didn't respond. She didn't move her lips away when I touched them with mine but made no corresponding movement, she allowed herself to be kissed but was indifferent and, of course, she never opened her mouth to let me swallow her saliva. Her body, too, seemed like an iceberg when my hands caressed her waist, her shoulders, and paused at her hard little breasts with erect nipples. She remained still, passive, resigned to this effusiveness, like a queen accepting the homage of a vassal, until, at last, noticing that my caresses were becoming bolder, she casually pushed me away.

"This is my fourth declaration of love, Chilean girl," I said at the door to the little hotel on Rue Gay Lussac. "Is the answer finally yes?"

"We'll see." And she blew me a kiss and moved away. "Never lose hope, good boy."

For the ten days that followed this encounter, Comrade Arlette and I had something that resembled a honeymoon. We saw each other every day and I went through all the cash I still had from Aunt Alberta's money orders. I took her to the Louvre and the Jeu de Paume, the Rodin Museum and the houses of Balzac and Victor Hugo, the Cinémathèque on Rue d'Ulm, a performance at the National Popular Theater directed by Jean Vilar (we saw Chekhov's *Ce fou de Platonov*, in which Vilar himself played the protagonist), and on Sunday we rode the train to Versailles, where, after visiting the palace, we took a long walk in the woods and were caught in a rainstorm and soaked to the skin. In those days anyone would have taken us for lovers because we always held hands and I used any excuse to kiss and caress her. She allowed me to do this, at times amused, at other times indifferent, always putting an end to my effusiveness with an impatient expression. "That's enough now, Ricardito." On rare occasions she would take the initiative and arrange or muss my hair with her hand or pass a slender finger along my nose or mouth as if she wanted to smooth them, a caress like that of an affectionate mistress with her poodle.

From the intimacy of those ten days I came to a conclusion: Comrade Arlette didn't give a damn about politics in general or the revolution in particular. Her membership in the Young Communists and then in the MIR was probably a lie, not to mention her studies at Catholic University. She not only never talked about political or university subjects, but when I brought the conversation around to that terrain, she didn't know what to say, was ignorant of the most elementary things, and managed to change the subject very quickly. It was evident she had obtained this guerrilla fighter's scholarship in order to get out of Peru and travel around the world, something that as a girl of very humble origins— that much was glaringly obvious—she never could have done otherwise. But I didn't have the courage to question her about any of this; I didn't want to put her on the spot and force her to tell me another lie.

On the eighth day of our chaste honeymoon she agreed, unexpectedly, to spend the night with me at the Hôtel du Sénat. It was something I had asked for—had begged for—in vain, on all the previous days. This time, she took the initiative.

"I'll go with you today, if you like," she said at night as we were eating a couple of baguettes with Gruyère cheese (I didn't have the money for a restaurant) in a *bistrot* on Rue de Tournon. My heart raced as if I had just run a marathon.

After an awkward negotiation with the watchman at the Hôtel du Sénat—"*Pas de visites nocturnes à l'hôtel, monsieur!*"—which left Comrade Arlette undaunted, we climbed the five flights with no elevator up to my garret. She let herself be kissed, caressed, undressed, always

33

with that curious attitude of nonparticipation, not allowing me to lessen the invisible distance she kept from my kisses, embraces, and affection, even though she surrendered her body to me. It moved me to see her naked on the narrow bed in the corner of the room where the ceiling sloped and the light from the single bulb barely reached. She was very thin, with well-proportioned limbs and a waist so narrow I thought I could have encircled it with my hands. Under the small patch of hair on her pubis, the skin seemed lighter than on the rest of her body. Her olive skin, with Oriental reminiscences, was soft and cool. She allowed herself to be kissed from head to toe, maintaining her usual passivity, and she heard, like someone listening to the rain, Neruda's "Material nupcial," which I recited into her ear, along with my stammered words of love: this was the happiest night of my life, I had never wanted anyone the way I wanted her, I would always love her.

"Let's get under the blanket, it's very cold," she interrupted, bringing me down to mundane reality. "It's a wonder you don't freeze in here."

I was about to ask if she ought to take care of me, but I didn't, confused by her attitude of self-assurance, as if she'd had centuries of experience in these encounters and I was the novice. We made love with difficulty. She gave herself without the slightest embarrassment, but she was very narrow, and in each of my efforts to penetrate she shrank back, grimacing in pain: "Slower, slower." Finally, I did make love to her and was happy loving her. It was true my greatest joy was to be there with her, it was true that in my few and always fleeting affairs I'd never felt the combination of tenderness and desire that

34

she inspired in me, but I doubt this was also the case for Comrade Arlette. Instead, throughout it all she gave the impression of doing what she did without really caring about it.

The next morning, when I opened my eyes, I saw her at the foot of the bed, washed and dressed and observing me with a look that revealed a profound uneasiness.

"Are you really in love with me?"

I said I was, several times, and extended my hand to take hers, but she didn't hold hers out to me.

"Do you want me to stay here and live with you, in Paris?" she asked in the tone of voice she might have used to suggest going to the movies to see one of the nouvelle vague films by Godard, Truffaut, or Louis Malle, which were at the height of their popularity.

Again I said yes, totally disconcerted. Did that mean the Chilean girl had fallen in love with me?

"It isn't for love, why lie to you?" she replied coldly. "But I don't want to go to Cuba, and I want to go back to Peru even less. I'd like to stay in Paris. You can help me get out of my commitment to the MIR. Talk to Comrade Jean, and if he releases me, I'll come and live with you." She hesitated a moment and, with a sigh, made a concession: "I might even end up falling in love with you."

On the ninth day I talked to fat Paúl during our midday meeting, this time at Le Cluny, with two *croque monsieurs* and two espressos in front of us. He was categorical.

"I can't release her, only the MIR leadership could do that. But even so, just proposing this would create a huge damn problem for me. Let her go to Cuba, take the course, and demonstrate she's in no physical or psychological condition for armed struggle. Then I could suggest to the leadership that she stay here as my assistant. Tell her that, and above all, tell her not to discuss this with anybody. I'm the one who'd be fucked, *mon vieux.*"

With an aching heart I went to tell Comrade Arlette Paúl's answer. And, worst of all, I encouraged her to follow his advice. Our having to separate hurt me more than her. But we couldn't harm Paúl, and she had to avoid antagonizing the MIR because that could cause her problems in the future. The course lasted a few months. Right from the beginning she would need to demonstrate complete ineptitude for guerrilla life and even pretend to faint. In the meantime, here in Paris, I'd find work, rent a small apartment, and be waiting for her . . .

"I know, you'll cry, you'll miss me, you'll think about me day and night," she interrupted with an impatient gesture, her eyes hard and her voice icy. "All right, I can see there's no other way. We'll see each other in three months, Ricardito."

"Why are you saying goodbye now?"

"Didn't Comrade Jean tell you? I leave for Cuba early tomorrow, by way of Prague. Now you can begin to shed your goodbye tears."

She did, in fact, leave the next day, and I couldn't go with her to the airport because Paúl forbade it. At our next meeting, the fat man left me totally demoralized when he announced I couldn't write to Comrade Arlette or receive letters from her because, for reasons of security, the scholarship recipients had to cut off all communication during training. Once the course had ended, Paúl wasn't even sure if Comrade Arlette would pass through Paris again on her way back to Lima.

For days I was like a zombie, reproaching myself day and night for not having had the courage to tell Comrade Arlette that in spite of Paúl's prohibition she should stay with me in Paris, instead of urging her to go on with this adventure that would end only God knew how. Until, one morning, when I left my garret to have breakfast at the Café de la Marie on Place Saint-Sulpice, Madame Auclair handed me an envelope with a UNESCO imprint. I had passed the exam, and the head of the department of translators had made an appointment with me at his office. He was a gray-haired, elegant Spaniard whose family name was Charnés. He was very amiable. He laughed readily when he asked me about my "long-term plans" and I said, "To die of old age in Paris." There was no opening yet for a permanent position, but he could hire me as a "temp" during the general assembly and when the agency was overwhelmed with work, something that happened with some frequency. From then on I was certain that my constant dream— well, at least since I'd had the use of my reason—of living in this city for the rest of my life was beginning to become a reality.

My existence did a somersault after that day. I began to cut my hair twice a month and put on a jacket and tie every morning. I took the Métro at Saint-Germain or l'Odéon to ride to the Ségur station, the one closest to UNESCO, and I stayed there, in a small cubicle, from nine thirty to one and from two thirty to six, translating into Spanish generally ponderous documents regarding the removal of the temples of Abu Simbel on the Nile or the preservation of fragments of cuneiform writing discovered in caves in the Sahara desert, near Mali.

Curiously, as my life changed, so did Paúl's. He was still my best friend, but we began to see each other less and less frequently because of the obligations I had recently assumed as a bureaucrat, and because he began to travel the world, representing the MIR at congresses or meetings for peace, for the liberation of the Third World, for the struggle against nuclear armaments, against colonialism and imperialism, and a thousand other progressive causes. At times Paúl felt dazed, living in a dream—when he was back in Paris he'd call and we would have a meal or a cup of coffee two or three times a week—and he'd tell me he had just come back from Beijing, from Cairo, from Havana, from Pyongyang, from Hanoi, where he had to speak about the outlook for revolution in Latin America before fifteen hundred delegates from fifty revolutionary organizations in some thirty countries in the name of a Peruvian revolution that hadn't even begun yet.

Often, if I hadn't known so well the integrity that oozed from his pores, I would have believed he was exaggerating just to impress me. How was it possible that this South American in Paris, who just a few months ago had earned his living as a kitchen boy in the México Lindo, was now a figure in the revolutionary jet set, making transatlantic flights and rubbing elbows with the leaders of China, Cuba, Vietnam, Egypt, North Korea, Libya, Indonesia? But it was true. Paúl, as a result of imponderables and the strange tangle of relationships, interests, and confusions that constituted the revolution, had been transformed into an international figure. I confirmed this in 1962 when there was a minor journalistic upheaval over an attempt to assassinate the Moroccan revolutionary leader Ben Barka, nicknamed the Dynamo, who, three years later, in October 1965, was abducted and disappeared forever as he left the Brasserie Lipp, a restaurant on Saint-Germain. Paúl met me at midday at UNESCO, and we went to the cafeteria for a sandwich. He was pale and had dark circles under his eyes, an agitated voice, a kind of nervousness very unusual in him. Ben Barka had been presiding at an international congress of revolutionary forces on whose executive council Paúl also served. The two of them had been seeing a good deal of each other and traveling together during the past few weeks. The attempt on Ben Barka could only be the work of the CIA, and the MIR now felt at risk in Paris. Could I, for just a few days, while they took certain necessary steps, keep a couple of suitcases in my garret?

"I wouldn't ask you to do something like this if I had another alternative. If you tell me you can't, it's not a problem, Ricardo."

I'd do it if he told me what was in the suitcases.

"In one, papers. Pure dynamite: plans, instructions, preparations for actions in Peru. In the other, dollars."

"How much?"

"Fifty thousand."

I thought for a moment.

"If I turn the suitcases over to the CIA, will they let me keep the fifty thousand?"

39

"Just think, when the revolution triumphs, we could name you ambassador to UNESCO," said Paúl, following my lead.

We joked for a while, and when night fell he brought me the two suitcases, which we put under my bed. I spent a week with my hair on end, thinking that if some thief decided to steal the money, the MIR would never believe there had been a robbery, and I'd become a target of the revolution. On the sixth day, Paúl came with three men I didn't know to take away those troublesome lodgers.

Whenever we saw each other I asked about Comrade Arlette, and he never tried to deceive me with false news. He was very sorry but hadn't been able to learn anything. The Cubans were extremely strict where security was concerned, and they were keeping her whereabouts an absolute secret. The only certainty was that she hadn't come through Paris yet, since he had a complete record of the scholarship recipients who returned to Paris.

"When she comes through, you'll be the first to know. The girl really has a hold on you, doesn't she? But why, *mon vieux*, she isn't even that pretty."

"I don't know why, Paúl. But the truth is she does have a tight hold on me."

With Paúl's new kind of life, Peruvian circles in Paris began to speak ill of him. These were writers who didn't write, painters who didn't paint, musicians who didn't play or compose, and café revolutionaries who vented their frustration, envy, and boredom by saying that Paúl had become "sensualized," a "bureaucrat of the revolution." What was he doing in Paris? Why wasn't he over there with those kids he was sending to receive military training and then sneak into Peru to begin guerrilla actions in the Andes? I defended him in heated arguments. I said that in spite of his new status, Paúl continued to live with absolute modesty. Until very recently, his wife had been cleaning houses to support the family. Now the MIR, taking advantage of her Spanish passport, used her as a courier and frequently sent her to Peru to accompany returning scholarship recipients or to carry money and instructions, on trips that filled Paúl with worry. But from his confidences I knew that the life imposed on him by circumstances, which his superior insisted he continue, irritated him more and more each day. He was impatient to return to Peru, where actions would begin very soon. He wanted to help prepare them on-site. The leadership of the MIR wouldn't authorize this, and it infuriated him. "This is what comes of knowing languages, damn it," he'd protest, laughing in the midst of his bad temper.

Thanks to Paúl, during those months and years in Paris I met the principal leaders of the MIR, beginning with its head and founder, Luis de la Puente Uceda, and ending with Guillermo Lobatón. The head of the MIR was a lawyer from Trujillo, born in 1926, who had repudiated the Aprista Party. He was slim, with glasses, light skin, and light hair that he always wore slicked back like an Argentine actor. The two or three times I saw him, he was dressed very formally in a tie and a dark leather coat. He spoke quietly, like a lawyer at work, giving legalistic details and using the elaborate vocabulary of a judicial argument. I always saw him surrounded by two or three brawny types who must have been his bodyguards, men who looked at him worshipfully and never offered an opinion. In everything he said there was something so cerebral, so abstract, that it was hard for me to imagine him as a guerrilla fighter with a machine gun over his shoulder, climbing up and down steep slopes in the Andes. And yet he had been arrested several times, was exiled in Mexico, lived a clandestine life. But he gave the impression that he had been born to shine in forums, parliaments, tribunals, political negotiations, that is, in everything he and his comrades scorned as the shady double-talk of bourgeois democracy.

Guillermo Lobatón was another matter. Of the crowd of revolutionaries I met in Paris through Paúl, none seemed as intelligent, well educated, and resolute as he. He was still very young, barely in his thirties, but he already had a rich past as a man of action. In 1952 he had been the leader of the great strike at the University of San Marcos against the Odría dictatorship (that was when he and Paúl became friends), and as a result he was arrested, sent to the fronton that was used as a political prison, and tortured. This was how his studies in philosophy had been cut short at San Marcos, where, they said, he was in competition with Li Carrillo, Heidegger's future disciple, for being the most brilliant student at the School of Letters. In 1954 he was expelled from the country by the military government, and after countless difficulties arrived in Paris, where, while he earned his living doing manual labor, he resumed his study of philosophy at the Sorbonne. Then the Communist Party obtained a scholarship for him in East Germany, in Leipzig, where he continued his philosophical studies at a school for the party's cadres. While he was there he was caught off guard by the Cuban Revolution. What happened in Cuba led him to think very critically about the strategy of Latin American Communist parties and the dogmatic spirit of Stalinism. Before I met him in person, I had read a work of his that circulated around Paris in mimeographed form, in which he accused those parties of cutting themselves off from the masses because of their submission to the dictates of Moscow, forgetting, as Che Guevara had written, "that the first duty of a revolutionary is to make the revolution." In this work, where he extolled the example of Fidel Castro and his comrades as revolutionary models, he cited Trotsky. Because of this citation he was subjected to a disciplinary tribunal in Leipzig and expelled in the most infamous way from East Germany and from the Peruvian Communist Party. This was how he came to Paris, where he married a French girl, Jacqueline, who was also a revolutionary activist. In Paris he met Paúl, his old friend from San Marcos, and became affiliated with the MIR. He had received guerrilla training in Cuba and was counting the hours until he could return to Peru and move into action. During the time of the invasion of Cuba at the Bay of Pigs, I saw him everywhere, attending every demonstration of solidarity with Cuba and speaking at several of them, in good French and with devastating rhetoric.

He was a tall, slim boy, with light ebony skin and a smile that displayed magnificent teeth. Just as he could argue for hours, with great intellectual substance, about political subjects, he was also capable of becoming involved in impassioned dialogues on literature, art, or sports, especially soccer and the feats of his team, the

Alianza Lima. There was something in his being that communicated his enthusiasm, his idealism, his generosity, and the steely sense of justice that guided his life, something I don't believe I had seen—especially in so genuine a way—in any of the revolutionaries who passed through Paris during the sixties. That he had agreed to be an ordinary member of the MIR, where there wasn't anyone with his talent and charisma, spoke very clearly to the purity of his revolutionary vocation. On the three or four occasions I talked to him, I was convinced, despite my skepticism, that if someone as lucid and energetic as Lobatón were at the head of the revolutionaries, Peru could be the second Cuba in Latin America.

It was at least six months after she left that I had news of Comrade Arlette, through Paúl. Since my contract as a temp left me with a good amount of free time, I began to study Russian, thinking that if I could also translate from that language—one of the four official languages of the United Nations and its subsidiary agencies at the time—my work as a translator would be more secure. I was also taking a course in simultaneous interpretation. The work of interpreters was more intense and difficult than that of translators, but for this reason they were more in demand. One day, as I left my Russian class at the Berlitz School on Boulevard des Capucines, I found fat Paúl waiting for me at the entrance to the building.

"News about the girl, finally," he said by way of greeting, wearing a long face. "I'm sorry, but it isn't good, *mon vieux*."

I invited him to one of the *bistrots* near the Opéra for a drink to help me digest the bad news. We sat outside, on the terrace. It was a warm spring twilight, with early stars, and all of Paris seemed to have poured out onto the street to enjoy the good weather. We ordered two beers.

"I suppose that after so much time you're not still in love with her," Paúl said to prepare me.

"I suppose not," I replied. "Tell me once and for all and don't fuck around, Paúl."

He had just spent a few days in Havana, and Comrade Arlette was the talk of all the young Peruvians in the MIR because, according to excited rumors, she was having a passionate love affair with Comandante Chacón, second-in-command to Osmani Cienfuegos, the younger brother of Camilo, the great hero of the Cuban Revolution who had disappeared. Comandante Osmani Cienfuegos was head of the organization that lent assistance to all revolutionary movements and related parties, and the man who coordinated rebel actions in every corner of the world. Comandante Chacón, veteran of the Sierra Maestra, was his right arm.

"Can you imagine, that tremendous piece of news was the first thing I heard." Paúl scratched his head. "That skinny thing, that absolutely ordinary girl, having an affair with one of the historic comandantes! Comandante Chacón, no less!"

"Couldn't it just be gossip, Paúl?"

He shook his head remorsefully, and patted my arm in encouragement.

"I was with them myself at a meeting in Casa de las Américas. They're living together. Comrade Arlette, even

45

if you don't believe it, has become an influential person, sharing bed and table with the comandantes."

"It's just wonderful for the MIR," I said.

"But shit for you." Paúl gave me another little pat. "I'm damn sorry to have to give you the news, *mon vieux*. But it's better for you to know, isn't it? Okay, it's not the end of the world. Besides, Paris is full of damn fine women. Just look around."

After attempting a few jokes, with absolutely no success, I asked Paúl about Comrade Arlette.

"As the companion of a comandante of the revolution she doesn't need a thing, I suppose," he said evasively. "Is that what you want to know? Or if she's richer or uglier than when she was here? Just the same, I think. A little more tanned by the Caribbean sun. You know, I never thought she was anything special. I mean, don't make that face, it's not that important, my friend."

Often, in the days, weeks, and months that followed that meeting with Paúl, I tried to imagine the Chilean girl transformed into Comandante Chacón's lover, dressed as a guerrilla fighter with a pistol at her waist, a blue beret, boots, alternating with Fidel and Raúl Castro in the big parades and demonstrations of the revolution, doing voluntary work on weekends and toiling like a slave in the cane fields while her small hands with their delicate fingers struggled to hold the machete and, perhaps, with that facility of hers for phonetic metamorphosis which I already knew about, speaking with that lingering, sensual music of people from the Caribbean. The truth is, I couldn't envision her in her new role: her image trickled away as if it were liquid.

Had she really fallen in love with this comandante? Or had he been the instrument for her getting out of guerrilla training and, above all, out of her commitment to the MIR to wage revolutionary war in Peru? It did me no good at all to think about Comrade Arlette, since each time I did I felt as if a new ulcer had opened in the pit of my stomach. To avoid this, and I wasn't completely successful, I dedicated myself zealously to my classes in Russian and simultaneous interpretation whenever Señor Charnés, with whom I got on very well, had no contract for me. And I had to tell Aunt Alberta—to whom I'd confessed in a letter, in a moment of weakness, that I was in love with a girl named Arlette, and who was always asking for her photograph—that we had broken up and from now on she should put the matter out of her mind.

It must have been six or eight months following the afternoon that Paúl gave me the bad news about Comrade Arlette when, very early one morning, the fat man, whom I hadn't seen for a while, came by the hotel so we could have breakfast together. We went to Le Tournon, a *bistrot* on the street of the same name, at the corner of Rue de Vaugirard.

"Even though I shouldn't tell you, I've come to say goodbye," he said. "I'm leaving Paris. Yes, *mon vieux*, I'm going to Peru. Nobody knows about it here, so you don't know anything either. My wife and Jean-Paul are already there."

The news left me speechless. And suddenly I was filled with a terrible fear, which I tried to conceal.

"Don't worry," Paúl said to calm me, with that smile that puffed up his cheeks and made him look like a clown. "Nothing will happen to me, you'll see. And when the revolution triumphs, we'll make you ambassador to UNESCO. That's a promise!"

For a while we sipped our coffee in silence. My croissant was on the table, untouched, and Paúl, bent on making jokes, said that since something apparently was taking away my appetite, he'd make the sacrifice and take care of that crusty half-moon.

"Where I'm going the croissants must be awful," he added.

Then, unable to control myself any longer, I told him he was going to commit an unforgivable act of stupidity. He wasn't going to help the revolution, or the MIR, or his comrades. He knew it as well as I did. His weight, which left him gasping for breath after walking barely a block on Saint-Germain, would be a tremendous hindrance to the guerrillas in the Andes, and for that same reason, he'd be one of the first the soldiers would kill as soon as the uprising began.

"You're going to get yourself killed because of the stupid gossip of a few rancorous types in Paris who accuse you of being an opportunist? Think it over, Fats, you can't do something as mindless as this."

"I don't give a damn what the Peruvians in Paris say, compadre. It isn't about them, it's about me. This is a question of principle. It's my obligation to be there."

And he started to crack jokes again and assure me that, in spite of his 120 kilos, he had passed all the tests in his military training and, furthermore, had demonstrated excellent marksmanship. His decision to return to Peru had provoked arguments with Luis de la Puente and the leadership of the MIR. They all wanted him to stay in Europe as the movement's representative to friendly organizations and governments, but he, with his bulletproof obstinacy, finally got his way. Seeing there was nothing I could do, and that my best friend in Paris had practically decided to commit suicide, I asked him if his departure meant that the insurrection would break out soon.

"It's a question of a couple of months, maybe less."

They had set up three camps in the mountains, one in the department of Cuzco, another in Piura, and the third in the central region, on the eastern slope of the Cordillera, near the edge of the Junín forest. Contrary to my prophecies, he assured me that the great majority of scholarship recipients had gone to the Andes. Fewer than ten percent had deserted. With an enthusiasm that sometimes verged on euphoria, he told me the recipients' return operation had been a success. He was happy because he had directed it himself. They had gone back one by one or two by two, following complicated trajectories that made some of the kids go halfway around the world to hide their tracks. No one had been found out. In Peru, De la Puente, Lobatón, and the rest had established urban support networks, formed medical teams, installed radio stations at the camps and at scattered hiding places for supplies and explosives. Contacts with the peasant unions, especially in Cuzco, were excellent, and they expected that once the rebellion began, many members of the village communities would join the struggle. He spoke with joy and certainty, convinced of what he was saying, exalted. I couldn't hide my sorrow.

"I know you don't believe me at all, Don Incredulous," he finally murmured.

"I swear I'd like nothing better than to believe you, Paúl. And have your enthusiasm."

He nodded, observing me with his affectionate, full-moon smile.

"And you?" he asked, grasping my arm. "What about you, *mon vieux*?"

"Not me, not ever," I replied. "I'll stay here, working as a translator for UNESCO, in Paris."

He hesitated for a moment, afraid that what he was going to say might hurt me. It was a question he undoubtedly had been biting his tongue over for a long time.

"Is this what you want out of life? Nothing but this? All the people who come to Paris want to be painters, writers, musicians, actors, theater directors, or get a doctorate, or make a revolution. You only want this, to live in Paris? I confess, *mon vieux*, I never could swallow it."

"I know you couldn't. But it's the truth, Paúl. When I was a boy, I said I wanted to be a diplomat, but that was only so they'd send me to Paris. That's what I want: to live here. Does it seem like a small thing to you?"

I pointed at the trees in the Luxembourg Gardens: heavy with green, they overflowed the fences and looked elegant beneath the overcast sky. Wasn't it the best thing that could happen to a person? To live, as Vallejo said in one of his lines, among "the leafy chestnut trees of Paris"?

"Admit that you write poetry in secret," Paúl insisted. "That it's your hidden vice. We've talked about it often, with other Peruvians. Everybody thinks you write and don't dare admit it because you're self-critical. Or timid. Every South American comes to Paris to do

50

great things. Do you want me to believe that you're the exception to the rule?"

"I swear I am, Paúl. My only ambition is to go on living here, just as I'm doing now."

I walked with him to the Métro station at Carrefour de l'Odéon. When we embraced, I couldn't stop my eyes from filling with tears.

"Take care of yourself, Fats. Don't do anything stupid up there, please."

"Yes, yes, of course I will, Ricardo." He gave me another hug. And I saw that his eyes were wet too.

I stood there, at the entrance to the station, watching him go down the steps slowly, held back by his round, bulky body. I was absolutely certain I was seeing him for the last time.

Fat Paúl's departure left me feeling empty because he was the best friend I had during those uncertain times of my settling in Paris. Fortunately, the temp contracts at UNESCO and my classes in Russian and simultaneous interpretation kept me very busy, and at night I returned to my garret in the Hôtel du Sénat and hardly had the energy to think about Comrade Arlette or fat Paúl. Without intending to, at that time I believe I began to move away unconsciously from the Peruvians in Paris, whom I had previously seen with a certain degree of frequency. I didn't look for solitude, but after I became an orphan and my aunt Alberta took me in, it hadn't been a problem for me. Thanks to UNESCO, I no longer worried about surviving; my translator's salary and occasional money orders from my aunt were enough for me to live on and to pay for my Parisian pleasures: movies, art shows, plays, and books. I was a steady customer at

La Joie de Lire bookshop, on Rue Saint-Séverin, and at the bouquinistes on the quays along the Seine. I went to the National Popular Theater, the Comédie-Française, l'Odéon, and from time to time to concerts at the Salle Pleyel.

And during that time I also had the beginnings of a romance with Carmencita, the Spanish girl who, dressed in black from head to toe like Juliette Gréco, sang and accompanied herself on the guitar at L'Escale, the little bar on Rue Monsieur le Prince frequented by Spaniards and South Americans. She was Spanish but had never set foot in her country because her republican parents couldn't or wouldn't go back while Franco was alive. The ambiguity of that situation tormented her and frequently appeared in her conversation. Carmencita was tall and slim, with hair cut *à la garçon* and melancholy eyes. She didn't have a great voice, but it was very melodious, and she gave marvelous performances of songs based on roundels, poems, verses, and refrains of the Golden Age, murmuring them with very effective pauses and emphasis. She had lived for a couple of years with an actor, and the break with him hurt her so much that—she told me this with the bluntness I initially found so shocking in my Spanish colleagues at UNESCO—she didn't "want to hook up with any guy right now." But she agreed to my taking her to the movies, to supper, and to the Olympia one night to hear Léo Ferré, whom we both preferred to Charles Aznavour and Georges Brassens, the other popular singers of the moment. When we said good night after the concert, at the Opéra Métro station, she said, brushing my lips, "I'm beginning to like you, my little Peruvian." Absurdly enough, whenever I went out with Carmencita I was filled with disquiet, the feeling I was being unfaithful to the lover of Comandante Chacón, an individual I imagined as sporting a huge mustache and strutting around with a pair of pistols on his hips. My relationship with the Spanish girl went no further because one night I discovered her in a corner of L'Escale melting with love in the arms of a gentleman with a neck scarf and heavy sideburns.

A few months after Paúl left, Señor Charnés began to recommend me as a translator at international conferences and congresses in Paris or other European cities when there wasn't work for me at UNESCO. My first contract was at the International Atomic Energy Agency, in Vienna, and the second, in Athens, at an international cotton congress. These trips, lasting only a few days but well paid, allowed me to visit places I never would have gone to otherwise. Though this new work cut into my time, I didn't abandon my Russian studies or interpreting classes but attended them in a more sporadic way.

It was on my return from one of those short business trips, this time to Glasgow and a conference on customs tariffs in Europe, that I found a letter at the Hôtel du Sénat from a first cousin of my father's, Dr. Ataúlfo Lamiel, an attorney in Lima. This uncle once removed, whom I barely knew, informed me that my aunt Alberta had died of pneumonia and had made me her sole heir. It was necessary for me to go to Lima to expedite the formalities of the inheritance. Uncle Ataúlfo offered to advance me the price of a plane ticket against the inheritance, which, he said, would not make me a millionaire but would help out nicely during my stay in Paris. I went to the post office on Vaugirard to send him a telegram, saying I'd buy the ticket myself and leave for Lima as soon as possible.

Aunt Alberta's death left me in a black mood for many days. She had been a healthy woman, not yet seventy. Though she was as conservative and judgmental as one could be, this spinster aunt, my father's older sister, had always been very loving toward me, and without her generosity and care I don't know what would have become of me. When my parents died in a senseless car accident, hit by a truck that fled the scene as they were traveling to Trujillo for the wedding of a daughter of some close friends—I was ten—she took their place. Until I finished my law studies and came to Paris, I lived in her house, and though her anachronistic manias often exasperated me, I loved her very much. From the time she adopted me, she devoted herself to me body and soul. Without Aunt Alberta, I'd be as solitary as a toadstool, and my connections to Peru would eventually vanish.

That same afternoon I went to the offices of Air France to buy a round-trip ticket to Lima, and then I stopped at UNESCO to explain to Señor Charnés that I had to take a forced vacation. I was crossing the entrance lobby when I ran into an elegant lady wearing very high heels and wrapped in a black fur-trimmed cape, who stared at me as if we knew each other.

"Well, well, isn't it a small world," she said, coming close and offering her cheek. "What are you doing here, good boy?"

"I work here, I'm a translator," I managed to stammer, totally disconcerted by surprise, and very conscious of the lavender scent that entered my nostrils when I kissed her. It was Comrade Arlette, but you had to make a huge effort to recognize her in that meticulously made-up face, those red lips, tweezed eyebrows, silky curved lashes shading mischievous eyes that black pencil lengthened and deepened, those hands with long nails that looked as if they had just been manicured.

"How you've changed since I saw you last," I said, looking her up and down. "It's about three years, isn't it?"

"Changed for the better or the worse?" she asked, totally self-assured, placing her hands on her waist and making a model's half turn where she stood.

"For the better," I admitted, not yet recovered from the impact she'd had on me. "The truth is, you look wonderful. I suppose I can't call you Lily the Chilean girl or Comrade Arlette the guerrilla fighter anymore. What the hell's your name now?"

She laughed, showing me the gold ring on her right hand.

"Now I use my husband's name, the way they do in France: Madame Robert Arnoux."

I found the courage to ask if we could have a cup of coffee for old times' sake.

"Not now, my husband's expecting me," she said, mockingly. "He's a diplomat and works here in the French delegation. Tomorrow at eleven, at Les Deux Magots. You know the place, don't you?"

I was awake for a long time that night, thinking about her and about Aunt Alberta. When I finally managed to get to sleep, I had a wild nightmare about the two of them ferociously attacking each other, indifferent to my pleas that they resolve their dispute like civilized people. The fight was due to my aunt Alberta accusing the Chilean girl of stealing her new name from a character in Flaubert. I awoke agitated, sweating, while it was still dark and a cat was yowling.

When I arrived at Les Deux Magots, Madame Robert Arnoux was already there, at a table on the terrace protected by a glass partition, smoking with an ivory cigarette holder and drinking a cup of coffee. She looked like a model out of *Vogue*, dressed all in yellow, with white shoes and a flowered parasol. The change in her was truly extraordinary.

"Are you still in love with me?" was her opening remark, to break the ice.

"The worst thing is that I think I am," I admitted, feeling my cheeks flush. "And if I weren't, I'd fall in love all over again today. You've turned into a very beautiful woman, and an extremely elegant one. I see you and don't believe what I see, bad girl."

"Now you see what you lost because you're a coward," she replied, her honey-colored eyes glistening with mocking sparks as she intentionally exhaled a mouthful of smoke in my face. "If you had said yes that time I proposed staying with you, I'd be your wife now. But you didn't want to get in trouble with your friend Comrade Jean, and you sent me off to Cuba. You missed the opportunity of a lifetime, Ricardito."

"Can't this be resolved? Can't I search my conscience, suffer from heartache, and promise to reform?"

"It's too late now, good boy. What kind of match for the wife of a French diplomat can a little pissant translator for UNESCO be?"

She didn't stop smiling as she spoke, moving her

mouth with a more refined flirtatiousness than I remembered. Contemplating her prominent, sensual lips, lulled by the music of her voice, I had an enormous desire to kiss her. I felt my heart beat faster.

"Well, if you can no longer be my wife, there's always the possibility of our being lovers."

"I'm a faithful spouse, the perfect wife," she assured me, pretending to be serious. And with no transition: "What happened to Comrade Jean? Did he go back to Peru to make the revolution?"

"Several months ago. I haven't heard anything about him or the others. And I haven't read or heard of any guerrillas there. Those revolutionary castles in the air probably turned into smoke. And all the guerrillas went back home and forgot about it."

We talked for almost two hours. Naturally, she assured me the love affair with Comandante Chacón had been nothing but the gossip of the Peruvians in Havana; in reality, she and the comandante had only been good friends. She refused to tell me anything about her military training, and, as always, avoided making any political comments or giving me details regarding her life on the island. Her only Cuban love had been the chargé d'affaires at the French embassy, Robert Arnoux, now her husband, who had been promoted to advisory minister. Weak with laughter and retrospective anger, she told me about the bureaucratic obstacles they had to overcome to marry, because it was almost unthinkable in Cuba that a scholarship recipient would leave her training. But in this regard it was certainly true that Comandante Chacón had been "loving" and helped her defeat the damn bureaucracy.

"I'd wager anything you went to bed with that damn comandante."

"Are you jealous?"

I said yes, very. And that she was so attractive I'd sell my soul to the devil, I'd do anything if I could make love to her, or even just kiss her. I grasped her hand and kissed it.

"Be still," she said, looking around in fake alarm. "Are you forgetting I'm a married woman? Suppose somebody here knows Robert and tells him about this?"

I said I knew perfectly well that her marriage to the diplomat was a mere formality to which she had resigned herself in order to leave Cuba and settle in Paris. Which seemed fine to me, because I too believed one could make any sacrifice for the sake of Paris. But, when we were alone, she shouldn't play the faithful, loving wife, because we both knew very well it was a fairy tale. Without becoming angry in the least, she changed the subject and said there was a damn bureaucracy here too and she couldn't get French nationality for two years, even though she was legally married to a French citizen. And they had just rented a nice apartment in Passy. She was decorating it now, and as soon as it was presentable she'd invite me over to introduce me to my rival, who, in addition to being congenial, was a very cultured man.

"I'm going to Lima tomorrow," I told her. "How can I see you when I get back?"

She gave me her telephone number and address and asked if I was still living in that little room in the garret of the Hôtel du Sénat, where she had been so cold.

"It's hard for me to leave it because I had the best

experience of my life there. And that's why, for me, that hole is a palace."

"This experience is the one I think it is?" she asked, bringing her face, where mischief was always mixed with curiosity and coquetry, close to mine.

"The same."

"For what you said just now, I owe you a kiss. Remind me the next time we see each other."

But a moment later, when we said goodbye, she forgot her marital precautions and instead of her cheek she offered me her lips. They were full and sensual, and in the seconds I had them pressed against mine, I felt them move slowly, provocatively, in a supplementary caress. When I already had crossed Saint-Germain on the way to my hotel, I turned to look at her and she was still there, on the corner by Les Deux Magots, a bright, golden figure in white shoes, watching me walk away. I waved goodbye and she waved the hand holding the flowered parasol. I only had to see her to discover that in these past few years I hadn't forgotten her for a single moment, that I loved her as much as I did the first day.

When I arrived in Lima in March 1965, shortly before my thirtieth birthday, photographs of Luis de la Puente, Guillermo Lobatón, fat Paúl, and other leaders of the MIR were in all the papers and on television—by now there was television in Peru—and everybody was talking about them. The MIR rebellion had an undeniable romantic aspect. The Miristas themselves had sent the photos to the media, announcing that in view of the iniquitous exploitative conditions that made victims of peasants and workers, and the surrender of the Belaúnde

Terry government to imperialism, the Movement of the Revolutionary Left had decided to take action. The leaders of the MIR showed their faces and appeared with long hair and full-grown beards, with rifles in their hands and combat uniforms consisting of black turtleneck sweaters, khaki trousers, and boots. I noticed that Paúl was as fat as ever. In the photograph that *Correo* published on the front page, he was surrounded by four other leaders and was the only one smiling.

"These wild men won't last a month," predicted Dr. Ataúlfo Lamiel in his study on Calle Boza in the center of Lima, on the morning I went to see him. "Turning Peru into another Cuba! Your poor aunt Alberta would have fainted dead away if she could see the outlaw faces of our brand-new guerrillas."

My uncle didn't take the announcement of armed actions very seriously, a feeling that seemed widespread. People thought it was a harebrained scheme that would end in no time. During the weeks I spent in Peru, I was crushed by a sense of oppressiveness and felt like an orphan in my own country. I lived in my aunt Alberta's apartment on Calle Colón in Miraflores, which still was filled with her presence and where everything reminded me of her, of my years at the university, of my adolescence without parents. It moved me when I found all the letters I had written to her from Paris, arranged chronologically, in her bedside table. I saw some of my old Miraflores friends from the Barrio Alegre, and with half a dozen of them went one Saturday to eat at the Kuo Wha Chinese restaurant near the Vía Expresa to talk about old times. Except for our memories, we didn't have much in common anymore, since their lives as young professionals and businessmen—two were working in their fathers' companies—had nothing to do with my life in France. Three were married, one had begun to have children, and the other three had girlfriends who would soon be their brides. In the jokes we told one another—a way of filling empty spaces in the conversation—they all pretended to envy me for living in the city of pleasure and fucking those French girls who were famous for being wild women in bed. How surprised they would have been if I confessed that in the years I spent in Paris, the only girl I went to bed with was a Peruvian, Lily of all people, the false Chilean girl of our childhood. What did they think of the guerrillas and their announcement in the papers? Like Uncle Ataúlfo, they didn't think they were important. Those Castristas sent here by Cuba wouldn't last very long. Who could believe that a Communist revolution would triumph in Peru? If the Belaúnde government couldn't stop them, the military would come in again and impose order, something they didn't look forward to.

That's what Dr. Ataúlfo Lamiel was afraid of too. "The only thing these idiots will achieve by playing guerrilla is to hand the military an excuse for a coup d'état on a silver platter. And stick us with another eight or ten years of military dictatorship. Who even thinks about making a revolution against a government that's not only civilian and democratic, but that the entire Peruvian oligarchy, beginning with *La Prensa* and *El Comercio*, accuses of being Communist because it wants agrarian reform? Peru is confusion, nephew, you did the right thing when you went to live in the country of Cartesian clarity."

61

Uncle Ataúlfo was a lanky, mustachioed man in his forties who always wore a jacket and bow tie and was married to Aunt Dolores, a kind, pale woman who had been an invalid for close to ten years and whom he looked after with devotion. They lived in a nice house, full of books and records, in Olivar de San Isidro, where they invited me to lunch and dinner. Aunt Dolores bore her illness without bitterness and amused herself by playing the piano and watching soap operas. When we recalled Aunt Alberta, she started to cry. They had no children and he, in addition to his law practice, taught classes in mercantile law at Catholic University. He had a good library and was very interested in local politics, not hiding his sympathies for the democratic reform movement incarnated, to his mind, in Belaúnde Terry. He was very kind to me, expediting the formalities of the inheritance as much as he could and refusing to charge me a cent for his services: "Don't be silly, nephew, I was very fond of Alberta and your parents." Those were tedious days of abject appearances before notaries and judges and carrying documents back and forth through the labyrinthine Palace of Justice, which left me sleepless at night and increasingly impatient to return to Paris. In my free time I reread Flaubert's *Sentimental Education* because now, for me, Madame Arnoux in the novel had not only the name but also the face of the bad girl. Once the taxes on the inheritance had been deducted and the debts left behind by Aunt Alberta had been paid, Uncle Ataúlfo announced that with the apartment sold and the furniture put up for auction, I'd receive something like sixty thousand dollars, maybe a little more. A handsome sum I never thought I'd have. Thanks to Aunt Alberta, I could buy a small apartment in Paris.

As soon as I was back in France, the first thing I did after climbing up to my garret in the Hôtel du Sénat and even before I unpacked was to call Madame Robert Arnoux.

She made an appointment with me for the next day and said that if I wanted to, we could have lunch together. I picked her up at the entrance to the Alliance Française, on Boulevard Raspail, where she was taking an accelerated course in French, and we went to have a curry *d'agneau* at La Coupole, on Boulevard Montparnasse. She was dressed simply, slacks and sandals and a light jacket. She wore earrings whose colors matched those in her necklace and bracelet and a bag hanging from her shoulder, and each time she moved her head, her hair swung gaily. I kissed her cheeks and hands, and she greeted me with: "I thought you'd come back more tanned from the Lima summer, Ricardito." She had really turned into an extremely elegant woman: she combined colors and applied her makeup very tastefully. I observed her, still stupefied by her transformation. "I don't want you to tell me anything about Peru," she said, so categorically I didn't ask why. Instead, I told her about my inheritance. Would she help me find an apartment?

She approved enthusiastically.

"I love the idea, good boy. I'll help you furnish and decorate it. I've had practice with mine. It's turning out so well, you'll see."

After a week of frantic afternoon appointments after her French classes, which took us to agencies and apartments in the Latin Quarter, Montparnasse, and the fourteenth arrondissement, I found an apartment with two rooms, a bath, and a kitchen on Rue Joseph Granier, in an art deco building from the 1930s that had geometrical designs—rhombuses, triangles, and circles—on the façade, in the vicinity of the École Militaire in the seventh arrondissement, very close to UNESCO. It was in good condition, and even though it faced an interior courtyard and for the moment you had to climb four flights of stairs to reach it—the elevator was under construction—it had a great deal of light, since in addition to two good-sized picture windows, a large concave skylight exposed it to the Paris sky. It cost close to seventy thousand dollars, but I had no difficulty when I went to the Société Générale, the bank where I kept my account, and asked for a mortgage. During those weeks when I was looking for the apartment and then making it livable, cleaning, painting, and furnishing it with a few bits and pieces purchased at La Samaritaine and the Marché aux Puces, I saw Madame Robert Arnoux every day, Monday through Friday—she spent Saturdays and Sundays in the country, with her husband—from the time she left her classes until four or five in the afternoon. She enjoyed helping me with all my chores, practicing her French with real estate agents and concierges, and she displayed such good humor that—as I told her—it seemed the small apartment to which she was giving life was for the two of us to share.

"It's what you'd like, isn't it, good boy?"

We were in a *bistrot* on Avenue de Tourville, near Les Invalides, and I kissed her hands and searched for her mouth, mad with love and desire. I nodded several times.

"The day you move we'll have a premiere," she promised.

She kept her promise. It was the second time we made love, on this occasion in the full light of day that came pouring in through the large skylight, where curious pigeons observed us, naked and embracing on the mattress without sheets that had recently been liberated from the plastic wrapping in which the truck from La Samaritaine had brought it. The walls smelled of fresh paint. Her body was as slim and well formed as I remembered it, with her narrow waist that I thought could be encircled by my hands, and her pubis with sparse hair, its skin whiter than her smooth belly or thighs, which darkened and shaded to a pale green luster. Her entire body gave off a delicate fragrance, accentuated in the warm nest of her depilated underarms, behind her ears, and in her small, wet sex. On her curved groin thin blue veins were visible under the skin, and it moved me to imagine her blood flowing slowly through them. As she did the last time, with total passivity she allowed herself to be caressed and listened silently, feigning an exaggerated attention or pretending she didn't hear anything and was thinking about something else, to the intense, hurried words I said into her ear or mouth as I struggled to spread her labia.

"Make me come first," she whispered in a tone that concealed a command. "With your mouth. Then it'll be easier for you to enter. And don't you come yet. I like to feel irrigated."

She spoke with so much coldness that she didn't seem like a girl making love but a doctor formulating a technical description, detached from pleasure. I didn't care, I was totally happy, as I hadn't been in a long time, perhaps not ever. "I'll never be able to repay so much happiness, bad girl." I spent a long time with my lips pressed against her contracted sex, feeling the pubic hairs tickling my nose, licking her tiny clitoris avidly, tenderly, until I felt her moving, becoming excited, and finishing with a quivering of her lower belly and legs.

"Come in now," she whispered in the same imperious voice.

It wasn't easy this time either. She was narrow, she shrank away, she resisted me, she moaned, until at last I was successful. It felt as if my sex were being broken, strangled by that throbbing interior passage. But it was a marvelous pain, a vertigo into which I sank, tremulous. I ejaculated almost immediately.

"You come very fast," Madame Arnoux reprimanded me, pulling my hair. "You have to learn to hold off if you want to please me."

"I'll learn everything you want, guerrilla fighter, but be quiet now and kiss me."

That same day, as we said goodbye, she invited me to supper to introduce me to her husband. We had drinks in their pretty apartment in Passy, decorated in the most bourgeois style one could imagine, with velvet drapes, deep carpets, antique furniture, end tables holding little porcelain figures, and, on the walls, engravings of mordant scenes by Gavarni and Daumier. We went to eat at a nearby *bistrot* where the specialty, according to the diplomat, was coq au vin. And for dessert, he suggested the tarte Tatin.

Monsieur Robert Arnoux was a short, bald man who had a small brush mustache that moved when he talked and eyeglasses with thick lenses, and who must have been twice the age of his wife. He treated her with great consideration, pulling out her chair and pushing it in and helping her with her raincoat. He was alert all night, pouring wine when her glass was empty and passing her the basket if she had no bread. He wasn't very congenial, but rather arrogant and cutting, though he did actually seem cultured and spoke of Cuba and Latin America with great accuracy. His Spanish was perfect, with a slight inflection that revealed the years he had served in the Caribbean. In reality he wasn't part of the French delegation to UNESCO but had been loaned by the Quai d'Orsay as an adviser and chief of staff to the director general, René Maheu, a colleague of Jean-Paul Sartre and Raymond Aron at the École Normale, about whom it was said that he was a circumspect genius. I had seen him a few times, always escorted by this squint-eyed little bald man who turned out to be the husband of Madame Arnoux. When I told him I worked as a temp translator for the department of Spanish, he offered to recommend me to "Charnés, an excellent person." He asked what I thought about events in Peru, and I said I hadn't received news from Lima for some time.

"Well, those guerrillas in the sierra," he said with a shrug, as if he didn't give them too much importance. "Robbing farms and assaulting the police. How absurd! Especially in Peru, one of the few Latin American countries trying to build a democracy."

So the first actions of the Mirista guerrilla war had taken place.

"You have to leave that gentleman right away and marry me," I told the Chilean girl the next time we saw each other. "Do you want me to believe you're in love with a Methuselah who not only looks like your grand-father but is very ugly too?"

"Another slander against my husband and you won't see me again," she threatened, and in one of those light-ning changes that were her specialty, she laughed. "Does he really look very old next to me?"

My second honeymoon with Madame Arnoux ended shortly after that meal, because as soon as I moved to the École Militaire district, Señor Charnés renewed my con-tract. Then, because of my schedule, I could see her only for short periods, an occasional midday when, during that free hour and a half between one and two thirty, instead of going up to the UNESCO cafeteria, I ate a sandwich with her in some *bistrot*, or a few evenings when, I don't know with what excuse, she freed herself from Monsieur Arnoux to go to the movies with me. We'd watch the film holding hands, and I would kiss her in the darkness. "*Tu m'embêtes*," she said, practicing her French. "*Je veux voir le film, grosse bête*." She made rapid progress in the language of Montaigne, began to speak it without the slightest embarrassment, and her errors in syntax and phonetics were amusing, one more charming trait in her personality. We didn't make love again until many weeks later, after a trip she took to Switzerland alone, when she returned to Paris several hours earlier than planned so she could spend some time with me in my apartment on Rue Joseph Granier.

Everything in the life of Madame Arnoux remained extremely mysterious, as it had been in the lives of Lily the Chilean girl and Arlette the guerrilla fighter. If what she told me was true, she now led an intense social life of receptions, dinners, and cocktail parties, where she rubbed elbows with *le tout* Paris; for example, yesterday she had met Maurice Couve de Murville, General de Gaulle's minister of foreign relations, and last week she had seen Jean Cocteau at a private screening of *To Die in Madrid*, a documentary by Frédéric Rossif, on the arm of his lover, the actor Jean Marais, who, by the way, was extremely handsome, and tomorrow she was going to a tea given by friends for Farah Diba, the wife of the Shah of Iran, who was on a private visit to Paris. Mere delusions of grandeur and snobbery, or had her husband in fact introduced her to a world of luminaries and frivolity that she found dazzling? And she was constantly making, or she told me she was making, trips to Switzerland, Germany, Belgium, for just two or three days, and for reasons that were never clear: expositions, gala events, parties, concerts. Since her explanations seemed so obviously fantastic to me, I chose not to ask more questions about her trips, pretending to believe absolutely the reasons she occasionally deigned to give me for those glittering excursions.

One afternoon in the middle of 1965, at UNESCO, a colleague at the office, an old Spanish republican who years ago had written "a definitive novel on the Civil War that corrected Hemingway's errors," entitled *For Whom the Bells Don't Toll*, handed me the copy of *Le Monde* he was leafing through. The guerrillas of the Túpac Amaru column of the MIR, led by Lobatón and operating in the provinces of La Concepción and Satipo, in the department of Junín, had plundered the powder magazine of a mine, blown up a bridge across the Moraniyoc River, occupied the Runatullo ranch, and distributed the provisions to the peasants. And a couple of weeks later, it ambushed a detachment of the Civil Guard in the narrow Yahuarina pass. Nine guards, among them the major in command of the patrol, died in the fighting. In Lima, there had been bombing attacks on the Hotel Crillón and the Club Nacional. The Belaúnde government had decreed a state of siege throughout the central sierra. I felt my heart shrink. That day, and the days that followed, I was uneasy, the face of fat Paúl etched in my mind.

Uncle Ataúlfo wrote to me from time to time—he had replaced Aunt Alberta as my only correspondent in Peru—his letters filled with commentary on the political situation. Through him I learned that although the guerrilla war was very sporadic in Lima, military actions in the central and southern Andes had convulsed the country. *El Comercio* and *La Prensa*, and Apristas and Odristas now allied against the government, were accusing Belaúnde Terry of weakness in the face of the Castrista rebels, and even of secret complicity with the insurrection. The government had made the army responsible for suppressing the rebels. "This is turning ugly, nephew, and I'm afraid there may be a coup at any moment. You can hear the sound of swords crossing in the air. When don't things go badly in our Peru!" To his affectionate letters Aunt Dolores would always add a message in her own hand.

In a totally unexpected way, I ended up getting along very well with Monsieur Robert Arnoux. He showed up one day at the Spanish office at UNESCO to suggest that, when it was time for lunch, we go to the cafeteria to have a sandwich together. For no special reason, just to chat for a while, the time needed to have a filtered

Gitane, the brand we both smoked. After that, he stopped by from time to time, when his commitments allowed, and we'd have coffee and a sandwich while we discussed the political situation in France and Latin America, and cultural life in Paris, about which he was also very knowledgeable. He was a man who read and had ideas, and he complained that even though working with René Maheu was interesting, the problem was that he had time to read only on weekends and couldn't go to the theater and concerts very frequently.

Because of him I had to rent a dinner jacket and wear formal dress for the first and undoubtedly the last time in my life in order to attend a benefit for UNESCO—a ballet, followed by dinner and dancing—at the Opéra. I had never been inside this imposing building, adorned with the frescoes Chagall had painted for the dome. Everything looked beautiful and elegant to me. But even more beautiful and elegant was the ex–Chilean girl and ex–guerrilla fighter, who, in an ethereal strapless gown of white crepe with a floral print, an upswept hairdo, and jewels at her throat, ears, and fingers, left me open-mouthed with admiration. The old men who were friends of Monsieur Arnoux came up to her all night, kissed her hand, and stared at her with glittering, covetous eyes. *"Quelle beauté exotique!"* I heard one of those excited drones say. At last I was able to ask her to dance. Holding her tight, I murmured in her ear that I'd never even imagined she could ever be as beautiful as she was at that moment. And it tore my heart out to think that, after the dance, in her house in Passy, it would be her husband and not me who would undress her and make love to her. The *beauté exotique* let herself be adored with a condescending little smile and then finished me off with a cruel remark: "What cheap, sentimental things you say to me, Ricardito." I inhaled the fragrance that floated all around her and wanted her so much I could hardly breathe.

Where did she get the money for those clothes and jewels? I was no expert in luxury items, but I realized that to wear those exclusive models and change outfits the way she did—each time I saw her she was wearing a new dress and exquisite new shoes—one needed more money than a UNESCO functionary could earn, even if he was the director's right hand. I tried to learn the secret by asking her if, besides occasionally deceiving Monsieur Robert Arnoux with me, she wasn't also deceiving him with some millionaire thanks to whom she could dress in clothes from the great shops and wear jewels from the *Arabian Nights*.

"If you were my only lover, I'd walk around like a beggar, little pissant," she replied, and she wasn't joking.

But she immediately offered an explanation that seemed perfect, though I was certain it was false. The clothes and jewels she wore weren't bought but lent by the great modistes along Avenue Montaigne and the jewelers on Place Vendôme; as a way to publicize their creations, they had chic ladies in high society wear them. And so because of her social connections, she could dress and adorn herself like the most elegant women in Paris. Or did I think that on the miserable salary of a French diplomat she'd be able to compete with the grandes dames in the City of Light?

A few weeks after the dance at the Opéra, the bad girl called me at my office at UNESCO.

"Robert has to go with the director to Warsaw this weekend," she said. "You won the lottery, good boy! I can devote all of Saturday and Sunday to you. Let's see what you arrange for me."

I spent hours thinking about what would surprise and amuse her, what odd places in Paris she didn't know, what performances were being offered on Saturday, what restaurant, bar, or *bistrot* might appeal to her because of its originality or secret, exclusive character. Finally, after shuffling through a thousand possibilities and discarding all of them, I chose for Saturday morning, if the weather was good, an excursion to the Asnières dog cemetery on a tree-filled little island in the middle of the river, and supper at Allard, on Rue de Saint-André-des-Arts, at the same table where one night I had seen Pablo Neruda eating with two spoons, one in each hand. To enhance its stature in her eyes, I'd tell Madame Arnoux it was the poet's favorite restaurant and invent the dishes he always ordered. The idea of spending an entire night with her, making love to her, enjoying on my lips the flutter of her "sex of nocturnal eyelashes" (a line from Neruda's poem "Material nupcial" that I had murmured in her ear the first night we were together in my garret at the Hôtel du Sénat), feeling her fall asleep in my arms, waking on Sunday morning with her warm, slim body curled up against mine, kept me, for the three or four days I had to wait until Saturday, in a state in which hope, joy, and fear that something would frustrate our plan barely allowed me to concentrate on my work. The reviewer had to correct my translations several times.

That Saturday was a glorious day. At midmorning, in

the new Dauphine I had bought the previous month, I drove Madame Arnoux to the Asnières dog cemetery, which she had never seen. We spent more than an hour wandering among the graves—not only dogs but cats, rabbits, and parrots were buried there—and reading the deeply felt, poetic, cheerful, and absurd epitaphs with which owners had bid farewell to their beloved animals. She really seemed to be having a good time. She smiled and kept her hand in mine, her eyes the color of dark honey were lit by the springtime sun, and her hair was tousled by a breeze blowing along the river. She wore a light, transparent blouse that revealed the top of her breasts, a loose jacket that fluttered with her movements, and brick-red high-heeled boots. She spent some time contemplating the statue to the unknown dog at the entrance, and with a melancholy air lamented having "so complicated" a life, otherwise she would adopt a puppy. I made a mental note: that would be my gift on her birthday, if I could find out when it was.

I put my arm around her waist, pulled her to me, and said that if she decided to leave Monsieur Arnoux and marry me, I'd undertake to see that she had a normal life and could raise all the dogs she wanted.

Instead of answering, she asked, in a mocking tone, "The idea of spending the night with me makes you the happiest man in the world, Miraflores boy? I'm asking so you can tell me one of those cheap, sentimental things you love saying so much."

"Nothing could make me happier," I said, pressing my lips to hers. "I've been dreaming about it for years, guerrilla fighter."

"How many times will you make love to me?" she continued in the same mocking tone.

"As many as I can, bad girl. Ten, if my body holds out."

"I'll allow you only two," she said, biting my ear. "Once when we go to bed, and another when we wake up. And no getting up early. I need a minimum of eight hours' sleep so I'll never have wrinkles."

She had never been as playful as she was that morning. And I don't think she ever was again. I didn't remember having seen her so natural, giving herself up to the moment without posing, without inventing a role for herself, as she breathed in the warmth of the day and let herself be penetrated and adored by the light that filtered through the tops of the weeping willows. She seemed much younger than she actually was, almost an adolescent and not a woman close to thirty. We had a ham sandwich with pickles and a glass of wine at a *bistrot* in Asnières, on the banks of the river, and then went to the Cinémathèque on Rue d'Ulm to see Marcel Carné's *Les enfants du paradis*, which I had seen but she hadn't. When we came out she spoke about how young Jean-Louis Barrault and María Casares looked, and how they didn't make movies like that anymore, and she confessed that she had cried at the end. I suggested we go to my apartment to rest until it was time for supper, but she refused: going home now would give me ideas. Instead, the afternoon was so nice we ought to walk for a while. We went in and out of the galleries along Rue de Seine and then sat down at an open-air café on Rue de Buci for something cold to drink. I told her I had seen André Breton around there one morning, buying fresh fish. The streets and cafés were full of people, and the Parisians had those open, pleasant expressions they wear on the rare days when the weather's nice. I hadn't felt this happy, optimistic, and hopeful for a long time. Then the devil raised his tail and I saw the headline in *Le Monde*, which the man next to me was reading: ARMY DESTROYS HEADQUARTERS OF PERUVIAN GUERRILLAS. The subtitle said: "Luis de la Puente and Other MIR Leaders Killed." I hurried to buy the paper at the stand on the corner. The byline was Marcel Niedergang, the paper's correspondent in South America, and there was an inset by Claude Julien explaining what the Peruvian MIR was and giving information about Luis de la Puente and the political situation in Peru. In August 1965, special forces of the Peruvian army had surrounded Mesa Pelada, a hill to the east of the city of Quillabamba, in the Cuzcan valley of La Convención, and captured the Illarec ch'aska (morning star) camp, killing a good number of guerrillas. Luis de la Puente, Paúl Escobar, and a handful of their followers had managed to escape, but the commandos, after a long pursuit, surrounded and killed them. The article indicated that military planes had bombed Mesa Pelada, using napalm. The corpses had not been returned to their families or shown to the press. According to the official communiqué, they had been buried in a secret location to prevent their graves from becoming destinations for revolutionary pilgrimages. The army showed reporters the weapons, uniforms, documents, as well as maps and radio equipment the guerrillas had stored at Mesa Pelada. In this way the Pachacútec column, one of the rebel focal points of the Peruvian revolution, had been wiped out. The army was hopeful that the Túpac Amaru column, headed by Guillermo Lobatón and also under siege, would soon fall.

"I don't know why you're making that face, you knew this would happen sooner or later," Madame Arnoux said in surprise. "You yourself told me so many times that this was the only way it could turn out."

"I said it as a kind of magic charm, so it wouldn't happen."

I had said it and thought it and feared it, of course, but it was different knowing it had happened and that Paúl, the good friend and companion of my early days in Paris, was now a corpse rotting in some desolate wasteland in the eastern Andes, perhaps after being executed—and no doubt tortured if the soldiers had captured him alive. I overcame my feelings and proposed to the Chilean girl that we drop the subject and not let the news ruin the gift from the gods of my having her to myself for an entire weekend. She managed that with no difficulty; for her, it seemed to me, Peru was something she had very deliberately expelled from her thoughts like a mass of bad memories (poverty, racism, discrimination, being disregarded, multiple frustrations?), and, perhaps, she had made the decision a long time ago to break forever with her native land. But in spite of my efforts, I couldn't forget the damn news in *Le Monde* and concentrate on the bad girl. Throughout supper at Allard, the ghost of my friend took away my appetite and my good humor.

"It seems to me you're in no mood to *faire la fête*," she said with compassion when we were having dessert. "Do you want to leave it for another time, Ricardito?"

I insisted I didn't and kissed her hands and swore that in spite of the awful news, spending a night with her was the most wonderful thing that had ever happened to me. But when we reached my apartment on Joseph Granier, and she took a coquettish baby-doll, her toothbrush, and a change of clothes for the next day out of her overnight case, and we lay down on the bed—I had bought flowers for the living room and bedroom—I began to caress her and realized, to my embarrassment and humiliation, that I was in no condition to make love to her.

"This is what the French call a fiasco," she said, laughing. "Do you know this is the first time it's happened to me with a man?"

"How many have you been with? Let me guess. Ten? Twenty?"

"I'm terrible at math," she said in anger. And she took her revenge with a command: "Make me come with your mouth. I have no reason to be in mourning. I hardly knew your friend Paúl, and besides, remember it was his fault I had to go to Cuba."

And just like that, as casually as she would have lit a cigarette, she spread her legs and lay back, her arm across her eyes, in that total immobility, that deep concentration into which, forgetting about me and the world around her, she sank to wait for her pleasure. She always took a long time to become excited and finish, but that night she took even longer than usual, and two or three times my tongue cramped and for a few moments I had to stop kissing and sucking her. Each time her hand admonished me, pulling my hair or pinching my shoulder. At last I felt her move and heard the quiet little purr that seemed to move up from her belly to her mouth, and I felt her limbs contract and heard her long, satisfied sigh. "Thank you, Ricardito," she murmured. She fell asleep almost immediately. I was awake for a long time, my throat tight with anguish. My sleep was restless, and I had nightmares I could barely recall the next day.

I awoke at about nine. The sun was no longer shining. Through the skylight I could see the overcast sky, the color of a burro's belly, the eternal Parisian sky. She slept, her back to me. She seemed very young and fragile with her girl's body, quiet now, hardly stirred by her light, slow breathing. No one, seeing her like this, could have imagined the difficult life she must have had since she was born. I tried to picture her childhood, being poor in the hell that Peru is for the poor, and her adolescence, perhaps even worse, the countless difficulties, defeats, sacrifices, concessions she must have suffered in Peru, in Cuba, in order to move ahead and reach the place she was now. And how hard and cold having to defend herself tooth and nail against misfortune had made her, all the beds she'd had to pass through to avoid being crushed by a life her experiences had convinced her was a battlefield. I felt immense tenderness toward her. I was sure it was my good fortune, and also my misfortune, that I would always love her. Seeing her and feeling her breathe excited me. I began to kiss her on the back, very slowly, her pert little ass, her neck and shoulders, and, turning her toward me, her breasts and mouth. She pretended to sleep but was already awake, since she arranged herself on her back to receive me. She was wet, and for the first time I could enter her without

79

difficulty, without feeling I was making love to a virgin. I loved her, I loved her, I couldn't live without her. I begged her to leave Monsieur Arnoux and come to me, I'd earn a lot of money, I'd pamper her, I'd satisfy her every whim, I'd . . .

"Well, you've redeemed yourself," and she burst into laughter, "and you even held out longer than usual. I thought you'd become impotent after last night's fiasco."

I proposed fixing breakfast, but she wanted us to go out, she was longing for *un croissant croustillant*. We showered together, she let me wash and dry her and, as I sat on the bed, watch her dress, comb her hair, and put on makeup. I slipped her shoes onto her feet, first kissing her toes one by one. We walked hand in hand to a *bistrot* on Avenue de la Bourdonnais where, in fact, the half-moons crunched as if they had just come out of the oven.

"If instead of sending me to Cuba that time you had let me stay with you here in Paris, how long would we have lasted, Ricardito?"

"All our lives. I'd have made you so happy you never would have left me."

She stopped joking and looked at me, very serious, and somewhat contemptuous.

"How naïve you are, what a dreamer." She enunciated each syllable, defying me with her eyes. "You don't know me. I'd only stay forever with a man who was very, very rich and powerful, which you'll never be, unfortunately."

"And what if money wasn't happiness, bad girl?"

"Happiness, I don't know and I don't care what it is, Ricardito. What I am sure about is that it isn't the romantic, vulgar thing it is for you. Money gives you security, it protects you, it lets you enjoy life thoroughly and not worry about tomorrow. It's the only happiness you can touch."

She sat looking at me, wearing the cold expression that intensified sometimes in a strange way and seemed to freeze the life around her.

"You're very nice but you have a terrible defect: lack of ambition. You're satisfied with what you have, aren't you? But it isn't anything, good boy. That's why I couldn't be your wife. I'll never be satisfied with what I have. I'll always want more."

I didn't know how to respond, because though it hurt me, she had said something that was true. For me, happiness was having her and living in Paris. Did that mean you were unredeemably mediocre, Ricardito? Yes, probably. Before we went back to the apartment, Madame Robert Arnoux went to make a phone call. She came back with a worried face.

"I'm sorry, but I have to go, good boy. Things have become difficult."

She offered no explanations and wouldn't let me take her to her house or wherever she had to go. We went up for her overnight bag and I accompanied her to the taxi stand next to the École Militaire Métro station.

"In spite of everything it was a nice weekend," she said, brushing my lips. "Ciao, *mon amour*."

When I returned home, surprised at her abrupt departure, I discovered she had left her toothbrush in the bathroom. A beautiful little brush that had the name of the manufacturer stamped on the handle: Guerlain. Forgotten? Probably not. Probably a deliberate oversight in order to leave me a memento of the sad night and happy waking.

That week I couldn't see or talk to her, and the following week, without being able to say goodbye—she didn't answer the phone no matter what time I called—I left for Vienna to work for two weeks at the International Atomic Energy Agency. I loved that baroque, elegant, prosperous city, but a temp's work during those periods when international organizations have congresses, general sessions, or annual conferences—which is when they need extra translators and interpreters—is so intense it didn't leave me time for museums, concerts, or the opera, except one afternoon when I made a fast visit to the Albertina. At night I was exhausted and barely had the energy to go into one of the old cafés, the Central, the Landtmann, the Hawelka, the Frauenhuber, with their belle époque decor, to have a wiener schnitzel, the Austrian version of the breaded steak my aunt Alberta used to make, and a glass of foaming beer. I was groggy when I got into bed. I called the bad girl several times but nobody answered, or the phone was busy. I didn't dare call Robert Arnoux at UNESCO, afraid I'd arouse his suspicions. At the end of the two weeks, Señor Charnés telegraphed me proposing a ten-day contract in Rome for a seminar followed by a conference at the Food and Agriculture Organization, so that I traveled to Italy without passing through Paris. I couldn't reach her from Rome, either. I called her as soon as I was back in France. Without success, of course. What was going on? I began to have anguished thoughts of an accident, an illness, a domestic tragedy.

My nerves were so on edge because I couldn't communicate with Madame Arnoux that I had to read the most recent letter from Uncle Ataúlfo twice; I found it waiting for me in Paris. I couldn't concentrate or get the Chilean girl out of my mind. Uncle Ataúlfo gave me long interpretations of the political situation in Peru. The Túpac Amaru column of the MIR, led by Lobatón, hadn't been captured yet, though army communiqués reported constant clashes in which the guerrillas always suffered losses. According to the press, Lobatón and his people had gone deep into the forest and made alliances among the Amazonian tribes, principally the Asháninka, dispersed throughout the region bounded by the Ene, Perené, Satipo, and Anapati rivers. There were rumors that the Asháninka communities, seduced by Lobatón's personality, identified him with a mythical hero, Itomi Pavá, the atavistic dispenser of justice who, according to legend, would come back one day to restore the power of their nation. Military planes had bombed forest villages on the suspicion they were hiding Miristas.

After more fruitless attempts to speak with Madame Arnoux, I decided to go to UNESCO and see her husband, using the pretext of inviting them to supper. I went first to say hello to Señor Charnés and my colleagues in the Spanish office. Then I went up to the sixth floor, the sanctum sanctorum, where the head offices were located. From the door I could see Monsieur Arnoux's ravaged face and brush mustache. He gave a strange start when he saw me and seemed gruffer than ever, as if my presence displeased him. Was he ill? He seemed to have aged ten years in the few weeks I hadn't seen him. He extended a reluctant hand without saying a word and waited for me to speak, giving me a penetrating stare with his rodent eyes.

"I've been working away from Paris this past month, in Vienna and Rome. I'd like to invite the two of you to have supper one night when you're free."

He kept looking at me, not answering. He was very pale now, his expression desolate, and he pursed his lips as if it were difficult for him to speak. My hands began to tremble. Was he going to tell me that his wife had died?

"Then you haven't heard," he murmured drily. "Or are you playing a game?"

I was disconcerted and didn't know how to answer.

"All of UNESCO knows," he added, quietly, sarcastically. "I'm the laughingstock of the agency. My wife has left me, and I don't even know for whom. I thought it was you, Señor Somocurcio."

His voice broke before he finished pronouncing my name. His chin quivered and his teeth seemed to be chattering. I stammered that I was sorry, I hadn't heard anything, and stupidly repeated that this month I had been working away from Paris, in Vienna and Rome. And I said goodbye, but Monsieur Arnoux didn't respond.

I was so surprised and chagrined that I felt a wave of nausea in the elevator and had to throw up in the bathroom in the corridor. With whom had she gone away? Could she still be living in Paris with her lover? One thought accompanied me in the days that followed: the weekend she had given me was her goodbye. So I'd have something special to pine for. The leavings you throw to the dog, Ricardito. Some calamitous days followed that brief visit to Monsieur Arnoux. For the first time in my life, I suffered from insomnia. I was in a sweat all night, my mind blank, as I clutched the Guerlain toothbrush that I kept like a charm in my night table, chewing on my despair and jealousy. The next day I was a wreck, my body shaken by chills, without energy for anything, and I didn't even want to eat. The doctor prescribed Nembutal, which didn't put me to sleep so much as knock me out. I awoke distraught and shaking, as if I had a savage hangover. I kept cursing myself for how stupid I had been when I sent her off to Cuba, putting my friendship with Paúl ahead of the love I felt for her. If I had held on to her we would still be together, and life wouldn't be this sleeplessness, this emptiness, this bile.

Señor Charnés helped me out of the slow emotional dissolution in which I found myself by giving me a month's contract. I wanted to fall on my knees and thank him. With the routine of work at UNESCO, I was slowly emerging from the crisis I had been in since the disappearance of the ex-Chilean girl, the ex-guerrilla fighter, the ex-Madame Arnoux. What did she call herself now? What personality, what name, what history had she adopted for this new stage in her life? Her new lover must be very important, much more important than the adviser to the director of UNESCO, who was too modest for her ambitions now, and who was devastated by her leaving. She had given me clear warning that last morning: "I'd only stay forever with a man who was very, very rich and powerful." I was certain I wouldn't see her again this time. You had to pull yourself together and forget the Peruvian girl with a thousand faces, good boy, convince yourself she was no more than a bad dream.

But a few days after I had gone back to work at UNESCO, Monsieur Arnoux appeared in the cubicle that was my office as I was translating a report on bilingual education in sub-Saharan Africa.

"I'm sorry I was short with you the other day," he said, uncomfortably. "I was in a very bad state of mind just then."

He proposed that we have supper. And though I knew this supper would be catastrophic for my own state of mind, my curiosity to hear about her and find out what had happened were stronger, and I accepted.

We went to Chez Eux, a restaurant in the seventh arrondissement, not far from my house. It was the tensest, most difficult supper I've ever had. But fascinating too, because I learned many things about the ex-Madame Arnoux and also discovered how far she had gone in her search for the security she identified with wealth.

We ordered whiskey with ice and Perrier as an aperitif, and then red wine with a meal we barely tasted. Chez Eux had a fixed menu consisting of exquisite food that came in deep pans, and our table was filling up with pâtés, snails, salads, fish, meat, which the amazed waiters took away almost untouched to make room for a great variety of desserts, one bathed in bubbling chocolate, not understanding why we slighted all those delicacies.

Robert Arnoux asked me how long I had known her. I lied and said only since 1960 or 1961, when she passed through Paris on her way to Cuba as one of the recipients of a scholarship from the MIR to receive guerrilla training.

"In other words, you don't know anything about her past, her family," Monsieur Arnoux said with a nod, as if he were talking to himself. "I always knew she lied. About her family and her childhood, I mean. But I forgave her. They seemed like pious lies intended to disguise a childhood and adolescence that embarrassed her. Because she must have come from a very humble social class, don't you agree?"

"She didn't like talking about it. She never told me anything about her family. But yes, undoubtedly a very humble class—"

"It made me sad, I could guess at the mountain of prejudices in Peruvian society, the great family names, the racism," he interrupted me. "She said she had attended the Sophianum, the best nuns' academy in Lima, where the daughters of high society were educated. That her father owned a cotton plantation and she had broken with her family out of idealism, in order to be a revolutionary. She never cared about the revolution, I'm sure of that! From the time I met her, she never expressed a single political opinion. She would have done anything to get out of Cuba. Even marry me. When we left, I suggested a trip to Peru to meet her family. She told me more stories, of course. That because she had been in the MIR and in Cuba, if she set foot in Peru she would be arrested. I forgave these fantasies. I understood they were born of her insecurity. She had been infected with the social and racial prejudices that are so strong in South American countries. That's why she invented the

87

biography for me of the aristocratic girl she had never been."

At times I had the impression that Monsieur Arnoux had forgotten about me. Even his gaze was lost at some point in the void, and he spoke so softly his words became an inaudible murmur. At other times he recovered, looked at me with suspicion and hatred, and pressed me to tell him if I'd known she had a lover. I was her compatriot, her friend, hadn't she ever confided in me?

"She never said a word. I never suspected anything. I thought you two got along very well, that you were happy."

"I thought so too," he murmured, crestfallen. He ordered another bottle of wine. And added, his eyes veiled and his voice acerbic: "She didn't need to do what she did. It was ugly, it was dirty, it was disloyal to behave like that with me. I gave her my name, I went out of my way to make her happy. I endangered my career to get her out of Cuba. That was a real via crucis. Disloyalty can't reach these extremes. So much calculation, so much hypocrisy, it's inhuman."

Abruptly he stopped speaking. He moved his lips, not making a sound, and his rectangular little mustache twisted and stretched. He had gripped his empty glass and was squeezing it as if he wanted to crush it. His eyes were bloodshot and filled with tears.

I didn't know what to say to him, any consolatory phrase would have sounded false and ridiculous. Suddenly, I understood that so much desperation was not due only to her abandoning him. There was something else he wanted to tell me but was finding difficult.

"My life's savings," Monsieur Arnoux whispered,

looking at me accusingly, as if I were responsible for his tragedy. "Do you follow? I'm an older man, I'm in no condition to rebuild my whole life. Do you understand? Not only to deceive me with some gangster who must have helped her plan the crime, but to do that too: withdraw all the money from the account we had in Switzerland. I gave her that proof of my trust, do you see? A joint account. In case I had an accident, or died suddenly. So inheritance taxes wouldn't take everything I'd saved in a lifetime of work and sacrifice. Do you understand the disloyalty, the vileness? She went to Switzerland to make a deposit and took everything, everything, and ruined me. *Chapeau, un coup de maître!* She knew I couldn't denounce her without accusing myself, without ruining my reputation and my position. She knew if I denounced her I'd be the first one injured, for keeping secret accounts, for evading taxes. Do you understand how well planned it was? Can you believe she could be so cruel toward someone who gave her only love and devotion?"

He kept returning to the same subject, with intervals in which we drank wine in silence, each of us absorbed in his own thoughts. Was it perverse of me to wonder what hurt him more, her leaving him or her stealing his secret bank account in Switzerland? I felt sorry for him, and I felt remorse, but I didn't know how to comfort him. I limited myself to interjecting occasional brief, friendly phrases. In reality, he didn't want to converse with me. He had invited me to supper because he needed someone to listen to him, he needed to say aloud, before a witness, things that had been scorching his heart ever since the disappearance of his wife.

"Forgive me, I needed to unburden myself," he said at last when all the other diners had left and we were alone, watched with impatient eyes by the waiters in Chez Eux. "I thank you for your patience. I hope this catharsis does me some good."

I said that with time, all of this would be behind him, no trouble lasts a hundred years. And as I spoke, I felt like a total hypocrite, as guilty as if I had planned the flight of ex–Madame Arnoux and the plundering of his secret account.

"If you ever run into her, please tell her. She didn't need to do that. I would have given her everything. Did she want my money? I would have given it to her. But not like this, not like this."

We said goodbye in the doorway of the restaurant, in the brilliance of the lights on the Eiffel Tower. It was the last time I saw the mistreated Monsieur Robert Arnoux.

The Túpac Amaru column of the MIR, under the command of Guillermo Lobatón, lasted some five months longer than the column that had made its headquarters on Mesa Pelada. As it had done with Luis de la Puente, Paúl Escobar, and the Miristas who perished in the valley of La Convención, the army gave no details regarding how it annihilated all the members of that guerrilla band. In the second half of 1965, helped by the Asháninka of Gran Pajonal, Lobatón and his companions eluded the persecution of the special forces of the army that mobilized in helicopters and on land and savagely punished the indigenous settlements that hid and fed the guerrillas. Finally, the decimated column, twelve men devastated by mosquitoes, fatigue, and disease, fell in the vicinity of the Sotziqui River on January 7, 1966. Did they die in combat or were they captured alive and executed? Their graves were never found. According to unverifiable rumors, Lobatón and his second-in-command were taken up in a helicopter and thrown into the forest so the animals would devour their corpses. For several years Lobatón's French partner, Jacqueline, attempted without success, by means of campaigns in Peru and other countries, to have the government reveal the location of the graves of the rebels in that ephemeral guerrilla war. Were there survivors? Were they living clandestinely in the convulsed, divided Peru of Belaúnde Terry's final days? As I slowly recovered from the disappearance of the bad girl, I followed these distant events through the letters of Uncle Ataúlfo. He seemed more and more pessimistic about the possibility that democracy would not collapse in Peru. "The same military that defeated the guerrillas is preparing now to defeat the legitimate state and have another kind of uprising," he assured me.

One day in Germany, in the most unexpected way, I ran into a survivor of Mesa Pelada: none other than Alfonso the Spiritualist, the boy sent to Paris by a theosophical group in Lima, the one fat Paúl had snatched away from spirits and the next world to turn him into a guerrilla fighter. I was in Frankfurt, working at an international conference on communications, and during a break I escaped to a department store to make some purchases. At the register, someone took my arm. I recognized him instantly. In the four years since I'd seen him he had put on weight and let his hair grow very long—the new style in Europe—but his dead-white face with its reserved, rather sad expression was the same. He had been in Germany a few months, obtained political refugee status, and was living with a girl from Frankfurt whom he had met in Paris when Paúl was there. We went to have coffee in the department-store cafeteria full of matrons with fat little children who were being waited on by Turks.

Alfonso the Spiritualist had been miraculously saved from the army commando attack that leveled Mesa Pelada. Luis de la Puente had sent him to Quillabamba a few days earlier: communications with urban support bases were not working well, and in the field they hadn't heard anything about a group of five trained boys whose arrival had been expected weeks before.

"The support base in Cuzco had been infiltrated," he told me, speaking with the same calm I remembered. "Several people were captured, and somebody talked under torture. That's how they got to Mesa Pelada. The truth was, we hadn't begun operations. Lobatón and Máximo Velando had moved plans forward in Junín. And after the ambush in Yahuarina, when they killed so many police, they threw the army at us. Those of us in Cuzco hadn't begun to move yet. De la Puente's idea wasn't to stay in the field but to keep moving. 'The guerrilla focus is perpetual movement,' that's what Che taught. But they didn't give us time and we were caught in the security zone."

The Spiritualist spoke with a curious distance from what he was saying, as if it had occurred centuries earlier. He didn't know by what conjunction of circumstances he had escaped the dragnets that demolished the MIR's support bases in Quillabamba and Cuzco. He hid in the house of a Cuzcan family, whom he had known long ago through his theosophical sect. They treated him very well even though they were afraid. After a couple of months, they got him out of the city and to Puno, hiding in a freight truck. From there it was easy to reach Bolivia, where, after a long series of procedures and formalities, he arranged for East Germany to admit him as a political refugee.

"Tell me about fat Paúl, up there in Mesa Pelada."

Apparently he had adapted well to the life and to the altitude of 3,800 meters. His spirits never flagged, though at times, on marches exploring the territory around the camp, his body played some bad tricks on him. Above all when he had to climb up mountains or down precipices in torrential rains. One time he fell on a slope that was a quagmire and rolled twenty, thirty meters. His companions thought he had cracked open his skull, but he got up as good as new, covered in mud from head to toe.

"He lost a lot of weight," Alfonso added. "The morning I said goodbye to him, in Illarec ch'aska, he was almost as thin as you. Sometimes we talked about you. 'I wonder what our ambassador to UNESCO is doing?' he'd say. 'Do you think he decided to publish those poems he was secretly writing?' He never lost his sense of humor. He always won the joke contests we had at night to keep from being bored. His wife and son are living in Cuba now."

I would have liked to spend more time with Alfonso the Spiritualist, but I had to go back to the conference.

93

We said goodbye with a hug, and I gave him my number so he could call me if he ever came through Paris.

A little while before or after this conversation, the grim prophecies of my uncle Ataúlfo came true. On October 3, 1968, the military, headed by General Juan Velasco Alvarado, initiated the coup that ended the democracy presided over by Belaúnde Terry, who was sent into exile, and a new military dictatorship began in Peru that would last for twelve years.

Painter of Horses in Swinging London

In the second half of the 1960s, London displaced Paris as the city of styles and trends that moved into Europe and then spread all over the world. Music replaced books and ideas as a center of attraction for the young, above all with the Beatles but also including Cliff Richard, the Shadows, the Rolling Stones with Mick Jagger, other English bands and singers, and hippies and the psychedelic revolution of the flower children. As they had once gone to Paris to make the revolution, many Latin Americans immigrated to London to join the partisans of cannabis, pop music, and the promiscuous life. Carnaby Street supplanted Saint-Germain as the navel of the world. London was the birthplace of the miniskirt, long hair, the eccentric outfits commemorated by the musicals *Hair* and *Jesus Christ Superstar*, the popularization of drugs, beginning with marijuana and ending with LSD, the fascination with Hindu spiritualism and Buddhism, the practice of free love, the emergence of homosexuals from the closet, gay pride campaigns, as well as a total rejection of the bourgeois establishment, in the name not of the socialist revolution, to which the hippies were indifferent, but of a hedonistic and anarchic pacifism, tamed by a love for nature and animals and a disavowal of traditional morality. Debates regarding La Mutualité, the nouveau roman, refined singer-song-writers like Léo Ferré or Georges Brassens, and Parisian art cinemas were no longer the points of reference for young rebels, but rather Trafalgar Square and the parks where they demonstrated behind Vanessa Redgrave and Tariq Ali against the war in Vietnam, between crowded concerts by their great idols and tokes of Colombian herb, and pubs and discotheques, symbols of the new culture that like a magnet attracted millions of young people of both sexes to London. In England these were also the years of theatrical splendor, and the mounting of Peter Weiss's *Marat/Sade* in 1964, directed by Peter Brook, best known for his revolutionary stagings of Shakespeare, was an event throughout all of Europe. I've never seen anything onstage since then that etched itself so deeply in my mind.

Through one of those strange conjunctions woven by fate, it turned out that in the late sixties I was spending long periods of time in England and living in the very heart of swinging London: in Earl's Court, an extremely lively and cosmopolitan section west of Kensington which, because of the many New Zealanders and Australians, was known as Kangaroo Valley. In fact, the adventure of May 1968, when the young people of Paris filled the Latin Quarter with barricades and declared that one had to be a realist by choosing the impossible, found me in London, where, because of the strikes that paralyzed train stations and airports in France, I was stranded for a few weeks, unable to find out if anything had happened to my little apartment near the École Militaire.

When I returned to Paris, I discovered that my apartment was intact, for the revolution of May 1968 had not spilled over the perimeter of the Latin Quarter and Saint-Germain-des-Prés. Contrary to what many people prophesied during those euphoric days, it did not have significant political consequences except to accelerate the fall of de Gaulle, inaugurate the brief five-year era of Pompidou, and reveal the existence of a left more modern than the French Communist Party ("*la crapule stalinienne*," according to the phrase of Cohn-Bendit, one of the leaders of '68). Customs became freer, but from the cultural point of view, with the disappearance of an entire illustrious generation—Mauriac, Camus, Sartre, Aron, Merleau-Ponty, Malraux—there was a discreet cultural retraction during those years, when instead of creators, the *maîtres à penser* became the critics, first the structuralists in the style of Michel Foucault and Roland Barthes, and then the deconstructionists, like Gilles Deleuze and Jacques Derrida, with their arrogant, esoteric rhetoric, isolated in cabals of devotees and removed from the general public, whose cultural life, as a consequence of this development, became increasingly banal.

Those were years when I was working very hard, though, as the bad girl might have said, with only moderate achievements: the move from translator to interpreter. As I had done the first time, I filled the emptiness of her disappearance by taking on countless obligations. I resumed my classes in Russian and simultaneous interpretation, to which I devoted myself tenaciously after my hours of work at UNESCO. I spent two summers in the USSR, for two months each time, the first in Moscow and the second in Leningrad, taking special intensive Russian-language courses for interpreters in secluded university areas where we felt as if we were at a Jesuit boarding school.

Some two years after my final supper with Robert Arnoux, I had a rather subdued relationship with Cécile, a functionary at UNESCO, an attractive, pleasant woman but a nondrinker, a vegetarian, and a devout Catholic, with whom I got along perfectly well only when we made love, because in everything else we were polar opposites. At one point we contemplated the possibility of living together, but both of us became frightened—I above all—at the prospect of cohabitation when we were so different and there was not, deep down, even the shadow of true love between us. Our relationship languished from tedium, and one day we stopped seeing and calling each other.

It was difficult for me to obtain my first contracts as an interpreter in spite of excelling at all the exams and having the corresponding diplomas. But this was a tighter network than that of translators, and the professional associations, real mafias, admitted new members by the eyedropper. I achieved membership only when I could add Russian to English and French as the languages I translated into Spanish. My interpreting contracts kept me traveling a great deal in Europe, and frequently to London, especially for economic conferences and seminars. One day in 1970, at the Peruvian consulate on Sloane Street, where I had gone to renew my passport, I ran into Juan Barreto, a childhood friend and classmate at the Colegio Champagnat in Miraflores, who was also renewing his passport.

He had become a hippie, not the tattered kind but an elegant one. He wore his silky, graying hair hanging loose down to his shoulders and had a rather sparse beard that created a carefully tended muzzle around his mouth. I remembered him as chubby and short, but now he was taller than me by a few centimeters and was as slim as a model. He wore cherry-colored velvet trousers and sandals that seemed to be made of parchment, not leather, a printed silk Oriental tunic, a blaze of color framed by his loose, open jacket that reminded me of the ones worn by Turkoman shepherds in a documentary on Mesopotamia I had seen at the Palais de Chaillot in the series *Connaissance du monde*, which I attended every month.

We went for coffee in the vicinity of the consulate, and our conversation was so agreeable I invited him to have lunch at a pub in Kensington Gardens. We spent more than two hours together, he speaking and I listening and interjecting monosyllables.

His story was novelesque. I recalled that in his last years at school, Juan began to work at Radio El Sol as a commentator and soccer announcer, and his Marist friends predicted a great future for him as a sports journalist. "But that was really a child's game," he told me. "My true vocation was always painting." He attended the School of Fine Arts in Lima and took part in a group show at the Institute of Contemporary Art on Jirón Ocoña. Then his father sent him to take a course in design and color at St. Martin's School of Arts in London. As soon as he arrived in England, he decided the city was his ("Brother, it seemed to be waiting for me") and he would never leave it. When he told his father he wasn't returning to Peru, his father cut off his allowance. Then he began a poverty-stricken existence as a street artist, making portraits of tourists in Leicester Square or in the doorways of Harrods, and drawing with chalk on the sidewalks of Parliament, Big Ben, or the Tower of London and then passing the hat among the onlookers. He slept at the YMCA and in miserable bed-and-breakfasts and, like other dropouts, on winter nights he took refuge in religious shelters for human rejects and stood in long lines at churches and charitable institutions where they gave out bowls of hot soup twice a day. He often spent the night outdoors, in parks or inside cartons in the vestibules of stores. "I was desperate, but never once in all that time did I feel fucked-up enough to ask my father for a ticket back to Peru."

In spite of their insolvency, he and other vagabond hippies managed to travel to Kathmandu, where he discovered that in spiritual Nepal it was more difficult to survive without money than in materialistic Europe. The solidarity of his migratory companions was decisive in keeping him from dying of hunger or disease, because in India he contracted a Maltese fever that brought him to within an inch of departing this world. The girl and two boys traveling with him took turns watching over him as he convalesced in a filthy hospital in Madras where the rats wandered among the patients lying on the floor on straw mats.

"I'd become totally accustomed to the life of a tramp, to my home being on the street, when my luck changed."

He was making charcoal portraits for a couple of pounds each at the entrance to the Victoria and Albert Museum on Brompton Road, when a lady carrying a parasol and wearing net gloves unexpectedly asked him to draw the portrait of the dog she was walking, a female King Charles spaniel, with white and coffee-colored spots, that was brushed, washed, and combed with the airs of a lady. The dog's name was Esther. The lady was delighted with the double drawing Juan made, "full face and in profile." When she went to pay him, she discovered she didn't have any money, either because her wallet had been stolen or because she had left it at home. "It doesn't matter," said Juan. "It's been an honor to work for so distinguished a model." The lady, confused and grateful, left. But after taking a few steps, she returned and handed Juan a card. "If you're ever in the area, knock on the door so you can greet your new friend." She pointed at the dog.

Mrs. Stubard, a retired nurse and childless widow, became a fairy godmother whose magic wand took Juan Barreto off the London streets and gradually cleaned him up ("One of the consequences of being a tramp is that you never bathe, and you don't even smell as dirty as you really are"), fed him, dressed him, and finally catapulted him into the most English of English environments: the world of owners, riders, trainers, and enthusiasts at the Newmarket Riding Club, where the most famous racehorses in Great Britain, and perhaps the world, are born, grow up, die, and are buried.

Mrs. Stubard lived alone with little Esther in a red-brick house, with a small garden that she tended herself and kept beautiful, in a quiet, prosperous section of St. John's Wood. She had inherited it from her husband, a pediatrician who had spent his entire life in the wards and consulting rooms of Charing Cross Hospital caring for other people's children though he never could have one of his own. Juan Barreto knocked on the widow's door one afternoon when he was hungrier, lonelier, and more anguished than usual. She recognized him immediately.

"I've come to see how my friend Esther is getting along. And, if it's not too much trouble, to ask you for a piece of bread."

"Come in, artist," she said with a smile. "Would you mind shaking off those disgusting sandals you're wearing? And take the opportunity to wash your feet at the faucet in the garden."

"Mrs. Stubard was an angel come down from heaven," said Juan Barreto. "She had framed my charcoal drawing of the dog and kept it on an end table in the living room. It looked very nice." She also had Juan wash his hands with soap and water ("From the beginning she adopted the air of a bossy mother that she still uses with me") and fixed him a couple of tomato, cheese, and cucumber sandwiches and a cup of tea. They talked for a long time, and she urged Juan to tell her his life from A to Z. She was alert and avid to know everything about the world, and she insisted that Juan describe in detail what the hippies were like, where they came from, and what kinds of lives they led.

"You won't believe it, but I was fascinated by the old lady. I went to see her not only so she could feed me but because I had a great time talking to her. She had a seventy-year-old body but a fifteen-year-old spirit. And this'll kill you, I turned her into a hippie."

Juan stopped by the little house in St. John's Wood once a week, bathed and combed Esther, helped Mrs.

Stubard prune and water the garden, and sometimes went shopping with her at the nearby Sainsbury's market. The bourgeois residents of St. John's Wood must have been surprised to see the mismatched pair. Juan helped her cook—he taught her Peruvian recipes for stuffed potato, shredded chicken and chili, ceviche—and washed the dishes for her, and then they had after-dinner conversations during which Juan played music by the Beatles and the Rolling Stones for her, and recounted a thousand and one adventures and anecdotes about the hippies, male and female, he had met on his wanderings around London, India, and Nepal. Mrs. Stubard's curiosity was not satisfied with Juan's explanations of how cannabis sharpened one's lucidity and sensitivity, principally for music. At last, overcoming her prejudices—she was a practicing Methodist—she gave Juan some money so she could try marijuana. "She was so restless, I swear she would have tried a cap of LSD if I had encouraged her to." Their marijuana session was carried out against the musical background of the soundtrack of *Yellow Submarine*, the Beatles picture Mrs. Stubard and Juan had gone arm in arm to see at a theater in Piccadilly Circus. My friend was afraid his protector and friend would have a bad trip and, in fact, eventually she complained of a headache and fell asleep faceup on the living-room carpet after two hours of extraordinary excitement when she chattered like a parrot, bursting into laughter and doing ballet steps before the stupefied eyes of Juan and Esther.

Their relationship turned into something more than friendship, a fraternal companionship of accomplices in spite of the differences in age, language, and background. "I felt as if she were my mother, my sister, my buddy, my guardian angel."

As if Juan's testimony regarding the hippie subculture were not enough for her, one day Mrs. Stubard suggested he invite two or three of his friends for tea. He had all kinds of doubts. He feared the consequences of that effort to mix water and oil, but finally he arranged for the meeting. He chose three of the more presentable of his hippie friends and told them if they gave Mrs. Stubard a hard time, or stole anything from her house, he'd break his pacifist vows and strangle them. The two girls and the boy—René, Jody, and Aspern—sold incense and bags woven according to supposed Afghani patterns on the streets of Earl's Court. They behaved fairly well and made short work of the strawberry shortcake and almond pastries Mrs. Stubard had prepared for them, but when they lit a stick of incense, explaining to the lady of the house that this would purify the atmosphere spiritually and that the karma of each person present would improve, it turned out that Mrs. Stubard was allergic to the purifying smoke: she suffered an attack of loud, unstoppable sneezes that reddened her eyes and nose and set off Esther's barking. When this incident had been overcome, the get-together proceeded fairly well until René, Jody, and Aspern told Mrs. Stubard they formed a love triangle and that the three of them making love was their homage to the Holy Trinity—the Father, the Son, and the Holy Spirit—and an even more determined way of putting into practice the slogan "Make love not war," approved at the last demonstration in Trafalgar Square against the war in Vietnam by no less a personage than the philosopher and mathematician

Bertrand Russell. Within the Methodist morality she had been taught, a three-way love was something Mrs. Stubard had not imagined even in her most salacious nightmare. "The poor woman's jaw dropped and she spent the rest of the afternoon staring in a catatonic stupor at the trio I had brought to her house. Later, she confessed with a melancholy air that, having been brought up as English girls of her generation were brought up, she had been deprived of many curious things in life. And she told me she never had seen her husband naked, because from the first day to the last they made love in the dark."

From visiting her once a week, Juan passed on to two, then three visits, and finally he moved in with Mrs. Stubard, who fixed up the small room that had been her late husband's, since in his final years they'd had separate bedrooms. Contrary to what Juan had feared, their cohabitation was perfect. She never tried to interfere in any way in Juan's life, or ask why he slept elsewhere on certain nights or came home when the residents of St. John's Wood were leaving for work. She gave him a key to the house. "The only thing she worried about was my taking a bath a couple of times a week," Juan said with a laugh. "Because you may not believe it, but after almost three years as a street hippie, I had lost the habit of showering. In Mrs. Stubard's house, I gradually rediscovered the Miraflores perversion of a daily shower."

In addition to helping her in the garden and kitchen, and taking Esther for walks and putting the trash can out on the street, Juan had long, intimate conversations with Mrs. Stubard, always with a cup of tea in their hands and a platter of gingersnaps in front of them. He told her about Peru and she talked of an England that, from the perspective of swinging London, seemed prehistoric: boys and girls who stayed in harsh boarding schools until they were sixteen and where, except for the disreputable districts of Soho, St. Pancras, and the East End, life ended at nine o'clock at night. The only diversion Mrs. Stubard and her husband allowed themselves was to go occasionally to hear a concert or an opera at Covent Garden. During summer vacation they spent a week in Bristol, in the house of her brother and sister-in-law, and another week in the Scottish Highlands, which her husband loved. Mrs. Stubard had never been out of Great Britain. But she was interested in the world: she read *The Times* carefully, beginning with the obituaries, and listened to BBC newscasts on the radio at one in the afternoon and at eight in the evening. It never had occurred to her to buy a television set, and she went to the movies only rarely. But she had a phonograph and listened to the symphonies of Mozart, Beethoven, and Benjamin Britten.

One day her nephew Charles, her only close relative, came for tea. He was a horse trainer at Newmarket, quite a character, according to his aunt. And he must have been, judging by the red Jaguar he parked at the door to the house. Young and jovial, with curly blond hair and red cheeks, he was amazed there wasn't a single bottle of good Scotch in the house and that he had to make do with a glass of the sweet muscatel Mrs. Stubard regaled him with after tea, the inevitable cucumber sandwiches, and the cheese and lemon cake. He was very cordial to Juan, though he had difficulty locating in the world the exotic country the hippie of the house came from—he confused Peru with Mexico—something he criticized himself for with a sporting spirit: "I'm going to buy a map of the world and a geography manual so I won't stick my foot in my mouth again the way I did today." He stayed until nightfall, telling anecdotes about the thoroughbred he was training for the races at Newmarket. And he confessed he had become a trainer because he couldn't be a jockey, given his husky build. "Being a jockey is a terrible sacrifice, but it's also the most beautiful profession in the world. Winning the Derby, victory at Ascot, just imagine! Better than winning first prize in the lottery."

Before he left he stood looking, with great satisfaction, at the charcoal sketch Juan Barreto had made of Esther. "This is a work of art," he declared. "I laughed at him to myself, taking him for a yokel," Juan Barreto said in self-recrimination.

A short while later my friend received a note that, second only to his street encounter with Mrs. Stubard and Esther, definitively changed the direction of his life. Would the "artist" be interested in painting a portrait of Primrose, the mare Charles was training, the star of Mr. Patrick Chick's stable, whose owner, happy with the rewards she brought him at the track, wanted to eternalize her in an oil painting? He was offering two hundred pounds if he liked the painting; if not, Juan could keep the canvas and receive fifty pounds for his efforts. "My ears still buzz with the vertigo I felt as I read that letter from Charles." Juan rolled his eyes with retrospective emotion.

Thanks to Primrose, Charles, and Mr. Chick, Juan stopped being an insolvent hippie and became a salon hippie, whose talent for immortalizing on canvas fillies, mares, breeders, and racers ("animals about which I was completely ignorant") gradually opened to him the doors of the Newmarket owners and trainers. Mr. Chick liked the oil painting of Primrose and gave an astounded Juan Barreto the two hundred pounds he had promised. The first thing Juan did was to buy Mrs. Stubard a little flowered hat and matching umbrella.

That had been four years ago. Juan still did not completely believe the fantastic change in his luck. He had painted at least a hundred oils of horses and made countless drawings, sketches, and studies in pencil and in charcoal, and he had so much work that the stable owners at Newmarket were obliged to wait weeks before he could take care of their requests. He bought a little house in the country halfway between Cambridge and Newmarket, and a pied-à-terre in Earl's Court for his visits to London. Whenever he came to the city he went to visit his fairy godmother and take Esther out for a walk. When the little dog died, he and Mrs. Stubard buried her in the garden.

I saw Juan Barreto several times in the course of that year, on all my visits to London, and I put him up for a few days in my apartment in Paris during a vacation he took to see a show dedicated to "Rembrandt's Century" at the Grand Palais. The hippie style had just come to France, and people would turn around on the street to look at Juan's clothes. He was an excellent person. Every time I went to London to work I let him know in advance, and he arranged to leave Newmarket and give me at least one night of pop music and London dissipation. Thanks to him I did things I'd never done, spent blanked-out nights in discotheques or at hippie parties where the smell of pot filled the air, and where brownies made with hashish were served that hurled a novice like me into hypersensitive trips, sometimes amusing and sometimes nightmarish.

The most surprising thing for me—and the most pleasant, why deny it?—was how easy it was at those parties to caress and make love to any girl. Only then did I discover how much I had absorbed the moral framework that my aunt Alberta taught me, which, in a sense, still regulated my life in Paris. In the world's imagination, French girls were known for being free, without prejudices, and not too finicky when it was time to go to bed with a man, but in fact, the ones who carried that freedom to an unprecedented extreme were the girls and boys of the London hippie revolution who, at least in Juan Barreto's circle of acquaintances, would go to bed with the stranger they had just danced with and come back after a while as if nothing had happened and go on with the party and taste the same dish again.

"The life you've lived in Paris is the life of a UNESCO bureaucrat, Ricardo," Juan said mockingly, "a Miraflores puritan. I assure you that in many places in Paris the same freedom exists as here."

This was certainly true. My life in Paris—my life in general—had been fairly sober, even during the times I had no contract, when instead of kicking up my heels, I would dedicate myself to perfecting Russian with a private teacher because, though I could interpret it, I didn't feel as confident with the language of Tolstoy and Dostoyevsky as I did with English and French. I had taken a liking to it and read more in Russian than in any other language. Those occasional weekends in England, taking part in nights of pop music, pot, and sex in swinging London, marked a modulation in what had been before (and would go on being afterward) a very austere life. But on those London weekends, which I gave to myself as a present after finishing a contract, and thanks to the painter of horse portraits, I did things that made it hard for me to recognize myself: dancing barefoot, with disheveled hair, smoking pot or chewing peyote seeds, and almost always, as the finishing touch to those agitated nights, making love, often in the most unlikely places, under tables, in tiny bathrooms, in closets, in gardens, with some girl, at times very young, with whom I barely exchanged a word and whose name I wouldn't remember afterward.

Juan insisted, after our first meeting, that whenever I came to London I stay at his pied-à-terre in Earl's Court. He was almost never there because he spent most of his time in Newmarket, transferring real equines to canvas. I'd be doing him a favor if I aired out his apartment from time to time. If we were in London at the same time, that wouldn't be a problem either because he could sleep at Mrs. Stubard's—he still had his room there—and, as a last resort, he could set up a folding cot in the bedroom of his pied-à-terre. He was so insistent that finally I agreed. Since he wouldn't allow me to pay even a penny in rent, I tried to make it up to him by always bringing from Paris a bottle of good Bordeaux, some Camembert or Brie, and tins of pâté de foie gras, which made his eyes sparkle. Juan was now a hippie on no special diet, one who didn't believe in vegetarianism.

I liked Earl's Court very much and fell in love with its

fauna. The district breathed youth, music, lives lived without caution or calculation, great doses of ingenuousness, the desire to live for the day, removed from conventional morality and values, a search for pleasure that rejected the old bourgeois myths of happiness—money, power, family, position, social success—and found it in simple, passive forms of existence: music, artificial paradises, promiscuity, and an absolute lack of interest in the other problems that were shaking society. With their tranquil, peaceable hedonism, the hippies harmed no one, and they didn't proselytize, didn't want to convince or recruit people they had broken with in order to live their alternative lives: they wanted to be left in peace, absorbed in their frugal egotism and their psychedelic dream.

I knew I'd never be one of them because, though I thought of myself as a person fairly free of prejudices, I would never feel comfortable letting my hair grow down to my shoulders, or dressing in capes, necklaces, and iridescent shirts, or engaging in group sexual encounters. But I felt a great fondness for and even a melancholy envy of those boys and girls, given over without the slightest apprehension to the confused idealism that guided their conduct, never imagining the risks all of that was obliging them to take.

In those years, though not for much longer, the employees of banks, insurance companies, and financial firms in the City wore the traditional attire of striped trousers, black jacket, bowler hat, and the inescapable black umbrella under the arm. But on the backstreets of Earl's Court, with their two- or three-story houses and little gardens front and back, you could see people dressed as if they were going to a masquerade ball, even in rags and often barefoot, but always with a keen esthetic sense and sly, humorous details, seeking out what was showy, exotic, distinctive. I was astounded by my neighbor Marina, a Colombian who had come to London to study dance. She had a hamster that would constantly escape into Juan's pied-à-terre and scare me half to death, since it usually climbed into bed and curled up in the sheets. Marina, though she lived in poverty and must have had very little clothing, rarely dressed the same way twice: one day she appeared in huge clown's overalls and a derby on her head, and the next day in a miniskirt that left practically no secret of her body to the imagination of passersby. One day I ran into her in the Earl's Court station mounted on stilts, her face disfigured by a Union Jack painted from ear to ear.

Many hippies, perhaps the majority, came from the middle or upper class, and their rebellion was familial, directed against the well-regulated lives of their parents and what they considered the hypocrisy of puritanical customs and social façades behind which they hid their egotism, insular spirit, and lack of imagination. Their pacifism, naturism, vegetarianism, their eager search for a spiritual life that would give transcendence to their rejection of a materialist world corroded by class, social, and sexual prejudices, a world they wanted nothing to do with—this was sympathetic. But all of it was anarchic, thoughtless, without a center or direction, even without ideas, because the hippies—at least the ones I knew and observed up close—though they claimed to identify with the poetry of the beatniks (Allen Ginsberg gave a reading of his poems in Trafalgar Square in which he sang and performed Indian dances, and thousands of young people attended), in fact read very little or nothing at all. Their philosophy wasn't based on thought and reason but on sentiment, on feeling.

One morning I was in Juan's pied-à-terre, dedicated to the prosaic task of ironing some shirts and undershorts I had just washed in the Earl's Court Laundromat, when someone rang the doorbell. I opened and saw half a dozen boys with shaved heads, commando boots, short trousers, leather jackets with a military cut, some wearing crosses and combat medals on their chests. They asked about the Swag and Tails pub, which was just around the corner. They were the first skinheads I had seen. After that, these gangs would appear in the neighborhood from time to time, sometimes armed with clubs, and the benign hippies who spread their blankets on the sidewalks to sell handcrafted trinkets had to run, some with their babies in their arms, because the skinheads professed an obstinate hatred for them. It wasn't only hatred for the way they lived but also class hatred, because these hoodlums, playing at being SS, came from working-class and marginal areas and embodied their own kind of rebellion. They became the shock troops of a tiny party, the racist National Front, which demanded the expulsion of blacks from England. Their idol was Enoch Powell, a conservative parliamentarian who, in a speech that caused an uproar, had prophesied in an apocalyptic manner that "rivers of blood would run in Great Britain" if there wasn't a halt to immigration. The appearance of the skinheads had created a certain tension, and there were some acts of violence in the district, but they were isolated. As far as I was concerned, I really enjoyed all those short stays in Earl's Court. Even Uncle Ataúlfo noticed it. We wrote to each other with some frequency; I recounted my London discoveries, and he complained about the economic disasters that the dictatorship of General Velasco Alvarado was beginning to cause in Peru. In one of his letters, he said, "I see you're having a very good time in London and that the city makes you happy."

The neighborhood had filled with small cafés, vegetarian restaurants, and houses where all the varieties of Indian tea were offered, staffed by hippie girls and boys who prepared the perfumed infusions in front of the patron. The hippies' scorn for the industrial world had led them to revive handicrafts of every kind and to mythologize manual labor: they wove bags and made sandals, earrings, necklaces, tunics, headscarves, and pendants. I loved to go to the teahouses and read, as I did in the *bistrots* of Paris, but how different the atmosphere was, especially in a garage with four tables where the waitress was Annette, a French girl with long hair held back in a braid and very pretty feet; I had long conversations with her about the differences between asanas and pranayama yoga, about which she seemed to know everything and I nothing.

Juan's pied-à-terre was tiny, happy, and inviting. It was on the ground floor of a two-story house, divided and subdivided into small apartments, and it consisted of a single bedroom, a small bathroom, and a kitchenette built into a wall. The room was spacious, with two large windows that assured good ventilation and an excellent view of Philbeach Gardens, a small street in the shape of a half-moon, and the interior garden, which lack of care had turned into an overgrown thicket. At one time there was a Sioux tent in that garden where a hippie couple lived with two crawling babies. She would come to the pied-à-terre to heat her children's bottles, and she showed me a way of breathing that entailed holding the air and passing it through the entire body, which, she said very seriously, dissolved all the warlike tendencies in human nature.

In addition to the bed, the room had a large table full of strange objects bought by Juan Barreto on Portobello Road and, on the walls, a multitude of prints, some images of Peru—the inevitable Machu Picchu in a preferred spot—and photographs of Juan with different people in a variety of places. And a tall case where he kept books and magazines. There were also some books on a shelf, but what abounded in the place were records: he had an excellent collection of rock-and-roll and pop music, both English and American, arranged around a first-rate radio and record player.

One day when I was examining Juan's photographs for the third or fourth time—the most amusing was one taken in the equine paradise of Newmarket, in which my friend appeared on a superb-looking thoroughbred crowned with a horseshoe of acanthus flowers, its reins held by a jockey and a splendid gentleman, undoubtedly the owner, both laughing at the poor rider who seemed very uncertain on this Pegasus—one of the pictures attracted my attention. Taken at a party of three or four very well-dressed couples, smiling and looking at the camera and holding glasses in their hands. What? Merely a resemblance. I looked again and rejected the idea. That day I went back to Paris. For the next two months, when I didn't return to London, the suspicion haunted me until it became a fixed idea. Could it be that the ex–Chilean girl, the ex–guerrilla fighter, the ex–Madame Arnoux was now in Newmarket? I asked myself this very often, caressing the little Guerlain toothbrush she left in my apartment on the last day I saw her and which I always kept with me, like an amulet. Too improbable, too coincidental, too everything. But I couldn't get the suspicion—the hope—out of my head. And I began to count the days until a new contract would return me to the pied-à-terre in Earl's Court.

"Do you know her?" Juan asked in surprise when I finally showed him the photograph and asked him about it. "She's Mrs. Richardson, the wife of that flamboyant man you see there, he's something of a glutton. She's Mexican, I think. She speaks a very funny English, you'd die laughing if you heard her. Are you sure you know her?"

"No, it isn't the person I thought it was."

But I was absolutely certain it was. What he said about her "very funny English" and her "Mexican" background convinced me. It had to be her. And though in the four years that had passed since she disappeared from Paris, I had often told myself it was much better this way because that little Peruvian adventurer had already caused enough disarray in my life, when I was sure she had reappeared in a new incarnation of her mutable identity only fifty miles from London, I felt an irresistible, restless need to go to Newmarket and see her again. Juan was sleeping at Mrs. Stubard's and I spent a good number of nights wide awake, in a state of anxiety that made my heart pound as if I were suffering an attack of tachycardia. Could she possibly have gone there? What adventures, entanglements, audacities had catapulted her into an enclave of the most exclusive society in the world? I didn't dare ask Juan Barreto more questions about Mrs. Richardson. I was afraid that if he confirmed the identity of our compatriot, she'd find herself embroiled in an extremely difficult situation. If she was passing herself off as Mexican in Newmarket, it had to be for some dark and troubled reason. I devised a secretive strategy. Indirectly, without mentioning in any way the lady in the photograph, I would try to have Juan take me to that Eden of horse racing. During a long night of palpitations and sleeplessness, not to mention a violent erection, at one point I even had an attack of jealousy of my friend. I imagined that the equine portrait painter not only did oil paintings in Newmarket but also entertained the bored wives of stable owners in his idle moments and, perhaps, that among his conquests was Mrs. Richardson.

Why didn't Juan have a steady partner, like so many other hippies? At the parties he took me to he almost always disappeared with a girl, sometimes with two. But one night I was amazed to see him caress and kiss on the mouth with a good deal of passion a redheaded boy, as slim as a reed, whom he crushed in his arms with amorous frenzy.

"I hope you weren't shocked by what you saw," he said to me later, somewhat peevishly.

I said that at the age of thirty-five nothing in the world shocked me, least of all whether human beings made love from the front or the back.

"I do it both ways and that makes me happy, my friend," he confessed, proudly. "I think I like girls better than boys, but in any case I wouldn't fall in love with one or the other. The secret to happiness, at least to peace of mind, is knowing how to separate sex from love. And, if possible, eliminating romantic love from your life, which is the love that makes you suffer. That way, I assure you, you live with greater tranquility and enjoy things more."

A philosophy the bad girl would have subscribed to down to the crossed t's and dotted i's, since she no doubt had always practiced it. I believe this was the only time we spoke—I should say, that he spoke—about intimate matters. He led a totally free and promiscuous life, but at the same time he preserved that widespread urge among Peruvians to avoid confidences in sexual matters and always to touch on the subject in a veiled, indirect way. Our conversations dealt principally with far-off Peru, where the news we received was increasingly disastrous regarding the sweeping nationalizations of farms and businesses by the military dictatorship of General Velasco Alvarado, which, according to my uncle Ataúlfo's letters, were more and more demoralizing and would drive us back to the Stone Age. On this occasion Juan also confessed that though in London he pursued every opportunity to satisfy his appetites ("So I've seen," I joked), in Newmarket he behaved like a chaste gentleman even though there was no lack of possibilities for amusement. But he didn't want some bedroom complication to compromise the work that had provided him with the security and income he never thought he'd attain. "I'm thirty-five, too, and as you've seen, here in

Earl's Court that counts as old age." It was true: the physical and mental youth of the inhabitants of this London neighborhood sometimes made me feel prehistoric.

It cost me a good amount of time and a delicate tangle of insinuations and apparently innocent questions to keep pushing Juan Barreto to take me to Newmarket, the celebrated town in Suffolk that since the middle of the eighteenth century had incarnated the English passion for thoroughbreds. I asked him endless questions. What were the people like there, the houses where they lived, the rituals and traditions that surrounded them, the relations among owners, jockeys, and trainers. And what happened at the auctions at Tattersalls, where extraordinary sums were paid for star horses, and how was it possible to auction a horse by parts, as if it could be disassembled. In response to what he told me, I did everything but applaud—"Man, that's interesting"—and put on an enthusiastic face: "How lucky you are, old friend, to know a world like that from the inside."

At last it produced results. After an end-of-season horse auction, an Italian breeder married to an Englishwoman, Signor Ariosti, was giving a dinner in his house to which he had invited Juan. My friend asked if he could bring along a compatriot, and the host said he'd be delighted. I recall that for the seventeen days I had to wait until the moment arrived, I was in a daze and suffered sudden cold sweats, an adolescent's excitement as I imagined seeing the Peruvian girl, and a few sleepless nights during which I did nothing but reproach myself: I was a hopeless imbecile to still be in love with a madwoman, an adventurer, an unscrupulous female with whom no man, I least of all, could maintain a stable relationship without eventually being stepped on. But in the intervals between these masochistic soliloquies, others came into play, full of joy and hope: Had she changed very much? Did she still have the bold manner that attracted me so much, or had life in the stratified English world of horses domesticated and nullified it? The day we took the train to Newmarket—we had to change lines at the Cambridge station—I was assailed by the notion that all of this was a figment of my imagination and Mrs. Richardson was in fact nothing more or less than some ordinary woman of Mexican background. What if you've been chasing an illusion all this time, Ricardito.

Juan Barreto's house in the country, a few miles from Newmarket, was a one-story wooden structure surrounded by willows and hydrangeas that looked more like an artist's studio than a residence. Crowded with jars of paint, easels, canvases mounted on stretchers, sketchbooks, and books about art, there were also a good number of records strewn on the floor around a wonderful sound system. Juan had a Mini Minor that he never brought to London, and that afternoon he gave me a ride in his small vehicle around Newmarket, a mysterious, scattered city with practically no center. He took me to see the blue-blood Jockey Club and the National Horseracing Museum. The real city wasn't the handful of houses around Newmarket High Street where there was a church, a few shops, some Laundromats, and a couple of restaurants, but the beautiful residences dispersed over the flat countryside and surrounded by the stables, outbuildings, and training tracks that Juan pointed out to me, naming their owners and recounting anecdotes about them. I barely heard him. All my attention was focused on the people we passed in the hope that the female form I was searching for would suddenly appear among them.

She didn't appear, not on that drive, and not in the small Indian restaurant where Juan took me that night for tandoori curry, and not the next day, either, during the long, interminable auction of mares and fillies and racehorses and studhorses held at Tattersalls under a huge canvas tent. I was stupendously bored. It surprised me to see the number of Arabs, some in jellabas, who raised the bids at each sale and sometimes paid astronomical sums that I never suspected could be paid for a quadruped. None of the many people Juan introduced me to during the auction, or the rest periods when attendees drank champagne from paper cups and ate carrots, cucumbers, and sardines from paper plates, mentioned the name I was waiting for: Mr. David Richardson.

But that night, as soon as I entered the sumptuous mansion of Signor Ariosti, I suddenly felt my throat go dry and my finger- and toenails begin to ache. There she was, less than ten meters away, sitting on the arm of a sofa, holding a tall glass in her hand. Before I could say a word or get close enough to her face to kiss her cheek, she extended an indifferent hand and greeted me in English as if I were a perfect stranger: "How do you do?" And without giving me time to reply, she turned her back and resumed her conversation with the people around her. Soon I heard her recounting, with absolute confidence and in an approximate but very expressive

English, how, when she was a girl, her father would take her to Mexico City every week to a concert or the opera. In this way he instilled in her an early passion for classical music.

She hadn't changed very much in these four years. She had the same slim, graceful appearance, with a narrow waist, slender shapely legs, and ankles as fine and delicate as wrists. She seemed more sure of herself and more confident than before, and she moved her head at the end of each sentence with studied nonchalance. She had lightened her hair a little and wore it longer than in Paris, with waves I didn't recall; her makeup was simpler and more natural than the heavy application Madame Arnoux was in the habit of using. She wore a skirt that was fashionably short and showed her knees, and a low-cut blouse that bared her smooth, silky shoulders and emphasized her throat, an elegant column encircled by a thin silver chain from which hung a precious stone, perhaps a sapphire, that with her movements swayed roguishly over the opening where arrogant breasts peeked out. I saw the wedding band on the ring finger of her left hand, in the Protestant manner. Had she converted to Anglicanism too? Mr. Richardson, to whom Juan introduced me in the next room, was an exuberant man in his sixties wearing an electric-yellow shirt and a handkerchief of the same color that spilled out over his smart blue suit. Drunk and euphoric, he was telling jokes about his travels in Japan, which greatly amused the circle of guests around him as he filled their glasses from a bottle of Dom Pérignon that appeared and reappeared in his hands as if by magic. Juan explained that he was a very rich man who spent part of the year in Asia on business, but that the guiding star of his life was the aristocratic passion par excellence: horses.

The hundred or so people, who filled the rooms and the veranda that opened onto a vast garden with a lighted tiled swimming pool, corresponded more or less to what Juan Barreto had described: a very English world that had been joined by some foreign horse people, like the owner of the house, Signor Ariosti, or my exotic compatriot disguised as a Mexican, Mrs. Richardson. Everyone had consumed a fair amount of drink, and they all seemed to know one another very well and communicate in a coded language whose recurrent theme was horse racing. Once, when I had managed to sit in the group around Mrs. Richardson, I learned that several of them, including the bad girl and her husband, had recently flown to Dubai in a private plane as the guests of an Arab sheikh for the opening of a racetrack. They had been treated like royalty. As for Muslims not drinking alcohol, they said, it might be true for poor Muslims, but the others, the horse people of Dubai, for instance, drank and served their guests the most exquisite French wine and champagne.

In spite of my efforts, in the course of the long night I couldn't exchange a single word with Mrs. Richardson. Each time I approached her, observing certain forms, she moved away on the pretext of wanting to greet someone, or to go to the buffet or the bar, or to have a private chat with a friend. I couldn't exchange glances with her either, and though I had no doubt she was perfectly aware of my constantly following her with my eyes, she never looked at me but always arranged to show me her back or her profile. What Juan Barreto had said was true: her English was elementary and at times incomprehensible, full of mistakes, but she spoke with so much freshness and conviction, and her Latin American musicality was so attractive, that the result was charming as well as expressive. To fill in the gaps she constantly accompanied her words with gestures, looks, and expressions that were a consummate display of coquetry.

Charles, Mrs. Stubard's nephew, turned out to be a charming boy. He told me that because of Juan, he had begun to read books by English travelers to Peru and was planning to spend a vacation in Cuzco and hike up to Machu Picchu. He wanted to persuade Juan to go with him. If I wanted to join the adventure, I was welcome.

At about two in the morning, as people were beginning to say good night to Signor Ariosti, on a sudden impulse that must have been brought on by the countless glasses of champagne I had consumed, I moved away from a couple who were asking me about my experiences as a professional interpreter, avoided my friend Juan Barreto, who, for the fourth or fifth time that evening, wanted to pull me into a room to admire the full-length portrait he had painted of Belicoso, one of the stars of the stables belonging to the master of the house, and crossed the salon to the group that included Mrs. Richardson. I grasped her arm with some force, smiled, and obliged her to move away from the people around her. She looked at me with a displeasure that twisted her mouth, and I heard her pronounce the first swear word I had ever heard her use.

"Let go of me, you fucking beast," she whispered through clenched teeth. "Let go of me, you'll make trouble for me."

"If you don't call me, I'll tell Mr. Richardson you're married in France and are wanted by the Swiss police for emptying out the secret bank account of Monsieur Arnoux."

And I put a piece of paper in her hand with the telephone number of Juan's pied-à-terre in Earl's Court. After a moment of astonishment and silence—her face frozen in a rictus—she burst into laughter, opening her eyes wide.

"Oh my God! You're learning, good boy," she exclaimed in a tone of professional approval, recovering from her surprise.

She turned and went back to the small group I had pulled her away from.

I was absolutely sure she wouldn't call me. I was a discomfiting witness to a past she wanted to erase at any cost; if not, she never would have behaved as she had all evening, avoiding me. But she did call me at Earl's Court two days later, very early. We could barely speak because, as always, she did nothing but give orders.

"I'll wait for you tomorrow at three, at the Russell Hotel. Do you know it? In Russell Square, near the British Museum. English punctuality, please."

I was there half an hour early. My hands were perspiring and it was hard for me to breathe. The place couldn't have been better. The old belle époque hotel, its façade and long hallways in the Oriental pompier style, seemed half empty, especially the bar with its high ceiling, wood-paneled walls, small widely spaced tables, some of them hidden among screens, and thick carpets that muffled footsteps and conversation. Behind the bar, a waiter leafed through the *Evening Standard*.

She arrived a few minutes late, dressed in a tailored outfit of mauve suede, shoes and handbag of black crocodile, a single strand of pearls, and on her hand a flashing solitaire. Over her arm she carried a gray raincoat and an umbrella of the same color and fabric. How far Comrade Arlette had come! Without greeting me, or smiling, or extending her hand, she sat across from me, crossed her legs, and began to berate me.

"The other night you did something so stupid I can't forgive you. You shouldn't have said a word to me, you shouldn't have taken my arm, you shouldn't have spoken to me as if you knew me. You might have compromised me. Didn't you realize you had to pretend? Where's your head, Ricardito?"

It was the bad girl, no question about that. We hadn't seen each other for four years and she didn't think to ask me how I was, what I had been doing, or even to give me a smile or a pleasant word on our meeting. She went straight to what concerned her without being distracted by anything else.

"You look very pretty," I said, speaking with some difficulty because of my emotions. "Even prettier than four years ago when your name was Madame Arnoux. I forgive your insults the other night and your insolent remarks now because of how pretty you look. Besides, in case you want to know, yes, I'm still in love with you. In spite of everything. Crazy about you. More than ever. Do you remember the toothbrush you left me as a memento the last time we saw each other? Here it is. Since then I carry it everywhere in my pocket. I've become a fetishist because of you. Thanks for being so pretty, Chilean girl."

She didn't laugh, but the ironic gleam of past times flashed in her eyes the color of dark honey. She took the toothbrush, examined it, and returned it to me, murmuring, "I don't know what you're talking about." With no discomfort at all she allowed me to look at her as she observed me, studying me. My eyes looked her over from top to bottom, from bottom to top, stopping at her knees, her throat, her ears half covered by locks of her now light-colored hair, her carefully tended hands and long nails with natural polish, her nose that seemed to have sharpened. She allowed me to take her hands and kiss them but with her proverbial indifference, without the slightest gesture of reciprocity.

"Was that a serious threat you made the other night?" she finally asked.

"Very serious," I said, kissing each finger, the knuckles, the back and palm of each hand. "Over the years I've become like you. Anything to get what you want. Those are your words, bad girl. And as you know very well, the only thing I really want in this world is you."

She slipped one of her hands from mine and passed it over my head, mussing my hair, in that slightly pitying semi-caress she had used with me on other occasions.

"No, you're not capable of those things," she said quietly, as if lamenting a lack in my personality. "But yes, it must be true you're still in love with me."

She ordered tea with scones for two and said her husband was a very jealous man and, what was worse, sick with retrospective jealousy. He sniffed out her past like a predatory wolf. Which was why she needed to be very careful. If he had suspected the other night that we knew each other, he would have made a scene. I hadn't been imprudent enough to tell Juan Barreto who she was, had I?

"I wouldn't have been able to tell him even if I wanted to," I reassured her. "Because the truth is, I still don't have the slightest idea who you are."

Finally she laughed. She let me hold her head in both my hands and bring our lips together. Beneath mine, which kissed her avidly, tenderly, with all the love I felt for her, hers were unyielding.

"I want you," I murmured, nibbling the edge of her ear. "You're more beautiful than ever, Peruvian girl. I love you, I want you with all my heart, with all my body. In these four years all I've done is dream about you, and want you, and love you. And curse you too. Each day, each night, every day."

After a moment she moved me away with her hands.

"You must be the last person on earth who still says those things to women," she said with a smile, amused, looking at me as if I were an exotic animal. "What cheap sentimental things you tell me, Ricardito!"

"The worst thing isn't that I say them. The worst thing is that I feel them. It's true. You turn me into a character in a soap opera. I've never said them to anybody but you."

"Nobody can ever see us like this," she said suddenly, changing her tone, very serious now. "The last thing I want is my pain of a husband to have a jealous fit. And now I have to go, Ricardito."

"Will I have to wait another four years to see you again?"

"Friday," she specified immediately with a mischievous little laugh, passing her hand over my hair again.

And after a dramatic pause: "Right here. I'll reserve a room in your name. Don't worry, little pissant, I'll pay for it. Bring an overnight bag, to make it look good."

I said that was fine but I'd pay for the room myself. I didn't intend to trade my honest profession of interpreter for that of kept man.

She burst out laughing, spontaneously this time.

"Of course!" she exclaimed. "You're a good little Miraflores gentleman and gentlemen don't take money from women."

For the third time she ran her hand through my hair and this time I caught her hand and kissed it.

"Did you think I'd go to bed with you in the dump that fag Juan Barreto lent you in Earl's Court? You haven't realized yet that I'm at the top now."

A minute later she was gone, after telling me not to leave the Russell Hotel for another quarter of an hour, because with David Richardson everything was possible, including his having her followed every time she came to London by one of those detectives who specialized in adultery.

I waited fifteen minutes and then, instead of the tube, I took a long walk under a cloudy sky and intermittent showers. I went to Trafalgar Square, crossed St. James's Park and Green Park, smelling the wet grass and watching the branches of fat oaks dripping water, went down almost all of Brompton Road, and an hour and a half later reached the half-moon of Philbeach Gardens, tired and happy. The long walk had calmed me and allowed me to think without the tumult of chaotic ideas and sensations I had experienced since my visit to Newmarket. How could seeing her again after so much time upset you so much, Ricardito? Because everything I told her was true: I was still crazy about her. It was enough for me to see her to realize that, despite my knowing that any relationship with the bad girl was doomed to failure, the only thing I really wanted in life with the passion others bring to the pursuit of fortune, glory, success, power, was having her, with all her lies, entanglements, egotism, and disappearances. A cheap, sentimental thing, no doubt, but also true that I wouldn't do anything until Friday but curse how slowly the hours went by until I could see her again.

On Friday, when I arrived at the Russell Hotel with my overnight bag, the receptionist, an Indian, confirmed that the room had been reserved for the day in my name. It had already been paid for. He added that "my secretary" had told them I came in from Paris with some frequency, and in that case the hotel would find a way to give me the special price they used for regular clients, "except in high season." The room overlooked Russell Square, and though it wasn't small it seemed so because it was crowded with objects: end tables, lamps, miniature animals, prints, and paintings of Mongol warriors with popping eyes, twisted beards, and curved scimitars who seemed to be rushing the bed with very evil intentions.

The bad girl arrived half an hour after me, wrapped in a close-fitting leather coat, a little matching hat, and knee-high boots. In addition to her handbag she carried a portfolio filled with notebooks and textbooks for classes on modern art that, she told me later, she took three times a week at Christie's. Before looking at me she glanced around the room and nodded briefly in approval. When, finally, she deigned to look at me, I already had her in my arms and had begun to undress her.

"Be careful," she instructed. "Don't wrinkle my clothes."

I took them off with all the precaution in the world, studying each thing she wore as if it were a precious, unique object, kissing with devotion every centimeter of skin that came into view, breathing in the soft, lightly perfumed aura that emanated from her body. Now she had a small, almost invisible scar near her groin because her appendix had been removed, and her pubis had even less hair than before. I felt desire, emotion, tenderness as I kissed her insteps, her fragrant underarms, the suggestion of little bones in her spine, and her motionless buttocks, as delicate to the touch as velvet. I kissed her small breasts at length, mad with happiness.

"You haven't forgotten what I like, good boy," she finally whispered in my ear.

And, without waiting for my reply, she turned on her back, spreading her legs to make a place for my head as she covered her eyes with her right arm. I felt her begin to move farther and farther from me, the Russell Hotel, London, in order to concentrate totally, with an intensity I'd never seen in any other woman, on the solitary, personal, egotistical pleasure my lips had learned to give her. Licking, sucking, kissing, nibbling her small sex, I felt her grow wet and vibrate. It took her a long time to finish. But how delicious and exciting it was to feel her purring, moving, rocking, submerged in the vertigo of desire, until at last a long wail shook her body from head to toe. "Now, now," she whispered in a choked voice. I entered her easily and embraced her with so much strength that she came out of the inertia in which the orgasm had left her. She groaned, twisting, trying to slip out from under my body, complaining, "You're crushing me."

With my mouth pressed against hers, I pleaded, "For once in your life, tell me you love me, bad girl. Even if it isn't true, say it. I want to know how it sounds, just once."

Afterward, when we had finished making love and were talking, lying naked on the yellow spread, menaced by the fierce Mongol warriors, and I was caressing her breasts, her waist, and kissing the almost invisible scar and playing with her smooth belly, pressing my ear to her navel and listening to the deep sounds of her body, I asked her why she hadn't made me happy, saying that small lie into my ear. Hadn't she said it so many times to so many men?

"That's why," she replied immediately, pitiless. "I've never said 'I love you, I adore you' and really meant it. Never. I've only said those things as a lie. Because I've never loved anybody, Ricardito. I've lied to all of them, always. I think the only man I've never lied to in bed is you."

"Well, coming from you, that's a declaration of love."

Did she finally have what she had wanted for so long, now that she was married to a rich and powerful man?

A shadow veiled her eyes, and her voice thickened.

"Yes and no. Because even though I have security now and can buy whatever I want, I'm obliged to live in Newmarket and spend my life talking about horses."

She said this with a bitterness that seemed to come

from the bottom of her soul. And then, suddenly, she was sincere with me in an unexpected way, as if she could no longer keep everything inside. She despised horses with all her heart, along with her friends and acquaintances in Newmarket, and the owners, trainers, jockeys, stableboys, grooms, dogs, cats, and every person who directly or indirectly had anything to do with equines, damn monsters that were the only topic of conversation and concern of the horrible people who surrounded her. Not only at the races, the training tracks, the stables, but also at dinners, receptions, weddings, birthday parties, and casual encounters, the people in Newmarket talked about the diseases, accidents, trial runs, victories, or defeats of those awful quadrupeds. This life had soured her days, and even her nights, because recently she'd been having nightmares about the horses of Newmarket. And even though she didn't say so, it was easy to guess that her immeasurable hatred for horses and Newmarket had not skipped over her husband. Mr. David Richardson, moved by his wife's suffering and depression, had given her permission a few months ago to come to London—a city that the fauna of Newmarket detested and where they rarely set foot— and take mini-courses on art history at Christie's and Sotheby's, classes in flower arranging at Out of the Bloom in Camden, and even sessions in yoga and Transcendental Meditation at an ashram in Chelsea that distracted her a little from the psychological devastation caused in her by horses.

"Well, well, bad girl," I said mockingly, delighted to hear what she was telling me. "Have you discovered that money isn't always happiness? Can I hope, then, that one day you'll say goodbye to Mr. Richardson and marry me? Paris is more amusing than the horsey hell of Suffolk, as you know."

But she was in no mood for joking. The repugnance she felt for Newmarket was even more serious than it seemed on that occasion, a real trauma. I think that never, not once on all the many afternoons we saw each other and made love over the next two years in various rooms of the Russell Hotel—I had the impression she knew them all by heart—never did the bad girl fail to vent her anger in a rant against the horses and people of Newmarket, whose life she thought monotonous, stupid, the emptiest in the world. Why, if she was so unhappy with the life she led, didn't she put an end to it? Why was she waiting to leave David Richardson, a man she clearly had not married for love?

"I don't dare ask him for a divorce," she confessed on one of those afternoons. "I don't know what would happen to me."

"Nothing would happen to you. You're legally married, aren't you? Couples here get unmarried without any problem."

"I don't know," she said, going a little further with her confidences than usual. "We were married in Gibraltar and I'm not sure if the marriage is valid here. And I don't know how to check that without David finding out. Good boy, you don't know the rich. Least of all David. To marry me he worked out a divorce with his lawyers that almost left his first wife in the street. I don't want the same thing to happen to me. He has the best lawyers, the best connections. And in England I'm less than nobody, a poor shit."

I never could learn how she had met him, when and in what way her romance with David Richardson had blossomed and catapulted her from Paris to Newmarket. It was clear she had miscalculated when she thought that with this conquest she would also conquer the unlimited freedom she associated with a fortune. Not only was she not happy, but apparently she had been happier as the wife of the French functionary she had abandoned. When, on another afternoon, she brought up Robert Arnoux and insisted I recount in exact detail the conversation we'd had on the night he invited me to supper at Chez Eux, I did as she asked, omitting nothing, even telling her how her ex-husband's eyes had filled with tears when he told me she had fled with all his savings in their joint account in a Swiss bank.

"Like a good Frenchman, the only thing that hurt him was the money," she said, not at all impressed. "His savings! A few measly francs that weren't enough for me to live on for a year. He used me to sneak money out of France. Not only his but his friends' money too. I could have been arrested if I had been caught. Besides, he was a miser, the worst thing anybody can be in this life."

"Since you're so cold and perverse, why don't you kill David Richardson, bad girl? You'll avoid the risks of a divorce and inherit his fortune."

"Because I wouldn't know how to do it without getting caught," she replied, not smiling. "Do you want to do it? I'd give you ten percent of the inheritance. It's an awful lot of money."

We were playing, but when I heard her say those outrageous things to me so openly, I couldn't help shuddering. She was no longer the vulnerable girl who had gone through a thousand difficulties and come out of them thanks to uncommon boldness and determination; now she was a grown woman, convinced that life was a jungle where only the worst triumphed, and ready to do anything not to be conquered and to keep moving higher. Even sending her husband to the next world in order to inherit his money, if she could do it with an absolute guarantee of impunity? "Of course," she said with that fierce, mocking look. "Do I scare you, good boy?"

She enjoyed herself only when David Richardson took her on his business trips to Asia. According to what she said, something fairly vague, her husband was a broker, the middleman for various commodities that Indonesia, Korea, Taiwan, Thailand, and Japan exported to Europe, which is why he made frequent trips to meet with the suppliers. She didn't always go with him; when she did, she felt emancipated. Seoul, Bangkok, Tokyo were the compensations that allowed her to endure Newmarket. While he had his dinners and business meetings, she was a tourist, visiting temples and museums and buying clothes or decorative objects for her house. For example, she had a marvelous collection of Japanese kimonos and a great variety of the articulated marionettes used in Balinese theater. Sometime when her husband was traveling, would she let me come to Newmarket and see her house? No, never. I should never show up there again, even if Juan Barreto invited me. Except, of course, if I decided to take her homicidal proposition seriously.

Those two years when I spent long periods of time in swinging London sleeping at Juan Barreto's pied-à-terre in Earl's Court and seeing the bad girl once or twice a week were the happiest I'd ever had. I earned less money as an interpreter because, for the sake of London, I turned down many contracts in Paris and other European cities, including Moscow, where international conferences and congresses became more frequent at the end of the sixties and the beginning of the seventies, but I did accept fairly low-paying jobs whose only attraction was that they took me to England. But not for anything in the world would I have traded the joy of arriving at the Russell Hotel, where I came to know all the staff by name, and waiting, in a trance, for Mrs. Richardson. She surprised me each time with a new dress, lingerie, perfume, or shoes. One afternoon, as I'd asked her to do, she brought several kimonos from her collection in a bag and put on a show for me, walking and moving around the room with her feet very close together and wearing the stereotyped smile of a geisha. I always had noticed an Asian trace in her small body and the slightly greenish tinge of her skin, the inheritance of some ancestor she knew nothing about, and that afternoon it seemed more obvious than ever.

We made love, we talked while we were naked and I toyed with her hair and body, and on occasion, if time allowed, we took a walk in a park. If it was raining we went to the movies and watched the picture holding hands. Or we'd have tea with the scones she liked at Fortnum and Mason, and once we had the famous, elaborate tea served at the Hotel Ritz, but we never went back because as we were leaving she spotted a couple from Newmarket at one of the tables. I saw her turn pale. In those two years I became convinced that, in my case at least, it wasn't true that love diminished or disappeared with use. Mine grew each day. I studied carefully the galleries, museums, art cinemas, expositions, recommended itineraries—the oldest pubs in the city, the antiques fairs, the settings for Dickens's novels—so I could suggest walks that would amuse her, and each time I also surprised her with some little gift from Paris that would impress her for its originality, if not its price. At times, when she was happy with the gift, she would say, "You deserve a kiss," and place her lips on mine for a second. Resting there quietly, they let themselves be kissed but didn't respond.

Did she come to love me a little in those two years? She never said so, of course, that would have been a demonstration of weakness for which she never could have forgiven herself—or me. But I think she became accustomed to my devotion, to feeling flattered by the love I poured over her with both hands, more than she ever would have confessed, even to herself. She liked my giving her pleasure with my mouth and then, as soon as she'd had an orgasm, penetrating and "irrigating" her. And my telling her all the possible forms and thousand ways I loved her. "What cheap, sentimental things are you going to tell me today?" was sometimes her greeting.

"That the most exciting thing in you, after this tiny clitoris of yours, is your Adam's apple. When it goes up, but principally when it dances down your throat."

If I managed to make her laugh I felt fulfilled, the way I had when I was a boy after the daily good deed the brothers at the Colegio Champagnat in Miraflores recommended we do in order to sanctify the day. One afternoon we had a curious incident, with some consequences. I was working at a congress organized by British Petroleum, in a conference hall at Uxbridge on the outskirts of London, and I couldn't leave to meet her—I had asked permission to be away in the afternoon—because the colleague who was supposed to replace me fell ill. I called her at the Russell Hotel, giving her all kinds of excuses. Without saying a word she hung up on me. I called again and she wasn't in the room.

The following Friday—generally we saw each other on Wednesdays and Fridays, the days of her supposed art classes at Christie's—she made me wait more than two hours without calling to explain the delay. Finally she showed up, frowning, when I no longer thought she was coming.

"Couldn't you have called?" I protested. "You've set my nerves—"

I couldn't finish because a slap, delivered with all her strength, closed my mouth.

"You don't stand me up, little pissant." She quivered with indignation, and her voice broke. "If you have a date with me—"

I didn't let her finish the sentence because I threw myself at her and with all the weight of my body pushed her onto the bed. She defended herself a little at first, but soon she stopped resisting. And almost immediately I felt her kissing and embracing me, and helping me take off her clothes. She'd never done anything like it before. For the first time I felt her body embracing me, entwining her legs with mine, her lips pressing against mine, her tongue struggling with mine. Her hands dug into my back, my neck. I asked her to forgive me, it would never happen again, I thanked her for making me so happy and showing me for the first time that she loved me too. Then I heard her sob and saw that her eyes were wet.

"My love, darling, don't cry, it's too silly." And I fondled her, kissing away her tears. "It won't happen again, I promise. I love you, I love you."

Afterward, when we dressed, she remained silent, her expression rancorous, regretting her weakness. I tried to improve her mood by joking.

"Did you stop loving me so soon?"

She looked at me angrily for a long time, and when she spoke her voice sounded very hard.

"Make no mistake, Ricardito. Don't think I made that scene because I'm crazy about you. No man matters very much to me, and you're no exception. But I have my pride, and nobody stands me up in a hotel room."

I said she was sorry I had discovered that in spite of all her boasting, defiance, and insults, she did feel something for me. It was the second serious error I had committed with the bad girl since the day when, instead of keeping her in Paris, I encouraged her to go to Cuba for guerrilla training. She looked at me very gravely, said nothing for some time, and finally murmured, full of haughtiness and scorn, "Is that what you think? You'll find out it isn't true, little pissant."

She left the room without saying goodbye. I thought it was a passing fit of bad temper, but I didn't hear from her the next week. I spent Wednesday and Friday waiting for her in vain, accompanied in my solitude by the belligerent Mongols. The following Wednesday, when I arrived at the Russell Hotel, the Indian concierge handed me a note. Very direct, it informed me she was leaving for Japan with "David." She didn't even say for how long or that she would call me as soon as she returned to England. I was filled with evil presentiments and cursed my faux pas. Knowing her, this two-sentence note could be a long and, perhaps, definitive goodbye.

In those two years my friendship with Juan Barreto had grown closer. I spent a good number of days at his pied-à-terre in Earl's Court, always hiding from him my meetings with the bad girl, of course. At about this time, in 1972 or '73, the hippie movement went into rapid decline and became a bourgeois style. The psychedelic revolution turned out to be less profound and serious than its followers believed. Its music, the most creative thing it produced, was rapidly absorbed by the establishment and transformed into a part of official culture, making millionaires and multimillionaires out of old rebels and nonconformists and their representatives and recording companies, beginning with the Beatles and ending with the Rolling Stones. Instead of the liberation of the spirit, "the indefinite expansion of the human mind" promised by the guru of LSD and former Harvard professor Dr. Timothy Leary, drugs and a promiscuous, unrestrained life caused a good number of problems and some personal and familial misfortunes. Nobody lived this change of circumstances as viscerally as my friend Juan Barreto.

He had always been very healthy but suddenly began to complain of frequent, debilitating grippes and colds, accompanied by acute attacks of neuralgia. His doctor in Cambridge advised a vacation in a warmer climate than England. He spent ten days in Ibiza and came back to London tanned and happy, full of risqué anecdotes about hot nights in Ibiza, "something I never would have imagined in a country with Spain's reputation for prudery."

It was at this time that Mrs. Richardson left for Tokyo with her husband. I didn't see Juan for about a month. I was working in Geneva and Brussels and when I called him, in London and in Newmarket, he didn't answer the phone. During those four weeks I heard nothing from the bad girl either. When I returned to London, my neighbor in Earl's Court, the Colombian Marina, told me Juan had been admitted to Westminster Hospital a few days earlier. They had him in the infectious diseases wing, and he was undergoing all kinds of tests. He had lost a great deal of weight. I found him unshaven, under a mountain of blankets, and in distress because "these quacks can't manage to diagnose my disease." At first they said he had genital herpes that had developed complications, and then that it probably was a form of sarcoma. Now they told him nothing but generalities. His eyes burned when he saw me approach his bed.

"I feel more abandoned than a dog, brother," he confessed. "You don't know how happy I am to see you. I've discovered that even though I know a million gringos, you're the only friend I have. A friend in a Peruvian friendship, the kind that goes down to the marrow of your bones, I mean. The truth is that friendships here are very superficial. The English don't have time for friendship."

Mrs. Stubard had left her house in St. John's Wood a few months earlier. Her health was fragile and she had retired to an old-age home in Suffolk. She came to visit Juan once, but it was too much of a trip for her, and she hadn't returned. "The poor thing has a bad back, and getting here was a real act of heroism for her." Juan was a different person; illness had made him lose his optimism and certainty, and filled him with fears.

"I'm dying and they don't know from what," he said in a cavernous voice the second or third time I went to see him. "I don't think they're hiding it from me so as not to frighten me, English doctors always tell you the truth no matter how awful it is. The fact is they don't know what's happening to me."

The tests showed nothing conclusive, and the doctors suddenly began to talk about an elusive, unidentified virus that attacked the immune system, making Juan susceptible to all kinds of infections. He was exceedingly weak, with sunken eyes, bluish skin, protruding bones. He kept passing his hands over his face as if to prove he was still there. I was with him during all the hours visitors were authorized. I saw him being consumed more and more each day as he sank into despair. One day he asked me to find him a Catholic priest because he wanted to confess. It wasn't easy. The priest at the Brompton Oratory with whom I spoke said it was impossible for him to visit hospitals. But he gave me the phone number of a Dominican convent that offered this service. I had to go in person to arrange the matter. A red-faced, good-natured Irish priest came to see Juan, and my friend had a long conversation with him. The Dominican came back two or three times to see him. Those dialogues calmed him for a few days. And as a result he made a transcendental decision: he would write to his family, with whom he'd had no contact for more than ten years.

He was too weak to write, and so he dictated a long, deeply felt letter to me in which he told his parents about his career as a painter in Newmarket, with humorous details. He said that though he often wanted to write and make peace with them, he always had been held back by a stupid streak of pride, which he regretted. Because he loved and missed them very much. In a postscript he added something that would make them happy, he was sure: after being estranged from the Church for many years, God had allowed him to return to the faith he had been brought up in, which now brought peace to his life. He didn't say a word about his illness.

Without telling Juan, I requested an appointment with the head of the Department of Infectious Diseases at Westminster Hospital. Dr. Rotkof was an older, fairly dry man with a graying beard and tuberous nose, who before answering my questions wanted to know my relationship to the patient.

"We're friends, Doctor. He has no family here in England. I'd like to be able to write to his parents in Peru and tell them the truth about Juan's condition."

"I can't tell you very much, except that it's extremely serious," he said abruptly, with no preambles. "He can die at any moment. His organism lacks defenses and a cold could kill him."

It was a new disease, and a fair number of cases had been detected in the United States and the United Kingdom. It attacked with special virulence homosexual communities, people addicted to heroin and all intravenous drugs, and hemophiliacs. Except for the fact that sperm and blood were the principal means of transmitting the "syndrome"—nobody was talking about AIDS yet—very little was known about its origin and nature. It devastated the immune system and exposed the patient to every sort of disease. A constant was the kind of lesion on the legs and abdomen that was tormenting my friend. Stunned by what I'd just heard, I asked Dr. Rotkof to advise me what to do. Should I tell Juan? He shrugged and pouted. That depended entirely on me. Maybe yes, maybe no. Though perhaps yes, if my friend had to make any arrangements with regard to his passing.

I was so affected by my conversation with Dr. Rotkof that I didn't have the courage to return to Juan's room, certain he would see everything in my face. I felt terribly sorry for him. What I wouldn't have given to see Mrs. Richardson that afternoon and feel her, if only for a few hours, at my side. Juan Barreto had told me a profound truth: though I also knew hundreds of people here in Europe, the only friend I had "in the Peruvian style" was about to die. And the woman I loved was on the other side of the world with her husband, and true to form, had given no sign of life for more than a month. She had carried out her threat, showing the insolent little pissant that she absolutely was not in love and could dispose of him like a useless trinket. For days I had been tormented by the suspicion that she would disappear again without leaving a trace. Is this why you dreamed about escaping from Peru and living in Europe since the time you were a boy, Ricardo Somocurcio? During those days in London I felt as lonely and sad as a stray dog.

Without saying anything to Juan, I wrote a letter to his parents, explaining that he was in a very delicate condition, the victim of an unknown disease, and telling them what Dr. Rotkof had told me: he could meet a fatal end at any moment. I said that though I lived in Paris, I would stay in London as long as necessary to be with Juan. I gave them the phone number and address of the pied-à-terre in Earl's Court and asked for their instructions.

They called as soon as they received my letter, which arrived at the same time as the one Juan had dictated to me. His father was devastated by the news, but, at the same time, happy to have recovered his prodigal son. They made arrangements to come to London. They asked me to reserve a room at a modest hotel, since they didn't have much money at their disposal. I reassured them; they would stay at Juan's pied-à-terre, where they could cook, making their stay in London less expensive. We agreed that I would prepare Juan for their imminent arrival.

Two weeks later the engineer Clímaco Barreto and his wife, Eufrasia, were installed in Earl's Court and I had moved to a bed-and-breakfast in Bayswater. The arrival of his parents had an immensely positive effect on Juan. He recovered his hope and humor, and seemed to improve. He even managed to keep down some of the food the nurse brought him morning and evening, though before that everything he put in his mouth nauseated him. The Barretos were fairly young—he had worked all his life at the Paramonga ranch, until the government of General Velasco Alvarado expropriated it, and then he resigned and found a job as a professor of mathematics at one of the new universities springing up in Lima like mushrooms—or else they were very well preserved, since they barely looked in their fifties. He was tall and had the athletic look of someone who has spent his life in the countryside, and she was a small, energetic woman whose manner of speaking, the soft tone and abundance of diminutives, the music of my old Miraflores neighborhood, made me nostalgic. As I listened to her, I felt I had left Peru a long time ago to live the European adventure. But spending time with them also confirmed that it would be impossible for me to go back and speak and think the way Juan's parents spoke and thought. Their comments on what they saw in Earl's Court, for example, revealed very graphically how much I had changed over the years. It wasn't an encouraging revelation. I undoubtedly had stopped being a Peruvian in many senses. What was I, then? I hadn't become a European either, not in France and certainly not in England. So what were you, Ricardito? Maybe what Mrs. Richardson called me in her fits of temper: a little pissant, nothing but an interpreter, somebody, as my colleague Salomón Toledano liked to define us, who is only when he isn't, a hominid who exists when he stops being what he is so that what other people think and say can pass through him more easily.

With Juan Barreto's parents in London, I could go back to Paris and work. I accepted the contracts I was offered, even if they were for only one or two days, because, as a result of the time I had spent in England with Juan, my income had taken a nosedive.

Even though Mrs. Richardson had forbidden me to do so, I began calling her house in Newmarket to find out when the couple would return from their trip to Japan. The person who answered, a Filipina maid, didn't know. Each time I pretended to be a different person, but I suspected that the Filipina recognized my voice and was slamming the phone in my face: "They aren't back yet."

Until one day, when I despaired of ever seeing her again, Mrs. Richardson herself answered the phone. She recognized me instantly because there was a long silence. "Can you talk?" I asked. She replied in a cutting voice, full of contained fury, "No. Are you in Paris? I'll call you at UNESCO or at home as soon as I can." And she banged down the phone, emphasizing her annoyance. She called me that same night at my apartment near the École Militaire.

"Because I stood you up one time, you hit me and made that commotion," I complained in an affectionate voice. "What must I have done not to hear anything from you for three months?"

"Don't ever call Newmarket again," she reprimanded me with a displeasure that raged in her words. "This isn't a joke. I'm having a very serious problem with my husband. We shouldn't see each other or talk for a while. Please. I beg you. If it's true you love me, do this for me. We'll see each other when this is all over, I promise. But don't ever call me again. I'm in trouble and I have to take care of myself."

"Wait, wait, don't hang up. At least tell me how Juan Barreto is."

"He died. His parents took his remains back to Lima. They came to Newmarket to put his cottage up for sale. Another thing, Ricardo. Avoid coming to London for a while, if you don't mind. Because if you come, without meaning to you can create a very serious problem for me. I can't say anything else for now."

And she hung up without saying goodbye. I was left empty and distraught. I felt so angry, so demoralized, so contemptuous of myself that I resolved—once again!—

to uproot Mrs. Richardson from my memory and my heart, to use the kind of cheap sentimental phrase that made her laugh. It was stupid to go on loving someone so insensitive, someone who was sick of me, who played with me as if I were an idiot, who never showed me the slightest consideration. This time you must absolutely free yourself from that Peruvian, Ricardo Somocurcio!

Several weeks later I received a few lines from Juan Barreto's parents in Lima. They thanked me for helping them and apologized for not having written or called me, as I had asked them to do. But Juan's death, which was so sudden, had left them stunned, half crazed, unable to do anything. The formalities involved in repatriating his remains were horrible, and if it hadn't been for the people at the Peruvian embassy, they would never have been able to take him home and bury him in Peru as he wished. At least they had succeeded in doing that for their adored son, whose loss had left them inconsolable. In any case, in the midst of their sorrow, it was a comfort to know Juan had died like a saint, reconciled with God and religion, in a true angelic state. That's what the Dominican priest who administered the last rites had told them.

Juan Barreto's death affected me deeply. Again I was left without a close friend, for in a way he had replaced fat Paúl. Since Paúl had disappeared in the guerrilla war, I hadn't known anyone in Europe whom I esteemed as much and to whom I felt as close as the Peruvian hippie who became a painter of horses in Newmarket. London, England—they wouldn't be the same without him. Another reason not to go back there for a good long while.

I tried to put my decision into practice with the usual recipe: loading myself down with work. I accepted every contract and spent weeks and months traveling from one European city to another, working as an interpreter at conferences and congresses on all imaginable topics. I had acquired the skill of the good interpreter, which consists in knowing the equivalents of words without necessarily understanding their contents (according to Salomón Toledano, understanding them was a hindrance), and I continued to perfect Russian, the language I loved, until I acquired a sureness and naturalness in it equivalent to my skills in French and English.

Even though I'd had a residency permit in France for years, I began to take the steps necessary to obtain French nationality, since with a French passport greater possibilities for work would open to me. A Peruvian passport aroused suspicion in some organizations when it was time to hire an interpreter, for they had difficulty situating Peru in the world and determining its status in the community of nations. Further, beginning in the 1970s, an attitude of rejection and hostility toward immigrants from poor countries became widespread throughout western Europe.

One Sunday in May, as I was shaving and getting ready to take advantage of the spring day and stroll along the quays of the Seine to the Latin Quarter, where I intended to have couscous for lunch in one of the Arab restaurants on Rue Saint-Séverin, the phone rang. Without saying "Hello" or "Good morning," the bad girl shouted at me, "Did you tell David I was married in France to Robert Arnoux?"

I was about to hang up. Four or five months had gone by since our last conversation. But I controlled my anger.

"I should have but it didn't occur to me, Señora Bigamist. You can't know how sorry I am that I didn't. They arrested you, didn't they?"

"Answer me and don't play the fool," her voice insisted, giving off sparks. "I'm in no mood for jokes now. Was it you? You once threatened to tell him, don't think I've forgotten that."

"No, it wasn't me. What's going on? What kind of trouble are you in now, you savage?"

There was a pause. I heard her anxious breathing. When she spoke again, she seemed weak, tearful.

"We were getting a divorce and things were going well. But suddenly, in these past few days, I don't know how, my marriage to Robert came up. David has the best lawyers. Mine is a nobody and now he says that if they prove I'm married in France, my marriage to David in Gibraltar will automatically be nullified and I can find myself in big trouble. David won't give me a cent, and if he reaches an agreement with Robert, they can bring criminal charges against me, demand compensation for damages, and I don't know what else. I might even go to jail. And they'll throw me out of the country. Are you sure it wasn't you who told? Good, I'm glad, you didn't seem like the kind of person who does those things."

There was another long pause, and she sighed, as if choking back a sob. As she talked she seemed sincere, speaking without a hint of self-pity.

"I'm very sorry," I said. "The truth is, your last call hurt me so much I decided not to see you, or talk to you, or look for you, or think about your existence ever again."

"Aren't you in love with me anymore?" she said with a laugh.

"Yes, I am, apparently. Too bad for me. What you've told me breaks my heart. I don't want anything to happen to you, I want you to go on doing every mean thing in the world to me. Can I help you somehow? I'll do whatever you ask. Because I still love you with all my heart, bad girl."

She laughed again.

"At least I still have those cheap, sentimental things you say," she exclaimed. "I'll call you so you can bring me oranges in jail."

4

The Dragoman of Château Meguru

Salomón Toledano boasted of speaking twelve languages and being able to interpret all of them in both directions. He was a short, thin little man, half lost in baggy suits that looked as if he bought them too big intentionally, and he had tortoise-like eyes hovering between wakefulness and sleep. His hair was thinning, and he shaved only every two or three days, so there was always a grayish shadow staining his face. No one looking at him—so unprepossessing, the perfect nobody— could have imagined the extraordinary facility he had in learning languages and his phenomenal aptitude for interpreting. International and transnational organizations, as well as governments, argued over him, but he never accepted a permanent position because as a freelancer he felt more liberated and earned more money. Not only was he the best interpreter I had met in all the years I earned a living practicing the "profession of phantoms"—that's what he called it—but he was also the most original.

Everyone admired and envied him, but very few of our colleagues liked him. They were annoyed by his loquacity, his lack of tact, his childishness, and the avidity with which he monopolized the conversation. He spoke in an ostentatious and sometimes crude manner, because although he knew the generalities of languages, he was ignorant of local nuances, tones, and usages, which often made him seem dull or coarse. But he could be entertaining, recounting anecdotes and memories of his family and his travels around the world. I was fascinated by his personality—that of a childish genius—and since I spent hours listening to him, he developed a fair amount of esteem for me. Whenever we met in the interpreters' booths at some conference or congress, I knew I'd have Salomón Toledano sticking to me like a leech.

He had been born into a Ladino-speaking Sephardic family from Smyrna, and for that reason he considered himself "more Spaniard than Turk, though with a five-century lag." His father must have been a very prosperous businessman and banker because he sent Salomón to study in private schools in Switzerland and England and to attend universities in Boston and Berlin. Before obtaining his degrees he already spoke Turkish, Arabic, English, French, Spanish, Portuguese, Italian, and German, and after specializing in Romanic and Germanic philology, he lived for some years in Tokyo and Taiwan, where he learned Japanese, Mandarin, and the Taiwanese dialect. With me he always spoke a chewed-over and slightly archaic Spanish in which, for example, he gave us "interpreters" the name "dragomans." That was why we nicknamed him the Dragoman. Sometimes, without realizing it, he passed from Spanish to French or English, or to more exotic languages, and then I had to interrupt and ask that he confine himself to my limited (compared to his) linguistic world. When I met him he was learning Russian, and after a year of effort he read and spoke it more fluently than I, who had spent five years scrutinizing the mysteries of the Cyrillic alphabet.

Though he generally translated into English, when necessary he also interpreted into French, Spanish, and other languages, and I always marveled at the fluency of his expression in my language in spite of his never having lived in a Spanish-speaking country. He wasn't a man who read very much, and he wasn't especially interested in culture except for grammar books and dictionaries, and unusual pastimes like collecting stamps and toy soldiers, subjects in which he said he was as well versed as in languages. The most extraordinary thing was to hear him speak Japanese, because then, like a true chameleon but without being aware of it, he adopted the postures, bows, and gestures of an Asian. Thanks to him, I discovered that the predisposition for languages is as mysterious as the inclination of certain people for mathematics or music and has nothing to do with intelligence or knowledge. It is something separate, a gift that some possess and others don't. Salomón Toledano's was so developed that in spite of his inoffensive, innocuous air, he seemed outrageous to his colleagues. Because when it wasn't a question of languages, he was so undefended in his ingenuousness that he was a man-child.

We had met earlier for reasons having to do with work, but our friendship really was born during the time in my life when I had lost contact once again with the bad girl. Her separation from David Richardson was catastrophic when he proved to the court hearing the suit for divorce that Mrs. Richardson was a bigamist, for she was also married legally in France to a functionary at the Quai d'Orsay, whom she had never divorced. The bad girl, seeing that the battle was lost, chose to escape England and the hated horses of Newmarket, destination unknown. But she passed through Paris—at least, that's what she wanted me to believe—and in March 1974 she called to say goodbye from the new Charles de Gaulle Airport. She told me things had gone very badly for her, her ex-husband had won in every sense of the word, and, sick to death of courts and lawyers who made the little money she had disappear, she was going where no one could try her patience any further.

"If you want to stay in Paris, my house is yours," I told her in all seriousness. "And if you want to marry again, we'll get married. I don't give a damn if you're a bigamist or a trigamist."

"Stay in Paris so Monsieur Robert Arnoux can denounce me to the police or do something worse? I'm not that crazy. Thanks anyway, Ricardito. We'll see each other again, when the storm passes."

Knowing she wouldn't tell me, I asked where she was going and what she planned to do now with her life.

"I'll tell you the next time we see each other. Here's a kiss, and don't cheat on me too much with the Frenchwomen."

I was sure this time too that I'd never hear from her again. As I had the previous times, I made the firm resolution, at the age of thirty-eight, to fall in love with someone less evasive and complicated, a normal girl with whom I could have a relationship free of unexpected alarms, maybe even marry and have children. But that didn't happen, because in this life things rarely happen the way we little pissants plan them.

I soon was in a routine of work that bored me at times but wasn't unpleasant. I thought being an interpreter was an innocuous profession, but one that also posed few moral problems to the person who practiced it. And it allowed me to travel, earn a decent amount of money, and take time off when I wanted to.

My only contact with Peru, for by now I rarely saw Peruvians in Paris, continued to be the increasingly desperate letters from Uncle Ataúlfo. Aunt Dolores always sent me regards in her own hand, and from time to time I would send her scores, for playing the piano was the great diversion in her invalid's life. Uncle Ataúlfo said that the eight years of General Velasco Alvarado's military dictatorship, with its nationalizations, agrarian reform, industrial collectivization, and state control of the economy, had provided erroneous solutions to the problems of social injustice, inequality, and the exploitation of the majority by a privileged minority, and this had served only to inflame and further impoverish everyone, frighten away investments, eradicate savings, and increase unrest and violence. Though populism had been reined in somewhat in the second stage of the dictatorship, led during its last four years by General Francisco Morales Bermúdez, newspapers and television and radio stations were still state controlled, political life nullified, and there was no hint that democracy would be reestablished. The bitterness distilled in Uncle Ataúlfo's letters made me sorry for him and other Peruvians of his generation who, when they reached old age, saw their lifelong dream of Peru making progress fade instead of materialize. Peruvian society was sinking deeper and deeper into poverty, ignorance, and brutality. I had done the right thing by coming to Europe, even though my life as an obscure dragoman was somewhat solitary.

I was also losing interest in current French politics, which I once followed passionately. In the seventies, during the governments of Pompidou and Giscard d'Estaing, I barely read the day's news. In the daily and weekly papers I turned almost exclusively to the cultural pages. I always went to art shows and concerts but less to the theater, which had degenerated a good deal in comparison with the previous decade, though I did go to the movies, sometimes twice a week. Happily, Paris was still a paradise for cinephiles. With regard to literature, I was no longer up-to-date because, like the theater, the novel and essay had taken a nosedive in France. I never could read with enthusiasm the intellectual idols of those years, Barthes, Lacan, Derrida, Deleuze, and others whose verbose books dropped from my hands, except for Michel Foucault. His history of madness had a powerful effect on me, as did his essay on the prison system (*Surveiller et punir*), though I wasn't convinced by his theory that the history of western Europe was one of multiple institutionalized repressions—prisons, hospitals, gender, the police, laws—by a power that colonized every area of liberty in order to annihilate dissent and nonconformity. In fact, during those years I read dead authors for the most part, especially the Russians.

I was always very busy working and doing other things, but in the seventies, when I examined my life, trying to be objective, for the first time it seemed sterile and my future that of a confirmed bachelor and outsider who would never be truly integrated into his beloved France. And I always thought of Salomón Toledano's sudden apocalyptic observation when, one day in the interpreters' room at UNESCO, he asked, "If we suddenly felt ourselves dying and asked ourselves, 'What trace of our passage through this dog's life of drudgery will we leave behind?,' the honest answer would be: 'None, we haven't done anything except speak for other people.' Otherwise, what does it mean to have translated millions of words and not remember a single one of them, because not a single one deserved to be remembered?" It wasn't strange that the Dragoman was unpopular among people in the profession.

One day I told him I hated him because that sentence, which came back to me from time to time, had convinced me of the total uselessness of my existence.

"We dragomans are merely useless, dear friend," he consoled me. "But we don't harm anyone with our work. In every other profession great damage can be done to the species. Think about lawyers and doctors, for example, not to mention architects and politicians."

We were having a beer in a *bistrot* on Avenue de Suffren after a day of work at UNESCO, which was holding its annual conference. In an attack of confidentiality, I had just told him, without specific details or names, that for many years I had been in love with a woman who came and went in my life like a will-o'-the-wisp, lighting it up with happiness for short periods of time and then leaving it dry, sterile, immune to any other enthusiasm or love.

"Falling in love is a mistake," was Salomón Toledano's judgment, echoing my vanished friend Juan Barreto, who shared that philosophy but without my colleague's verbal mannerisms. "Grab the woman by her hair and drag her to bed. Make her see all the stars in the firmament as quick as a wink. That's the correct theory. I cannot practice it, *hélas*, on account of my weak physique. Once I tried to play macho with a wild woman and she wrecked my face with a single slap. Which is why, despite my thesis, I treat ladies, above all prostitutes, as if they were queens."

"I don't believe you've never been in love, Dragoman."

He acknowledged falling in love once in his life, when he was a university student in Berlin. With a Polish girl, so Catholic that every time they made love she cried with remorse. The Dragoman proposed. The girl accepted. It was a tremendous effort for them to obtain their families' blessings. They managed it after a complicated negotiation in which they decided on a double wedding, one Jewish, the other Catholic. In the midst of preparations for the wedding, without warning the bride ran off with an American officer who had concluded his service in Berlin. The Dragoman, maddened by despair, engaged in a strange inquisition: he burned his magnificent collection of stamps. And decided he would never fall in love again. In the future, love for him would be purely mercenary. He kept his word. After that episode, he frequented only prostitutes. And instead of stamps, now he collected toy soldiers.

A few days later, thinking he was doing me a favor, he involved me in a weekend trip with two Russian courtesans who, according to him, would not only allow me to practice my Russian but would introduce me to the "emanations and bruises of Slavic love." We went for supper to Le Grand Samovar, a restaurant in Batignolles, and then to a narrow, dark, suffocatingly smoky boîte de nuit near Place de Clichy, where we met the nymphs. We drank a good deal of vodka, so that my memories blurred almost from the time we walked into the cave called Les Cosaques, and the only thing I remember clearly was that of the two Russians, fate, or I should say the Dragoman, gave me Natasha, the fatter and more heavily made-up of the two Rubenesque women in their forties. My companion was stuffed into a brilliant pink dress with net trim, and when she laughed or moved, her tits shook like belligerent balloons. She looked like an escapee from a painting by Botero. Until my memory vanished into an alcoholic mist, my friend talked like a parrot in a Russian larded with obscenities, which the two courtesans celebrated with loud laughter.

The next morning I awoke with an aching head and sore bones: I had slept on the floor at the foot of the bed where the supposed Natasha was snoring, fully dressed and wearing her shoes. By day she was even fatter than at night. She slept placidly until noon, and when she awoke she looked in astonishment at the room, the bed she was occupying, and me, who wished her good afternoon. She immediately demanded three thousand francs, about six hundred dollars at the time, which is what she charged for a full night. I had nothing like that much money and an unpleasant discussion ensued in which I finally convinced her to take all the cash I had with me, which came to half that amount, and some little porcelain figures that adorned the room. She left, shouting curses, and I spent a long time under the shower, swearing never again to engage in this kind of dragomanic adventure.

When I told Salomón Toledano about my nocturnal fiasco, he said that by contrast he and his friend had made love until they passed out in a display of strength worthy of pages in *The Guinness Book of World Records*. He never dared propose to me another nocturnal excursion with exotic ladies.

What distracted me and occupied many of my hours in those final years of the seventies were the stories of Chekhov in particular and Russian literature in general. I never had considered doing literary translations because I knew they were very badly paid in every language, and surely worse in Spanish than in others. But in 1976 or 1977, through a mutual friend, I met a Spanish publisher, Mario Muchnik, at UNESCO, and we became friends. When he learned I knew Russian and was very fond of reading, he encouraged me to prepare a small anthology of Chekhov's stories, which I had raved to him about, assuring him that Chekhov was as good a storywriter as he was a dramatist, though the mediocre translations of his stories meant he was not valued very highly as a narrator. Muchnik was an interesting case. Born in Argentina, he studied sciences and began a career as a researcher and academic but soon abandoned it to devote himself to publishing, his secret passion. He was a publisher by vocation, for he loved books and published only good literature, which, he said, guaranteed him all the failure in the world, financially speaking, but the greatest personal satisfaction. He spoke of the books he brought out with an enthusiasm so contagious that, after thinking about it for a while, I accepted his offer to translate an anthology of Chekhov's stories, for which I requested unlimited time. "You have it," he said, "and besides, even though you earn a pittance, you'll have more fun than a pig in mud."

It took a very long time, but I did, in fact, enjoy myself, reading all of Chekhov, choosing his most beautiful stories, and bringing them over into Spanish. It was more delicate than translating the speeches and papers to which I was accustomed in my work. I felt less ghostlike as a literary translator than I did as an interpreter. I had to make decisions, explore Spanish searching for nuances and cadences that corresponded to the semantic subtleties and tonalities—the marvelous art of allusion and elusion in Chekhov's prose—and to the rhetorical sumptuousness of Russian literary language. A real pleasure to which I devoted entire Saturdays and Sundays. I sent Mario Muchnik the promised anthology almost two years after he hired me. I'd had such a good time with it that I almost didn't accept the check he sent as my fee. "Perhaps this will be enough for you to buy a nice edition of some good writer, Chekhov, for example," he said.

When, sometime later, I received copies of the anthology, I gave one, with a dedication, to Salomón Toledano. We had a drink together occasionally, and sometimes I went with him to shops that sold toy soldiers, or to philatelic or antiquarian stores, which he inspected thoroughly though he rarely bought anything. He thanked me for the book but advised energetically against my continuing on this "very dangerous path."

"Your livelihood is at risk," he warned. "A literary translator aspires to be a writer; that is, he's a frustrated pencil pusher. Somebody who'll never be resigned to disappearing into his work, as good interpreters do. Don't

163

renounce your status as a nonexistent gentleman, dear friend, unless you wish to end up a clochard."

Contrary to my belief that polyglots owed their skill to a good musical ear, Salomón Toledano didn't have the slightest interest in music. In his apartment in Neuilly I didn't even see a phonograph. His excellent ear was tuned specifically for languages. He told me that in Smyrna, Turkish and Spanish—well, Ladino, which he had shaken off completely during a summer in Salamanca—were spoken interchangeably in his family, and that he inherited his linguistic aptitude from his father, who could speak half a dozen languages, which was very useful in his business. Ever since he was a boy he had dreamed of traveling, visiting cities, and that had been the great incentive for his learning languages, thanks to which he became what he was now: a citizen of the world. That same nomadic vocation made him the precocious stamp collector he had been until his traumatic engagement in Berlin. Collecting stamps was another way of visiting countries, of learning geography and history.

The toy soldiers didn't cause him to travel but they did amuse him very much. His apartment was filled with them, from the entrance hall to the bedroom, including the kitchen and bathroom. He specialized in the battles of Napoleon. He had them very well arranged and classified, with tiny cannon, horses, and standards, so that as you walked through his apartment you followed the military history of the First Empire until Waterloo, whose protagonists surrounded his bed on all four sides. In addition to toy soldiers, Salomón Toledano's house was filled with dictionaries and grammars of every possible language. And, an extravagance, the small television set that rested on a shelf facing the toilet. "Television is a powerful laxative for me," he explained.

Why did I develop so much fondness for Salomón Toledano, while all our colleagues avoided him for being unbearably tiresome? Perhaps because his solitude resembled mine, though we were different in many other ways. We told each other we never could live in our countries again, for he in Turkey and I in Peru would surely feel more foreign than we did in France, where we also felt like outsiders. And we were both very conscious that we would never be integrated into the country where we had chosen to live and which had even granted us passports (both of us had acquired French citizenship).

"It isn't the fault of France if we're still a couple of foreigners, dear friend. It's our fault. It's a vocation, a destiny. Like our profession as interpreters, another way of always being a foreigner, of being present without being present, of existing but not existing."

No doubt he was right when he said these lugubrious things. Those conversations with the Dragoman always left me somewhat demoralized, and at times they wouldn't let me sleep. Being a phantom was not something that left me unfazed, but it didn't seem to matter very much to him.

That was why, in 1979, when an excited Salomón Toledano announced that he had accepted an offer to travel to Tokyo and work for a year as the exclusive interpreter for Mitsubishi, I felt a certain relief. He was a good person, an interesting specimen, but something in him saddened and alarmed me because it revealed certain secret pathways in my own destiny.

I saw him off at Charles de Gaulle, and when I shook his hand next to the Japan Airlines counter I felt him slip a small metallic object between my fingers. It was a hussar of the emperor's guard. "I have a duplicate," he said. "It will bring you luck, dear friend." I put it on my night table, next to my amulet, that exquisite Guerlain toothbrush.

A few months later, the military dictatorship in Peru finally ended, elections were held, and in 1980 Peruvians, as if making amends, reelected as president Fernando Belaúnde Terry, the head of state deposed by the military coup of 1968. Uncle Ataúlfo was happy and decided to celebrate by doing something extravagant: he would take a trip to Europe, where he had never set foot. He tried to persuade Aunt Dolores to accompany him, but she claimed her invalidism would keep him from enjoying the trip and turn her into a hindrance. And so Uncle Ataúlfo came alone. He arrived in time for us to celebrate my forty-fifth birthday together.

I put him up in my apartment near the École Militaire, giving him the bedroom while I slept on the sofa bed in the small living-dining room. He had aged a great deal since the last time I had seen him fifteen years earlier. He was over seventy, and the years weighed heavily on him. He had almost no hair left, and he shuffled when he walked and tired easily. He took pills for his blood pressure, and his dentures must have been uncomfortable because he was constantly moving his mouth as if trying to make them fit properly over his gums. But he was clearly delighted to be in Paris at last, an old desire of his. He was ecstatic looking at the streets, the quays along the Seine, the old stones, and he kept murmuring, "Everything's more beautiful than in photographs." I accompanied Uncle Ataúlfo to Notre Dame, the Louvre, Les Invalides, the Panthéon, Sacré-Coeur, galleries, museums. This city, in fact, was the most beautiful in the world, and having spent so many years here had made me forget that. I lived surrounded by so many lovely things, almost without seeing them. And so for a few days I enjoyed being a tourist in my adopted city as much as he did. We had long conversations, sitting on the terraces of *bistrots*, having a glass of wine as an aperitif. He was happy with the end of the military regime and the restoration of democracy in Peru but had few illusions regarding the immediate future. According to him, Peruvian society was a boiling cauldron of tensions, hatreds, prejudices, and resentments that had grown much worse in the twelve years of military government. "You wouldn't recognize your country, nephew. There's a latent menace in the air, a feeling that at any moment something catastrophic can explode." His words were prophetic this time too. Soon after he returned to Peru following his trip to France and a short excursion by bus through Castile and Andalusia, Uncle Ataúlfo sent me clippings of newspaper articles from Lima accompanied by cruel photographs: in the center of the capital, unknown Maoists had hung from utility poles some poor dogs to which they had attached signs with the name Teng Hsiao-p'ing, whom they accused of betraying Mao and ending the Cultural Revolution in the People's Republic of China. This was the beginning of the armed rebellion of Shining Path, which would last throughout the eighties and provoke an unprecedented bloodbath in Peruvian history: more than sixty thousand dead and disappeared.

A few months after his departure, Salomón Toledano wrote me a long letter. He was very happy with his stay in Tokyo, though the Mitsubishi people had him working so much that at night he collapsed in exhaustion on his bed. But he had brought his Japanese up-to-date, met nice people, and didn't miss rainy Paris at all. He was going out with a lawyer in the firm who was divorced, beautiful, and didn't have knock-knees, like so many Japanese women, but did have very shapely legs and a direct, profound gaze that "delved into his soul." He went on to say: "Don't worry, dear friend, faithful to my promise, I won't fall in love with this Nipponese Jezebel. But, except for falling in love, I propose doing everything else with Mitsuko." Beneath his signature he had written a laconic postscript: "Regards from the bad girl." When I reached that sentence, I dropped the Dragoman's letter and had to sit down, overcome by vertigo.

Was she in Japan? How the hell had Salomón and the mischievous Peruvian managed to meet in densely populated Tokyo? I rejected the idea that she was the lawyer with the dark gaze whom my colleague seemed taken with, though with the ex-Chilean, ex-guerrilla fighter, ex-Madame Arnoux, and ex-Mrs. Richardson nothing was impossible, even her going around now disguised as a Japanese lawyer. That reference to the "bad girl" revealed a certain degree of familiarity between her and Salomón; the Chilean girl must have told him something of our long, syncopated relationship. Had they made love? I discovered in the days that followed that the unfortunate postscript had turned my life upside down and returned me to the sickly, stupid love-passion that had consumed me for so many years, preventing me from living normally. And yet, in spite of my doubts, my jealousy, my anguished questions, knowing the bad girl was there, real and alive, in a concrete place though so far from Paris, filled my head with fantasies. Again. It was like leaving the limbo in which I had lived these past six years, ever since she called from Charles de Gaulle Airport (well, she said she was calling from there) to tell me she was escaping England.

So, Ricardo Somocurcio, are you still in love with your elusive compatriot? No doubt about it. Ever since that postscript from the Dragoman, day and night I kept seeing her dark face, insolent expression, eyes the color of dark honey, and my whole body ached with desire to hold her in my arms.

Salomón Toledano's letter had no letterhead, and the Dragoman didn't bother to give me his address or phone number. I made inquiries at the Paris office of Mitsubishi and they advised me to write to him at the firm's Department of Human Resources in Tokyo, and gave me the address. That's what I did. My letter was very indirect, telling him first about my own work; I said the emperor's hussar had brought me luck, because in recent weeks I'd had excellent contracts, and I congratulated him on his new conquest. Finally I came to the point. I was agreeably surprised to learn he had met an old friend of mine. Was she living in Tokyo? I had lost track of her years ago. Could he send me her address? Her phone number? I'd like to be in touch with my compatriot again after so much time.

I sent the letter without too much hope it would reach him. But it did, and his answer was almost lost on the roads of Europe. The Dragoman's letter landed in Paris when I was in Vienna, working at the International Atomic Energy Agency, and my concierge in École Militaire, following my instructions in the event I had a letter from Tokyo, forwarded it to Vienna. When the letter arrived in Austria I was on my way back to Paris. In short, what normally would have taken a week took close to three.

When I finally held Salomón Toledano's letter in my hands, I trembled from head to toe as if I were suffering an attack of tertian fever. And my teeth were chattering. It was a letter several pages long. I read it slowly, spelling it out, so as not to miss a syllable of what it said. From the beginning he became involved in an impassioned apology for Mitsuko, his Japanese lawyer, confessing, in some embarrassment, that his promise not to fall in love again, undertaken as a result of his "sentimental mishap in Berlin," had been shattered after thirty years of being rigorously respected, because of the beauty, intelligence, delicacy, and sensuality of Mitsuko, a woman the Shinto gods had wanted to use to revolutionize his life ever since he had the fortunate idea of returning to this city where, for the past few months, he had been the happiest man on earth.

Mitsuko had rejuvenated him, filling him with vigor. Not even in the flower of his youth did he make love with the drive he had now. The Dragoman had rediscovered passion. How terrible to have wasted so many years, so much money, so much sperm in mercenary affairs! But perhaps not; perhaps everything he had done until now had been an ascesis, a training of his spirit and body in order to deserve Mitsuko.

As soon as he returned to Paris, the first thing he

would do would be to toss into the fire and watch the fusing of those cuirassiers, hussars, plumed horsemen, sappers, artillerymen, on whom, over the years, in an activity as onerous and absorbing as it was useless, he had wasted his existence, turning his back on the happiness of love. He never would collect anything again; his only pastime would be learning by heart, in all the languages he knew, erotic poems to whisper into Mitsuko's ear. She liked to hear them, though she didn't understand them, after the marvelous "joys" they had each night in a variety of settings.

Then, in prose overloaded with feverish excitement and pornography, he went on to describe Mitsuko's amatory feats and secret charms, among them a very subdued, inoffensive, tender, and sensual form of the fearful *vagina dentata* of Greco-Roman mythology. Tokyo was the most expensive city in the world, and though his salary was high, it was disappearing in nocturnal trips to the Ginza, the Tokyo district of the night, which the Dragoman and Mitsuko, by visiting restaurants, bars, cabarets, and especially houses of assignation, had made the jewel in their crown of Japanese nightlife. But who cared about money when happiness was in the balance! Because all the exquisite refinement of Japanese culture shone not in the prints of the Meiji period, or the Noh theater, or Kabuki, or the Bunraku puppets, as I surely believed, but in the houses of assignation or *maisons closes*, called by the Frenchified name of *châteaux*, the most famous of which was the Château Meguru, a true paradise of carnal pleasure, given over completely to the Japanese genius for combining the most advanced technology with sexual wisdom and rites ennobled by tradition. Everything was possible in the chambers of the Château Meguru: excesses, fantasies, phantoms, extravagances all had a setting, and the instrumentality to become concrete. Mitsuko and he had lived through unforgettable experiences in the discreet reserved rooms of the Château Meguru: "There we felt like gods, dear friend, and on my honor, I do not exaggerate and am not delirious."

At last, when I was afraid the man in love wouldn't say a word about the bad girl, the Dragoman turned his attention to my request. He had seen her only once after receiving my letter. It was very difficult for him to talk to her alone because, "for obvious reasons," he didn't want to refer to me "in front of the gentleman with whom she lives, or at least with whom she goes out and with whom she is usually seen," a "personage" of bad reputation and worse appearance, someone you only had to see to feel a chill run down your spine and to say to yourself: "I wouldn't want this individual for an enemy."

But finally, with Mitsuko's help, he managed to speak privately to her and give her my message. She told him that "since her *petit ami* was jealous," it would be better if I didn't write to her directly so he wouldn't make a scene (or knock her down). But, if I wanted to write to her through the Dragoman, she would be delighted to hear from me. Salomón Toledano added: "Do I need to tell you, dear friend, that nothing would make me happier than being your go-between? Our profession is a disguised form of procuring, pimping, or being a go-between, and so I am prepared for so noble a mission. I shall do it, taking all the precautions in the world to keep your letters from ever falling into the hands of that thug the girl of your dreams is going around with. Forgive me, dear friend, but I have guessed everything: Am I wrong, or is she the love of your life? And by the way, congratulations: she is no Mitsuko—no one is Mitsuko—but her exotic beauty shines with an aura of mystery in her face that is very seductive. Be careful!" He signed it: "A hug from the Dragoman of Château Meguru!"

Who was the Peruvian girl involved with now? A Japanese, no doubt about that. Perhaps a gangster, one of the Yakuza bosses who had amputated part of his little finger, the gang's countersign. Nothing surprising about it. She undoubtedly had met him on the trips she made to the Orient with Mr. Richardson, another gangster, except he wore a shirt and tie and had stables in Newmarket. The Japanese was a sinister character, judging from the Dragoman's jokes. Was he referring only to his physical appearance when he said there was something frightening about him? Or was it his background? The only thing missing in the Chilean girl's résumé: lover of a boss in the Japanese mafia. A man with power and money, of course, indispensable qualities for winning her. And a few corpses behind him. I was eaten alive by jealousy, yet at the same time an odd feeling had taken possession of me, a mixture of envy, curiosity, and admiration. It was clear, the bad girl's indescribable audacity would never cease to amaze me.

Twenty times I told myself not to be so idiotic as to write her or try to reestablish some kind of relationship with her, because I would be burned and spat upon, as always. But less than two days after reading the Dragoman's letter, I wrote her a note and began to devise a way to travel to the Land of the Rising Sun.

My letter was completely hypocritical, since I didn't want to cause her any difficulty (I was sure that this time, in Japan, she had sunk her feet into muddier waters than on other occasions). I was very happy to have had news of her through my colleague, our mutual friend, and to know things were going well for her and she was so happy in Tokyo. I told her about my life in Paris, the work routine that sometimes took me to other European cities, and, I said, what a coincidence that in the not too distant future I would be traveling to Tokyo, contracted as an interpreter at an international conference. I hoped to see her and recall old times. Because I didn't know what name she was using now, all I said in the salutation was this: "Dear Peruvian girl." And I included a copy of my anthology of Chekhov, with a dedication that read: "To the bad girl, with the unchanging affection of the little pissant who translated these stories." I mailed the letter and book to Salomón Toledano's address, along with a few lines thanking him for his help, confessing my envy at knowing how happy and how much in love he was, and asking that if he heard of any conference or congress that might need good interpreters who spoke Spanish, French, English, and Russian (though not Japanese) to let me know, because suddenly I felt an irresistible urge to visit Tokyo.

My efforts to find a job that would take me to Japan failed. Not knowing Japanese excluded me from many local conferences, and for the moment there were no meetings in Tokyo of any UN agency where only the official languages of the United Nations were required. Going on my own, as a tourist, would cost an arm and a leg. Would I vaporize in just a few days most of the funds

I had been able to save in recent years? I decided to do it. But as soon as I made the decision and was ready to go to a travel agency, I received a phone call from my old boss at UNESCO, Señor Charnés. He had retired but was working on his own as the head of a private agency for translators and interpreters with which I was always in contact. He had a conference for me in Seoul, for five days. That meant I now had my round-trip fare. It would be cheaper to get to Tokyo from Korea. From that moment on, my life was caught up in a whirlwind: arranging visas, finding guidebooks for Korea and Japan, and constantly repeating to myself that I was taking a totally stupid step since the most likely thing was that I wouldn't even be able to see her in Tokyo. The bad girl probably had moved somewhere else or would avoid me so the Yakuza boss wouldn't slit her open from head to toe and throw her body to the dogs, as the villain had done in a Japanese film I had just seen.

During those feverish days, the phone woke me in the middle of the night.

"Are you still in love with me?"

The same voice, the same mocking, amused tone as before, and, at bottom, that trace of the Lima accent she never had lost completely.

"I must be, bad girl," I replied, wide awake now. "Otherwise, ever since I found out you're in Tokyo, why would I keep knocking on doors for a contract that would take me there, even if only for a day? I finally have one, for Seoul. I'll leave in a couple of weeks. From there I'll go to Tokyo to see you. Even if that Yakuza boss you're with, according to what my spies tell me, shoots me dead. Are these symptoms of my being in love?"

"Yes, I think so. It's just as well, good boy. I thought, after so much time, you'd forgotten me. Did your colleague Toledano tell you that? That I'm with a mafia boss?"

She burst into laughter, delighted with these credentials. But she changed the subject almost immediately and spoke to me in an affectionate way.

"I'm glad you're coming. Even though we don't see each other often, I always think about you. Shall I tell you why? Because you're the only friend I have left."

"I'm not and never will be your friend. Don't you realize that yet? I'm your lover, your suitor, the person who, since he was a boy, has been crazy about the Chilean girl, the guerrilla fighter, the bureaucrat's wife, the wife of the horse breeder, the gangster's mistress. The little pissant who lives only to desire you and think about you. In Tokyo I don't want us to remember anything. I want to hold you in my arms, kiss you, smell you, bite you, make love to you."

She laughed again, this time more willingly.

"Do you still make love?" she asked. "Good, just as well. Nobody has said those things to me since the last time we saw each other. Will you tell me a lot of them when you come, Ricardito? Go on, tell me another, as an example."

"On nights when there's a full moon I go out to bay at the sky and then I see your face painted up there. Right now I'd give ten years of my life to see myself reflected at the back of your eyes, your eyes the color of dark honey—"

She was laughing, amused, but suddenly she became frightened and interrupted me.

"I have to hang up."

I heard the receiver click. I couldn't close my eyes again, overcome by a mixture of elation and uneasiness that kept me awake until seven in the morning, the hour when I normally got up to prepare my usual breakfast—black coffee and a slice of toast with honey—when I didn't go out to eat at the counter of a nearby café on Avenue de Tourville.

I spent the remaining two weeks before my trip to Seoul occupied by the kinds of things, I suppose, that sweethearts full of illusions did long ago in the days preceding the wedding, when both of them would lose their virginity: buying clothes and shoes, having my hair cut (not by the low-priced barber behind UNESCO where I always went but at a deluxe barbershop on Rue Saint-Honoré), and, above all, going to boutiques and ladies' shops to find a discreet gift the bad girl could hide in her own wardrobe and that was, at the same time, original and delicate, one that would tell her the tender, sweet things I longed to whisper in her ear. Every hour I spent looking for the gift, I told myself that I was now even more imbecilic than I had been before, and deserved to be kicked and trampled in the dirt again by the lover of the Yakuza boss. At last, after much searching, I bought one of the first things I had seen and liked, at Vuitton: a dressing case with a collection of crystal flasks for perfumes, creams, and lipsticks, and a pocket diary and mother-of-pearl pencil concealed in a false bottom. There was something vaguely adulterous about this hiding place in a cosmetics case.

The conference in Seoul was draining. It dealt with patents and tariffs, and the speakers had recourse to a very technical vocabulary, which made it twice as difficult for me. The excitement of recent days, jet lag, and the time difference between Paris and Korea kept me awake, my nerves on edge. On the day I arrived in Tokyo, early in the afternoon, I was overcome by fatigue, and in the tiny room the Dragoman had reserved for me at a small hotel in the center of the city, I collapsed with exhaustion. I slept four or five uninterrupted hours, and that night, after a long, cold shower to wake me up, I went out for supper with my friend and his Japanese love. From the first moment I sensed that Salomón Toledano was much more in love with Mitsuko than she was with him. The Dragoman looked rejuvenated and elated. He wore a bow tie I'd never seen before and a suit with a modern, youthful cut. He joked, showered attention on his friend, and on any pretext kissed her on the cheeks or mouth and put his arm around her waist, which seemed to make her uncomfortable. She was much younger than he, pleasant and rather charming, in fact: nice legs and a porcelain face in which large, vivacious eyes sparkled. She couldn't hide an expression of displeasure each time Salomón drew her close. She spoke English very well, but her naturalness and cordiality experienced a kind of shutdown whenever my friend made these ostentatious displays of affection. He seemed not to notice. We went first to a bar on Kabuki-cho, in Shinjuku, a district filled with cabarets, erotic shops, restaurants, discotheques, massage parlors, and a dense crowd circulating among all of them. Deafening music poured out of every establishment, and there was a real aerial forest of lights, banners, and advertisements. It made me dizzy. Later we ate in a quieter place, in Nishi-Azabu, where, for the first time, I tasted Japanese food and drank the tepid, bitter sake. Throughout the evening my impression grew that the relationship between Salomón and Mitsuko was far from working as smoothly as the Dragoman had claimed in his letters. But, I told myself, this is surely because Mitsuko, sparing in her displays of affection, wasn't yet accustomed to the expansive, Mediterranean manner in which Salomón exhibited to the world the passion she had awakened in him. She'd soon become used to it.

Mitsuko took the initiative of talking about the bad girl. She did it halfway through the meal, and in the most natural maneuver, asking if I wanted her to call my compatriot to let her know I had arrived. I asked her to do that, and gave her the phone number of my hotel. That was better than my calling her, keeping in mind that the gentleman with whom she lived was, apparently, a Japanese Othello and, perhaps, a killer.

"Is that what this man told you?" Mitsuko said with a laugh. "How silly. Mr. Fukuda is a little strange, they say he's involved in some rather obscure business in Africa. But I've never heard that he's a criminal or anything like that. It's true he's very jealous. At least, that's what Kuriko says."

"Kuriko?"

"The bad girl."

She said "bad girl" in Spanish, and she herself celebrated her small linguistic accomplishment by applauding. In other words, now her name was Kuriko. Well then.

That night, when we said goodbye, the Dragoman managed to have a very brief private conversation with me. Pointing at Mitsuko, he asked, "What do you think?"

"Very attractive, Dragoman. You were absolutely right. She's charming."

"And you're only seeing her dressed," he said, winking and hitting his chest. "We have to have a long talk, dear friend. You'll be amazed at the plans I have brewing. I'll call you tomorrow. Sleep, dream, and recover."

But the one who called, early, was the bad girl. She gave me an hour to shave, shower, and dress. When I went down she was waiting for me, sitting in one of the armchairs in the reception area. She wore a light-colored raincoat, and under that a brick-colored blouse and dark brown skirt. You could see her round, beautiful knees and slender legs. She was slimmer than I remembered and her eyes were rather tired. But no one in the world would have thought she was past forty. She looked fresh and beautiful. From a distance, she could have been taken for one of those delicate, tiny Japanese women who float silently down the street. Her face brightened when she saw me, and she stood for me to embrace her. I kissed her cheeks and she didn't move her lips away when I brushed them with mine.

"I love you very much," I stammered. "Thank you for still being so young and good-looking, Chilean girl."

"Come, we'll take the bus," she said, grasping my arm. "I know a nice place to talk. It's a park where all of Tokyo goes to have picnics and get drunk when the cherry blossoms come out. There you can tell me some more cheap, sentimental things."

Holding my arm, she led me to a bus stop two or

three blocks from the hotel, where we climbed onto a bus that was sparkling clean. Both the driver and the woman who took the fares had on the face masks I was surprised to see so many people wearing on the street. In many ways, Tokyo resembled a clinic. I gave her the Vuitton case I had brought for her and she accepted it without too much enthusiasm. She examined me, half amused, half curious.

"You've become Japanese. In the way you dress, your gestures, your movements, even the color of your skin. How long have you been calling yourself Kuriko?"

"My friends gave me the name, I don't know whose idea it was. I must have some Asian in me. You told me that once in Paris, don't you remember?"

"Of course I remember. Do you know, I was afraid you'd become ugly."

"But you've turned gray. And you have some wrinkles, here under your lids." She pressed my arm and her eyes filled with mischief. She lowered her voice. "Do you wish I were your geisha, good boy?"

"Yes, that too. But above all, my wife. I've come to Tokyo to ask you for the umpteenth time to marry me. This time I'll convince you, I'm warning you. And by the way, how long have you been riding buses? Can't the Yakuza boss give you a car with a driver and body-guard?"

"Even if he could, he wouldn't," she said, still holding my arm. "It would be ostentatious, what the Japanese hate most. People here disapprove of differen-tiating yourself from others, in any way. That's why the rich masquerade as poor and the poor as rich."

We got off in a park filled with people, office workers

using the midday break to eat sandwiches and have a drink under the trees, surrounded by grass and pools of brightly colored fish. The bad girl took me to a teahouse in a corner of the park. There were small tables with comfortable chairs among screens that offered a certain amount of privacy. As soon as we sat down I kissed her hands, her mouth, her eyes. I had been observing her for a long time, breathing her in.

"Do I pass the test, Ricardito?"

"With outstanding grades. But you look a little tired, Japanese girl. Is it the emotion of seeing me after totally abandoning me for six years?"

"And the tension in my life as well," she added, very seriously.

"What wicked things are you doing to make your life so tense?"

She sat looking at me, not answering, and she passed her hand over my hair in her usual affectionate gesture, half loving and half maternal.

"You have so many gray hairs," she repeated, examining me. "I gave you some, didn't I? Soon I'll have to call you good old man instead of good boy."

"Are you in love with this Fukuda? I hoped you were with him only out of self-interest. Who is he? Why does he have such a bad reputation? What does he do?"

"A lot of questions at one time, Ricardito. First tell me some of those things from soap operas. Nobody's done that for years."

I spoke to her very quietly, looking into her eyes and occasionally kissing the hand I held in mine.

"I haven't lost hope, Japanese girl. Even if you think I'm an utter cretin, I'll keep insisting until you come and

182

live with me. In Paris, and if you don't like Paris, wherever you want. As an interpreter I can work anywhere in the world. I swear I'll make you happy, Japanese girl. Too many years have gone by for you to have any doubts: I love you so much I'll do anything to keep you with me when we're together. Do you like gangsters? I'll become a robber, a kidnapper, a swindler, a drug trafficker, whatever you want. Six years without hearing anything from you, and now I can hardly speak, hardly think, I'm so moved to feel you close to me."

"Not bad," she said with a laugh as she brought her face forward and gave me a bird's rapid peck on the lips.

She ordered tea and some cakes in a Japanese that the waitress had her repeat several times. After the order had been brought and she poured me a cup of tea, she gave a delayed response to my question.

"I don't know if what I feel for Fukuda is love. But never in my life have I depended so much on anyone the way I depend on him. The truth is he can do whatever he wants with me."

She didn't say this with the joy or euphoria of someone, like the Dragoman, who had discovered a love-passion. Instead she was alarmed, surprised at something like this happening to a person like her, who had thought herself immune to those weaknesses. There was something anguished in her eyes the color of dark honey.

"Well, if he can do whatever he wants with you, that means you've finally fallen in love. You're a glacial woman, and I hope this Fukuda makes you suffer the way you've made me suffer for so many years . . ."

I felt her grasp my hand and rub it.

"It isn't love, I swear. I don't know what it is, but it can't be love. More a sickness, a vice. That's what Fukuda is for me."

The story she told me may have been true, though she surely left many things in the shadows, and dissimulated, softened, and embellished others. It was difficult for me to believe anything she said, because ever since I met her she had always told me more lies than truths. And I believe that, unlike the common run of mortals, by this time the new Kuriko found it very difficult to differentiate the world in which she lived from the one she claimed to live in. As I imagined, she had met Fukuda years earlier, on one of the trips she made to the Orient with David Richardson, who, in fact, had business dealings with the Japanese. Fukuda once told the bad girl it was a shame a worldly woman like her, with so much character, had settled for being Mrs. Richardson, because she could have had a great career in the world of business. The phrase kept sounding in her ears. When she felt her world collapsing because her ex-husband had found out about her marriage to Robert Arnoux, she called Fukuda, told him what had happened, and proposed working for him in any capacity. The Japanese sent her a ticket on a flight from London to Tokyo.

"When you called me from the airport in Paris to say goodbye, were you going to join him?"

She nodded. "Yes, but in fact I called from the airport in London."

On the very night she arrived in Japan, Fukuda made her his mistress. But he didn't have her live with him for another couple of years. Until then she lived alone, in a boardinghouse, in a minuscule room with a bathroom and a wall kitchen, "tinier than the room my Filipina maid had in Newmarket." If she hadn't traveled so much, "running errands for Fukuda," she would have gone mad with claustrophobia and loneliness. She was Fukuda's mistress, but one among several. The Japanese never hid the fact that he slept with other women. He brought her sometimes to spend the night with him, but then weeks could go by without his inviting her to his house. During those periods, their relationship was strictly that of employee and employer. What were Mr. Fukuda's "errands"? Smuggling drugs, diamonds, paintings, weapons, money? Often not even she knew. She carried what he prepared for her, in suitcases, packages, bags, or briefcases, and so far—she knocked the wooden table—she had always gotten past customs, borders, and police without too much difficulty. Traveling this way through Asia and Africa, she discovered what panicked fear meant. At the same time, she never had lived with so much intensity and the kind of energy that on each trip made her feel that life was a marvelous adventure. "How different living this way is from that limbo, that slow death surrounded by horses in Newmarket!" After two years of working for him, Fukuda, satisfied with her services, rewarded her with a promotion: "You deserve to live under my roof."

"You're going to end up knifed, murdered, locked up for years and years in some horrible jail," I said. "Have you lost your mind? If you're telling me the truth, what you're doing is stupid. When you're caught smuggling drugs or something worse, do you think this gangster is going to worry about you?"

"I know he won't, he told me so himself," she interrupted. "At least he's very frank with me, you see. 'If they ever catch you, you're on your own. I don't know you and I've never known you. You're on your own.'"

"You see how much he loves you."

"He doesn't love me. Not me, not anybody. He's like me that way. But he has more character and he's stronger than I am."

We had been there more than an hour, and it was growing dark. I didn't know what to say. I felt demoralized. It was the first time she seemed to have given herself totally, body and soul, to a man. Now it was crystal clear: the bad girl would never be yours, little pissant.

"What an unhappy expression on your face," she said with a smile. "Does what I told you make you sad? You're the only person I could have told it to. Besides, I needed to tell somebody. But maybe I've done a bad thing. Will you forgive me if I give you a kiss?"

"It makes me sad that for the first time in your life, you really love somebody and it's not me."

"No, no, it's not love," she repeated, shaking her head. "It's more complicated, more like a sickness, I already told you that. He makes me feel alive, useful, active. But not happy. It's a kind of possession. Don't laugh, don't joke, sometimes I feel possessed by Fukuda."

"If you're so afraid of him, I imagine you won't dare make love to me. And I came to Tokyo expressly to ask you to take me to the Château Meguru."

She had been very serious telling me about her life with Fukuda, but now, opening her eyes wide, she burst into laughter.

"And how the hell do you know about the Château Meguru when you've only just come to Tokyo?"

"From my friend, the interpreter. Salomón calls himself 'the Dragoman of the Château Meguru.'" I grasped her hand and kissed it. "Would you dare, bad girl?"

She looked at her watch and was thoughtful for a few moments, calculating. Suddenly, decisively, she asked the waitress to call us a taxi.

"I don't have much time," she said. "But for some reason it makes me feel bad to see you with that face of a beaten dog. Let's go, though I'm taking a huge risk doing this."

The Château Meguru was a house of assignation operating in a labyrinthine building filled with hallways and dark stairs that led to rooms equipped with saunas, Jacuzzis, water beds, mirrors on the walls and ceilings, radios, and television sets, next to which were piles of pornographic videos with fantasies for every imaginable taste and a marked preference for sadomasochism. And in a small glass cabinet, condoms and vibrators of various sizes with features like rooster crests, tufts, and miters, as well as a rich paraphernalia of sadomasochistic toys, whips, masks, handcuffs, and chains. Like the buses, the streets, and the park, here too the cleanliness was meticulous and morbid. When I entered the room, I had the feeling I was in a laboratory or a space station. In fact, it was difficult for me to understand the enthusiasm of Salomón Toledano, who called these technological bedrooms and mini sex shops an Eden of pleasures.

When I began to undress Kuriko, and saw and touched her soft skin, and smelled her perfume, in spite

187

of my efforts to control myself, the anguish that had tightened my chest ever since she told me about her unconditional surrender to Fukuda overcame me. I burst into tears. She let me cry for a long time, not saying anything. Pulling myself together, I stammered some excuses, and I felt her caress my hair again.

"We haven't come here to be sad," she said. "Put your arms around me and tell me you love me, foolish boy."

When we were both naked I saw she really had become very thin. You could see the ribs on her chest and back, and the small scar on her belly had lengthened. But her shape was as harmonious as ever, and her small breasts firm. I kissed her slowly, for a long time, everywhere on her body—the faint perfume of her skin seemed to emanate from inside—whispering words of love. I didn't care about anything. Not even that she was bewitched by the Japanese. I was terrified that, because of the work he had her doing, she'd end up with her belly ripped open by bullets, or in an African jail. But then I would move heaven and earth to rescue her. Because, why deny it, I loved her more and more each day. And I would always love her, even if she deceived me with a thousand Fukudas, because she was the most beautiful and delicate woman in creation: my queen, my princess, my torturer, my liar, my Japanese girl, my only love. Kuriko had covered her face with her arm and said nothing, she didn't even listen to me, totally concentrated on her pleasure.

"What I like, good boy," she finally ordered, spreading her legs and drawing my head to her sex.

Kissing and sucking, relishing the fragrance that came

from the depths of her womb, made me as happy as it always had. For a few eternal minutes, submerged in a silent, feverish exaltation, swallowing the sweet juices I absorbed from inside her, I forgot about Fukuda and the thousand and one adventures she had told me about. After I felt her climax I lifted myself over her, and with the same difficulty as always I penetrated her, hearing her groan and seeing her frown. I was very excited but managed to hold off inside her, lost in a frenzied vertigo until I finally ejaculated. For a long time I gripped her, holding her tight against me. I caressed her, bit her hair, her perfect ears, I kissed her and begged her pardon for not being able to hold back longer.

"There's a remedy so you don't finish so quickly, so you keep your erection for a long time, for hours," she finally said into my ear in her old, mischievous voice. "Do you know what it is? No, what would you know about these things, you're such a saint. It's a powder prepared from ground elephant tusks and rhinoceros horns. Don't laugh, it isn't witchcraft, it's true. I'll give you a vial of it to remember me by in Paris. I'm telling you it's worth a fortune all over Asia. This way you'll think of Kuriko every time you go to bed with a Frenchwoman."

I raised my head from her neck to see her face: she looked very beautiful this way, pale, with bluish circles under her eyes and the languor she sank into after love.

"Is that what you smuggle on your trips through Asia and Africa, aphrodisiacs prepared from elephant tusks and rhinoceros horns to swindle the gullible?" I asked, shaking with laughter.

"It's the best business in the world, though you may not believe it," she said with a laugh, infected by my laughter. "The ecologists are to blame, they made the hunting of elephants, rhinoceroses, and who knows how many other animals illegal. Now those tusks and horns are worth a fortune in the countries here. I also bring in other things I don't intend to tell you about. But that's Fukuda's big business. And now I have to go, good boy."

"I don't plan to go back to Paris," I said as I watched her, her back to me, walking naked on tiptoe to the bathroom. "I'll live in Tokyo, and if I can't kill Fukuda, I'll settle for being your dog, just like you're that gangster's dog."

"Bowwow," the Chilean girl barked.

When I returned to my hotel, I found a message from Mitsuko. She wanted to see me alone on an urgent matter. Could I call her at her office early tomorrow?

I called as soon as I got up, and with interminable Japanese courtesies, the Dragoman's friend asked me to have coffee with her midmorning in the cafeteria at the Hotel Hilton, because she had something important to tell me. As soon as I hung up, the phone rang. It was Kuriko. She had told Fukuda that an old Peruvian friend was in Tokyo, and the Yakuza boss had invited me, along with the Dragoman and his girlfriend, to have a drink at their house tonight and then a dinner-show at the most popular musical in the Ginza. Had I heard right?

"And then I said I'd be showing you around for the next few days. He didn't object."

"How generous, how gallant," I responded, indignant at what she had just told me. "You, asking permission of a man! I don't recognize you, bad girl."

"You've made me blush," she murmured in some confusion. "I thought you'd be happy to know we could see each other for as long as you're in Tokyo."

"I'm jealous. Don't you realize that? Before it didn't matter, because your lovers or husbands didn't matter to you, either. But this Japanese does. You never should have told me he can do whatever he wants with you. That dagger in my heart will go with me to the grave."

She laughed, as if I had made a joke.

"I don't have time now for those cheap, sentimental things, good boy. I'll get rid of that jealousy of yours. I've made a wonderful plan for the day, you'll see."

I asked her to pick me up at the Hilton cafeteria at noon, and I went to my appointment with Mitsuko. When I arrived she was already there, smoking. She seemed very nervous. She apologized again for her audacity in calling me, but, she said, she had no one else to turn to. "The situation has become very difficult and I don't know what to do." Perhaps I could advise her.

"Are you referring to your relationship with Salomón?" I asked, suspecting what was to follow.

"I thought our affair would be a little flirtation," she agreed, exhaling smoke from her nose and mouth. "A pleasant, passing adventure, the kind that doesn't involve commitment. But Salomón doesn't understand it that way. He wants to turn this into a lifelong relationship. He insists we get married. I'll never marry again. I went through one failed marriage and I know what it means. Besides, I have a career ahead of me. The truth is, his obstinacy is driving me crazy. I don't know what to do to end this once and for all."

I wasn't happy to have my suspicions confirmed. The Dragoman had built castles in the air and was going to suffer the greatest frustration of his life.

"Since the two of you are such good friends and he thinks so highly of you, I thought, I mean, I hope it's not an imposition, I thought you could help me."

"But how can I help you, Mitsuko?"

"By talking to him. Explaining things to him. That I'll never marry him. That I don't want to and can't continue this relationship in the way he insists on having it. The truth is he's harassing me, crushing me. I have a great number of responsibilities at the company and this is affecting my work. It's been very difficult for me to get where I am at Mitsubishi."

All the smokers in Tokyo seemed to have congregated in the impersonal cafeteria of the Hotel Hilton. Clouds of smoke and a strong odor of tobacco filled the place. You could hear English spoken at almost every table. There were as many foreigners as Japanese.

"I'm very sorry, Mitsuko, but I won't do it. This isn't something third parties should interfere in, it's between you and him. You ought to talk to him, openly, and right away. Because Salomón is head over heels in love with you. As he's never been before with anybody else. And he's filled with illusions. He thinks you love him too."

I told her some of what the Dragoman had said in his letters. How meeting her had changed the way he had thought about love ever since that distant experience of his youth in Berlin, when his Polish fiancée left him in the midst of preparations for the wedding. I could see that what I was saying didn't move her in the least: she must have been sick of the poor Dragoman.

"I understand that girl," she remarked icily. "Your friend can be, I don't know how to say this in English, overwhelming, suffocating. Sometimes, when we're together, I feel I'm in prison. He doesn't give me any space to be myself, to breathe. He wants to touch me all the time. Even though I've explained to him that here in Japan we're not used to that kind of demonstrativeness in public."

She spoke in such a way that, within a few minutes, I thought the problem was even more serious: Mitsuko felt so sickened by the Dragoman's kissing and pawing in full view of everyone, and by who knows what kind of besiegement in private, that she had grown to detest him.

"Then, do you think I ought to talk to him?"

"I don't know, Mitsuko, don't make me give you advice about something so personal. The only thing I want is for my friend to suffer as little as possible. And I believe that if you aren't going to continue with him, if you've decided to break it off, it's better to do it right away. It'll be worse later."

When she left, with more excuses and courteous phrases, I felt uncomfortable and ill at ease. I would have preferred not to have had that conversation with Mitsuko, not to have learned that my friend was going to be brutally awakened from the dream he was in and returned to harsh reality. Fortunately, I didn't have to wait very long: Kuriko appeared in the doorway of the cafeteria and I went to meet her, happy to leave that smoke-filled den. She was wearing a little hat and a rain-coat of the same light checkered cloth, dark flannel trousers, a high-necked garnet-colored sweater, and sporty moccasins. Her face looked fresher and younger than it had the night before. An adolescent over forty. Just seeing her made my bad mood vanish. She offered her lips so I could kiss her, something she didn't usually do, I was always the one who searched out her mouth.

"Come, let's go, I'm going to take you to the Shinto temples, the nicest ones in Tokyo. In all of them there are animals roaming free, horses, roosters, doves. They're considered sacred, reincarnations. And tomorrow, the Zen Buddhist temples, with their gardens of sand and rocks that the monks rake and rearrange every day. They're beautiful too."

It was a day of intense activity, getting on and off buses, the aerodynamic subway, sometimes taxis. I entered and left temples, pagodas, and an enormous museum that had copies of Peruvian ceramics because—as a placard indicated—the institution, respectful of the prohibitions in Peru against taking objects from the archaeological patrimony out of the country, did not exhibit original pieces. But I don't think I paid much attention to what I was seeing, because my five senses were concentrated on Kuriko, who held my hand almost all the time and was unusually affectionate toward me. She joked, and flirted, and laughed freely, eyes shining, each time she whispered in my ear, "Now some more cheap, sentimental things, good boy," and I did as she asked. In midafternoon we sat at an isolated table in the cafeteria of the Museum of Anthropology to have a sandwich. She took off her checkered hat and smoothed her hair. She wore it very short and displayed her entire graceful neck with its hint of a little green snake of a vein.

"Anybody who doesn't know you would say you're in love with me, bad girl. I don't think you've ever been this affectionate since I first met you in Miraflores, when you were Chilean."

"I'm probably in love with you and don't know it yet," she said, passing her hand over my hair and bringing her face close so I could see how ironic and insolent her eyes were. "What would you do if I told you I am, and that we can live together?"

"I'd have a heart attack and die right here. Are you, Kuriko?"

"I'm happy because we can see each other every day you're in Tokyo. I was worried about that, how I'd manage to see you every day. That's why I dared tell Fukuda. And you see how well it turned out."

"The magnanimous gangster gave you permission to show your compatriot the charms of Tokyo. I hate your damn Yakuza boss. I would have preferred not to meet him, never to see him. Tonight I'll go through hell watching you with him. Can I ask you a favor? Don't touch him, don't kiss him in front of me."

Kuriko burst into laughter and covered my mouth with her hand.

"Be quiet, fool, he'd never do those things, not with me, not with anybody. No Japanese would. There's such a big difference here between what you do in public and in private that what seems natural to us they find shocking. He isn't like you. Fukuda treats me like his employee. At times, like his whore. But, what's true is true, you've always treated me like a princess."

"Now you're the one saying cheap, sentimental things."

I took her face between my hands and kissed her.

"And you shouldn't have told me that this Japanese treats you like his whore," I whispered in her ear. "Don't you see it's like skinning me alive?"

"I didn't tell you. Let's forget it, wipe it away."

Fukuda lived in a district far from the center of Tokyo, a residential area where very modern buildings of six or eight stories alternated with traditional houses that had tile roofs and tiny gardens and seemed about to be flattened by their tall neighbors. He had an apartment on the sixth floor of a building with a uniformed doorman who accompanied me to the elevator. This opened into the interior of the house, and after a small, bare reception room, there was a spacious dining room that had a large picture window through which you could see an infinite blanket of twinkling lights under a starless sky. The living room was soberly furnished, with blue ceramic plates on the walls, Polynesian sculptures on shelves, and carved ivory objects on a long, low table. Mitsuko and Salomón were already there, holding glasses of champagne. The bad girl was wearing a long, mustard-colored dress that left her shoulders bare, and a gold chain around her neck. She was made-up for a party and her hair was gathered in two knots. The hairstyle, which I hadn't seen her wear before, accentuated her Oriental appearance. She could be taken for Japanese, now more than ever. She kissed me on the cheek and said to Mr. Fukuda in Spanish, "This is Ricardo Somocurcio, the friend I told you about."

Mr. Fukuda made the well-known Japanese bow of greeting. And in fairly comprehensible Spanish, his greeting as he extended his hand was this: "The Yakuza boss welcomes you."

The witticism left me totally disconcerted, not only because I wasn't expecting it—I didn't imagine that Kuriko could have told him what I'd said about him—but because Mr. Fukuda joked (was he joking?) without smiling, with the same inexpressive, neutral, parchment-like face he maintained all night. A face that looked like a mask. When I stammered, "Ah, you speak Spanish," he shook his head and from then on spoke only a very hesitant, awkward English on the few occasions he did speak. He handed me a glass of champagne and indicated a seat next to Kuriko.

He was a short man, even smaller than Salomón Toledano, almost skeletal, so that compared to the svelte, slim bad girl, he seemed delicate. I had formed so different an idea of him that I had the impression he was an impostor. He wore round, dark glasses with wire frames that he didn't remove all night, which increased the discomfort he produced in me because I couldn't tell if his eyes—I imagined them as cold and belligerent—were observing me or not. He had gray hair plastered against his skull, perhaps pomaded, and combed back in the style of Argentine tango singers of the 1950s. He wore a dark suit and tie, which gave him a certain funereal air, and he could remain motionless and silent for a long time, his small hands resting on his knees, as if he were petrified. But perhaps his most pronounced physical trait was a lipless mouth that barely moved when he spoke, like a ventriloquist's. I felt so tense and uncomfortable that, uncharacteristically—I never could drink much because alcohol went to my head very quickly—

that night I drank to excess. When Mr. Fukuda stood to indicate it was time for us to leave, I'd had three glasses of champagne and my head was beginning to spin. And, somewhat removed from the conversation being held almost exclusively by the Dragoman as he spoke of the regional variants in Japanese he had begun to distinguish, I asked myself in stupefaction: "What does this insignificant old man have that makes the bad girl talk about him the way she does?" What did he say to her, what did he do to her, to make her say he's her vice, her sickness, that she's possessed by him, that he can do what he wants with her? Since I didn't find the answer, I felt more jealousy, more fury, more contempt for myself, and I cursed myself for having done something as stupid as coming to Japan. And yet, a second later, looking at her out of the corner of my eye, I told myself that only once before, at the dance at the Opéra in Paris, had she looked as desirable as she did tonight.

Two taxis were waiting at the entrance to the building. I went alone with Kuriko, because that was indicated with a single gesture of command by Mr. Fukuda, who climbed into the other cab with the Dragoman and Mitsuko. As soon as we drove away, I felt the bad girl grasp my hand and move it to her legs so I would touch her.

"Isn't he supposed to be jealous?" I said, pointing at the other taxi ahead of us. "Why does he let you ride alone with me?"

She pretended not to understand.

"Don't make that face, silly," she said. "Don't you love me anymore?"

"I hate you," I said. "I've never been as jealous as I

am now. Can that dwarf, that abortion of a man, be the great love of your life?"

"Stop talking nonsense and kiss me instead."

She threw her arms around my neck, offered me her mouth, and I felt the tip of her tongue become entangled with mine. She let me give her long kisses, and she responded with joy.

"I love you, damn you, I love you, I want you," I implored in her ear. "Come away with me, Japanese girl, come, I swear we'll be happy."

"Careful, we're almost there," she said. She moved away from me, took a tissue from her bag, and touched up her lips. "Wipe your mouth, my lipstick smeared a little."

The theater-restaurant was a music hall with a gigantic stage, large and small tables arranged along a ramp that opened like a fan, and immense chandeliers that shed a powerful light on the enormous room. The table reserved by Fukuda was fairly close to the stage and had a magnificent sight line. The show began almost immediately after we arrived. It recalled the great Broadway hits, with numbers that were sometimes parodic, sometimes mimetic, the footwork and figures performed by a large group of dancers. There were also acts by clowns, magicians, and contortionists, and songs in English and Japanese. The emcee seemed to know almost as many languages as the Dragoman, though, according to Salomón, he spoke them all badly.

This time too Mr. Fukuda, with commanding gestures, decided our places. Again he sat me next to Kuriko. As soon as the lights went down—the table was lit by bulbs half hidden among the floral arrangements—

I felt the bad girl's foot on mine. I looked at her and, with the most natural air in the world, she was talking to Mitsuko in a Japanese that, to judge by the efforts Mitsuko made to understand her, must have been as approximate as her French and English. She looked very attractive in this semidarkness, with her burnished hair, pale skin, rounded shoulders, long neck, shining honey-colored eyes, well-defined lips. She took off her shoe so I could feel the sole of her foot, which was on mine for almost the entire meal, moving at times to rub my ankle and remind me she was there, aware of what she was doing, defying her lord and master. He, hieratic, watched the show or conversed with the Dragoman, barely moving his mouth. Only once, I believe, did he turn to me to ask in English how things were going in Peru and if I knew people in the Japanese colony there, which, apparently, was fairly large. I told him I hadn't been in Peru for many years and didn't know much about what was going on in the country where I was born. And had never known any Japanese Peruvians, though there certainly were many of them, since Peru had been the second country in the world, after Brazil, to open its borders to Japanese immigration at the end of the nineteenth century.

Supper had already been ordered and the dishes, nicely presented and very bland miniatures of vegetables, shellfish, and meat, came in endless succession. I hardly tasted them, just enough to be polite. On the other hand, I drank several tiny porcelain cups in which the gangster served us the warm, syrupy sake. I felt dizzy before the first part of the show was over. But, at least, my initial uneasiness had disappeared. When the lights went on, to my surprise the bad girl's bare foot was still there, touching me. I thought: "She knows I'm suffering horrible jealousy and she's trying to make amends." That was it: each time I turned to look at her, trying not to betray what I was feeling, I told myself that I had never seen her look so beautiful or desirable. For example, her ear was a miracle of minimalist architecture with its gentle curves and the slight bend in the upper part of the lobe.

At one point there was a minor incident between Salomón and Mitsuko, though I don't know how it began. Suddenly she stood and left without saying goodbye to anyone or giving any explanation. The Dragoman jumped up and followed her.

"What happened?" I asked Mr. Fukuda, but he sat looking at me, immutable, not saying anything.

"She doesn't like to be touched or kissed in public," said Kuriko. "Your friend has wandering hands. Mitsuko will leave him soon. She told me so."

"Salomón will die if she leaves him. He loves Mitsuko like a mooning calf. Head over heels in love."

The bad girl laughed, her mouth open, her full lips very red now with makeup.

"In love like a mooning calf! Head over heels in love!" she repeated. "I haven't heard those laughable things for ages. Do they still say them in Peru, or are there other Peruvianisms for being in love?"

And passing from Spanish to Japanese, she began to explain to Fukuda what those expressions meant. He listened to her, rigid and inscrutable. From time to time, like an articulated puppet, he would pick up his glass, raise it to his mouth without looking at it, take a sip, and return it to the table. Unexpectedly, a short while later the Dragoman and Mitsuko came back. They had made peace, for they were smiling and holding hands.

"Nothing like arguments to keep love alive," Salomón said with the smile of a satisfied man, winking at me. "But the man has to discipline the woman occasionally to keep her in her place."

When we left there were two taxis waiting for us again, and as he had earlier, Mr. Fukuda decided with a gesture that I would get into one of them with Kuriko. He left with Salomón and Mitsuko. I began to like the hated Japanese because of the privileges he granted me.

"At least let me have the shoe for the foot you've been touching me with all night. I'll go to bed with it, since I can't do that with you. And I'll keep it next to the Guerlain toothbrush."

But to my surprise, when we reached Fukuda's building, Kuriko, instead of saying good night, took me by the hand and invited me to go up with her to have "one for the road" in her apartment. In the elevator I kissed her desperately. As I kissed her I said I would never forgive her for looking so beautiful on this night in particular, when I had discovered that her ears were miraculous minimalist creations. I adored them and would like to cut them off, embalm them, and carry them around the world in the jacket pocket closest to my heart.

"Go on, go on with your cheap, sentimental things, you sentimental man." She looked pleased, smiling, very much in control.

Fukuda wasn't in the living room. "I'll see if he's back," she murmured, after pouring me a glass of whiskey on the rocks. She returned right away, her face afire with a provocative expression.

"He hasn't come back. You have what you wanted, good boy, that means he won't come back at all. He'll sleep somewhere else."

She didn't seem very sorry that her sickness, her vice, had abandoned her. On the contrary, it seemed to make her happy. She explained that Fukuda would disappear suddenly like this after a supper or going to the movies, not saying anything to her. And the next day, when he came back, he wouldn't explain anything.

"Do you mean he's going to spend the night with another woman? Having the most beautiful woman in the world in his house, the imbecile is capable of spending the night with someone else?"

"Not all men have your good taste," said Kuriko, dropping onto my knees and throwing her arms around my neck.

As I embraced her and caressed her and kissed her on the neck, the shoulders, the ears, she said it wasn't possible that fate, or the gods, or whatever, had been so generous with me, chasing away the Yakuza boss and granting me so much happiness.

"Are you sure he won't come back?" I asked after a moment, in a sudden attack of lucidity.

"No, I know him, if he hasn't come back it's because he won't spend the night here. Why, Ricardito? Are you afraid?"

"No, not afraid. If you asked me today to kill him, I'd kill him. I've never been so happy in my life, Japanese girl. And you've never been as beautiful as you are tonight."

"Come, come."

I followed her, resisting my vertigo. The objects in the

living room moved around me in slow motion. I felt so happy as I passed the picture window through which you could see the city, that I thought if I went through one of the panes and threw myself into the void, I'd float like a feather over the interminable blanket of lights. A hallway in the semidarkness had erotic prints on the walls. A room in shadows, carpeted, where I stumbled and fell onto a large, soft bed with a number of pillows. Without my asking, Kuriko began to take off her clothes. And when she had finished, she helped me to strip.

"What are you waiting for, silly?"

"Are you sure he won't come back?"

Instead of answering, she pressed her body to mine, wrapped herself around me, searched for my mouth, and filled it with her saliva. Never had I felt so excited, so moved, so fortunate. Was all this really happening? The bad girl never had been so ardent, so enthusiastic, never had taken so many initiatives in bed. She always had adopted a passive, almost indifferent attitude, seeming to resign herself to being kissed, caressed, loved, with no contribution on her part. Now she was the one kissing and nibbling my entire body, responding to my caresses instantly, with a resolution that astonished me. "Don't you want me to do what you like?" I murmured. "First me," she replied, pushing me with affectionate hands so I'd lie down on my back and spread my legs. She squatted between my knees, and for the first time since we made love in that *chambre de bonne* in the Hôtel du Sénat, she did what I had begged her to do so many times and she had always refused: to put my sex in her mouth and suck it. I heard myself moan, overwhelmed by the

204

immeasurable pleasure that was disintegrating me piece by piece, atom by atom, transforming me into pure sensation, into music, into crackling flame. Then, in one of those seconds or minutes of miraculous suspension, when I felt my entire being concentrated in that piece of grateful flesh the bad girl was licking, kissing, sucking, swallowing, while her fingers caressed my testicles, I saw Fukuda.

He was half hidden in the shadows beside a large television set, as if he were separated by the darkness in that corner of the bedroom, two or three meters at the most from the bed where Kuriko and I were making love, sitting on a chair or a bench, as motionless and mute as a sphinx, with his eternal movie gangster's dark glasses and both hands in his fly.

Grabbing her by the hair, I obliged the bad girl to let go of the sex she had in her mouth—I heard her complain about my pulling her hair—and completely shaken by surprise, fear, and confusion, I stupidly said in her ear, in a very quiet voice: "But, he's there, Fukuda's there." Instead of jumping out of the bed, putting on a horrified expression, starting to run, going mad, screaming, after a second's vacillation during which she began to turn her head toward the corner but thought better of it, I saw her do the only thing I never would have suspected or wanted her to do: put her arms around me, press against me with all her strength to keep me in the bed, seek out my mouth, bite me, pass me her saliva mixed with my semen, and say desperately, hurriedly, in anguish, "And what do you care if he's here or not, silly? Aren't you enjoying it, aren't I making you enjoy it? Don't look at him, forget about him."

Paralyzed by astonishment, I understood everything: Fukuda hadn't surprised us, he was there with the complicity of the bad girl, enjoying a show prepared by the two of them. I had fallen into a trap. The surprising things that had happened were clarified, they had been carefully planned by the Japanese and executed by her, submissive to his orders and desires. I understood the reason for how effusive Kuriko had been with me these two days and, above all, tonight. She hadn't done it for me, or for herself, but for him. To please her lord. For the enjoyment of her master. My heart pounded as if it would burst, and I could hardly breathe. I was no longer dizzy, and I felt my penis go flaccid, slipping away, shrinking, as if it were ashamed. I shoved her away and partially sat up, restrained by her, as I shouted, "I'll kill you, you son of a bitch! Damn you!"

But Fukuda was no longer in the corner, or in the room, and now the bad girl's mood had changed and she insulted me, her voice and face distorted by rage.

"What's wrong with you, you idiot? Why are you making a scene?" She hit me on the face, the chest, wherever she could, with both hands. "Don't be ridiculous, don't be provincial. You always have been and always will be a sorry bastard, what else could I expect from you, little pissant."

In the semidarkness, as I tried to move her away, I looked for my clothes on the floor. I don't know how I found them, or got dressed, or put on my shoes, or how long the farcical scene lasted. Kuriko had stopped hitting me, but she sat on the bed and screeched, hysterical, mixing sobs and insults.

"Did you think I'd do this for you, you pauper, you

failure, you imbecile? But who are you, who did you think you were? Ah, you'd die if you knew how much I despise you, how much I hate you, you coward."

At last I finished dressing and almost ran down the hall with the erotic prints, wanting Fukuda to be waiting for me in the living room with a revolver in his hand and two bodyguards armed with clubs, because then I'd rush him, try to pull off those hateful glasses, spit in his face so they would kill me right away. But nobody was in the living room or the elevator. Downstairs, in the doorway of the building, trembling with cold and rage, I had to wait a long time for the taxi that the uniformed doorman called for me.

In my hotel room I lay on my bed, fully dressed. I felt exhausted, distressed, offended, and I didn't even have the energy to take off my clothes. I was awake for hours, my mind a blank, feeling like human junk saturated with a stupid innocence, a naïve imbecility. I kept repeating, like a mantra: "It's your fault, Ricardo. You knew her. You knew what she was capable of. She never loved you, she always despised you. What are you crying about, little pissant? What are you complaining about, what are you grieving for, dimwit, prick, imbecile? That's what you are, everything she called you and more. You ought to be happy, and like assholes and modern, intelligent people do, tell yourself you got what you wanted. Didn't you fuck her? Didn't she suck your dick? Didn't you come in her mouth? What else do you want? What do you care if that midget, that Yakuza was there, watching you fuck his whore? What do you care about what happened? Who told you to fall in love with her? You're to blame for everything, Ricardito, you and no one else."

When day broke I shaved, showered, packed my bag, and called Japan Airlines to move up my return to Paris, which I was obliged to do by way of Korea. I managed to arrange a seat on the noon plane to Seoul, so I had just enough time to get to Narita Airport. I called the Dragoman to say goodbye, telling him it was urgent I return to Paris because I had just been offered a good contract. He insisted on seeing me off even though I did everything I could to talk him out of it.

When I was at reception, paying the bill, I received a phone call. As soon as I heard the voice of the bad girl saying "Hello, hello," I hung up. I went out to the street to wait for the Dragoman. We took a bus that picked up passengers from different hotels, so it took more than an hour to reach Narita. On the way, my friend asked if I'd had some problem with Kuriko or with Fukuda, and I assured him I hadn't, that my impetuous departure was due to the excellent contract Señor Charnés had offered me by fax. He didn't believe me but didn't insist.

And then, turning to his own affairs, he began to talk to me about Mitsuko. He had always been allergic to matrimony, he considered it a surrender for any free person like himself. But, since Mitsuko was so insistent on their marrying, and had turned out to be such a nice girl, and had treated him so well, he was thinking about sacrificing his liberty, giving her that pleasure, and marrying. "In the Shinto rite, if necessary, dear friend."

I didn't dare even to suggest it probably would be a good idea for him to wait a while before taking so transcendental a step. As he talked to me, I felt sorry down to the marrow of my bones, thinking about how much he was going to suffer when, one of these days, Mitsuko found the courage to tell him she wanted to break it off because she didn't love him and even had grown to detest him.

At Narita, as I gave the Dragoman a hug when they announced my flight to Seoul, I felt, absurdly enough, my eyes fill with tears when I heard him say, "Would you agree to be a witness at my wedding, dear friend?"

"Of course, old man, it would be an honor."

Two days later I arrived in Paris, a physical and moral ruin. I hadn't closed my eyes or had a bite of food in forty-eight hours. But I arrived, also decided—I had reflected on this resolution during the entire trip—not to allow myself to be completely disheartened, to overcome the depression that was undermining me. I knew the recipe. This could be cured by working and filling my free time with occupations that would at least be absorbing if they couldn't be creative or useful. Feeling that my will was dragging my body behind it, I asked Señor Charnés to find me a good number of contracts because I needed to pay off an important debt. He did, with the benevolence he had always shown for as long as I had known him. In the months that followed, I was not in Paris very often. I worked at all kinds of conferences and meetings in London, Vienna, Italy, the Scandinavian countries, and a couple of times in Africa, in Cape Town and in Abidjan. In every city, after work I would sweat blood at a gym, doing abdominal exercises, running on the treadmill, pedaling on a stationary bike, swimming or doing aerobics. And I continued to perfect my Russian, on my own, and to translate, slowly, for my own pleasure, the stories of Ivan Bunin, which, after Chekhov's, were the ones I liked best. When I had three translated, I sent them to my friend Mario Muchnik, in Spain. "With my insistence on publishing only master-pieces, I've already bankrupted four publishing houses," he replied. "And even though you may not believe it, I'm persuading a suicidal entrepreneur to finance the fifth. That's where I'll publish your Bunin and even pay you some rights that will be enough for a few coffees. The contract will follow." This incessant activity gradually took me out of the emotional disorder caused by my trip to Tokyo. But it couldn't do away with a certain inner sadness, a certain profound disillusionment that accompanied me for a long time, like a double, and corroded like acid any enthusiasm or interest I might begin to feel for anything or anyone. And on many nights I had the same filthy nightmare in which, on a background dense with shadows, I would see the weak little figure of Fukuda, motionless on his bench, as inexpressive as a Buddha, masturbating and ejaculating a shower of semen that fell on the bad girl and me.

After about six months, when I returned to Paris from one of those conferences, they handed me a letter from Mitsuko at UNESCO. Salomón had taken his life, swallowing a bottle of barbiturates in the small, rented apartment where he lived. His suicide had come as a surprise, because shortly after I left Tokyo, when Mitsuko, following my advice, found the courage to speak to him, explaining that they couldn't go on together because she wanted to dedicate herself fully to her career, Salomón took it very well. He seemed under-standing and didn't make a scene. They had maintained a distant friendship, which was inevitable considering the hectic pace in Tokyo. They would see each other occasionally in a tearoom or restaurant and spoke frequently on the phone. Salomón let her know that once his contract with Mitsubishi had ended, he didn't intend to renew it; he would return to Paris, "where he had a good friend." That was why she and everyone who knew him had been disconcerted by his decision to end his life. The firm had covered all the funeral costs. Fortunately, in her letter Mitsuko made no mention at all of Kuriko. I didn't answer or send her my condolences. I simply kept her letter in the little drawer in the night table where I kept the toy hussar the Dragoman had given me on the day he left for Tokyo, and the Guerlain toothbrush.

5

The Child Without a Voice

In spite of all the years I lived there, I had made no friends among my neighbors until Simon and Elena Gravoski moved into the art deco building on Rue Joseph Granier. I had thought Monsieur Dourtois was a friend. He was a functionary at the SNCF, the French rail system, married to a retired schoolteacher, a woman with yellowish hair and a grim expression. He lived across from me, and on the landing, or the staircase, or in the vestibule at the entrance, we would exchange nods or say good morning, and as the years passed we began to shake hands and make comments on the weather, a perennial concern of the French. Because of these fleeting conversations, I came to believe we were friends, but one night I learned we weren't when I came home after a concert by Victoria de los Angeles at the Théâtre des Champs-Élysées and discovered I had forgotten my apartment key. At that hour, no locksmith was open. I made myself as comfortable as I could on the landing and waited for five in the morning, the time my very punctual neighbor left for work. I supposed that when he found me there, he would invite me into his house to wait for daylight. But at five o'clock, when Monsieur Dourtois appeared and I explained why I was there, stiff after a sleepless night, he limited himself to expressing his sorrow, looking at his watch, and saying, "You'll have to wait another three or four hours until a locksmith opens, *mon pauvre ami.*"

With his conscience now at rest, he left. Sometimes I passed other residents of the building on the stairs, and I forgot their faces immediately and their names vanished as soon as I learned them. But when the Gravoskis and Yilal, their nine-year-old adopted son, came to the building because the Dourtoises had moved to the Dordogne, it was another matter. Simon, a Belgian physicist, worked as a researcher at the Pasteur Institute, and Elena, a Venezuelan, was a pediatrician at the Hôpital Cochin. They were cheerful, pleasant, easygoing, curious, cultured, and from the day I met them in the middle of their move and offered to give them a hand and tell them about the neighborhood, we became friends. We would have coffee together after supper, lend each other books and magazines, and occasionally go to the La Pagode cinema, which was nearby, or take Yilal to the circus, the Louvre, or other museums in Paris.

Simon was barely forty, though his heavy red beard and prominent belly made him look older. He dressed haphazardly, wearing a jacket whose pockets bulged with notebooks and papers and carrying a satchel full of books. He wore glasses for myopia, which he cleaned frequently with his wrinkled tie. He was the incarnation of the careless, absentminded intellectual. Elena, on the other hand, was somewhat younger, flirtatious, smartly dressed, and I don't recall ever seeing her in a bad mood. She was enthusiastic about everything in life: her work at the Hôpital Cochin and her young patients, about whom she told amusing anecdotes, but also the article she had just read in *Le Monde* or *L'Express*, and she would prepare to go to the movies or to eat at a Vietnamese restaurant the following Saturday as if she were attending the Oscars. She was short, slim, expressive, and she exuded congeniality from every pore. They spoke French to each other, but with me they used Spanish, which Simon knew perfectly.

Yilal had been born in Vietnam, and that was the only thing they knew about him. They adopted him when the boy was four or five years old—they weren't even certain of his age—through Caritas, after a Kafkaesque application procedure on the basis of which Simon, in laughing soliloquies, had founded his theory regarding the inevitable decay of humanity as a result of bureaucratic gangrene. They had named him Yilal after one of Simon's Polish ancestors, a mythic figure who, according to my neighbor, was decapitated in prerevolutionary Russia because he had been caught in flagrante with no less a personage than the czarina. Not only had this ancestor been a royal fornicator, but he had also been a theologian of the kabbalah, a mystic, a smuggler, a counterfeiter, and a chess player. Their adopted child was mute, the result not of organic deficiencies—his vocal cords were intact—but of a trauma in his infancy, perhaps a bombing or some other terrible event in the war in Vietnam that had left him an orphan. They had seen specialists and all agreed that in time he would recover the power of speech, but for the moment it wasn't worth inflicting more treatments on him. The therapeutic sessions were a torture for the boy and seemed to reinforce, in his wounded spirit, the desire to remain silent. He had been at a school for deaf-mutes for a few months, but they took him out because the teachers themselves advised his parents to send him to an ordinary school. Yilal wasn't deaf. He had a fine ear and enjoyed music; he followed the rhythm with his foot and with movements of his hands or head. Elena and Simon spoke to him aloud and he responded with signs and expressive gestures, and sometimes in writing, on a slate he wore around his neck.

He was very thin and somewhat frail, but not because he was reluctant to eat. He had an excellent appetite, and when I came to his house with a box of chocolates or a cake, his eyes would sparkle and he would devour the treats with signs of pleasure. But except for rare occasions, he was a withdrawn child who gave the impression of being submerged in a somnolence that distanced him from the reality around him. He could spend long periods of time with his lost gaze, enclosed in his private world, as if everything in his surroundings had disappeared.

He wasn't very affectionate but gave the impression that caresses annoyed him and he submitted to them with more resignation than happiness. Something soft and fragile emanated from him. The Gravoskis didn't have television—at that time many Parisians of the intellectual class still believed television shouldn't be in their houses because it was anticultural—but Yilal didn't share those prejudices and asked his parents to buy a television set as the families of his classmates had done. I proposed that if they were determined not to have this object that impoverished sensibilities in their house, Yilal could come to my apartment sometimes to watch a soccer match or a children's program. They agreed, and from then on, three or four times a week, after doing his homework, Yilal would cross the landing and come into my house to watch the program his parents or I had recommended to him. He seemed petrified for the hour he spent in my combined living-dining room, his eyes glued to the small screen as he watched cartoons, quiz shows, or a sports program. His gestures and expressions revealed total submission to the images. Occasionally, when the program was over, he spent some time with me and we talked. That is, he asked me questions about every imaginable thing and I responded, or read him a poem or a story from his reading book or my own library. I grew fond of him but tried not to show it too much, for Elena had warned me: "You have to treat him like a *normal* child. Never like a victim or an invalid, because that would do him great harm." When I wasn't at UNESCO and had contracts outside Paris, I left the key to my apartment with the Gravoskis so Yilal wouldn't miss his programs.

When I returned from one of those working trips, this one to Brussels, Yilal showed me this message on his slate: "When you were on your trip, the bad girl called you." The sentence was written in French, but "bad girl" was in Spanish.

It was the fourth time she had called in the couple of years since the episode in Japan. The first was three or four months after my hurried departure from Tokyo, when I was still struggling to recover from an experience that had left a wound in my memory that still festered at times. I was checking something in the library at UNESCO, and the librarian transferred a call for me

217

from the interpreters' room. Before I said "Hello" I recognized her voice.

"Are you still angry with me, good boy?"

I hung up, feeling my hand shake.

"Bad news?" the librarian asked, a Georgian woman who spoke Russian with me. "How pale you are."

I had to go into a UNESCO bathroom and throw up. For the rest of the day I was agitated by the call. But I had made a decision not to see the bad girl again or talk to her, and I was going to stick to it. It was the only way I would be cured of the dead weight that had conditioned my life ever since the day I helped my friend Paúl and went to pick up three aspiring guerrilla fighters at Orly Airport. I managed to forget her only partially. Devoted to my work, to the obligations it imposed on me—among which perfecting my Russian always headed the list—I sometimes spent weeks without thinking about her. But suddenly something would bring her to mind, and it was as if a hermit crab had taken up residence in my intestines and begun to devour my enthusiasm and energy. I would fall into a depression, and there was no way to get out of my head the image of Kuriko overwhelming me with caresses that had a fire she had never shown before, only to please her Japanese lover, who watched us, masturbating, from the shadows.

Her second call surprised me at the Hotel Sacher, in Vienna, during the only affair I had in those two years, with a colleague at a conference of the International Atomic Energy Agency. My lack of sexual appetite had been absolute since the episode in Tokyo, to the point where I wondered if I hadn't been left impotent. I had almost become accustomed to living without sex when, on the same day we met, Astrid, a Danish interpreter, proposed with disarming naturalness, "If you like, we can see each other tonight." She was a tall redhead, athletic, uncomplicated, with eyes so light they seemed liquid. We went to have some *Tafelspitz* and beer at the Café Central in the Palais Ferstel, Herrengasse, with its columns from a Turkish mosque, domed ceiling, and red marble tables, and then, without need for prior arrangements, we went to bed in the luxurious Hotel Sacher, where the two of us were staying, since the hotel offered significant discounts to conference participants. She was still attractive, though age had begun to leave a few traces on her extremely white body. She made love and the smile didn't leave her face, not even when she had an orgasm. I enjoyed it and she enjoyed it too, but it seemed to me that this healthful way of making love had more to do with gymnastics than with what the late Salomón Toledano called, in one of his letters, "the disturbing and lascivious pleasure of the gonads." The second and last time we went to bed, the telephone on my night table rang when we had finished our acrobatics and Astrid was telling me about the accomplishments of one of her daughters in Copenhagen, who had made the move from ballet dancer to circus acrobat. I picked up the receiver, said "Hello," and heard the affectionate, kittenish voice.

"Are you going to hang up on me again, little pissant?"

I held the receiver for a few seconds while I mentally cursed UNESCO for giving her my phone number in Vienna, but I hung up when, after a pause, she began to say: "Well, at least this time . . ."

"Stories of past love?" guessed Astrid. "Shall I go to the bathroom so you can talk freely?"

No, no, it was a story over and done with. Since that night I hadn't had another sexual relationship, and the truth was, it didn't concern me in the least. At the age of forty-seven, I had verified that a man could lead a perfectly normal life without making love. Because my life was fairly normal, though empty. I worked a great deal and did my job to fill the time and earn a salary, but not because I was interested—that happened only rarely—and even my studies of Russian and the almost eternal translation of Ivan Bunin's stories, which I did over and over again, turned out to be a mechanical chore that seldom became pleasurable again. Even films, concerts, books, records were ways to kill time more than activities that excited me as they once had. Another reason for my still feeling rancorous toward Kuriko. Because of her, the illusions that make existence something more than the sum of its routines had been extinguished for me. At times I felt like an old man.

Perhaps because of this state of mind, the arrival of Elena, Simon, and Yilal Gravoski in the building on Rue Joseph Granier was providential. My neighbors' friendship infused a little humanity and emotion into my dull, flat life. The third call from the bad girl came to my house in Paris, at least a year after the call to Vienna.

It was early, four or five in the morning, and the loud rings of the phone pulled me out of sleep and filled me with alarm. It rang so many times that finally I opened my eyes and fumbled for the receiver.

"Don't hang up." Pleading and anger mixed in her voice. "I need to talk to you, Ricardo."

I hung up and, of course, couldn't close my eyes for the rest of the night. I was distraught, feeling ill, until I saw the streaks of a mouse-colored dawn in the Paris sky through the skylight in my bedroom. Why was she calling me periodically? Because I must be one of the few stable things in her intense life, the faithful idiot in love who was always there, waiting for the call that would make her feel she was still what she no doubt was beginning not to be anymore, what she soon would not be again: young, beautiful, loved, desirable. Or, perhaps, she needed something from me? It wasn't impossible. A gap had suddenly appeared in her life that the little pissant could fill. And with that icy character of hers, she wouldn't hesitate to look for me, certain there was no pain, no humiliation that she, with her infinite power over my feelings, couldn't erase after two minutes of conversation. Knowing her, it was certain she'd be obstinate; she'd go on insisting, every few months, or years. No, this time you're wrong. I won't talk to you again on the phone, Peruvian girl.

Now she had called for the fourth time. From where? I asked Elena Gravoski but, to my surprise, she said she hadn't answered that call or any other during my trip to Brussels.

"Then it was Simon. Hasn't he said anything to you?"

"He doesn't even set foot in your apartment. He comes home from the institute when Yilal is eating supper."

But then, was it Yilal who *spoke* to the bad girl?

Elena turned pale.

"Don't ask him," she said, lowering her voice. She

was as white as a sheet. "Don't make the slightest allusion to the message he gave you."

Was it possible Yilal had *spoken* to Kuriko? Was it possible the boy broke his silence when his parents weren't nearby and couldn't see or hear him?

"Let's not think about that, let's not talk about that," Elena repeated, making an effort to compose her voice and appear natural. "What has to happen, will happen. In its own time. If we try to force it, we'll make everything worse. I've always known it would happen, that it will happen. Let's change the subject, Ricardo. What's this about the bad girl? Who is she? Tell me about her."

We were drinking coffee in her house, after supper, and talking quietly so as not to disturb Simon, who was in the next room, his study, revising a report he had to present the following day at a seminar. Yilal had gone to bed a while ago.

"An old story," I replied. "I've never told anybody about it. But look, I think I'll tell you, Elena. So you'll forget what happened with Yilal."

And I did tell her. From start to finish, from the distant days of my childhood, when the arrival of Lucy and Lily, the false Chileans, disturbed the tranquil streets of Miraflores, to the night of passionate love in Tokyo—the most beautiful night of love in my life—abruptly cut off by the sight, in the shadows of the room, of Mr. Fukuda watching us from behind his dark glasses, his hands moving inside his fly. I don't know how long I talked. I don't know exactly when Simon appeared and sat down next to Elena and began to listen to me, as silent and attentive as she was. I don't know when I began to cry, and, embarrassed by this emotional outburst, fell silent.

It took me a while to regain my composure. As I stammered excuses, I saw Simon stand and then come back with glasses and a bottle of wine.

"It's the only thing I have, wine, a very cheap Beaujolais," he said in apology, patting me on the shoulder. "I imagine in cases like this a nobler drink would be more appropriate."

"Whiskey, vodka, rum, cognac, of course!" said Elena. "This house is a disaster. We never have what we ought to have. We're terrible hosts, Ricardo."

"I've messed up your report for tomorrow with my little performance, Simon."

"Something much more interesting than my report," he declared. "Aside from that, the nickname fits you like a glove. Not in the pejorative but in the literal sense. That's what you are, *mon vieux*, though you don't like it: a good boy."

"Do you know, it's a marvelous love story?" exclaimed Elena, looking at me in surprise. "Because that's what it is, basically. A marvelous love story. This melancholy Belgian has never loved me like that. I envy her, chico."

"I'd like to meet this Mata Hari," said Simon.

"Over my dead body," Elena threatened, tugging at his beard. "Do you have any pictures of her? Will you show them to us?"

"Not even one. As I recall, we never took a picture together."

"The next time she calls, I beg you to answer that phone," said Elena. "The story can't end like this, with a phone ringing and ringing, like something in Hitchcock's worst movie."

"Besides," said Simon, lowering his voice, "you have to ask her if Yilal *talked* to her."

"I'm mortified," I said, apologizing for the second time. "I mean, crying and everything."

"You didn't see it, but Elena shed a few tears too," Simon said. "I would have joined you two if I weren't Belgian. My Jewish ancestors inclined me to weeping. But the Walloon prevailed. A Belgian doesn't fall into the emotionalism of tropical South Americans."

"To the bad girl, to that fantastic woman!" said Elena, raising her glass. "Holy God, what a boring life I've had."

We drank the entire bottle of wine, and with the laughter and jokes, I felt better. To prevent my feeling uncomfortable, not once in the days and weeks that followed did my friends the Gravoskis make the slightest reference to what I had told them. In the meantime, I decided that if the Peruvian girl called again, I would talk to her. So she could tell me if the last time she called, she had *talked* with Yilal. Was that the only reason? Not the only one. Ever since I confessed my love affair to Elena Gravoski, it was as if sharing the story with someone had lifted the burden of rancor, jealousy, humiliation, and susceptibility that trailed behind it, and I began to wait for her phone call with anticipation, afraid that because of my rebuffs of the past two years, it might not happen. I assuaged my feelings of guilt by telling myself this would in no way signify a relapse. I would talk to her like a distant friend, and my coldness would be the best proof that I was truly free of her.

As for the rest, the wait had a fairly good effect on my state of mind. Between contracts at UNESCO or outside

Paris, I resumed the translation of Ivan Bunin's stories, gave them a final revision, and wrote a short prologue before sending the manuscript to my friend Mario Muchnik. "It's about time," he replied. "I was afraid arteriosclerosis or senile dementia would come to me before your Bunin." If I was at home when Yilal watched his television program, I would read him stories. He didn't like the ones I had translated very much, and he listened more out of politeness than interest. But he adored the novels of Jules Verne. At the rate of a couple of chapters a day, I read several to him in the course of that autumn. The one he liked best—the episodes made him jump up and down with delight—was *Around the World in Eighty Days*. Though he was also fascinated by *Michael Strogoff: A Courier to the Czar*. Just as Elena had requested, I never asked him about the call only he could have received, though I was devoured by curiosity. In the weeks and months that followed the message for me that he had written on his slate, I never saw the slightest indication that Yilal was capable of speaking.

The call came two and a half months after the previous one. I was in the shower, getting ready to go to UNESCO, when I heard the phone ring and had a premonition: "It's her." I ran to the bedroom and picked up the receiver, dropping onto the bed even though I was wet.

"Are you going to hang up on me this time too, good boy?"

"How are you, bad girl?"

There was a brief silence, and finally, a little laugh.

"Well, well, at last you deign to answer me. May I ask to what I owe this miracle? Did you get over your fit of anger or do you still hate me?"

I felt like hanging up on her when I heard the lightly mocking tone and triumphant irony in her words.

"Why are you calling?" I asked. "Why did you call those other times?"

"I need to talk to you," she said, changing her tone.

"Where are you?"

"I've been here in Paris for a while. Can we see each other for a moment?"

I was dumbfounded. I had been sure she was still in Tokyo, or in some distant country, and would never set foot in France again. Knowing she was here and that I could see her at any time plunged me into total confusion.

"Just for a little while," she insisted, thinking my silence was prelude to a refusal. "What I have to tell you is very personal, I prefer not to do it on the phone. No more than half an hour. Not too long for an old friend, is it?"

We made a date for two days later, when I left UNESCO at six, in La Rhumerie on Saint-Germain-des-Prés (the bar had always been called La Rhumerie Martiniquaise, but recently, for some mysterious reason, it had lost its nationality). When I hung up, my heart was pounding in my chest. Before going back to the shower, I had to sit for a while with my mouth open until my respiration returned to normal. What was she doing in Paris? Special little jobs for Fukuda? Opening the European market to exotic aphrodisiacs made of elephant tusks and rhinoceros horns? Did she need my help in her smuggling operations, money laundering, or other criminal business? It had been stupid of me to answer the phone. It would be the same old story all over again. We'd talk, I'd submit again to the power she always had over me, we'd have a brief false idyll, I'd have all kinds of illusions, and when least expected she would disappear and I'd be left battered and bewildered, licking my wounds as I had in Tokyo. Until the next chapter!

I didn't tell Elena and Simon about the call or our appointment, and I spent forty-eight hours in a somnambulistic state, alternating between spasms of lucidity and a mental fog that lifted occasionally so I could give myself over to a masochistic session of insults: imbecile, cretin, you deserve everything that happens to you, has happened to you, will happen to you.

The day of our appointment was one of those gray, wet, late-autumn Parisian days when there are almost no leaves on the trees or light in the sky, people's bad temper increases with the bad weather, and you see men and women on the street concealed by coats, scarves, gloves, umbrellas, hurrying along and filled with hatred for the world. When I left UNESCO I looked for a taxi, but since it was raining and there was no hope of finding one, I opted for the Métro. I got off at the Saint-Germain station, and from the door of La Rhumerie I saw her sitting on the terrace, with a cup of tea and a bottle of Perrier in front of her. When she saw me she stood and reached up to my cheeks.

"Can we give each other an *accolade,* or can't we do that either?"

The place was filled with people typical of the district: tourists, playboys with chains around their necks and flamboyant vests and jackets, girls in daring necklines and miniskirts, some of them made up as if for a gala party. I ordered grog. We were silent, looking at each other with some discomfort, not knowing what to say.

Kuriko's transformation was notable. She seemed not only to have lost ten kilos—she had become a skeleton of a woman—but to have aged ten years since that unforgettable night in Tokyo. She dressed with a modesty and neglect I only remembered seeing in her on that distant morning when I picked her up at Orly Airport at Paúl's request. She wore a threadbare jacket that could have been a man's, faded flannel trousers, shoes that were worn and unpolished. Her hair was disheveled, and on her very thin fingers the nails seemed badly cut, unfiled, as if she bit them. The bones of her forehead, cheeks, and chin were prominent, stretching her very pale skin and accentuating its greenish cast. Her eyes had lost their light, and there was something fearful in them that recalled certain timid animals. She didn't have on a single adornment or any trace of makeup.

"How hard it's been for me to see you," she said at last. She extended her hand, touched my arm, and attempted one of those flirtatious smiles from the old days, which didn't turn out well this time. "At least tell me if you're over your anger and hate me a little less."

"Let's not talk about that," I replied. "Not now, not ever. Why did you call me so many times?"

"You gave me half an hour, didn't you?" she said, letting go of my arm and sitting up straight. "We have time. Tell me about yourself. Are things going well? Do you have a girlfriend? Are you still doing the same work?"

"A little pissant until death," I said with a reluctant laugh, but she remained very serious, observing me.

"The years have made you touchy, Ricardo. Once your rancor wouldn't have lasted so long." The old light twinkled in her eyes for a second. "Are you still telling women cheap, sentimental things, or don't you do that anymore?"

"How long have you been in Paris? What are you doing here? Working for the Japanese gangster?"

She shook her head. I thought she was going to laugh, but instead her expression hardened and those full lips that were still prominent on her face trembled, though they too seemed somewhat faded now, like the rest of her.

"Fukuda dropped me more than a year ago. That's why I came to Paris."

"Now I understand why you're in this lamentable condition," I said ironically. "I never imagined I'd see you like this, so broken."

"I was much worse," she acknowledged harshly. "At one point I thought I was going to die. The last two times I tried to talk to you, that was the reason. So at least you would be the one to bury me. I wanted to ask you to have me cremated. The thought of worms eating my body horrifies me. Well, that's over."

She spoke calmly, though allowing glimpses of a contained fury in her words. She didn't seem to be putting on a self-pitying act to impress me, or if she was, it was done with supreme skill. Instead, she described things objectively, from a distance, like a police officer or a notary.

"Did you try to kill yourself when the great love of your life left you?"

She shook her head and shrugged.

229

"He always said that one day he'd get tired of me and drop me. I was prepared. He didn't talk to hear his own voice. But he didn't choose the best moment to do it, or the best reasons."

Her voice trembled and her mouth twisted into a grimace of hatred. Her eyes filled with sparks. Was all of this just another farce to make me feel sorry for her?

"If the subject makes you uncomfortable, we'll talk about something else," I said. "What are you doing in Paris, what are you living on? Did the gangster at least give you some compensation that will let you live for a while without difficulties?"

"I was in prison in Lagos, a couple of months that seemed like a century," she said, as if I suddenly were no longer there. "The most awful, ugly city, and the most evil people in the world. Never even think about going to Lagos. When I finally got out of prison, Fukuda wouldn't let me come back to Tokyo. 'You're burned, Kuriko.' Burned in both senses of the word, he meant. Because now I was on file with the international police. And burned because the blacks in Nigeria probably infected me with AIDS. He hung up on me, just like that, after telling me I shouldn't see him, or write to him, or call him ever again. That's how he dropped me, as if I were a mangy dog. He didn't even pay for my ticket to Paris. He's a cold, practical man who knows what suits him. I no longer suited him. He's the exact opposite of you. That's why Fukuda is rich and powerful and you are and always will be a little pissant."

"Thanks. After all you've told me, that's praise."

Was any of it true? Or was it another of those fabulous lies that marked all the stages of her life? She had regained her self-control. She held her cup in both hands, sipping and blowing on the tea. It was painful to see her so ruined, so badly dressed, looking so old.

"Is this great melodrama true? Isn't this another of your stories? Were you really in prison?"

"Not only in prison but also raped by the Lagos police," she said, fixing my eyes with hers, as if I were responsible for her misfortune. "Some blacks whose English I couldn't understand because they spoke pidgin. That's what David called my English when he wanted to insult me: pidgin. But they didn't give me AIDS. Just crabs and chancre. A horrible word, isn't it? Have you ever heard it? You probably don't even know what it is, little saint. Chancre, infectious ulcers. Something disgusting but not serious if you treat it in time with antibiotics. But in damn Lagos they didn't treat me properly and the infection almost killed me. I thought I was going to die. That's why I called you. Now, fortunately, I'm all right."

What she was telling me could be true or false, but the immeasurable rage that permeated everything she said was no pose. Though with her, a performance was always possible. A formidable pantomime? I felt disconcerted, confused. The last thing I expected from our meeting was a story like this.

"I'm sorry you went through that hell," I said at last, just to say something, because what can you say in response to this kind of revelation? "If what you're telling me is true. You see, something dreadful has happened to me where you're concerned. You've told me so many stories in my life, it's difficult for me to believe anything you say."

"It doesn't matter if you don't believe me," she said, grasping my arm again and making an effort to seem cordial. "I know you're still offended, that you'll never forgive me for what happened in Tokyo. It doesn't matter. I don't want you to feel sorry for me. I don't want money, either. What I want, in fact, is to call you once in a while and occasionally have a cup of coffee with you, the way we're doing now. That's all."

"Why don't you tell me the truth? For once in your life. Go on, tell me the truth."

"The truth is, for the first time I feel uncertain and don't know what to do. Very alone. It hasn't happened before, even though I've had extremely difficult moments. If you must know, I'm sick with fear." She spoke with a proud dryness, with a tone and attitude that seemed to give the lie to what she was saying. She looked into my eyes without blinking. "Fear's a sickness too. It paralyzes me, it nullifies me. I didn't know that and now I do. I know some people here in Paris, but I don't trust anybody. But I do trust you. That's the truth, whether you believe me or not. Can I call you from time to time? Can we see each other occasionally, in a *bistrot*, the way we're doing today?"

"That's no problem. Of course we can."

We talked for another hour until it grew dark and the shop windows and windows of the buildings on Saint-Germain lit up, and the red and yellow lights of the cars formed a luminescent river that flowed slowly along the boulevard past the terrace of La Rhumerie. Then I remembered. Who answered the phone in my house the last time she called? Did she remember?

She looked at me, intrigued, uncomprehending. But then she nodded.

"Yes, a young woman. I thought you had a lover, but then I realized she must have been a maid. Filipina?"

"A child. Did he talk to you? Are you sure?"

"He said you were away on a trip, I think. Nothing, a couple of words. I left a message, I see he gave it to you. Why are you asking about that now?"

"He talked to you? Are you sure?"

"A couple of words," she repeated, nodding. "Who's the boy? Did you adopt him?"

"His name's Yilal. He's nine or ten years old. He's Vietnamese, the son of neighbors who are friends of mine. Are you sure he spoke to you? Because the boy is mute. His parents and I have never heard his voice."

She was bewildered and for a long moment, half closing her eyes, consulted her memory. She made several affirmative movements with her head. Yes, yes, she remembered very clearly. They spoke French. His voice was so delicate it seemed feminine to her. High-pitched and exotic. They exchanged very few words. Just that I wasn't there, I was away on a trip. And when she asked him to say "the bad girl" had called—she said this in Spanish—the thin voice interrupted: "What? What?" She had to spell "bad girl" in Spanish for him. She remembered very well. The boy had spoken to her, there was no doubt about it.

"Then you performed a miracle. Thanks to you, Yilal began to speak."

"If I have those powers, I'm going to use them. I imagine witches must make a ton of money in France."

233

A short while later, when we said goodbye at the entrance to the Saint-Germain Métro station and I asked for her phone number and address, she wouldn't give them to me. She would call me.

"You'll never change. Always the same mysteries, the same stories, the same secrets."

"It's done me a lot of good to see you finally and talk to you." She silenced me. "You won't hang up on me again, I hope."

"That depends on how you behave."

She stood on tiptoe and I felt her mouth purse in a rapid kiss on my cheek.

I watched her disappear into the Métro entrance. From the back, so thin, in flat shoes, she didn't seem to have aged as much as she did from the front.

Though it was still drizzling and fairly cold, instead of taking the Métro or a bus, I decided to walk. It was my sole physical activity now; my visits to the gym had lasted only a few months. Exercises bored me, and I was even more bored by the kind of people I met running on the treadmill, chinning themselves, doing aerobics. On the other hand, I enjoyed walking around this city filled with secrets and marvels, and on days when emotions ran high, like this one, a long walk, even under an umbrella in the rain and wind, would do me good.

Of all the things the bad girl told me, the only thing undoubtedly true was that Yilal had exchanged a few words with her. This meant the Gravoskis' son could speak; perhaps he had done it before, with people who didn't know him, at school, on the street. It was a small mystery he would reveal to his parents one day. I imagined the joy of Simon and Elena when they heard the thin voice, a little high-pitched, that the bad girl had described to me. I was walking along Boulevard Saint-Germain toward the Seine, when just before the Juilliard bookstore I discovered a small shop that sold toy soldiers and reminded me of Salomón Toledano and his ill-fated Japanese love. I went in and bought Yilal a small case with six horsemen of the Imperial Russian Guard.

What else could be true in the bad girl's story? Probably that Fukuda had dumped her in a cruel way and that she had been—and perhaps still was—sick. It was obvious, it was enough to see her prominent bones, her pallor, the dark circles under her eyes. And the story about Lagos? Perhaps it was true that she'd had problems with the police. It was a risk she ran in the dirty business her Japanese lover had involved her in. Didn't she tell me that herself, enthusiastically, in Tokyo? She was ingenuous enough to believe that adventures as a smuggler and trafficker, and gambling her freedom on trips to Africa, added spice to her life, made it more succulent and entertaining. I remembered her words: "By doing these things, I live more intensely." Well, whoever plays with fire sooner or later gets burned. If she really had been arrested, it was possible the police had raped her. Nigeria had a reputation as the paradise of corruption; a military satrapy, its police force must be rotted through. Raped by God knows how many men, brutalized for hours and hours in a filthy hole, infected with a venereal disease and crabs, and then treated by quacks who used unsterilized instruments. I was assailed by a feeling of shame and anger. If all that happened to her, even only some of it, and she had been on the verge of death, my cold, incredulous response had been mean-spirited, the response of a rancorous man who wanted only to assuage his pride, wounded by that ugly time in Tokyo. I should have said something affectionate to her, pretended I believed her. Because even if the story about the rape and prison was a lie, in fact she was a physical ruin now. And, no doubt, half dead from hunger. You behaved badly, Ricardito. Very badly, if it was true she turned to me because she felt alone and uncertain and I was the only person in the world she trusted. This last must be correct. She had never loved me but did feel confidence in me, the affection awakened by a loyal servant. Among her lovers and passing pals, I was the most disinterested, the most devoted. The asshole, self-sacrificing and docile. That's why she chose you to cremate her body. And will you toss her ashes into the Seine or keep them in a small Sèvres porcelain vase on your night table?

I reached Rue Joseph Granier soaked from head to toe and dying of the cold. I took a hot shower, put on dry clothes, and prepared a ham and cheese sandwich that I ate with fruit yogurt. With the case of toy soldiers under my arm, I knocked on the Gravoskis' door. Yilal was already in bed, and they had just finished eating a supper of spaghetti with basil. They offered me some, but all I accepted was a cup of coffee. While Simon examined the toy soldiers and joked that with gifts like these I wanted to turn Yilal into a militarist, Elena noticed something strange in my reticence.

"Something's happened, Ricardo," she said, scrutinizing my eyes. "Did the bad girl call you?"

Simon looked up from the toy soldiers and stared at me.

"I've just spent an hour with her in a *bistrot*. She's living in Paris. She's a wreck and has no money, she's dressed like a beggar. She says the Japanese dumped her after the police in Lagos arrested her on one of those trips she made to Africa to help him in his trafficking. And raped her. And infected her with crabs and chancre. And then, in some foul hospital, they almost finished the job. It may be true. It may be false. I don't know. She says Fukuda dropped her because he was afraid Interpol had her on file and the blacks had infected her with AIDS. The truth or an invention? I have no way of knowing."

"The saga becomes more interesting every day," Simon exclaimed in stupefaction. "True or not, it's a terrific story."

He and Elena looked at each other and looked at me, and I knew very well what they were thinking. I agreed.

"She remembers very clearly the call she made to my house. A thin, high-pitched voice answered, in French, and she thought it belonged to an Asian woman. He had her repeat 'bad girl' several times in Spanish. She can't have invented that."

I saw Elena become agitated. She was blinking very rapidly.

"I always thought it was true," murmured Simon. His voice was excited and he became flushed, as if he were suffocating from the heat. He kept scratching at his red beard. "I turned it around and around and reached the conclusion it had to be true. How could Yilal invent anything like 'bad girl'? How happy you've made us with this news, *mon vieux*."

Elena agreed, holding my arm. She was smiling and crying at the same time.

"I always knew it too, knew that Yilal had talked to her," she said, sounding out each word. "But please, we mustn't do anything. Or say anything to the boy. It will all come on its own. If we try to force him, things may get worse. He has to do it, break that barrier by his own effort. He will, at the right time, he'll do it soon, you'll see."

"This is the moment to bring out the cognac," said Simon, winking at me. "You see, *mon vieux*, I took precautions. Now we're prepared for the surprises you give us periodically. An excellent Napoleon, you'll see!"

We each had a cognac, almost without speaking, deep in our own thoughts. The drink did me good, for the walk in the rain had chilled me. When I said good night, Elena walked out to the landing with me.

"I don't know, it just occurred to me," she said. "Maybe your friend needs a medical exam. Ask her. If she wants, I can arrange it at the Hôpital Cochin, with my *copains*. At no charge to her, I mean. I imagine she has no insurance or anything like that."

I thanked her. I'd ask the next time we spoke.

"If it's true, it must have been awful for the poor woman," she murmured. "A thing like that leaves dreadful scars in one's mind."

The next day, I hurried home from UNESCO so I would see Yilal. He was watching a cartoon on television, and beside him were the six horsemen of the Russian Imperial Guard lined up in a row. He showed me his slate: "Thank you for the nice gift, Uncle Ricardo." He shook my hand, smiling. I began to read *Le Monde* while he, his attention hypnotized, was involved in his program. Afterward, instead of reading to him, I told him about Salomón Toledano. I talked about his collection of toy soldiers that I had seen invading every inch of his house, and his incredible ability to learn languages. He had been the best interpreter in the world. When he asked on his slate if I could take him to Salomón's house to see his Napoleonic battles, and I said he had died very far from Paris, in Japan, Yilal became sad. I showed him the hussar I kept on my night table, the one Salomón had given me the day he left for Tokyo. A little while later, Elena came to take him home.

In order not to think too much about the bad girl, I went to a movie in the Latin Quarter. In the dark, warm theater filled with students, on Rue Champollion, as I distractedly followed the adventures in *Stagecoach*, John Ford's classic Western, the deteriorated, wretched image of the Chilean girl appeared and reappeared in my head. That day, and all the rest of the week, her figure was always on my mind, along with the question to which I never found a reply: Had she told me the truth? Was the story about Lagos and Fukuda true? I was tormented by the conviction that I would never know with any certainty.

She called me a week later, at home, again very early in the morning. After asking how she was— "Fine, I'm fine now, I told you that"—I proposed having supper that night. She agreed, and we arranged to meet at the old Procope, on Rue de l'Ancienne Comédie, at eight. I arrived before she did and waited for her at a table beside the window that overlooked the Rohan passage. She arrived right after me. Better dressed than the last time, but still shabby: under the ugly, asexual jacket she wore a dark blue dress, without a collar or sleeves, and her medium-heeled shoes were cracked but recently polished. It was very strange to see her without rings, bracelets, earrings, or makeup. At least she had filed her nails. How could she have gotten so thin? It looked as if she would shatter with a single misstep.

She ordered consommé and grilled fish and barely sipped at the wine during the meal. She chewed very slowly and reluctantly and had difficulty swallowing. Did she really feel all right?

"My stomach has shrunk and I can hardly tolerate food," she explained. "After two or three bites I feel full. But this fish is delicious."

In the end I drank the bottle of Côtes du Rhône by myself. When the waiter brought coffee for me and verbena tea for her, I said, holding her hand, "I beg you, by what you love most, swear that everything you told me the other day in La Rhumerie is true."

"You'll never believe anything I tell you again, I know that." She had an air of fatigue, of weariness, and didn't seem to care in the least if I believed her or not. "Let's not talk about it anymore. I told you so you would let me see you from time to time. Because even if you don't believe this either, talking to you does me good."

I felt like kissing her hand but controlled myself. I told her Elena's proposal. She sat looking at me, disconcerted.

"But, she knows about me, about us?"

I nodded. Elena and Simon knew everything. In an outburst I had told them "our" entire story. They were very good friends, she had nothing to fear from them. They wouldn't denounce her to the police as a trafficker in aphrodisiacs.

"I don't know why I confided in them. Perhaps because, like everybody, occasionally I need to share with someone the things that distress me or make me happy. Do you accept Elena's proposal?"

She didn't seem very enthusiastic. She looked at me uneasily, as if fearing a trap. That light, the color of dark honey, had disappeared from her eyes. Along with the mischief, the mockery.

"Let me think about it," she said at last. "We'll see how I feel. I'm feeling fine, now. The only thing I need is quiet, and rest."

"It's not true that you're fine," I insisted. "You're a ghost. You're so thin a simple grippe could send you to the grave. And I don't feel like attending to that sinister little chore of incinerating you, and so forth. Don't you want to be attractive again?"

She burst into laughter.

"Ah, so now you think I'm ugly. Thanks for your honesty." She pressed the hand I was still holding hers with, and for a second her eyes came alive. "But you're still in love with me, aren't you, Ricardito?"

"No, not anymore. And I'll never be in love with you again. But I don't want you to die."

"It must be true you don't love me anymore if you haven't said a single cheap, sentimental thing to me this time," she acknowledged, making a half-comic face. "What do I have to do to conquer you again?"

She laughed with the flirtatiousness of the old days, and her eyes filled with mischievous light, but suddenly, with no transition, I felt the pressure of her hand on mine weaken. Her eyes went blank, she turned livid and opened her mouth, as if she needed air. If I hadn't been beside her, holding her, she would have fallen to the floor. I rubbed her temples with a dampened napkin, had her drink some water. She recovered a little but was still very pale, almost white. And now there was an animal panic in her eyes.

"I'm going to die," she stammered, digging her nails into my arm.

"You're not going to die. I've allowed you every despicable thing in the world since we were children, but not dying. I forbid it."

She smiled weakly.

"It was time you said something nice to me." Her voice was barely audible. "I needed it, even if you don't believe that, either."

When, after a while, I tried to have her stand, her legs were trembling and she dropped, exhausted, onto the chair. I had a waiter at Le Procope bring a taxi from the stand on the corner of Saint-Germain to the door of the restaurant, and then help me walk her to the street. The two of us carried her, lifting her at the waist. When she heard me tell the driver to take us to the nearest hospital—"The Hôtel-Dieu on the Cité, all right?"— she grabbed me in despair. "No, no, not to a hospital, under no circumstances, no." I found myself obliged to rectify that and ask the driver to take us instead to Rue Joseph Granier. On the way to my house—I had her leaning on my shoulder—she lost consciousness again for a few seconds. Her body went slack and slipped in the seat. When I straightened her, I could feel all the bones in her back. At the door to the art deco building, I called Simon and Elena on the intercom and asked them to come down and help me.

The three of us got her up to my apartment and laid her on my bed. My friends asked nothing but looked at the bad girl with avid curiosity, as if she had risen from the dead. Elena lent her a nightgown and took her temperature and blood pressure. She had no fever, but her pressure was very low. When she was fully conscious again, Elena had her sip a cup of very hot tea, with two pills that, she said, were a simple restorative. When she said goodbye, she assured me she didn't see any imminent danger, but if, in the course of the night, the bad girl felt ill, I should wake her. Elena herself would call the Hôpital Cochin and have them send an ambulance. In view of her fainting spells, a complete medical examination was indispensable. She would arrange everything, but it would take a couple of days at least.

When I returned to the bedroom, I found her with eyes open wide.

"You must be cursing the hour you picked up the phone," she said. "I've done nothing but make problems for you."

"Ever since I've known you, you've done nothing but make problems for me. It's my destiny. And there's nothing you can do to fight destiny. Look, here it is in case you need it. It's yours. But you have to return it to me."

And I took the Guerlain toothbrush out of the night table. She examined it, amused.

"Do you mean you still have it? It's your second gallantry of the evening. What luxury. Where are you going to sleep, if you don't mind my asking?"

"The sofa in the living room is a sofa bed, so don't get your hopes up. There's no chance at all that I'll sleep with you."

She laughed again. But that small effort fatigued her, and curling up under the sheets, she closed her eyes. I covered her with the blankets and put my bathrobe at her feet. I went to brush my teeth, put on my pajamas, and pull out the sofa bed in the living room. When I returned to the bedroom, she was asleep, breathing normally. The light from the street that filtered through the skylight illuminated her face: still very pale, with its pointed nose and, through her hair, glimpses of her beautiful ears. Her mouth was half open, the sides of her nose palpitating, and her expression was languid, totally abandoned. When I brushed her hair with my lips I felt her breath on my face. I went to lie down. I fell asleep almost immediately but awoke a couple of times in the night, and both times I tiptoed in to see her. She was asleep, breathing evenly. The skin on her face was drawn tight and her bones stood out. As she breathed, her chest lightly moved the blankets up and down. I imagined her small heart, thought of it beating wearily.

The next morning, I was preparing breakfast when I heard her get up. I was brewing coffee when she appeared in the kitchen, wrapped in my robe. It was enormous on her, and she looked like a clown. Her bare feet were like a little girl's.

"I slept almost eight hours," she said in astonishment. "That hasn't happened for ages. Last night I fainted, didn't I?"

"Nothing but an act so I'd bring you home. And, as you can see, I did. And you even got into my bed. You know all the tricks from soup to nuts, bad girl."

"I ruined your night, didn't I, Ricardito?"

"And you'll ruin my day too. Because you're going to

stay here, in bed, while Elena arranges things at the Hôpital Cochin so they can give you a complete checkup. No arguments allowed. The time has come for me to impose my authority over you, bad girl."

"Wow, what progress. You talk as if you were my lover."

But this time I didn't make her smile. She looked at me, her face contorted, her eyes gloomy. She looked very comical this way, with her hair disheveled and the robe dragging on the floor. I approached and embraced her. She was trembling and felt very fragile. I thought that if I tightened the embrace a little she would break, like a baby bird.

"You're not going to die," I whispered in her ear, just kissing her hair. "They'll do the exam, and if something's wrong, they'll treat it. And you'll be attractive again, and we'll see if you can get me to fall in love with you again. And now come, let's have breakfast, I don't want to get to UNESCO late."

As we were having coffee and toast, Elena stopped in on her way to work. She took the bad girl's temperature again, and her blood pressure, and found her better than the night before. But she told her to stay in bed all day and eat light things. She would try to arrange everything at the hospital so she could be admitted tomorrow. Elena asked what she needed, and the bad girl requested a hairbrush.

Before I left, I showed her the food in the refrigerator and the cupboard, more than enough for her to fix some chicken or buttered noodles in the afternoon. I'd take care of supper when I got back. If she felt sick, she had to call me immediately at UNESCO. She nodded without saying anything, looking at everything with a lost expression, as if she hadn't really understood what was happening to her.

I called early in the afternoon. She felt well. A bubble bath in my tub had made her happy, because for at least six months she had taken only showers in public bathhouses, always in a rush. In the evening, when I returned, I found her and Yilal absorbed in a Laurel and Hardy movie that sounded absurd dubbed into French. But they seemed to be enjoying themselves and celebrated the clowning of the fat man and the thin man. She had put on a pair of my pajamas, and on top of that the bathrobe in which she seemed lost. Her hair was combed, and her face was fresh and smiling.

On his slate, Yilal asked, pointing at the bad girl: "Are you going to marry her, Uncle Ricardo?"

"Not a chance," I told him, putting on a horrified face. "That's what she'd like. She's been trying to seduce me for years. But I don't pay attention to her."

"Pay attention," Yilal replied, writing quickly on his slate. "She's nice and she'll be a good wife."

"What have you done to buy off this child, guerrilla fighter?"

"I told him things about Japan and Africa. He's very good in geography. He knows the capitals better than I do."

During the three days the bad girl stayed in my house, before Elena found a place for her at the Hôpital Cochin, my guest and Yilal became intimate friends. They played checkers and laughed and joked as if they were the same age. They had such a good time together that although they kept the television on for the sake of appearances, in reality they didn't even look at the screen as they concentrated on JanKenPo, a hand game I hadn't seen played since my childhood in Miraflores: the rock breaks the scissors, the paper encloses the rock, the scissors cuts the paper. Sometimes she began reading Yilal the stories of Jules Verne, but after a few lines she abandoned the text and began to tell a nonsensical version of the story until Yilal pulled the book from her hands, shaking with laughter. On all three nights we had supper at the Gravoskis' house. The bad girl helped Elena cook and wash the dishes, while they chatted and told jokes. It was as if the four of us were two couples who had been friends all our lives.

On the second night, she insisted on sleeping on the sofa bed and giving my bedroom back to me. I had to do as she asked, because she threatened to leave if I didn't. Those first two days she was in good spirits; at least, she seemed to be at nightfall, when I returned from UNESCO and found her playing on equal terms with Yilal. On the third day, I awoke while it was still dark, certain I heard someone crying. I listened and had no doubt: it was quiet, intermittent weeping, with parentheses of silence. I went to the living room and found her curled up in the sofa bed, covering her mouth, drenched in tears. She was trembling from head to toe. I wiped her face, smoothed her hair, brought her a glass of water.

"Do you feel sick? Do you want me to wake Elena?"

"I'm going to die," she said very quietly, whimpering. "They infected me with something in Lagos, and nobody knows what it is. They say it isn't AIDS, but then, what is it? I hardly have strength for anything. Not for eating, or walking, or lifting my arm. The same thing happened to Juan Barreto in Newmarket, don't you remember? And I always have a discharge down there that looks like pus. It isn't only the pain. It's that I feel so much disgust for my body and everything else since Lagos."

She sobbed for a long time, complaining of cold even though she was wrapped up. I dried her eyes and gave her some water, disheartened by a feeling of powerlessness. What should I give her, what should I say to her to take her out of this state? Until, at last, I felt her fall asleep. I went back to the bedroom with fear in my heart. Yes, she was very sick, perhaps with AIDS, and probably would end up like poor Juan Barreto.

That afternoon, when I got home from work, she was ready to go to the Hôpital Cochin the following morning. She had gone in a cab for her things and had a suitcase and an overnight bag in the closet. I berated her. Why hadn't she waited for me to go with her to pick up her luggage? She replied quickly that she was embarrassed to let me see the hole where she had been living.

The next morning, carrying only the small overnight bag, she left with Elena. When she said goodbye, she murmured in my ear something that made me happy.

"You're the best thing that ever happened to me, good boy."

The two days the medical examination was supposed to take lengthened into four, and I couldn't see her on any of them. The hospital was very strict about their schedule, and it was too late for visitors by the time I left UNESCO. And I couldn't talk to her on the phone. At night, Elena told me what she had been able to find out. The bad girl was enduring the examinations, analyses, questions, and needles with fortitude. Elena worked in another pavilion but had arranged to stop in and see her a couple of times a day. Furthermore, Professor Bourrichon, an internist, one of the luminaries at the hospital, had taken her case because of his interest in it. In the afternoons, when I saw Yilal in front of the television set, I would find this question on his slate: "When will she be back?"

On the night of the fourth day, after feeding Yilal and putting him to bed, Elena came to my house to give me news. Though they were still waiting for the results of a couple of tests, that afternoon Professor Bourrichon had told her a few conclusions in advance. The bad girl was suffering from extreme malnutrition and acute depressive dejection, a loss of the vital impulse. She required immediate psychological treatment to help her recover "hopefulness in life"; without it any program of physical recuperation would be useless. The story about the rape was probably true; she showed signs of lacerations and scars in her vagina as well as her rectum, and had a suppurating wound produced by a metal or wooden instrument—she didn't remember which—introduced by force, which had torn one of the vaginal walls very close to her womb. It was surprising that this badly treated lesion had not caused septicemia. A surgical intervention was necessary to clean the abscess and suture the wound. But the most delicate part of her clinical picture was the intense stress that, as a result of her experience in Lagos and the uncertainty of her current situation, made her depressed, insecure, lacking in appetite, and subject to attacks of terror. Her fainting spells were a consequence of that trauma. Heart, brain, and stomach were functioning normally.

"They'll perform a small surgical procedure on her womb early tomorrow," Elena added. "Dr. Pineau, the surgeon, is a friend and won't charge anything. Only the anesthetist and the medicines will have to be paid for. About three thousand francs, more or less."

"No problem, Elena."

"After all, the news isn't too bad, is it?" she said encouragingly. "It could have been much worse, keeping in mind the butchery performed on the poor woman by those savages. Professor Bourrichon recommends that she have absolute rest in a clinic where they have good psychologists. She mustn't fall into the hands of one of those Lacanians who could trap her in a labyrinth and make things more complicated for her than they already are. The problem is that those kinds of clinics tend to be very expensive."

"I'll take care of getting her what she needs. The important thing is to find her a good specialist who'll get her out of this so she can be what she was, not the corpse she's turned into."

"We'll find one, I promise," Elena said with a smile, patting my arm. "She's the great love of your life, isn't she, Ricardo?"

"The only one, Elena. The only woman I've loved, ever since she was a girl. I've done the impossible to forget her, but the truth is it's useless. I'll always love her. Life wouldn't have meaning for me if she died."

"What luck that girl has, inspiring love like this," my neighbor said with a laugh. "*Chapeau!* I'll ask her for the recipe. Simon's right: that nickname she gave you fits like a glove."

The next morning I asked permission at UNESCO to

go to the Hôpital Cochin during the minor operation. I waited in a frigid corridor, with very high ceilings, where an icy wind blew and nurses, doctors, and patients passed by and, occasionally, sick people lying on cots with oxygen pumps or bottles of plasma suspended over their heads. There was a "No Smoking" sign that nobody seemed to pay attention to.

Dr. Pineau spoke to me for a few minutes, in front of Elena, as he removed his latex gloves and meticulously scrubbed his hands with lathering soap in a stream of water that emitted steam. He was a fairly young man, sure of himself, who didn't beat around the bush.

"She'll be perfectly fine. But you already know her condition. Her vagina is damaged, prone to inflammation and bleeding. Her rectum is also damaged. You'll have to control yourself, my friend. Make love very carefully, and not very often. At least for the next two months, I recommend restraint. The best thing would be not to touch her. If that isn't possible, then with extreme delicacy. The woman has suffered a traumatic experience. It wasn't a simple rape, but from what I understand, a real massacre."

I was with the bad girl when they brought her from the operating room to the large ward where they put her in an area isolated by two screens. It was a spacious, badly lit place with stone walls and dark concave ceilings that made one think of bats' nests, scrupulously clean tile floors, and a strong odor of disinfectant and bleach. She was even paler and more cadaverous, and her eyes were half closed. When she recognized me, she extended her hand. When I held it in mine, it seemed as thin and small as Yilal's.

"I'm fine," she said emphatically, before I could ask her how she felt. "The doctor who operated on me was very nice. And good-looking."

I kissed her hair, her pretty ears.

"I hope you didn't start flirting with him. You're very capable of that."

She pressed my hand and fell asleep almost immediately. She slept the entire morning and didn't wake until early afternoon, complaining of the pain. On the doctor's instructions, a nurse came to give her an injection. A short while later Elena appeared, wearing a white lab coat, to bring her a bed jacket. She put it on over her nightgown. The bad girl asked about Yilal and smiled when she heard that the Gravoskis' son asked for her constantly. I was with her for a good part of the afternoon, and stayed with her as she ate from a small plastic tray: vegetable soup and a piece of poached chicken with boiled potatoes. She carried the spoonfuls to her mouth unwillingly, and only because of my urging.

"Do you know why everybody's so nice to me?" she said. "Because of Elena. Nurses and doctors adore her. She's the most popular person in the hospital."

A short while later, visitors had to leave. That night, at the Gravoskis', Elena had news for me. She had made inquiries and consulted with Professor Bourrichon. He suggested a small, private clinic in Petit Clamart, not very far from Paris, where he had sent other patients who were victims of depression and nervous disorders due to physical abuse, with good results. The director had been a classmate of his. If we wanted, he could recommend the bad girl's case to him.

"You don't know how grateful I am, Elena. It seems like the right place. Let's proceed, as soon as we can."

Elena and Simon looked at each other. We were having the inevitable cup of coffee after a supper of an omelet, a little ham, and salad, with a glass of wine.

"There are two problems," said an uncomfortable Elena. "The first, as you know, is that it's a private clinic and will be very expensive."

"I have some savings, and if that's not enough, I'll get a loan. And, if necessary, I'll sell the apartment. Money isn't a problem, the important thing is for her to get better. What's the other one?"

"The passport she presented at the Hôpital Cochin is false," said Elena, with an expression and a tone of voice that seemed to be begging my pardon. "I've had to do a lot of juggling to keep the administration from denouncing her to the police. But she has to leave the hospital tomorrow and not set foot there again, unfortunately. And I don't discount the possibility that as soon as she leaves, they'll tip off the authorities."

"That lady will never cease to astonish me," exclaimed Simon. "Do the two of you realize how dull our lives are compared to hers?"

"Can the question of her papers be straightened out?" Elena asked me. "I imagine it'll be difficult, of course. I don't know, it might be a huge obstacle at Dr. Zilacxy's clinic in Petit Clamart. They may not admit her if they find out her situation in France is illegal. They could even turn her in to the police."

"I don't think the bad girl has ever had her papers in order," I said. "I'm absolutely certain she has several passports, not just one. Maybe one of them looks less false than the others. I'll ask her."

"We'll all wind up in jail," said Simon with a laugh. "They'll prohibit Elena from practicing medicine and throw me out of the Pasteur Institute, and then we'll finally begin to live real life."

The three of us ended up laughing, and the laughter shared with my two friends did me good. It was the first night in the past four that I slept through until the alarm clock rang. The next day, when I came home from UNESCO, I found the bad girl installed in my bed, with the bouquet of flowers I had sent her in a vase of water on the night table. She was feeling better, without any pain. Elena had brought her from the Hôpital Cochin and helped her up to the apartment, but then she went back to work. Yilal was with her, very happy about her recent arrival. When the boy left, the bad girl spoke to me in a low voice, as if the Gravoskis' son could still hear her.

"Tell Simon and Elena to come here for coffee this time. After they put Yilal to bed. I'll help you prepare it. I want to thank them for everything Elena has done for me."

I wouldn't let her get up to help me. I prepared the coffee and a short while later the Gravoskis knocked on the door. I carried the bad girl—she didn't weigh anything, barely as much as Yilal—to sit with us in the living room, and I covered her with a blanket. Then, without even greeting them, with radiant eyes she came out with the news.

"Please don't faint from the shock. This afternoon, after Elena left us alone, Yilal put his arms around me

254

and said very clearly in Spanish: 'He loves you very much, bad girl.' He said 'he loves,' not 'I love.'"

And, so there wouldn't be the slightest doubt she was telling the truth, she did something I hadn't seen since my days as a student at the Colegio Champagnat in Miraflores: she raised two fingers in the shape of a cross to her mouth and kissed them as she said, "I swear to you, that's just what he said, down to the last letter."

Elena began to cry, and as she shed those tears she laughed, her arms around the bad girl. Had Yilal said anything else? No. When she tried to initiate a conversation with him, the boy returned to his mutism and to answering in French on his slate. But that sentence, spoken in the same thin little thread of a voice she remembered from the phone, proved once and for all that Yilal wasn't mute. For a long time we didn't talk about anything else. We drank coffee, and Simon, Elena, and I had a glass of malt whiskey that I'd had in my side-board since time immemorial. The Gravoskis decided on the strategy to follow. None of us should let on that we knew. Since the boy had spoken to the bad girl on his own initiative, she, in the most natural way, without any pressure on him at all, should try to establish a dialogue, asking him questions, speaking without looking at him, distractedly, avoiding at all costs any possibility that Yilal might feel watched over or subjected to a test.

Then Elena spoke to the bad girl about Dr. Zilacxy's clinic in Petit Clamart. It was rather small, in a well-tended park filled with trees, and the director, a friend and classmate of Professor Bourrichon, was a prestigious psychologist and psychiatrist who specialized in the treatment of patients suffering from depression and nervous disorders resulting from accidents, various kinds of abuse and trauma, as well as anorexia, alcoholism, and drug addiction. The conclusions of the examination were categorical. The bad girl needed to withdraw for a time to the right kind of place for absolute rest, where, as she followed a regimen of diet and exercise to recover her strength, she would receive psychological support that would help her wipe out the reverberations in her mind of that awful experience.

"Does this mean I'm crazy?" she asked.

"You always were," I said. "But now you're also anemic and depressed, and they can cure that at the clinic. You'll be hopelessly mad until the end of your days, if that's what's worrying you."

She didn't laugh but yielded rather reluctantly to my arguments and agreed to Elena requesting an appointment with the director of the clinic in Petit Clamart. Our neighbor would go with us. When the Gravoskis left, the bad girl looked at me reproachfully, filled with anxiety.

"And who's going to pay for this clinic when you know very well I don't have a pot to piss in?"

"Who but the usual imbecile?" I said, adjusting her pillows. "You're my praying mantis, didn't you know? The female insect devours the male while he's making love to her. He dies happy, apparently. My case exactly. Don't worry about the money. Don't you know I'm rich?"

She grasped one of my arms with both her hands.

"You're not rich, you're a poor little pissant," she said in a fury. "If you weren't, I wouldn't have gone to Cuba, or London, or Japan. I would have stayed with you after that time when you showed me around Paris and took me to those horrible restaurants for beggars. I've always left you for rich men who turned out to be trash. And this is how I've ended up, a ruin. Are you happy that I acknowledge it? Do you like to hear it? Are you doing all this to show me how superior you are to all of them, and what I lost in you? Why are you doing this, may I ask?"

"Why do you think, bad girl? Maybe I want to earn indulgences and go to heaven. And it could also be that I'm still in love with you. And now, enough riddles. It's time to sleep. Professor Bourrichon says that until you're completely recovered, you should try to sleep at least eight hours a night."

Two days later my seasonal contract with UNESCO ended and I could devote the entire day to caring for her. At the Hôpital Cochin they had prescribed a diet for her based on vegetables, poached fish and meat, fruit, and stews, and had prohibited alcohol, including wine, as well as coffee and all spicy condiments. She was to exercise and walk at least an hour a day. In the morning, after breakfast —I bought croissants fresh from the oven at a bakery on École Militaire—we would take a walk, arm in arm, to the foot of the Eiffel Tower, along the Champ de Mars, and sometimes, weather permitting, and if she was in the mood, we would go along the quays of the Seine to Place de la Concorde. I let her lead the conversation, but I did try to keep her from talking about Fukuda or the episode in Lagos. It wasn't always possible. Then, if she insisted on bringing up the subject, I listened to what she wanted to tell me and asked no questions. From things occasionally hinted at in those semi-monologues, I deduced that her capture in Nigeria took place on the day she was leaving the country. But her threadbare story always occurred in a kind of fog. She had already passed through customs at the airport and was in the line of passengers making their way toward the plane. A couple of policemen took her out of line, very courteously; their attitude changed completely as soon as they put her in a van with windows painted black, and especially when they took her into a foul-smelling building with barred cells and a stink of excrement and urine.

"I believe I wasn't found out, those police weren't capable of finding anything out," she'd say occasionally. "I was turned in. But who did it? Who? Sometimes I think it was Fukuda himself. But why would he have done that? It doesn't make any sense, does it?"

"It doesn't matter now. It's over. Forget about it, bury it. It's not good for you to torture yourself with those memories. The only thing that matters is that you survived and soon you'll be completely well. And never get involved again in the kinds of entanglements that have consumed half your life."

On the fourth day, a Thursday, Elena told us that Dr. Zilacxy, director of the clinic in Petit Clamart, would see us on Monday at noon. Professor Bourrichon had spoken with him by phone and given him all the results of the bad girl's medical examination, as well as his prescriptions and advice. On Friday I went to speak to Señor Charnés, who had asked the secretary of the translators' and interpreters' agency he headed to call me. He offered me a well-paid contract for two weeks in Helsinki. I accepted. When I returned home, I heard voices and giggles in the bedroom as soon as I opened the door. I stood still with the door half open, listening. They were speaking in French, and one of the voices belonged to the bad girl. The other, thin, high-pitched, a little hesitant, could only be Yilal's. Suddenly my hands were sweating. I was ecstatic. I couldn't hear what they were saying, but they were playing something, perhaps checkers, perhaps JanKenPo, and, to judge by the giggles, having a very good time. They hadn't heard me come in. I closed the door slowly and walked toward the bedroom, exclaiming in a loud voice, in French, "I bet you're playing checkers and the bad girl is winning."

There was an immediate silence, and when I took another step and went into the bedroom I saw that they had the checkerboard open in the middle of the bed and were sitting on either side, both of them leaning over the pieces. Yilal looked at me, his eyes flashing with pride. And then, opening his mouth very wide, he said in French, "Yilal wins!"

"He always wins, it's not fair." The bad girl applauded. "This kid is a champion."

"Let's see, let's see, I want to referee this match," I said, dropping onto a corner of the bed and examining the board. I tried to feign absolute naturalness, as if nothing extraordinary were happening, but I could hardly breathe.

Leaning over the pieces, Yilal was studying the next move. For an instant the bad girl's eyes met mine. She smiled and winked.

"He wins again!" Yilal exclaimed, applauding.

"Well, of course, *mon vieux*, she has no place to move. You won. Give me five!"

I shook his hand, and the bad girl gave him a kiss.

"I'm not playing checkers with you again, I'm sick of being beaten," she said.

"I've thought of a game that's even more fun, Yilal," I improvised. "Why don't we give Elena and Simon the surprise of their lives? Let's put on a show for them that your parents will remember for the rest of their days. Would you like to do that?"

The boy's expression had turned wary and he waited, motionless, for me to continue, not committing himself. As I laid out the plan I was inventing as I described it to him, he listened, intrigued and somewhat intimidated, not daring to reject it, attracted and repelled at the same time by my proposal. When I finished, he was motionless and silent for a long time, looking first at the bad girl and then at me.

"What do you think, Yilal?" I insisted, still speaking French. "Shall we give Simon and Elena a surprise? I promise you they won't forget it for the rest of their lives."

"All right," said Yilal's thin voice, his head nodding assent. "We'll give them a surprise."

We did just what I had improvised, caught up in the emotion and confusion that *hearing* Yilal had thrown me into. When Elena came to pick him up, the bad girl and I asked if she, Simon, and the boy would come back after supper because we had a delicious dessert we wanted to share with them. Somewhat surprised, Elena said all right, just for a little while, because otherwise it would be very hard for Yilal the sleepyhead to wake up the next day. I ran as if the devil were pursuing me to the corner of École Militaire, to the bakery with the croissants on the

Avenue de la Bourdonnais. Fortunately, it was open. I bought a cake with a lot of cream and fat, red strawberries on top. We were so excited we barely tasted the meal of vegetables and fish I shared with the convalescent.

When Simon, Elena, and Yilal—already in slippers and robe—arrived, we were waiting for them, the coffee ready and the cake cut into slices. I saw immediately that Elena suspected something. Simon, on the other hand, preoccupied with an article by a dissident Soviet scientist he had read that afternoon, was over the moon and told us, while the cream from the overly sweet dessert dirtied his beard, that not long ago the Soviet scientist visited the Pasteur Institute and all the researchers and scientists had been struck by his modesty and intellectual accomplishments. Then, following the nonsensical script I had devised, the bad girl asked in Spanish, "How many languages do all of you think Yilal speaks?"

I saw that Simon and Elena froze immediately and widened their eyes slightly, as if asking: "What's going on here?"

"I think two," I declared. "French and Spanish. And you two, what do you think? How many languages does Yilal speak, Elena? Simon, how many do you think?"

Yilal's eyes moved from his parents to me, from me to the bad girl, and back to his parents again. He was very serious.

"He doesn't speak any," Elena stammered, looking at us and not turning her head toward the boy. "At least, not yet."

"I think . . . ," said Simon, and then fell silent, overwhelmed, begging us with his eyes to tell him what he should say.

"In reality, it doesn't matter what we think," the bad girl interjected. "It only matters what Yilal says. What do you say, Yilal? How many do you speak?"

"He speaks French," said the thin, high-pitched voice. And, after a very brief pause, changing languages, "Yilal speaks Spanish."

Elena and Simon sat staring at him, struck dumb. The slice of cake Simon was holding slid off the plate and landed on his trousers. The boy burst into laughter, raising his hand to his mouth, and pointing at Simon's leg, he exclaimed in French, "You dirty trousers."

Elena rose to her feet and now, standing beside the boy, looking at him ecstatically, she caressed his hair with one hand and passed the other along his lips, over and over again, the way a pious old woman caresses the image of her patron saint. But, of the two, the more moved was Simon. Incapable of saying anything, he looked at his son, at his wife, at us, stupefied, as if asking us not to wake him but to let him go on dreaming.

Yilal said nothing else that night. His parents took him home a short while later, and the bad girl, acting as mistress of the house, wrapped up the rest of the cake and insisted the Gravoskis take it. I shook Yilal's hand when we said good night.

"It turned out very well, didn't it, Yilal? I owe you a present because of how well you did. Another six toy soldiers for your collection?"

He made affirmative movements with his head. When we closed the door behind them, the bad girl exclaimed, "Right now they're the happiest couple on earth."

Much later, when I was beginning to fall asleep, I saw a silhouette slip into the living room and silently approach the sofa bed. She took me by the hand.

"Come, come with me," she ordered.

"I can't, I mustn't," I said, getting up and following her. "Dr. Pineau has forbidden it. For two months at least I can't even touch you, let alone make love to you. And I won't touch you, or make love to you, until you're well again. Understood?"

We got into bed, she curled up against me and leaned her head on my shoulder. I felt her body, nothing but skin and bone, and her small, icy feet rubbing against my legs, and a shudder ran from my head down to my heels.

"I don't want you to make love to me," she whispered, kissing me on the neck. "I want you to hold me, keep me warm, take away my fear, I'm dying of terror."

Her body, a form full of angles, trembled like a leaf. I embraced her, rubbed her back, her arms, her waist, and for a long time whispered sweet things in her ear. I would never let anybody hurt her again, she had to do everything she could to get better soon and get back her strength, her desire to live and be happy. So she could be attractive again. She listened in silence, clinging to me, attacked at intervals by terrors that made her moan and writhe. Much later, I sensed she was sleeping. But throughout the night, as I dozed, I felt her shudder and groan, seized by recurrent attacks of panic. When I saw her like this, so helpless, images of what had happened in Lagos came into my mind, and I felt sadness, rage, and a fierce desire for vengeance against her torturers.

The visit to the Petit Clamart clinic of Dr. André Zilacxy, a Frenchman of Hungarian descent, turned out to be a country excursion. A brilliant sun that day made the tall poplars and plane trees in the woods shine. The clinic was at the far end of a park that had chipped statues and a pond with swans. We arrived at midday, and Dr. Zilacxy had us come into his office immediately. The old building was a nineteenth-century, two-story seigneurial house that had a marble staircase and balconies with grillwork but was modernized in the interior. A new pavilion that had large floor-to-ceiling windows had been added—perhaps it was a solarium or a gym with a swimming pool. Through the windows in Dr. Zilacxy's office, people could be seen in the distance moving about under the trees, among them the white coats of nurses or doctors. Zilacxy also seemed to come from the nineteenth century, with his square-cut beard framing a thin face and a gleaming bald head. He wore black, with a gray vest, a stiff collar that looked false, and instead of a tie, a four-in-hand held by a vermilion pin. He had a pocket watch with a gold chain.

"I've spoken with my colleague Bourrichon, and read the report from the Hôpital Cochin," he said, coming to the point right away, as if he couldn't allow himself to waste time in banalities. "You're fortunate, the clinic is always full and there are people who wait a long time to be admitted. But, as the lady is a special case because she comes recommended by an old friend, we can make a place for her."

He had a very well-modulated voice, and an elegant, somewhat theatrical way of moving and displaying his hands. He said the "patient" would follow a special diet planned by a dietician so she could regain the weight she had lost, and a personal trainer would monitor her physical exercise. Her head physician would be Dr. Roullin, a specialist in traumas of the kind the lady had suffered. She could have visitors twice a week, between five and seven in the evening. In addition to her treatment with Dr. Roullin, she would take part in group therapy sessions that he led. Unless there was some objection on her part, hypnosis might be used in her treatment, under his direction. And—here he paused so we would know an important statement was coming—if the patient at any point in her treatment felt "disappointed," she could stop immediately.

"It never has happened to us," he added, clicking his tongue. "But the possibility is there in case it ever does."

He said that after talking to Professor Bourrichon, they both had agreed in principle that the patient should remain at the clinic a minimum of four weeks. Then they would see if it was advisable for her to prolong her stay or if she could continue her convalescence at home.

He responded to all of Elena's questions and mine—the bad girl didn't open her mouth, she did no more than listen as if the matter had nothing to do with her—regarding the functioning of the clinic, his colleagues, and after a joke about Lacan and his fantastic combinations of structuralism and Freud, which, he pointed out with a smile in order to set our minds at ease, "we don't offer on our menu," he had a nurse take the bad girl to the office of Dr. Roullin, who was waiting to talk to her and show her around the establishment.

When we were alone with Dr. Zilacxy, Elena cautiously brought up the delicate matter of how much the month of treatment would cost. And she quickly indicated that "the lady" had no insurance or personal funds and the friend who was here now would assume the cost of her cure.

"One hundred thousand francs, approximately, not counting the medicines that—well, it is difficult to know ahead of time—probably would amount to twenty or thirty percent more, in the worst-case scenario." He paused for a moment and coughed before he added: "This is a special price, since the lady comes recommended by Professor Bourrichon."

He looked at his watch, rose to his feet, and said that if we had decided, we should stop by administration to fill out forms.

Three-quarters of an hour later, the bad girl reappeared. She was pleased by her conversation with Dr. Roullin, who seemed very sensible and amiable, and by the visit to the clinic. The room she would occupy was small, comfortable, very pretty, with views of the park, and all the facilities, the dining room, the gym, the warm-water pool, the small auditorium where they gave talks and showed documentaries and feature films, were extremely modern. Without further discussion, we went to administration. I signed a document stating that I agreed to be responsible for all expenses and wrote a check for ten thousand francs as a deposit. The bad girl handed a French passport to the administrator, a very thin woman who wore her hair in a bun and had an inquisitorial eye, and she asked for her identification card instead. Elena and I looked at each other uneasily, expecting a catastrophe.

"I don't have it yet," said the bad girl with absolute naturalness. "I've lived abroad for many years and just came back to France. I know I ought to get one. I'll do that right away."

The administrator wrote the data from the passport into a notebook and returned it to her.

"You'll check in tomorrow," she said as we were leaving. "Please get here before noon."

Taking advantage of the beautiful day, a little cold but golden and with a perfectly clear sky, we took a long walk through the woods of Petit Clamart, listening to the dead leaves of autumn rustling under our feet. We had lunch in a little *bistrot* at the edge of the woods, where a crackling fireplace warmed the room and reddened the faces of the patrons. Elena had to go to work, so she left us just outside Paris, at the first Métro station we came across. During the entire ride to École Militaire the bad girl was silent, her hand in mine. At times I felt her shiver. In the house on Joseph Granier, as soon as we walked in, the bad girl made me sit in the easy chair in the living room and then she sat on my knees. Her nose and ears were freezing, and she trembled so much she couldn't articulate a word. Her teeth were chattering.

"The clinic will do you good," I said, caressing her neck, her shoulders, warming her icy ears with my breath. "They'll take care of you, fatten you up, put an end to these attacks of fear. They'll make you pretty and you can turn back into the devil you've always been. And, if you don't like the clinic, you'll come back here right away. Whenever you say. It isn't a prison, but a place to rest."

She held me tight and didn't say anything, but she trembled a long time before she grew calm. Then I prepared tea with lemon for the two of us. We talked while she packed her bag for the clinic. I handed her an envelope in which I had placed a thousand francs in bills for her to take with her.

"It isn't a gift, it's a loan," I joked. "You'll pay me back when you're rich. I'll charge you high interest."

"How much is all this going to cost you?" she asked, not looking at me.

"Less than I thought. About a hundred thousand francs. What do I care about a hundred thousand francs if I can see you looking attractive again? I'm doing it out of sheer self-interest, Chilean girl."

She didn't say anything for a long time and kept packing her suitcase, looking annoyed.

"I've become that ugly?" she said suddenly.

"Awful," I said. "Forgive me, but you've turned into a real horror of a woman."

"That's a lie," she said, turning and throwing a sandal that landed on my chest. "I can't be that ugly when yesterday, in bed, your cock was hard the whole night. You had to put up with wanting to make love to me, hypocrite."

She burst into laughter and from that moment on was in better spirits. As soon as she finished packing, she came to sit on my lap again so I could gently massage her back and arms. She was still there, sound asleep, when Yilal came in around six to watch his television program. Since the night of the surprise for his parents, he would speak to them and to us, but only for a few moments, because the effort tired him. And then he would go back to the slate, which he still wore around his neck, along with a couple of pieces of chalk in a little bag. That night we didn't hear his voice until he said goodbye, in Spanish: "Good night, friends."

After supper, we went to the Gravoskis' for coffee, and they promised to visit her at the clinic, and asked her to call if she needed anything while I was in Finland. When we came back, she didn't let me pull out the sofa bed.

"Why don't you want to sleep with me?"

I embraced her and pressed her body against mine.

"You know very well why. It's a martyrdom to have you naked beside me, desiring you as I do, when I can't touch you."

"You're hopeless," she said, as indignant as if I'd insulted her. "If you were Fukuda, you'd make love to me all night and not give a damn if I gushed blood or died."

"I'm not Fukuda. Haven't you realized that yet, either?"

"Of course I have," she repeated, throwing her arms around my neck. "That's why tonight you're going to sleep with me. Because I don't enjoy anything as much as making you suffer. Haven't you realized that?"

"*Hélas*, yes," I said, kissing her hair. "I realized it all too well many years ago, and the worst thing is I never learn. I even seem to like it. We're the perfect pair: the sadist and the masochist."

We slept together, and when she tried to caress me I grasped her hands and moved them away.

"Until you're completely healed, we're as chaste as two cherubs."

"It's true, you're a *vrai con*. At least hold me tight so I'm not afraid."

The next morning we took the train at the Saint Lazare station, and during the entire trip to Petit Clamart she was silent and downcast. We said goodbye at the door of the clinic. She held on to me as if we were never going to see each other again, and she wet my face with her tears.

"At this rate, any moment now you'll wind up falling in love with me."

"I'll bet whatever you want that I never will, Ricardito."

I left for Helsinki that same afternoon, and for the two weeks I was working there I didn't stop speaking Russian, every day, morning and afternoon. This was a tripartite conference, with delegates from Europe, the United States, and Russia, to design a policy of aid and cooperation from the Western powers to what remained of the ruins of the Soviet Union. There were commissions dealing with the economy, institutions, social policy, culture, and sports, and on all of them, the Russian delegates expressed themselves with a freedom and spontaneity inconceivable just a short time ago in those monotonous robots, the apparatchiks sent to international conferences by the governments of Brezhnev and even Gorbachev. It was evident things were changing there. I wanted to go back to Moscow and to the rebaptized Saint Petersburg, where I hadn't been for many years.

We interpreters had a great deal of work and almost no time to walk around. It was my second trip to Helsinki. The first had been in spring, when it was possible to walk the streets, and go out to the countryside and see the forests of fir trees dotted with lakes, and pretty villages with wooden houses in a country where everything was beautiful: the architecture, the landscape, the inhabitants, and, above all, the old people. Now, however, with the snow and a temperature of twenty degrees below zero, during my free hours I preferred to stay in the hotel reading or practicing the mysterious rituals of the sauna, which had a delicious anesthetic effect on me.

After ten days in Helsinki I received a letter from the bad girl. She was settled into the clinic in Petit Clamart, to which she had adjusted with no difficulty. She wasn't on a diet, she was overfed, but since she had to do a good deal of exercise in the gym—and was also swimming, helped by an instructor because she never had learned to swim, only to float and paddle in the water like a puppy—her appetite was good. She'd already had two sessions with Dr. Roullin, who was quite intelligent, and they got on very well. She hadn't had occasion to talk to the other patients; she only exchanged greetings with some of them at meals. The only patient with whom she had talked two or three times was a German girl who was anorexic, very shy and timid, but a nice person. All she remembered of the hypnosis session with Dr. Zilacxy was that when she woke up, she felt very calm and rested. She also said she missed me, and that I shouldn't do "a lot of dirty things in those Finnish saunas, which, as everyone knows, are great centers of sexual degeneracy."

In two weeks, when I returned to Paris, Señor Charnés's agency had another five-day contract for me almost immediately, in Alexandria. I was in France barely a day, so I couldn't visit the bad girl. But we spoke on the phone, at dusk. I found her in good spirits, happy above all with Dr. Roullin, who, she said, was doing her "an enormous amount of good," and amused at the group therapy led by Dr. Zilacxy, "something like the confessions of priests, but in a group, and with sermons by the doctor." What did she want me to bring her from Egypt? "A camel." She added, seriously: "I know what: one of those dancing outfits with your belly exposed that Arab dancers wear." Was she planning to please me, when she left the clinic, with a performance of belly dancing just for me? "When I get out, I'm going to do some things you don't even know exist, little saint." When I said I missed her a great deal, she replied, "Me too, I think." She was getting better, no doubt about it.

That night I had supper at the Gravoskis' and gave Yilal a dozen toy soldiers I had bought in a store in Helsinki. Elena and Simon were beside themselves with joy. Though the boy sometimes sank back into mutism and wouldn't give up his slate, each day he spoke a little more, not only with them but also at school, where his classmates, who had called him "the Mute" before, now called him "the Chatterbox." It was a question of patience; he'd soon be totally normal. The Gravoskis had gone to visit the bad girl a couple of times and found her perfectly adjusted to the clinic. Elena spoke once on the phone with Dr. Zilacxy, and he read her a few lines in which Dr. Roullin made a very positive report on the patient's progress. She had gained weight and had more and more control of her nerves every day.

The next afternoon I left for Cairo, where, after five tedious hours of flying, I had to take another plane on an Egyptian airline to Alexandria. I was exhausted when I arrived. As soon as I was in my little room in a miserable

272

hotel called the Nile—it was my fault, I chose the cheapest one offered to the interpreters—I didn't feel like unpacking and fell asleep for almost eight hours, something that happened to me very rarely.

The next day, which I had free, I walked around the ancient city founded by Alexander, visited its museum of Roman antiquities and the ruins of its amphitheater, and took a long walk on the beautiful avenue by the coast, with its cafés, restaurants, hotels, shops for tourists, and talkative, cosmopolitan crowd. Sitting on one of the terraces that made me think of the poet Kaváfis—his house in the vanished, now Arabified Greek district could not be visited; a sign in English indicated it was being renovated by the Greek consulate—I wrote a long letter to the patient, telling her how glad I was to know she was happy at the clinic in Petit Clamart and offering, if she behaved herself and left the clinic totally cured, to take her for a week to some beach in the south of Spain so she could get a tan. Would she like to have a honeymoon with this little pissant?

I spent the afternoon reviewing all the documentation on the conference, which began the next day. It had to do with the economic cooperation and development of all the countries in the Mediterranean basin: France, Spain, Greece, Italy, Turkey, Cyprus, Egypt, Lebanon, Algeria, Morocco, Libya, and Syria. Israel had been excluded. They were five exhausting days, with no time for anything, immersed in confused and tedious papers and debates which, in spite of producing mountains of printed paper, seemed to serve no practical purpose. On the last day, one of the Arabic interpreters at the conference, a native of Alexandria, helped me find what the bad girl had asked for: an Arab dancer's outfit, full of veils and sequins. I imagined her wearing it, swaying like a palm tree on the desert sand, under the moon, to the rhythm of flageolets, flutes, finger cymbals, timbrels, mandolins, cymbals, and other Arabic musical instruments, and I wanted her.

The day after I arrived in Paris, even before I talked with the Gravoskis, I went to visit her at the clinic in Petit Clamart. It was a gray, rainy day, and the nearby woods had been stripped of leaves and almost entirely blasted by winter. The park with the stone fountain, without swans now, was covered by a wet, depressing mist. I was shown into a rather spacious room where some people were sitting in chairs in what looked like family groups. I waited beside a window through which I could see the fountain, and suddenly I saw her come in, wearing a bathrobe and sandals, a towel wrapped around her head like a turban.

"I made you wait, I'm sorry, I was in the pool, swimming," she said, standing on tiptoe to kiss me on the cheeks. "I had no idea you were coming. Just yesterday I received your note from Alexandria. Are we really going for a honeymoon to a beach in the south of Spain?"

We sat in the same corner, and she drew her chair close to mine until our knees were touching. She extended both her hands so I could grasp them, and that's how we sat, our fingers intertwined, for the hour our conversation lasted. The change was remarkable. She had, in fact, recovered, and her body again had a shape, the bones of her face were no longer visible under the skin of her face, her cheekbones were no longer prominent. In her eyes the color of dark honey, the old vivacity and mischief could be seen again, and the little blue vein wove along her forehead. She moved her full lips with a coquetry that reminded me of the bad girl of prehistoric times. I saw that she was confident, serene, happy because of how well she felt and because, she assured me, she had only very occasional attacks of the fear that in the past two years had brought her to the brink of madness.

"You don't need to tell me you're better," I said, kissing her hands and devouring her with my eyes. "I just have to see you to know. You're pretty again. I'm so overwhelmed I barely know what I'm saying."

"And imagine, you've caught me coming out of the pool," she responded, looking into my eyes in a provocative way. "Wait till you see me dressed and with my makeup on. It'll knock you flat, Ricardito."

I had supper with the Gravoskis that night and told them about the incredible improvement in the bad girl after three weeks of treatment. They had visited her the previous Sunday and had the same impression. They were still delighted with Yilal. The boy was more and more willing to speak, at home and in school, though on certain days he enclosed himself again in silence. But there could be no doubt: going back was not a possibility. He had left the prison where he had taken refuge and was increasingly integrated into the community of speaking individuals. That afternoon he greeted me in Spanish: "You have to tell me about the pyramids, Uncle Ricardo."

I devoted the next few days to cleaning, arranging, and beautifying the apartment on Rue Joseph Granier, preparing to receive the patient. I had the curtains and sheets washed and ironed, hired a Portuguese woman to help me clean and wax the floors, dust the walls, and wash the linens, and bought flowers for the four large vases in the house. I placed the package with the Egyptian dancing outfit on the bed in the bedroom, with a cheerful card. The night before she was to leave the clinic, I was as eager as a young kid going out with a girl for the first time.

We went to pick her up in Elena's car, accompanied by Yilal, who had no classes that day. In spite of the rain and the gray, dull air, I felt as if streams of golden light were pouring down from the sky over France. She was ready, waiting for us at the entrance to the clinic, her suitcase at her feet. She had arranged her hair carefully, put on a little lipstick and rouge, manicured her hands, and lengthened her lashes with mascara. She wore a coat I hadn't seen before, navy blue and belted, with a large buckle. When he saw her, Yilal's eyes lit up and he ran to embrace her. While the porter placed her luggage in Elena's car, I went to administration and the woman with her hair in a bun handed me the bill. It came to approximately the amount Dr. Zilacxy had predicted: 127,315 francs. I had deposited 150,000 in my account to pay it and sold all the treasury bonds where I kept my savings and obtained two loans, one from the professional credit union I belonged to, which charged very low interest, and another from my bank, the Société Générale, at higher rates. Everything indicated it had been an excellent investment: the patient looked so much better. The administrator told me to call the director's secretary for an appointment, since Dr. Zilacxy wanted to see me. "Alone," she added.

That was a very beautiful night. We had a light supper at the Gravoskis' apartment, though we did have a bottle of champagne, and as soon as we returned home, we embraced and kissed for a long time. At first tenderly, then avidly, passionately, desperately. I ran my hands over her entire body and helped her to undress. It was marvelous, her figure, which had always been slim, once again had curves, sinuous forms, and it was delicious to feel in my hands and on my lips her small breasts, warm, soft, shapely, with their erect nipples and puckered areolas. I never wearied of inhaling the perfume of her depilated underarms. When she was naked I picked her up and carried her to the bedroom. She watched me undress with one of those mocking little smiles from the old days.

"Are you going to make love to me?" she incited me, speaking in a singsong. "But the two months the doctor ordered aren't over yet."

"Tonight I don't care," I replied. "You're too beautiful, and if I don't make love to you I'll die. Because I love you with all my heart."

"I thought it strange that you hadn't told me any cheap, sentimental things yet," she said with a laugh.

While I kissed her body, slowly, with infinite delicacy and immense love, beginning with her hair and ending with the soles of her feet, I felt her purring, contracting and stretching with excitement. When I kissed her sex she was very wet, throbbing, swollen. Her legs tightened around me. But as soon as I entered her, she howled and burst into tears, her face distorted with pain.

"It hurts, it hurts," she whimpered, pulling me out with both hands. "I wanted to please you tonight, but I can't, it's tearing me apart, it hurts."

She cried, kissing me on the mouth in distress, and her hair and tears were in my eyes and nose. She trembled the way she had when she suffered a terror attack. I asked her to forgive me for having been a brute, an irresponsible egotist. I loved her, I'd never make her suffer, she was for me the most precious, the sweetest, most tender thing in life. Since the pain didn't lessen, I got up, naked, and brought from the bathroom a washcloth soaked in warm water, and with her I gently pressed it on her sex until, gradually, the pain began to disappear. We wrapped ourselves in the blanket, and she wanted me to finish in her mouth but I refused. I was sorry I had made her suffer. Until she was completely healed, what happened tonight would not be repeated: we would live a chaste life, her health was more important than my pleasure. She listened, not saying anything, holding me close, not moving a muscle. But much later, before she fell asleep, with her arms around my neck and her lips pressed to mine, she whispered, "I read your letter from Alexandria ten times at least. I slept with it every night, holding it between my legs."

The next morning, I called the clinic in Petit Clamart from the street, and Dr. Zilacxy's secretary gave me an appointment for two days later. She too specified that the director wanted to see me alone. In the afternoon I went to UNESCO to explore possibilities for a contract, but the head of interpreters said there was nothing for the rest of the month, and he proposed instead to recommend me for a three-day conference in Bordeaux. I didn't accept. Señor Charnés's agency didn't have anything for me in Paris or its outskirts, but since my old *patrón* saw I needed work, he gave me a pile of documents to translate from Russian and English, at fairly good pay. And so I settled in to work in my living room, with my typewriter and my dictionaries. I imposed a schedule of regular hours on myself. The bad girl prepared cups of coffee for me and took care of the meals. From time to time, like a newlywed attentive to her husband, she came over to embrace my shoulders and give me a kiss on my back, neck, or ear. But when Yilal arrived she forgot about me completely and devoted herself to playing with the boy as if they were the same age. At night, after supper, we listened to records before going to bed, and sometimes she fell asleep in my arms.

I didn't tell her I had an appointment at the clinic in Petit Clamart, and I left the house on the pretext of an interview for a possible job at a firm on the outskirts of Paris. I arrived at the clinic half an hour early, dying of the cold, and waited in the visitors' room, watching light snow fall on the grass. The bad weather had made the stone fountain and the trees disappear.

Dr. Zilacxy, dressed exactly the same as the first time I saw him a month earlier, was with Dr. Roullin. I liked her right away. She was a stout woman, still young, with intelligent eyes and an amiable smile that almost never left her lips. She held a folder and passed it, rhythmically, from one hand to the other. They were standing when they received me, and though there were chairs in the office, they didn't invite me to sit down.

"How does she seem to you?" the director asked by way of greeting, making the same impression he had before: he was someone unwilling to waste time in circumlocutions.

"Magnificent, Doctor," I replied. "She's another person. She's recuperated, and her shape and color have returned. I find her very serene. And the terror attacks that tormented her so have disappeared. She's very grateful to both of you. As am I, of course."

"Fine, fine," said Dr. Zilacxy, rubbing his hands together like a magician and shifting his weight. "Still, I caution you, in these things, one can never trust appearances."

"What things, Doctor?" I interrupted, intrigued.

"Things of the mind, my friend," he said with a smile. "If you prefer to call it the spirit, I have no objection. The lady is fine physically. Her organism, in fact, has recovered, thanks to a disciplined life, a good regimen of diet and exercise. Now we must try to have her follow the instructions we gave her regarding meals. She shouldn't abandon going to the gym and swimming, which have done her so much good. But, in matters of the psyche, you'll have to show a great deal of patience. She is well oriented, I think, though the road she still has to travel will be a long one."

He looked at Dr. Roullin, who hadn't said a word so far. She nodded. Something in her penetrating eyes alarmed me. I saw her open the folder and leaf through it quickly. Were they going to give me bad news? Only now did the director point to the chairs. They sat down too.

"Your friend has suffered a great deal," said Dr. Roullin, so pleasantly that she seemed to mean something very different. "She has real turmoil inside her head. As a result of how wounded she is. I mean, because of what she still is suffering."

"But I also find her much improved psychologically," I said, for the sake of saying something. The preambles of both physicians had frightened me. "Well, I suppose no woman ever recovers completely after an experience like the one in Lagos."

There was a brief silence and another rapid exchange of glances between the director and the doctor. Through the picture window that faced the park, the falling snowflakes were now denser and whiter. The garden, the trees, the fountain had disappeared.

"That rape probably never happened, Monsieur," Dr. Roullin said affably, with a smile. And made a gesture as if in apology.

"It's a fantasy constructed to protect someone, to wipe away clues," added Dr. Zilacxy, not giving me time to react. "Dr. Roullin suspected as much in their first interview. And then we confirmed it when I hypnotized her. The curious thing is her inventing this to protect someone who, for a long time, for years, systematically used and abused her. You were aware of that, weren't you?"

"Who is Mr. Fukuda?" Dr. Roullin asked gently. "She speaks of him with hatred and, at the same time, with reverence. Her husband? Her lover?"

"Her lover," I stammered. "A sordid individual involved in shady business dealings with whom she lived in Tokyo for several years. She told me he dropped her when he found out that the police who arrested her in Lagos had raped her. Because he thought they had infected her with AIDS."

"Another fantasy, this one to protect herself," said the director of the clinic, gesturing. "And that gentleman didn't drop her. She escaped from him. Her terrors originate there. A mixture of fear and remorse for having fled a person who exercised total control over her, deprived her of her sovereignty, self-determination, pride, self-esteem, and nearly her reason."

I opened my mouth in utter amazement. I didn't know what to say.

"Fear he could pursue her to take his revenge and punish her," Dr. Roullin continued in the same amiable, discreet tone. "But her daring to escape was a great thing, Monsieur. An indication that the tyrant hadn't destroyed her personality completely. Deep down she preserved her dignity. Her free will."

"But those wounds, those injuries," I asked, and immediately repented, guessing what they would say.

"He subjected her to all kinds of abuse, for his amusement," the director explained, getting directly to the point. "He was both an esthete and a technician in the administration of his pleasures. You must have a clear idea of what she endured in order to help her. I have no choice but to give you the unpleasant details. That's the only way you'll be in a position to provide all the support she needs. He whipped her with cords that leave no marks. He lent her to his friends and bodyguards during orgies and watched them, because he is also a voyeur. Worst of all, perhaps, the thing that has left the deepest scar in her mind, was breaking wind. It excited him very much, apparently. He had her drink a solution of powders that filled her with gas. It was one of the fantasies with which that eccentric gentleman gratified himself: having her naked, on all fours, like a dog, breaking wind."

"He not only destroyed her rectum and vagina, Monsieur," said Dr. Roullin, with the same gentleness and without renouncing her smile, "he destroyed her personality. Everything in her that was worthy and decent. Which is why I must tell you again: she has suffered and will still suffer a great deal, appearances to the contrary. And at times she'll behave irrationally."

My throat was dry, and as if he had read my mind, Dr. Zilacxy handed me a glass of sparkling water.

"All right, everything must be said. Make no mistake. She was not deceived. She was a willing victim. She endured everything knowing very well what she was doing." Suddenly, the director's eyes began to scrutinize me in an insistent way, measuring my reaction. "Call it twisted love, baroque passion, perversion, masochistic impulse, or simply submission to an overwhelming personality, one to whom she could offer no resistance. She was an obliging victim and readily accepted all that gentleman's whims. When she becomes aware of this now, it enrages her and throws her into despair."

"It will be an exceedingly slow and difficult convalescence," Dr. Roullin said. "Until she recovers her self-esteem. She agreed, she wanted to be a slave, or almost a slave, and she was treated as such, do you see? Until one day, I don't know how, I don't know why, and neither does she, she realized the danger. She felt, guessed, that if it continued, she would end very badly, crippled, insane, or dead. And then she fled. I don't know where she found the strength to do it. One must admire her for that, I assure you. People who reach that extreme of dependence almost never free themselves."

"Her panic was so great she invented the entire story about Lagos, being raped by the police, her torturer dropping her for fear of AIDS. And she even came to believe it. Living in the fiction gave her reasons to feel more secure, less threatened than living in the truth. It's more difficult for everyone to live in the truth than in a lie. And even harder for someone in her situation. It will cost her immense effort to become accustomed again to the truth."

He fell silent, and Dr. Roullin didn't speak either. Both looked at me with indulgent curiosity. I sipped at the water, incapable of saying anything. I felt flushed and sweaty.

"You can help her," said Dr. Roullin after a moment. "Something else, Monsieur. It may surprise you to hear that you're probably the only person in the world who can help her. Much more than we can, I assure you. The danger is that she'll fold in on herself, in a kind of autism. You can be her communicating bridge to the world."

"She trusts you, and no one else, I believe," the director said in agreement. "With you she feels, how can I say it . . ."

"Dirty," said Dr. Roullin, lowering her eyes politely for a moment. "Because to her, though you may not believe it, you're a kind of saint."

My laugh sounded very false. I felt foolish, stupid, I wanted to tell them both to go to hell, to say that the two of them justified the suspicion I'd always had of psychologists, psychiatrists, psychoanalysts, priests, wizards, and shamans. They looked at me as if they could read my mind and forgave me. Dr. Roullin's imperturbable smile was still there.

"If you have patience and, above all, a good deal of love, her spirit can heal just as her body has," said the director.

I asked them, because I didn't know what else to ask, if the bad girl had to return to the clinic.

"On the contrary," said the smiling Dr. Roullin. "She should forget about us, forget she was here, that this clinic exists. Begin her life again, from square one. A life very different from the one she's had, with someone who loves and respects her. Like you."

"One more thing, Monsieur," said the director, getting to his feet and indicating in this way that the interview was over. "You'll find this strange. But she, and all those who live a good part of their lives enclosed in fantasies they erect in order to abolish their real life, both know and don't know what they're doing. The border disappears for a while and then it reappears. I mean, sometimes they know and other times they don't know what they're doing. This is my advice: don't try to force her to accept reality. Help her, but don't force her, don't rush her. This apprenticeship is long and difficult."

"It could be counterproductive and cause a relapse," Dr. Roullin said with a cryptic smile. "Little by little, through her own efforts, she'll have to readjust and accept real life again."

I didn't understand very clearly what they were attempting to tell me, but I didn't try to find out. I wanted to go, to leave that place and never think again about what I had heard. Knowing very well it would be impossible. On the suburban train back to Paris, I felt profoundly demoralized. Anguish closed my throat. It wasn't surprising that she had invented the Lagos story.

Hadn't she spent her life inventing things? But it hurt me to know that the injuries to her vagina and rectum had been caused by Fukuda, whom I began to hate with all my strength. Subjecting her to what practices? Did he sodomize her with metal objects, with those notched vibrators placed at the disposal of clients at Château Meguru? I knew the image of the bad girl, naked and on all fours, her stomach swollen by those powders, loosing strings of farts because that sight and those noises and odors gave erections to the Japanese gangster—only to him, or were they shows he put on for his buddies too?— would pursue me for months, years, perhaps the rest of my life. Is that what the bad girl called—and with what feverish excitement she had said it to me in Tokyo— living intensely? She had lent herself to all of it. At the same time that she was his victim, she had been Fukuda's accomplice. That meant something as devious and perverse as the desires of the horrendous Japanese lived in her too. How could she not think the imbecile who had just gone into debt so she would be cured, so that after a while she could move on to someone richer or more interesting than the little pissant, was a saint! And in spite of all that rancor and fury I only wanted to get home soon to see her, touch her, and let her know I loved her more than ever. Poor thing. How much she had suffered. It was a miracle she was still alive. I would dedicate the rest of my life to getting her out of that pit. Imbecile!

Back in Paris, my concern was to force myself to put on a natural face and not let the bad girl suspect what was whirling around my head. When I walked into the apartment, I found Yilal teaching her to play chess. She complained that it was very difficult and required a lot of thought, and the game of checkers was simpler and more fun. "No, no, no," insisted the boy's high-pitched voice. "Yilal will learn you." "Yilal will teach you, not learn you," she corrected.

When the boy left, I began to work on the translations to hide my state of mind and typed until it was time for supper. Since the table was covered with my papers, we ate in the kitchen, at a small counter with two stools. She had prepared a cheese omelet and salad.

"What's wrong?" she asked suddenly, as we were eating. "You seem strange. You went to the clinic, didn't you? Why haven't you told me anything? Did they tell you something bad?"

"No, on the contrary," I assured her. "You're fine. What they said is that now you need to forget about the clinic, Dr. Roullin, and the past. That's what they told me: you should forget about them so your recovery can be complete."

In her eyes I saw that she knew I was hiding something, but she didn't insist. We went to have coffee with the Gravoskis. Our friends were very excited. Simon had received an offer to spend a couple of years at Princeton University, doing research, in an exchange program with the Pasteur Institute. Both of them wanted to go to New Jersey: in two years in the United States, Yilal would learn English and Elena could work at Princeton Hospital. They were finding out if the Hôpital Cochin would give her a two-year, unpaid leave of absence. Since they did all the talking, I almost didn't have to say anything, just listen, or rather, pretend I was listening, for which I was extremely grateful.

I worked very hard in the weeks and months that followed. To pay off the loans and at the same time meet ongoing expenses that had increased now that the bad girl was living with me, I had to accept all the contracts offered to me, and at the same time, at night or very early in the morning, spend two or three hours translating documents given to me by the office of Señor Charnés, who, as always, made a constant effort to help me. I traveled throughout Europe, working at all kinds of conferences and congresses, and I brought the translations with me and did them at night, in hotels and pensions, on a portable typewriter. I didn't care about the excessive work. The truth is I felt happy living with the woman I loved. She seemed completely recovered. She never spoke of Fukuda, or Lagos, or the clinic at Petit Clamart. We would go to the movies, or sometimes listen to jazz at a *cave* on Saint-Germain, and on Saturdays have supper at some restaurant that wasn't too expensive.

My only extravagance was the cost of the gym, because I was sure it did the bad girl a lot of good. I enrolled her in a gym on Avenue Montaigne that had a warm-water pool, and she went very willingly several times a week to take aerobics classes with a trainer and swim. Now that she knew how to swim, it was her favorite sport. When I was away, she spent a good deal of time with the Gravoskis, who, finally, now that Elena had obtained permission, were preparing to travel to the United States in the spring. Occasionally they would take her to see a movie, an art show, or to have supper at a restaurant. Yilal had succeeded in teaching her chess, and beat her just as he had in checkers.

One day the bad girl told me that since she was feeling perfectly fine, which seemed true, given her healthy appearance and the love of life she seemed to have recovered, she wanted to find a job, not waste her days, and help me with expenses. It mortified her that I was killing myself with work and she didn't do anything but go to the gym and play with Yilal.

But when she began to look for work, the problem of her papers resurfaced. She had three passports, a Peruvian one that had expired and a French and a British one, both false. They wouldn't give her a decent job anywhere if she was illegal. Least of all during those times when, in all of western Europe, and especially in France, paranoia with regard to immigrants from Third World countries had increased. Governments were restricting visas and beginning to persecute foreigners without work permits.

The British passport, which showed a photograph of her wearing makeup that changed her appearance almost completely, had been issued to a Mrs. Patricia Steward. She explained that since her ex-husband, David Richardson, had proven the bigamy that annulled her British marriage, she automatically lost the citizenship she had obtained when she married him. She didn't dare use the French passport acquired thanks to her earlier husband, because she didn't know if Monsieur Robert Arnoux had finally decided to denounce her, had begun a legal proceeding, or accused her of bigamy or something else to take his revenge. For her trips to Africa, along with the British one, Fukuda had procured a French passport issued to Madame Florence Milhoun; in it, the photograph showed her looking very young, with a hairdo entirely different from the one she normally wore. She had used this passport to enter France the last time. I was afraid that if she was found out, they would throw her out of the country, or worse.

In spite of this obstacle, the bad girl continued making inquiries, answering the want ads in *Les Echos* for tourist agencies, public relations offices, art galleries, and companies that worked with Spain and Latin America and needed personnel with a knowledge of Spanish. It didn't seem very likely that, given her precarious legal status, she would find a regular job, but I didn't want to disillusion her and encouraged her to continue her search.

A few days before the Gravoskis' departure for the United States, at a farewell supper we gave them at La Closerie des Lilas, and after listening to the bad girl recounting how difficult it was to find a job where they would accept her without papers, Elena had an idea.

"Why don't you two marry?" she said to me. "You have French nationality, don't you? Well, marry her and you give your nationality to your wife. Her legal problems will be over, chico. She'll be a nice, legal Frenchwoman."

She said it without thinking, as a joke, and Simon picked up the thread: that wedding would be worth waiting for, he wanted to attend and be a witness for the groom, and since they wouldn't return to France for two years, we had to shelve the project until then. Unless we decided to get married in Princeton, New Jersey, in which case he'd not only be a witness but the best man too, and so forth.

Back home, half serious and half in jest, I said to the

bad girl as she was undressing, "Suppose we follow Elena's advice? She's right: if we marry, your situation is resolved instantly."

She put on her nightgown and turned to look at me, with her hands on her hips, a mocking little smile, and the stance of a fighting cock. She spoke with all the irony she was capable of.

"Are you seriously asking me to marry you?"

"Well, I think so," I said, trying to joke. "If you want to. Just to solve your legal problems. We don't want them to expel you from France one day for being illegal."

"I marry only for love," she said, staring daggers at me and tapping her right foot, which was extended in front of her. "I'd never marry a clod who made a proposal of marriage as coarse as the one you've just made to me."

"If you want, I'll get down on my knees, and with my hand over my heart, I'll beg you to be my adored little wife until the end of time," I said in confusion, not knowing if she was joking or speaking seriously.

The short, transparent organdy nightgown showed her breasts, her navel, and the dark little growth of hair at her pubis. It only reached down to her knees and left her shoulders and arms bare. Her hair was loose and her face lit up by the performance she had initiated. The light from the bedside lamp fell on her back and formed a golden halo around her figure. She looked very attractive and audacious, and I desired her.

"Do it," she ordered. "On your knees, with your hands on your chest. Tell me the best cheap, sentimental things in your repertoire and let's see if you convince me."

I fell to my knees and begged her to marry me, while I kissed her feet, her ankles, her knees, caressed her buttocks, and compared her to the Virgin Mary, the goddesses on Olympus, Semiramis and Cleopatra, Ulysses' Nausicaa, Quixote's Dulcinea, and told her she was more beautiful and desirable than Claudia Cardinale, Brigitte Bardot, and Catherine Deneuve all rolled into one. Finally I grasped her waist and made her fall onto the bed. As I caressed and made love to her, I heard her laugh as she said into my ear, "I'm sorry, but I've received better requests for my hand than yours, little pissant."

Whenever we made love, I had to take great precautions not to hurt her. And though I pretended to believe her when she said she was getting better, the passage of time had convinced me it wasn't true, that the injuries to her vagina would never disappear entirely and would forever limit our sex life. I often avoided penetration, and when I didn't, I entered very carefully, withdrawing as soon as I felt her body contract and saw her face contort into a pained expression. But even so, this difficult and at times incomplete lovemaking made me immensely happy. Giving her pleasure with my mouth and hands, and receiving it from hers, justified my life and made me feel like the most privileged of mortals. Though she often maintained that distant attitude she'd always had in bed, she sometimes seemed to become animated and participate with enthusiasm and ardor, and I would say to her, "Even though you don't like to admit it, I think you're beginning to love me." That night, when we were exhausted and sinking into sleep, I admonished her.

"You haven't given me an answer, guerrilla fighter.

This must be the fifteenth declaration of love I've made to you. Are you going to marry me or not?"

"I don't know," she replied, very seriously, her arms around me. "I still have to think about it."

The Gravoskis left for the United States on a sunny spring day when the first green buds were coming out on the chestnuts, beeches, and Lombardy poplars of Paris. We saw them off at the Charles de Gaulle Airport. When she embraced Yilal, the bad girl's eyes filled with tears. The Gravoskis had left us a key to their apartment so we could look in once in a while and keep the dust from invading. They were good friends, the only ones with whom we had that South American kind of visceral friendship, and for the two years of their absence we would miss them very much. When I saw the bad girl so downhearted over Yilal's departure, I suggested that instead of going home we take a walk or go to a movie. Then I'd take her to have supper at a small *bistrot* on the Île Saint-Louis that she liked very much. She had become so fond of Yilal that as we strolled around Notre Dame on our way to the restaurant, I said, jokingly, that if she'd like, once we were married we could adopt a child.

"I've discovered a maternal vocation in you. I always thought you didn't want children."

"When I was in Cuba, with Comandante Chacón, I had my tubes tied because he wanted a child and the idea horrified me," she replied, drily. "Now I'm sorry."

"Let's adopt one," I encouraged her. "Isn't it the same thing? Haven't you seen the relationship Yilal has with his parents?"

"I don't know if it's the same," she murmured, and I heard her voice become hostile. "Besides, I don't even know if I'll marry you. Let's change the subject, please."

She was in a very bad mood, and I understood that, without meaning to, I had touched a wounded place deep inside her. I tried to distract her and took her to look at the cathedral, a sight that never failed to overwhelm me even after all the years I had been in Paris. And that night more than other times. A faint light, with a slightly pink aura, bathed the stones of Notre Dame. The large mass seemed light because of the perfect symmetry of its parts, delicately balanced and sustained so that nothing was disordered or disarranged. History and the sifted light charged the façade with allusions and resonances, images and references. There were many tourists taking pictures. Was this same cathedral the setting for so many centuries of French history, the inspiration for the novel by Victor Hugo that excited me so when I read it as a boy, in Miraflores, in my aunt Alberta's house? It was the same one and a different one that had accrued more recent mythologies and events. Extraordinarily beautiful, it transmitted an impression of stability and permanence, of having escaped the usury of time. The bad girl, lost in her own thoughts, heard me praise Notre Dame as if she were hearing the rain. During supper she was dejected, peevish, and hardly ate a bite. And that night she fell asleep without saying good night, as if I were responsible for Yilal's departure. Two days later, I went to London with a contract for a week's work. When I said goodbye, very early in the morning, I said, "It doesn't matter if we don't get married if you don't want to, bad girl. It isn't necessary. I have to tell you something before I leave. In my forty-seven years

I've never been as happy as in these months we've been together. I don't know how to repay the happiness you've given me."

"Hurry, you'll miss the plane, you tiresome man," she said, pushing me toward the door.

She was still in a bad mood, withdrawn day and night. Since the departure of the Gravoskis, I almost hadn't been able to talk to her. Did Yilal's leaving affect her so much?

My work in London was more interesting than at other conferences and congresses. The meeting had one of those innocuous titles, tirelessly repeated with different topics: "Africa: An Impetus to Development." It was sponsored by the Commonwealth, the United Nations, the Organization of African Unity, and several independent institutes. But unlike other debates, there were very serious testimonies by political, business, and academic leaders from African countries regarding the calamitous state in which the former French and British colonies had been left when they achieved independence, and the obstacles they were confronting now in their efforts to order society, stabilize institutions, eliminate militarism and local strongmen, integrate into harmonious unity the distinct ethnicities in each country, and move forward economically. The situation in almost all the represented nations was critical, yet the sincerity and lucidity with which the Africans, most of them very young, described their reality had something vibrant that injected a hopeful energy into their tragic condition. Though I was also using Spanish, for the most part I had to interpret from French to English or the reverse. And I did it with interest, curiosity, and a desire to take a vacation one day in Africa. I couldn't forget, however, that the bad girl had made her trips to that continent in the service of Fukuda.

Whenever I left Paris for a job, we spoke every other day. She called me since it was cheaper; hotels and pensions charged a fortune for international calls. But even though I left her the telephone number at the Hotel Shoreham, in Bayswater, the bad girl didn't call on my first two days in London. On the third, I called her, early, before I left for the Commonwealth Institute where the conference was being held.

She seemed very strange. Laconic, evasive, irritated. I was frightened, thinking the old panic attacks had returned. She assured me that they hadn't, that she felt fine. Then did she miss Yilal? Of course she missed him. And did she miss me a little too?

"Let's see, let me think," she said, but her tone wasn't that of a woman who's joking. "No, frankly, I don't miss you very much yet."

I had a bad taste in my mouth when I hung up. Well, everybody had periods of neurasthenia, when they chose to seem hateful in order to establish their disgust with the world. It would pass. Since she still hadn't called two days later, I called her again, very early this time too. She didn't answer. She couldn't possibly have gone out at seven in the morning: she never did that. The only explanation was that she was still in a bad mood—but over what?—and didn't want to answer, since she knew very well I was the one calling. I called again at night and she still didn't pick up the phone. I called four or five times in the course of a sleepless night: total silence. The intermittent screech of the phone pursued me for the next twenty-four hours until, as soon as the last session ended, I hurried to Heathrow Airport to catch my plane to Paris. All kinds of gloomy thoughts made the flight, followed by the cab ride from Charles de Gaulle to Rue Joseph Granier, seem infinite.

It was a little after two in the morning when, under a persistent drizzle, I opened the door to my apartment. It was dark, empty, and on the bed was a note written in pencil on the lined yellow paper we kept in the kitchen to jot down daily reminders. It was a model of laconic iciness: "I'm tired of playing the petit bourgeois housewife you'd like me to be. That's not what I am or what I'll ever be. I'm very grateful for everything you've done for me. I'm sorry. Take care of yourself and don't suffer too much, good boy."

I unpacked, brushed my teeth, lay down. And spent the rest of the night in thought, my mind wandering. You've been expecting this, fearing this, right? You knew it would happen sooner or later, ever since you moved the bad girl to Rue Joseph Granier seven months ago. Though out of cowardice you tried not to assume it, to avoid it, deceive yourself, tell yourself that finally, after those horrible experiences with Fukuda, she had renounced adventures, dangers, and resigned herself to living with you. But you always knew, in your heart of hearts, the illusion would last only as long as her convalescence. You knew the mediocre, boring life she had with you would weary her, and once she recovered her health and self-confidence, and remorse or her fear of Fukuda had vanished, she would arrange to meet someone more interesting, richer, less a creature of habit than you, and undertake a new escapade.

As soon as some light appeared in the skylight I got up, prepared coffee, and opened the little security box where I always kept cash for the month's expenses. She had taken it all, naturally. Well, in reality, it wasn't very much. Who could the lucky man be this time? When and how had she met him? During one of my business trips, no doubt. Perhaps at the gym on Avenue Montaigne while she was doing aerobics and swimming. Perhaps one of those playboys without an ounce of fat on his body, and good muscles, one of those who tan under ultraviolet lights and have their nails manicured and their scalps massaged in barbershops. Had they made love yet, while she, maintaining the pantomime of staying with me, prepared her flight in secret? Of course. And no doubt her new lover would be less careful than you, Ricardito, with her damaged vagina.

I looked through the apartment and there was no trace of her. She had taken everything down to the last pin. One could say she never had been here. I showered, dressed, and went out, fleeing those two and a half small rooms where, just as I told her when I said goodbye, I had been happier than anywhere else, and where from now on—once again!—I would be immensely miserable. But, isn't it what you deserved, Peruvian? Didn't you know, when you wouldn't answer her calls, that if you did, if you succumbed again to this stubborn passion, it would all end the way it has now? There was nothing to be surprised at: what you always knew would happen, had happened.

It was a nice day, with no clouds and a coldish sun, and spring had filled the streets of Paris with green. The parks blazed with flowers. I walked for hours, along the quays, through the Tuileries and the Luxembourg Gardens, going into a café for something when I felt as if I would drop with fatigue. At dusk I had a sandwich and a beer and then went into a movie without even knowing what film they were showing. I fell asleep as soon as I sat down and woke only when the lights went on. I don't remember a single image.

When I left night had fallen. I was filled with despair, afraid I would begin to cry. You're not only capable of saying cheap, sentimental things but of living them too, Ricardito. The truth, the truth was that this time I wouldn't have the strength necessary to pull myself together as I had the other times, to react and go on pretending I had forgotten about the bad girl.

I walked along the quays on the Seine to the distant Pont Mirabeau, trying to remember the first lines of the poem by Apollinaire, repeating them in a murmur:

> *Sous le Pont Mirabeau Coule la Seine*
> *Faut-il qu'il m'en souvienne*
> *de nos amours*
> *Ou après la joie*
> *Venait toujours la peine?*

I had decided coldly, unmelodramatically, that this was, after all, a worthy way to die: jumping off the bridge, dignified by good modernist poetry and the intense voice of Juliette Gréco, into the dirty waters of the Seine. Holding my breath or gulping down water, I would lose consciousness quickly—perhaps lose it with the force of my body hitting the water—and death would follow immediately. If you couldn't have the only thing you wanted in life, which was her, better to end it once and for all and do it this way, little pissant.

I reached the Pont Mirabeau literally soaked to the skin. I hadn't even realized it was raining. There were no pedestrians or cars anywhere nearby. I walked to the middle of the bridge and without hesitating climbed to the metal ledge, where, as I stood on tiptoe to jump—I swear I was going to do it—I felt a gust of wind in my face and, at the same time, two large hands encircling my legs and with a tug making me lose my balance and fall backward onto the asphalt of the bridge.

"Fais pas le con, imbécile!"

He was a clochard who smelled of wine and grime, half lost inside a large plastic raincoat that covered his head. He had an enormous beard that looked grayish, turning white. Without helping me up, he placed his bottle of wine in my mouth and made me swallow: something hot and strong that stirred up my intestines. A turned wine becoming vinegar. I felt a wave of nausea but didn't throw up.

"Fais pas le con, mon vieux," he repeated. And I saw him turn and move away, staggering, his bottle of sour wine dancing in his hand. I knew I would always remember his shapeless face, his bulging bloodshot eyes, his hoarse human voice.

I walked back to Rue Joseph Granier, laughing at myself, filled with gratitude and admiration for that drunken vagabond on the Pont Mirabeau who saved my life. I was going to jump, I'd have done it if he hadn't stopped me. I felt stupid, ridiculous, ashamed, and had begun to sneeze. All this cheap clownishness would end in a cold. The bones in my back ached because of my fall onto the pavement, and I wanted to sleep, sleep the rest of the night, the rest of my life.

As I was opening the door to my apartment I saw a thin line of light inside. I crossed the living room in two strides. From the door to the bedroom I saw the back of the bad girl, standing in front of the bureau mirror and trying on the Arab dancer's outfit I bought her in Cairo and didn't think she had put on before. She had to have heard me but didn't turn to look at me, as if a ghost had entered the room.

"What are you doing here?" I said, shouted, or roared, paralyzed in the doorway, hearing how strange my voice sounded, like a man being strangled.

Very calmly, as if nothing had happened and the entire scene was the most trivial in the world, the dark, half-naked figure, wrapped in veils, from whose waist hung strips that could have been leather or chains, turned slightly and looked at me, smiling.

"I changed my mind and here I am back again." She spoke as if she were telling me a bit of casual gossip. And, moving on to more important things, she pointed at her dress and said, "It was a little big but now I think it fits well. How do I look?"

She couldn't say anything else because I, I don't know how, crossed the room in a single stride and slapped her with all my strength. I saw a gleam of terror in her eyes, I saw her rock back, lean against the bureau, fall to the floor, and I heard her say, maybe shout, without losing any of her serenity, her theatrical calm, "You're learning how to treat women, Ricardito."

I dropped to the floor next to her and took hold of her shoulders and shook her, crazed, vomiting up my indignation, my fury, my stupidity, my jealousy.

"It's a miracle I'm not at the bottom of the Seine because of you, of you"—the words crowded together in my mouth, my tongue became thick. "These last twenty-four hours you've made me die a thousand times. What game are you playing with me, tell me, what game? Is that why you called me, looked for me, when I finally had freed myself of you? How long do you think I'll put up with it? I have my limits too. I could kill you."

At that moment, in fact, I realized I could have killed her if I went on shaking her. Frightened, I let her go. She was livid and looked at me openmouthed, protecting herself with both arms raised.

"I don't recognize you, you're not yourself," she murmured, and her voice broke. She began to rub her cheek and right temple, which, in the half-light, looked swollen.

"I was on the verge of killing myself over you," I repeated, my voice saturated with rancor and hate. "I climbed onto the railing of the bridge to throw myself in the river and a clochard saved me. A suicide, the thing that was missing in your résumé. Do you think you can go on playing with me this way? It's clear I'll be free of you forever only by killing myself or killing you."

"That's a lie, you don't want to kill yourself or kill me," she said, crawling toward me. "You just want to ball me. Isn't that right? And I want you to ball me too. Or if that language bothers you, to make love to me."

It was the first time I heard her use that word, a Peruvianism I hadn't heard for centuries.

302

She had risen partially to throw herself into my arms and touched my clothing, horrified. "You're soaked, you'll catch a cold, take off that wet clothing, idiot. If you like, you can kill me later, but right now make love to me." She had recovered her serenity and was mistress of the situation. My heart was in my mouth and I could barely breathe. I thought how stupid it would be for me to have a heart attack just at that moment. She helped me take off my jacket, trousers, shoes, shirt—everything looked as if it had just come out of the water—and as she helped me undress, she passed her hand over my hair in that single, rare caress she sometimes deigned to give me. "How your heart is pounding, you little fool," she said a moment later, placing her ear on my chest. "Have I done that to you?" I had begun to caress her too, even though I hadn't yet taken control of my rage. But those feelings were mixing now with a growing desire that she inflamed—she had pulled off the dancer's outfit and, stretching out on top of me, dried me by moving her body along mine, putting her tongue in my mouth, making me swallow her saliva, grasping my sex, caressing it with both hands, and, finally, curling around herself like an eel, placing it in her mouth. I kissed her, caressed her, embraced her, without the delicacy of other times but roughly, still wounded and hurt, and finally I forced her to take my sex out of her mouth and lie under me. She spread her legs, docilely, when she felt my hard sex forcing its way into her. I entered her brutally and heard her howl with pain. But she didn't push me away, and with her body tense, moaning, sobbing softly, she waited for me to ejaculate. Her tears wet my face and I kissed them away. She was pale, her eyes popping, her face distorted by pain.

"It's better if you go, if you really leave me," I implored, trembling from head to foot. "Today I was ready to kill myself and I almost killed you. I don't want that. Go on, find someone else, a man who'll make you live intensely, like Fukuda. A man who'll beat you, lend you to his pals, make you swallow powders so you'll fart in his filthy face. You're not the woman to live with a tiresome hypocrite like me."

She put her arms around my neck and kissed my mouth as I spoke. Her entire body moved to adjust to mine.

"I don't intend to leave now or ever," she whispered in my ear. "Don't ask me why, because I won't tell you even when I'm dead. I'll never tell you I love you even if I do love you."

At that moment I must have passed out, or fallen asleep suddenly, though after her last words, I felt all my strength drain away and everything begin to spin around me. I awoke much later, in the darkened room, feeling a warm body entangled with mine. We were lying under the sheets and blankets, and through the large skylight I saw a star twinkling. It must have stopped raining a while ago because the glass was no longer misted over. The bad girl was pressed against me, her legs entwined with mine and her mouth resting on my cheek. I could feel her heart; it was beating steadily inside me. My anger had vanished and now I was filled with remorse for having hit her and for making her suffer while I made love to her. I kissed her tenderly, trying not to wake her, and whispered soundlessly in her ear, "I love you, I love you, I love you." She wasn't sleeping. She held me closer and spoke to me, placing her lips on mine, while between words her tongue flickered against mine.

"You'll never live quietly with me, I warn you. Because I don't want you to get tired of me, to get used to me. And even if we marry to straighten out my papers, I'll never be your wife. I always want to be your lover, your lapdog, your whore. Like tonight. Because then I'll always keep you crazy about me."

She said these things kissing me without pause and trying to get completely inside my body.

6

Arquímedes, Builder of Breakwaters

Breakwaters are the greatest mystery in engineering,"
Alberto Lamiel exaggerated, spreading his arms wide.
"Yes, Uncle Ricardo, science and technology have solved
all the mysteries of the universe except this one. Didn't
anybody ever tell you that?"

Ever since Uncle Ataúlfo introduced me to his
nephew, an engineer who had graduated from MIT and
was considered the star of the Lamiel family, and who
called me "uncle" even though I wasn't, since I was
Ataúlfo's nephew from a different branch of the family, I
had felt a certain antipathy toward the triumphant
young man: he talked too much, and in an unbearably
pontificating tone. But, evidently, the antipathy wasn't
reciprocal, because since our meeting his attentions
toward me had increased, and he displayed an esteem as
effusive as it was incomprehensible. What interest could
an obscure expatriate translator, back in Peru after so
many years and looking at everything with a mixture of
nostalgia and stupefaction, hold for this brilliant, successful young man who was putting up buildings everywhere in the expansive Lima of the 1980s? I don't know
what it was, but Alberto spent a good deal of time with
me. He took me to see the new neighborhoods—Las

Casuarinas, La Planicie, Chacarilla, La Rinconada, Villa—and the vacation developments springing up like mushrooms on the southern beaches, and he showed me houses surrounded by parks, with lakes and pools, that looked like something in a Hollywood movie. Once, when he heard me say that one of the things I had envied most about my Miraflores friends when I was a boy was that many of them were members of Regatas—I'd had to sneak into the club or swim there from the neighboring beach of Pescadores—he invited me to have lunch at the old Chorrillos institution. Just as he had said, the club's facilities were now very modern, with tennis and jai alai courts, Olympic-size warm-water pools, and two new beaches reclaimed from the ocean thanks to two long breakwaters. It was also true that the Alfresco Restaurant at Regatas prepared a dish of rice and shellfish that was marvelous served with cold beer. The view on this gray, cloudy November afternoon in a winter that refused to leave, with the ghostly cliffs of Barranco and Miraflores half hidden by the fog, stirred up many images from the depths of my memory. What he had just said about breakwaters pulled me away from the idle thoughts that preoccupied me.

"Are you serious?" I asked, my curiosity piqued. "The truth is, I don't believe it, Alberto."

"I didn't believe it either, Uncle Ricardo. But I swear to you it's so."

He was a tall, gringo-looking, athletic boy—he came to Regatas to play racketball and jai alai every morning at six—who wore his dark hair cut very close to the scalp, and breathed self-sufficiency and optimism. He mixed English words into his sentences. He had a fiancée in Boston, whom he was going to marry in a few months, as soon as she completed her degree in chemical engineering. He had turned down several job offers in the United States after graduating with honors from MIT in order to come back to Peru to "serve his country," because if all the privileged Peruvians went abroad, "who'd put their shoulders to the wheel and move our country forward?" His fine patriotic sentiments made me feel guilty, but he didn't realize it. Alberto Lamiel was the only person in his social circle who displayed so much confidence in the future of Peru. During those final months of Fernando Belaúnde Terry's second government—the end of 1984—with runaway inflation, the terrorism of Shining Path, blackouts, kidnappings, and the prospect that APRA, with Alan García, would win next year's elections, there was a good deal of uncertainty and pessimism in the middle class. But nothing seemed to demoralize Alberto. He carried a loaded pistol in his van in case he was attacked, and always had a smile on his face. The possibility of Alan García coming to power didn't frighten him. He had attended a meeting of young entrepreneurs with the Aprista candidate and thought him "pretty pragmatic, not at all ideological."

"In other words, a breakwater doesn't turn out well or badly for technical reasons—correct or mistaken calculations, successes or defects in construction—but because of strange incantations and white or black magic," I said, teasing him. "Is that what you, an engineer from MIT, mean to tell me? Witchcraft has come to Cambridge, Massachusetts?"

"That's exactly right, if you want to put it that way," he said, enjoying the joke. But he became serious again and declared, with energetic movements of his head, "A breakwater works or doesn't work for reasons science can't explain. The subject is so fascinating that I'm writing a brief report for the journal at my university. You'd love meeting my source. His name is Arquímedes, and it fits him to a tee. A character right out of the movies, Uncle Ricardo."

After hearing Alberto's stories, the breakwaters at the Regatas Unión, which we could see from the terrace of the Alfresco, took on the legendary aura of ancestral monuments, stone buttresses erected there, cutting through the sea, not only to force it to withdraw and create an arc of beach for swimmers but as reminders of an ancient lineage, constructions that were half urban, half religious, and products of both expert workmanship and knowledge that was secret, sacred, and mythic rather than practical and functional. According to my presumptive nephew, to construct a breakwater, to determine the precise spot where that assemblage of blocks of stone, superimposed or joined with mortar, should be built, the smallest technical calculation was not sufficient or even necessary. What was indispensable was the "eye" of the practitioner—a kind of wizard, shaman, diviner, like the dowser who discovers deposits of hidden water beneath the surface of the earth, or the Chinese master of feng shui who decides the direction in which a house and its furnishings should be oriented so that future inhabitants can live in peace and enjoy it or otherwise feel harassed and pushed toward discord and friction—who detects on a hunch or by divine knowledge, as old Arquímedes had been doing for half a century along the coast of Lima, where to construct a breakwater so the water accepts it and doesn't overturn it, filling it with sand, undermining it, bending its sides, preventing it from fulfilling its duty of humbling the sea.

"The surrealists would have loved to hear something like this, nephew," I said, pointing to the Regatas' breakwaters, over which white gulls and black ducks were circling, along with a flock of pelicans with philosophical eyes and beaks like ladles. "The breakwater, a perfect example of the marvelous quotidian."

"After you explain to me who the surrealists are, Uncle Ricardo," said the engineer, calling the waiter and indicating to me in a peremptory way that he would pay the bill. "I can see, even though you play the skeptic, that my story about breakwaters has knocked you out."

Yes, I was very intrigued. Was he speaking in earnest? What Alberto told me stayed with me from that day on, leaving and returning to my mind periodically, as if I intuited that if I followed that faint track, I'd suddenly find myself at a cave filled with treasure.

I had returned to Lima for a few weeks, rather hurriedly, with the intention of saying goodbye to and burying Uncle Ataúlfo Lamiel, who had been taken as an emergency case to the American Clinic with his second heart attack, and subjected to open-heart surgery with little hope he'd survive the ordeal. But, surprisingly, he did survive, and in spite of his eighty years and four bypasses, even seemed to be recuperating well. "Your uncle has more lives than a cat," said Dr. Castañeda, the Lima cardiologist who performed the surgery. "The truth is, I didn't think he'd come out of this." Uncle Ataúlfo intervened to say it was my return to Lima that had given him back his life, not any quacks. He had already been discharged from the American Clinic and was convalescing at home, cared for by a full-time nurse and by Anastasia, the maid in her nineties who had been with him all his life. Aunt Dolores had died a few years earlier. Though I tried to stay in a hotel, he insisted on my coming to his small, two-story house, not far from Olivar de San Isidro, where he had more than enough room.

Uncle Ataúlfo had aged a great deal and was now a frail little man who shuffled his feet and was as thin as a broomstick. But he preserved the unrestrained cordiality he'd always had, and he was still alert and curious, reading three or four newspapers a day with the help of a philatelist's magnifying glass and listening to the news every night so he would know how the world we live in was getting on. Unlike Alberto, Uncle Ataúlfo had somber forebodings about the immediate future. He thought that Shining Path and the Túpac Amaru Revolutionary Movement would be with us for some time, and he mistrusted the triumph of APRA in the next elections predicted by the polls. "It will be the coup de grâce for poor Peru, nephew," he complained.

I had returned to Lima after almost twenty years. I felt like a complete stranger in a city where there was almost no trace left of my memories. My aunt Alberta's house had disappeared, and in its place stood an ugly, four-story building. The same thing had happened all over Miraflores, where only a handful of the small houses with gardens from my childhood resisted modernization. The entire neighborhood had been depersonalized with a profusion of buildings of various heights and the multiplication of businesses and aerial forests of neon signs competing with one another in vulgarity and bad taste. Thanks to Alberto Lamiel, the engineer, I had seen the neighborhoods out of *Arabian Nights* where the rich and well-to-do had moved. They were surrounded by the immense districts, now euphemistically called "new towns," the refuge of millions of peasants who came down from the mountains, fleeing hunger and violence—armed actions and terrorism were concentrated principally in the region of the central sierra—and barely getting by in hovels made of straw mats, sticks, tin, rags, whatever they could find, in settlements that for the most part had no water, light, sewers, streets, or transportation. This coexistence of wealth and poverty in Lima made the rich seem richer and the poor seem poorer. On many afternoons, when I didn't go out with my old friends from Barrio Alegre or my new nephew, Alberto Lamiel, I would stay and talk with Uncle Ataúlfo, and this topic returned obsessively to our conversation. It seemed to me that the economic differences between the very small minority of Peruvians who lived well and enjoyed the advantages of education, work, and entertainment, and those who barely survived in poor or wretched conditions, had been exacerbated in the past two decades. According to him, this was a false impression, due to the perspective I had brought from Europe, where the existence of an enormous middle class diluted and wiped away those contrasts between extremes. But in Peru, where the middle class was very small, huge contrasts had always existed. Uncle Ataúlfo was dismayed by the violence that was crushing Peruvian society. "I always suspected this might happen. And now it's here, it has happened. It's just as well poor Dolores didn't live to see it." The kidnappings, the terrorists' bombs, the destruction of bridges, highways, electrical powerhouses, the atmosphere of insecurity and vandalism, he lamented, would set back by many years the country's ascent toward modernity, in which Uncle Ataúlfo had never stopped believing. Until now. "I won't see the ascent now, nephew. I hope you do."

I never could give him a convincing explanation of why the bad girl refused to come to Lima with me, because I didn't have one. He accepted with concealed skepticism the story that she couldn't leave her job because it was precisely the time of year when the company had to handle an overwhelming demand from conventions, conferences, weddings, banquets, and all kinds of celebrations, which prevented her taking a couple of weeks' vacation. In Paris I didn't believe her either when she used this excuse for not coming with me, and I told her so. The bad girl then confessed it wasn't true, that in reality she didn't want to go to Lima. "And why is that, may I ask?" I said, trying to tempt her. "Don't you miss Peruvian food? Well, I propose a couple of weeks with all the delicacies of our national cuisine, ceviche of corvina, prawn stew, rice with duck, cracked ribs, potatoes and eggs with chilies and olives, kid stew, and anything else you might want." There was no way to convince her, she wouldn't accept my enticements, serious or humorous. She wouldn't go to Peru, not now, not ever. She wouldn't set foot there even for a couple of hours. And when I wanted to cancel the trip so she wouldn't be left alone, she insisted I go, claiming the Gravoskis would be in Paris then, and she could turn to them if she needed help at any time.

Finding that job had been the best remedy for her state of mind. It also helped her, I think, when after overcoming a thousand complications, we married and she became, according to what she sometimes told me at moments of intimacy, "a woman who, when she was almost forty-eight years old, had her papers in order for the first time in her life." I thought that for the restless, freewheeling person she always had been, working in a company that organized "social events" would soon bore her, and she would be an employee so incompetent they would fire her. This didn't happen. On the contrary, in a short time she earned the confidence of the woman who hired her. And she took very seriously being busy, doing things, taking on obligations, even if it was asking prices at hotels and restaurants, making comparisons and negotiating discounts, finding out what the businesses, associations, and families really wanted—what kinds of landscapes, hotels, menus, shows, orchestras—for their meetings, banquets, anniversaries. She worked not only at the office but at home as well. In the afternoons and evenings I heard her, glued to the telephone, discussing the details of contracts with infinite patience, or reporting to Martine, her employer, on the arrangements made that day. Sometimes she had to travel to the provinces—generally to Provence, the Côte d'Azur, or Biarritz—either with Martine or as her representative. Then she would call every night and tell me, with a wealth of detail, what she had done that day. It had been good for her to be occupied, acquire responsibilities, and earn money. Once again she dressed flirtatiously, went to hairdressers, masseuses, manicurists, pedicurists, and constantly surprised me with a change in makeup, hairdo, or outfit. "Do you do this to be fashionable or to keep your husband forever in love?" "I do it above all because clients love to see me looking attractive and elegant. Are you jealous?" Yes, I was. I still was head over heels in love with her, and I think she was with me too, because except for small, passing crises, since the night I almost threw myself into the Seine I had noticed details in our relationship that would have been unthinkable before. "This two-week separation will be a test," she said on the night I left. "We'll see if you love me even more or leave me for one of those mischievous Peruvian girls, good boy." "As far as mischievous Peruvian girls go, I have more than enough with you." She had kept her slender figure—on weekends she always went to the gym on Avenue Montaigne to exercise and swim—and her face was still fresh and animated.

Our marriage had been a true bureaucratic adventure. Though it calmed her to know she now had her situation normalized at last, I suspected that if one day, for whatever reason, the French authorities began to dig through her papers, they would discover that our marriage was invalid because it had so many defects in form and substance. But I didn't tell her that, least of all now, when the French government had just granted her citizenship two years after our marriage, not suspecting that the new Madame Ricardo Somocurcio had already been made a naturalized French citizen through an earlier marriage under the name of Madame Robert Arnoux.

In order for us to marry, we had to create false papers for her, using a name different from the one she had when she married Robert Arnoux. We wouldn't have managed without the help of Uncle Ataúlfo. When I described the problem for him, in very broad strokes, without giving him any explanations except the indispensable ones and avoiding the scandalous details of the bad girl's life, he responded immediately, saying he didn't need to know anything else. Underdevelopment has rapid, though somewhat complicated, solutions for cases like this. And no sooner said than done: in a few weeks he sent me birth and baptismal certificates, issued by the municipality and parish of Huaura, in the name of Lucy Solórzano Cajahuaringa, and with them, following his instructions, we appeared before the Peruvian consul in Brussels, who was a friend of his. Uncle Ataúlfo had told him earlier, in a letter, that Lucy Solórzano, the fiancée of his nephew Ricardo Somocurcio, had lost all her papers, including her passport, and needed a new one. The consul, a human relic wearing a waistcoat, watch chain, and monocle, received us with cool, prudent good breeding. He didn't ask a single question, by which I understood that Uncle Ataúlfo had told him more things than he appeared to know. He was courteous, impersonal, and respectful of all the forms. He communicated with the Ministry of Foreign Relations, and through the ministry with the government and police, and sent copies of my fiancée's birth and baptismal certificates, requesting authorization to issue a new document. At the end of two months the bad girl had a new passport and a new identity, with which we could obtain, in Belgium, a tourist visa for France, endorsed by me, a nationalized French citizen residing in Paris. We immediately began the application process at the mayor's office in the fifth arrondissement, on Place du Panthéon. There we finally were married on an autumn afternoon in October 1982, accompanied only by the Gravoskis, who acted as witnesses. There was no wedding banquet or any kind of celebration, because that same afternoon I left for Rome with a two-week contract at the Food and Agriculture Organization.

The bad girl was much better. At times it was difficult for me to see her leading a life that was so normal, enjoying her work and, it seemed to me, happy in, or at least resigned to, our petit bourgeois life, working hard all week, preparing supper at night, going to the movies, the theater, an art show, or a concert, and eating out on weekends, almost always by ourselves, or with the Gravoskis when they were here, for they were still spending several months a year in Princeton. We saw Yilal only in the summer; for the rest of the year he was in school in New Jersey. His parents had decided he should be educated in the United States. There was no trace of his old problem. He spoke and grew normally, and seemed very well integrated into the world of the United States. He sent us postcards or an occasional letter, and the bad girl wrote to him every month and was always sending him presents.

Though they say only imbeciles are happy, I confess that I felt happy. Sharing my days and nights with the bad girl filled my life. In spite of her affection toward me, compared to how icy she had been in the past, she had, in fact, succeeded in making me live in constant uneasiness, apprehensive that one day, when least expected, she would return to her old ways and disappear without saying goodbye. She always managed to let me know — or, I should say, guess — that there was more than one secret in her daily life, a dimension of her existence to which I had no access, one that could give rise at any moment to an earthquake that would topple our life together. I hadn't gotten it into my head yet that Lily, the Chilean girl, would accept the rest of her life being what it was now: the life of a middle-class Parisian, without surprises or mystery, submerged in strict routine and devoid of adventure.

We were never so close as in the months following what we might call our reconciliation on the night the anonymous clochard emerged from the rain and darkness on the Pont Mirabeau to save my life. "Wasn't it God himself who grabbed your legs, good boy?" she asked mockingly. She never fully believed I was on the verge of killing myself. "When people want to commit suicide, they do it, and there's no clochard who can stop them, Ricardito," she said more than once. During this time she still suffered occasionally from terror attacks. Then, pale as a ghost, with gray lips, ashen skin, and dark circles under her eyes, she would not move away from me for a second. She followed me around the house like a lapdog, holding my hand, clutching at my belt or shirt, because the physical contact gave her a minimum of security without which, she stammered, "I'd fall apart." Seeing her suffer like that made me suffer too. And, at times, the insecurity that possessed her during the crisis was so great that she couldn't even go to the bathroom alone; overwhelmed by embarrassment, her teeth chattering, she asked me to go in with her to the toilet and hold her hand while she did what she needed to do.

I never could get a clear idea of the nature of the fear that would suddenly invade her, undoubtedly because it had no rational explanation. Did it consist of vague images, sensations, presentiments, the foreboding that something terrible was about to crush and annihilate her? "That and much more." When she suffered one of the attacks of fear, which generally lasted a few hours, the bold woman with so much character became as defenseless and vulnerable as a little girl. I would sit her on my lap and have her curl up against me. I felt her trembling, sighing, clinging to me with a desperation that nothing could diminish. After a while, she would fall into a deep sleep. In one or two hours she awoke, feeling fine, as if nothing had happened. All my pleas that she return to the clinic in Petit Clamart were useless. In the end, I stopped insisting because the mere mention of the subject enraged her. During those months, in spite of being so close physically, we hardly ever made love, because not even in the intimacy of bed could she achieve the minimum of tranquility, the momentary surrender that would allow her to yield to pleasure.

Work helped her emerge from this difficult period. The crises didn't disappear all at once, but they did become less frequent and less intense. Now she seemed much better, almost transformed into a normal woman. Well, at heart I knew she'd never be a normal woman. And I didn't want her to be one, because what I loved in her were the indomitable and unpredictable aspects of her personality.

In the talks we had during his convalescence, Uncle Ataúlfo never asked me questions about my wife's past. He would send her his regards, he was delighted to have her in the family, he hoped that one day she would want to come to Lima so he could meet her, because if not, he would have no choice but to visit us in Paris. He had framed the photograph taken on the day of our marriage as we were leaving the mayor's office, with the Panthéon as a backdrop, and kept it on an end table in the living room.

In these conversations, generally in the afternoon after lunch and sometimes lasting for hours, we talked a great deal about Peru. He had been an enthusiastic Belaúndista all his life, but now, sorrowfully, he confessed that Belaúnde Terry's second government had disappointed him. Except for returning the newspapers and television stations expropriated by the military dictatorship of Velasco Alvarado, he hadn't dared to correct any of the pseudo-reforms that had impoverished and inflamed Peru even further and provoked an inflation that would give victory to APRA in the next elections. And, unlike his nephew Alberto Lamiel, my uncle had no illusions concerning Alan García. I told myself that in the country of my birth, from which I was disengaged in an increasingly irreversible way, there undoubtedly were many men and women like him, basically decent people who had dreamed all their lives of the economic, social, cultural, and political progress that would transform Peru into a modern, prosperous, democratic society with opportunities open to all, only to find themselves repeatedly frustrated, and, like Uncle Ataúlfo, had reached old age—the very brink of death—bewildered, asking themselves why we were moving backward instead of advancing and were worse off now, with more discrimination, inequality, violence, and insecurity than when they were starting out.

"How right you were to go to Europe, nephew," was his refrain, which he repeated as he smoothed the graying beard he had grown. "Imagine what would have happened to you if you had stayed here to work, with all these blackouts, bombs, and kidnappings. And the lack of work for young people."

"I'm not so sure, uncle. Yes, it's true, I have a profession that allows me to live in a marvelous city. But there I've become a person without roots, a phantom. I'll never be French, even though I have a passport that says I am. There I'll always be a *métèque*. And I'm no longer Peruvian, because I feel even more of a foreigner here than I do in Paris."

"Well, I suppose you know that according to a survey by the University of Lima, the primary ambition of sixty percent of young people is to go abroad, the immense majority to the United States and the rest to Europe, Japan, Australia, wherever. We can't reproach them, can we? If their country can't give them work, or opportunities, or security, it's legitimate for them to want to leave. That's why I admire Alberto so much. He could have stayed in the United States with a magnificent job but chose to come and break his heart in Peru. I hope he doesn't regret it. He has a great deal of esteem for you, you know that, don't you, Ricardo?"

"Yes, uncle, and I for him. Really, he's very amiable. Thanks to my nephew I've seen Lima's other faces. The faces of the millionaires and of the shantytowns."

Just at that moment the phone rang and it was Alberto Lamiel, calling me.

"Would you like to meet old Arquímedes, the breakwater builder I told you about?"

"Man, of course I would," I said enthusiastically.

"They're building a new jetty at La Punta, and the

322

municipal engineer, Chicho Cánepa, is a friend of mine. Tomorrow morning, if that's all right with you. I'll pick you up at eight. That isn't too early for you, is it?"

"I must be very old, Uncle Ataúlfo, even though I'm only fifty," I said when I hung up. "Because Alberto, being your nephew, is really my cousin. But he insists on calling me uncle. He must think I'm prehistoric."

"It isn't that," Uncle Ataúlfo said with a laugh. "Since you live in Paris, you inspire his respect. Living there is a credential for him, the equivalent of having triumphed in life."

The next morning, punctual as a clock, Alberto came by a few minutes before eight, accompanied by Cánepa, the engineer in charge of work at the Cantolao beach and the pier at La Punta, a mature man with dark glasses and a large beer belly. He got out of Alberto's Cherokee and gave me the front seat. The two engineers wore jeans, sport shirts, and leather jackets. I felt ridiculous in my suit, dress shirt, and tie next to those gentlemen in casual attire.

"Old Arquímedes will make a huge impression on you," Alberto's friend, whom he called "Chicho," assured me. "He's a wonderful madman. I've known him twenty years, and the stories he tells still leave me openmouthed. He's a magician, you'll see. And a terrific storyteller."

"Somebody ought to tape him, I swear, Uncle Ricardo," Alberto joined in. "His tales about breakwaters are terrific, I always try to get him to talk."

"I still can't wrap my mind around what you told me, Alberto," I said. "I keep thinking you were kidding. It seems impossible that to build an ocean jetty, you need a wizard more than you need an engineer."

"Well, you ought to believe it," said Chicho Cánepa with a laugh. "Because if anybody knows that, I do, from bitter experience."

I told him to stop using the formal *usted* with me, I wasn't that old, and from now on we'd use *tú*.

We were following the beach highway, heading for Magdalena and San Miguel at the foot of the naked cliffs, and to our left was a rough sea, half hidden by fog, where some surfers rode the waves in their rubber suits even though it was still winter. Silent, indistinct, they rode the ocean, some with their arms raised to keep their balance. Chicho Cánepa recounted what happened to him with one of the jetties at Costa Verde, which we had just passed, the one that was partially built and had a mast at the tip. The municipality of Miraflores had hired him to widen the road and build two breakwaters to create a beach on the ocean. He had no difficulty with the first one, which was built in the place Arquímedes advised. Chicho wanted the second one to be a symmetrical distance from the other, between the Costa Verde and La Rosa Náutica restaurants. Arquímedes objected: it wouldn't stand up, the sea would swallow it.

"There was no reason for it not to stand up," said the engineer Cánepa emphatically. "I know about these things, it's what I studied. The waves and currents were the same as the ones pounding the first. The backward rush of the water was identical, as well as the depth of the marine base. The laborers insisted I listen to Arquímedes, but it seemed like the whim of an old drunk to justify his pay. And I built it where I wanted to. An evil hour, Ricardo, my friend! I used twice the amount of stones and mortar as in the first, and the damn thing sanded up over and over again. It caused eddies that altered the entire environment and created currents and tides that made the beach dangerous for swimmers. In less than six months the ocean pulverized the damn jetty and left it the ruin you just saw. Each time I pass there my face burns. A monument to my shame! The municipality fined me and I ended up losing money."

"What explanation did Arquímedes give you? Why couldn't the breakwater be built there?"

"The explanations he gives aren't explanations," said Chicho. "They're simpleminded, like: 'The sea won't accept it there, it doesn't fit there, it's going to move there, and if it moves, the water will knock it over.' Nonsense like that, meaningless things. Witchcraft, as you say, or whatever it is. But after what happened to me at Costa Verde, I keep my mouth shut and do what the old man says. As far as breakwaters are concerned, engineering isn't worth anything: he knows more."

The truth was I felt impatient to meet this marvel of flesh and blood. Alberto hoped we would find him watching the ocean. Then Arquímedes became a spectacle: sitting on the beach, his legs crossed like a Buddha, immobile, frozen, he could spend hours scrutinizing the water, in a state of metaphysical communication with the hidden forces of the tides and the gods of the marine depths, questioning them, listening to them, or praying to them in silence. Until, at last, he seemed to come back to life. Muttering something he would rise to his feet and with an energetic gesture proclaim: "Yes, you can," or "No, you can't"—in which case you had to go and find another place favorable to the breakwater.

And then suddenly, when we reached the little square of San Miguel, wet with misty rain, not suspecting the turmoil that would be unleashed deep inside me, it occurred to the engineer Chicho Cánepa to say, "He's a marvelous, fanciful old man. He's always telling the wildest stories, because he also has delusions of grandeur. At one point he fabricated a story about having a daughter in Paris who was going to bring him over there to live with her, in the City of Light!"

It was as if the morning had suddenly turned dark. I felt the acid sometimes produced by an old duodenal ulcer, a sputtering of lights in my head, I don't exactly know what I felt but there were a number of things, and then I knew why, ever since Alberto Lamiel decided at the Regatas Unión to tell me the story of Arquímedes and the breakwaters of Lima, I'd had an uneasy feeling, the strange itch that precedes the unexpected, the premonition of a cataclysm or a miracle, as if the story contained something that deeply concerned me. I barely could control my desire to shower Chicho Cánepa with questions about what he had just said.

As soon as we got out of the van on the Figueredo de Punta seawall, facing the beach at Cantolao, I knew who Arquímedes was without their needing to point him out to me. He wasn't sitting still. He was walking with his hands in his pockets along the shore where gentle waves came to die on the little beach of black stones and pebbles that I hadn't seen since my adolescence. He was an ashen, wretched, emaciated cholo, a mestizo with thin, disheveled hair, someone who had surely passed long ago into the time when old age begins, the consolatory season when chronological distances disappear and a man can be seventy, eighty, even ninety years old without anyone noticing the difference. He wore a threadbare blue shirt with hardly a button left on it, which the wind of the cold, gray morning inflated like a sail, revealing the old man's hairless, bony chest as, slightly bent and stumbling over the stones on the beach, he went back and forth, striding like a heron and threatening to fall down at each step.

"That's him, isn't it?" I asked.

"Who else would it be?" said Chicho Cánepa. And cupping his hands, he shouted: "Arquímedes! Arquímedes! Come here, somebody wants to meet you. Just think, he came all the way from Europe to see your face."

The old man stopped and his head gave a jerk. He looked at us, disconcerted. Then he nodded and came toward us, balancing on the black and lead-colored stones on the beach. When he was closer, I could see him more clearly. His cheeks were sunken, as if he had lost all his teeth, and his chin was divided by a cleft that could very well have been a scar. The liveliest and most powerful part of his person was his eyes, small, watery, but intense and belligerent, which looked without blinking, with insolent fixity. He must have been very old, given the wrinkles on his forehead and around his eyes, the ones that gave his neck the appearance of a rooster's crest, and the gnarled hand with black nails he held out to greet us.

"You're so famous, Arquímedes, that even if you don't believe it, my uncle Ricardo has come from France to meet the great builder of breakwaters in Lima," Alberto said, slapping him on the back. "He wants you to explain to him how and why you know where to build a breakwater and where not to."

"You can't explain it," the old man said, shaking my hand and spraying saliva when he talked. "You feel it in your gut. Happy to meet you, caballero. Are you a Frenchy?"

"No, I'm Peruvian. But I've lived there for many years."

He had a faint, high-pitched voice and barely said the end of his words, as if he lacked the breath to pronounce all the letters. Almost without a pause, as soon as he greeted me he turned to Chicho Cánepa.

"I'm sorry, but I think you won't be able to build here, engineer."

"What do you mean, 'think'?" The engineer was furious and raised his voice. "Are you sure or not?"

"I'm not sure," the old man admitted, uncomfortable, wrinkling his face even more. He paused, and taking a quick look at the ocean, he added, "I mean, I don't even know if I'm sure. Don't get angry with me, but something's telling me no."

"Don't fuck around, Arquímedes," the engineer Cánepa protested, waving his arms. "You have to give me a definitive answer. Or I won't pay you, damn it."

"It's just that sometimes the ocean's a crafty female, one of those who say 'Yes, but no,' and 'No, but yes.'" The old man laughed, opening wide his large mouth where barely two or three teeth were visible. And then I realized his breath was saturated with the sharp, acrid smell of some very strong cane liquor, or pisco.

"You're losing your powers, Arquímedes," said my nephew Alberto, giving him another affectionate slap on the back. "You never had doubts about these things before."

"I don't think that's true, engineer," said Arquímedes, becoming very serious. He pointed at the greenish-gray water. "These are things of the sea, and the sea has its secrets, like everybody else. I almost always know at the first look if you can or you can't. But this Cantolao beach is fucked-up, it has its little tricks and throws me off."

The undertow and the noise of the waves breaking against the stones on the beach were very strong, and at times I couldn't hear the old man's voice. I noticed a tic: from time to time he would raise a hand to his nose and brush it very rapidly, as if chasing away an insect.

Two men approached wearing boots and canvas jackets with yellow letters printed on them that said "Municipality of Callao." Chicho Cánepa and Alberto took them aside. I heard Cánepa say to them, not caring if Arquímedes heard, "Now it seems the asshole isn't sure if we can or we can't. So we'll just have to make the decision ourselves."

The old man was next to me but didn't look at me. Again his eyes were fixed on the ocean, and at the same time he moved his lips slowly, as if praying or talking to himself.

"Arquímedes, I'd like to invite you to lunch," I said in a quiet voice. "So you can talk to me a little about breakwaters. It's a subject I'm very interested in. Just the two of us. All right?"

He turned his head and fixed his quiet, and now serious, eyes on me. My invitation had disconcerted him. A mistrustful expression appeared among his wrinkles and he frowned.

329

"Lunch?" he repeated, confused. "Where?"

"Wherever you want. Anyplace you like. You choose the spot and it's my treat. All right?"

"When?" The old man played for time, scrutinizing me with growing suspicion.

"Now. Today, for example. Let's say I pick you up right here, about twelve, and we go to have lunch anywhere you choose. All right?"

After a while he nodded, still looking at me as if I suddenly had turned into something that threatened him. "What the hell can this individual want with me?" his calm, liquid, yellowish-gray eyes were asking.

When, half an hour later, Arquímedes, Alberto, Chicho Cánepa, and the men from the Municipality of Callao had finished arguing, and my nephew and his friend walked up to the van they had parked on the Figueredo seawall, I told them I was staying. I wanted to walk around La Punta, remembering my youth, when I sometimes came to the dances at Regatas Unión with my friends from the Barrio Alegre to flirt with the little blond Lecca twins who lived nearby and took part in the summer sailing championships. I'd go back to Miraflores in a taxi. They were a little surprised, but finally they left, not without suggesting that I be very careful where I went, Callao was full of hoodlums, and muggings and abductions had recently become the order of the day.

I took a long walk along the Figueredo, Pardo, and Wiese seawalls. The large mansions from forty or fifty years ago looked faded, smaller, stained by dampness and time, their gardens withered. Though clearly in decline, the neighborhood retained traces of its former splendor, like an aged woman who trails behind her a shadow of the beauty she once had been. I peered through the fence at the installations of the Naval School. I saw one group of cadets marching in their ordinary white uniforms, and another at the end of the embarcadero, tying a launch up to the dock. And meanwhile I kept repeating to myself: "It's impossible. It's absurd. A wild idea that makes no sense. Forget about the fantasy, Ricardo Somocurcio." It was madness to suppose an association like that. But at the same time, I reflected that enough had happened to me in life for me to know nothing was impossible, that the most outlandish and unbelievable coincidences and incidents could occur when the woman who was now my wife was involved. In spite of the dozens of years I hadn't been back here, La Punta hadn't changed as much as Miraflores, it still had a seigneurial, out-of-fashion air, an impoverished elegance. Now some impersonal, oppressive buildings had appeared among the houses, as they had in my old neighborhood, but there weren't many of them, and they didn't completely destroy the general harmony. The streets were almost deserted except for an occasional maid coming home from shopping, an occasional housewife pushing a baby carriage or taking her dog out to urinate along the shore.

At twelve o'clock I returned to the beach at Cantolao, now almost entirely covered by fog. I saw Arquímedes in the posture Alberto had described to me: sitting like a Buddha, motionless, staring at the sea. He was so still that a flock of white gulls walked around him, indifferent to his presence, pecking between the rocks, looking for something to eat. The noise of the tide was stronger.

Periodically, the gulls screeched together: a sound between hoarse and shrill, at times strident.

"The breakwater can be built," said Arquímedes when he saw me, with a little smile of triumph. And he snapped his fingers. "I'll give Engineer Cánepa a nice surprise."

"So now you're certain?"

"Very certain, sure I am," he said, nodding several times and using a boastful tone. His eyes gleamed with satisfaction.

He pointed at the ocean with absolute conviction, as if showing me that the evidence was there for anyone who bothered to see it. But the only thing I saw was a line of greenish-gray water, stained with foam, crashing against the stones, making a symmetrical, clamorous noise for a few moments then withdrawing, leaving behind tangles of dark brown seaweed. The fog was advancing and soon would envelop us.

"You amaze me, Arquímedes. What talents you have! What happened between this morning, when you were doubtful, and now, when you're finally sure? Have you seen something? Heard something? Was it a hunch, a premonition?"

I saw that the old man was having difficulties getting up, and I helped him, taking his arm. It was very thin, with no muscles and soft bones, like the limb of an amphibian.

"I *felt* they could," Arquímedes explained, then immediately fell silent, as if that verb could clarify the entire mystery.

In silence we climbed the stony beach toward the Figueredo seawall. The old man's shoes, riddled with holes, sank into the stones, and since he seemed about to fall, I took his arm again to hold him up, but he pulled away with a gesture of annoyance.

"Where do you want to go for lunch, Arquímedes?"

He hesitated for a second and then pointed toward the blurred, ghostly horizon of Callao.

"There, in Chucuito, I know a place," he said doubtfully. "The Chim Pum Callao. They make good ceviches, with nice, fresh fish. Sometimes Engineer Chicho goes there to down pork and onion sandwiches."

"Terrific, Arquímedes. Let's go there. I like ceviche a lot and haven't had a pork and onion sandwich in ages."

As we walked toward Chucuito accompanied by a cold wind, listening to the screech of the gulls and the clamor of the ocean, I told Arquímedes that the name of the restaurant reminded me of the fans of the Sport Boys, the famous soccer team of Callao, who, at matches in the Estadio Nacional on Calle José Díaz, would deafen the stands when I was a boy with the thundering cry "Chim Pum! Callao! Chim Pum! Callao!" And in spite of all the years that had passed, I always remembered that miraculous pair of forwards on the Sport Boys, Valeriano López and Jerónimo Barbadillo, the terror of all the defensive players who faced that lineup of pink shirts.

"I knew Barbadillo and Valeriano López when we were all kids," the old man said; he walked somewhat timidly, looking down at the ground, and the wind blew through his thin, whitish hair. "We even kicked a ball around together sometimes in the Estadio del Potao where the Sport Boys trained, or in empty lots in Callao. Before they became famous, I mean. Back then, soccer players played just for glory. Maybe they got a few tips once in a while. I liked soccer a lot. But I never was a good player, I didn't have the stamina. I got tired fast, and by the second quarter I'd be panting like a dog."

"Well, you have other skills, Arquímedes. Very few people in the world know what you've mastered: where to build breakwaters. It's a skill that's yours alone, I assure you."

The Chim Pum Callao was a ramshackle little food stand on one of the corners of the Parque José Gálvez. The surrounding area was full of bums and kids selling candies, lottery tickets, peanuts, or candied apples from little wooden carts or planks laid on sawhorses. Arquímedes must have gone there frequently because he waved at passersby, and some street dogs approached and wrapped themselves around his feet. When we walked into the Chim Pum Callao, the owner, a fat black woman with her hair in rollers who was working behind the counter, a long board resting on two barrels, greeted him affectionately: "Hello, Old Man Breakwater." There were about ten rough tables, with benches for seats, and only part of the roof was covered with galvanized metal; through the other part you could see the winter sky, cloudy and sad. A radio played "Pedro Navaja," a salsa by Rubén Blades, at top volume. We sat at a table near the door, ordered ceviches, pork and onion sandwiches, and an ice-cold Pilsen beer.

The black owner with the rollers was the only woman in the place. Almost all the tables were occupied by two, three, or four patrons, men who probably worked nearby because some had on the smocks that employees of the cold-storage plants wore, and at one table there were electricians' helmets and bags at the end of the benches.

"What is it you wanted to know, caballero?" Arquímedes opened fire. He looked at me, full of curiosity, and at regular intervals raised his hand to his nose to brush it and chase away a nonexistent insect. "I mean, why this invitation?"

"How did you learn you had the ability to read the ocean's intentions?" I asked. "Were you a boy? A young man? Tell me. I'm very interested in everything you can tell me."

He shrugged, as if he didn't remember or the matter wasn't worth thinking about. He murmured that once a reporter from *La Crónica* came to interview him about it, and it seemed he said nothing. Finally, he murmured, "These aren't things that go through my head, and that's why I can't explain it. I know where they can and where they can't. But sometimes I'm in the dark. I mean, I don't feel anything." He fell silent again for a long time. But as soon as they brought the beer and we toasted each other and had a drink, he began to talk and tell me about his life with a fair amount of fluency. He was born not in Lima but in the sierra, in Pallanca, though his family came down to the coast when he had just begun to walk, so he had no memory of the sierra and it was as if he'd been born in Callao. In his heart he felt like a real Callaoan. He learned to read and write at District School Number 5, in Bellavista, but didn't finish primary school because, to "fill the stew pot for the family," his father put him to work selling ice cream, riding a tricycle for La Deliciosa, a very famous ice-cream shop that was gone now but once had been on Avenida Sáenz Peña. As a boy and a young man he had done a little of everything: carpenter's helper, bricklayer, errand boy for a customs office, until finally he went to work as a helper on a fishing boat based at the Terminal Marítimo. There he began to discover, without knowing how or why, that he and the sea "understood each other like a team of oxen." He could smell out before anybody else did where to throw the nets because that's where schools of anchovies would come looking for food, and also where not to because jellyfish would frighten away the fish and not even a miserable catfish would go for the hook. He remembered very well the first time he helped build a jetty in the Callao sea, up around La Perla, more or less where Avenida de las Palmeras ends. All the efforts of the foremen to make the structure stand up to the surf failed. "What the hell's going on, why does this damn son of a bitch sand up all the time?" The contractor, a Chinese-cholo grouch from Chiclayo, was tearing his hair out and telling the ocean and everybody else to go fuck themselves. But no matter how much he goddamned and go-fucked, the ocean said no. And, caballero, when the ocean says no, it's no. Back then he wasn't twenty yet and was feeling jumpy because he still could be called up for military service.

Then Arquímedes started to think, to reflect, and instead of calling it a whore, it occurred to him "to talk to the ocean." And, even more important, "to listen to it the way you listen to a friend." He raised his hand to his ear and adopted an attentive, humble expression, as if he were receiving the secret confidences of the ocean right now. The priest from the Church of Carmen de la Legua once said, "Do you know who it is you're listening to,

Arquímedes? It's God. He tells you the wise things you say about the sea." Well, maybe, maybe God lived in the sea. And that's how it happened. He began to listen, and then, caballero, the sea made him feel that instead of building there, where the sea didn't want the breakwater, if they built fifty meters to the north, toward La Punta, "the sea would accept it." He went and told the contractor. At first the Chiclayan almost pissed himself laughing, you can imagine. But then, in sheer desperation, he said, "Let's give it a try, damn it." They tried in the spot Arquímedes suggested, and the breakwater stopped the sea cold. It's still there, all of it, resisting the rough surf. Word got around and Arquímedes acquired a reputation as a "wizard," a "magician," a "breakwater conjuror." Since then no breakwater was built anywhere in Lima bay without the foremen or engineers consulting him. Not only in Lima. They had taken him to Cañete, Pisco, Supe, Chincha, lots of places, for him to advise on the construction of jetties. He was proud to say that in his long professional life, he had made very few mistakes. Though sometimes he had, because the only one who's never wrong is God, caballero, and maybe the devil.

The ceviche burned as if the chili it contained were Arequipa *rocoto*. When the bottle of beer was empty, I ordered another, which we drank slowly, enjoying some excellent pork sandwiches on French bread with a wonderful sauce of lettuce, onion, and chilies. Animated by the glasses of beer, during one of Arquímedes' silences I finally dared ask the question that had been burning my throat for the past three hours.

"They told me you have a daughter in Paris. Is that true, Arquímedes?"

337

He sat looking at me, intrigued at my knowing intimate details about his family. And gradually the expansive expression on his face turned sour. Before answering he brushed his nose furiously and with a crack of his hand chased away the invisible insect.

"I don't want to know anything about that heartless girl," he growled. "And I want to talk about her even less, caballero. I swear, even if she repented and came to see me, I'd slam the door in her face."

When I saw how angry he was, I apologized for my impertinence. I had heard about his daughter from one of the engineers this morning, and since I lived in Paris too, I became curious and wondered if I knew her. I wouldn't have mentioned it if I thought it would irritate him.

Without responding at all to my explanations, Arquímedes kept eating his sandwich and sipping his beer. Since he hardly had any teeth, it was difficult for him to chew, and he made noises with his tongue and took a long time to swallow each mouthful. Uncomfortable with the long silence, convinced I had committed an error by asking about his daughter—what were you expecting to hear, Ricardito?—I raised my hand to call over the black woman in rollers and ask for the check. And at that moment, Arquímedes began talking again.

"Because she's an unfeeling girl, I swear," he declared, frowning with a very severe expression. "She didn't send money even for her mother's funeral. An egotist is what she is. She went over there and turned her back on us. She must think she's moved up in the world and that gives her the right to despise us now. As if she didn't carry the blood of her father and mother in her veins."

He was in a rage. When he spoke he grimaced, and that wrinkled his face even more. Again I murmured that I was sorry I had brought up the subject, it hadn't been my intention to make him angry, we ought to talk about something else. But he wasn't listening to me. In his staring eyes the pupils were gleaming, liquid and incandescent.

"I lowered myself and asked her to bring me over there when I could have ordered her to, I'm her father after all," he said, banging the table. His lips were trembling. "I lowered myself, I humbled myself. She didn't have to support me, nothing like that. I'd work at anything. Like helping to build breakwaters. Don't they build breakwaters in Paris? Well, then, I could work doing that. If I'm good here, why not there? The only thing I asked her for was a ticket. Not for her mother, not for her brothers. Just for me. I'd break my back, I'd earn and save and slowly bring over the rest of the family little by little. Was that too much to ask? It was very little, almost nothing. And what did she do? She never answered another letter. Not one, ever again, as if the idea of seeing me turn up there terrified her. Is that what a daughter does? I know why I say she became an unfeeling girl, caballero."

The black woman in rollers approached the table, swinging her hips like a panther, but instead of the check I asked her for another cold bottle of beer. Old Arquímedes had spoken so loudly that people at several tables turned to look at him. When he realized this he apologized, coughed, and lowered his voice.

"At first she did remember her family, I have to say that too. Well, only once in a while, but something's better than nothing," he continued more calmly. "Not when she was in Cuba; there, it seems, because of political things, she couldn't write letters. At least, that's what she said later, when she went to live in France and was already married. And then yes, from time to time, for the Patriotic Festival, or my birthday, or Christmas, she'd send a letter and a check. What a mess trying to cash it. Taking identity papers to the bank, and the bank charging I don't know how much in commissions. But in those days, though it didn't happen too often, she remembered she had a family. Until I asked her for the ticket to France. That's when she cut it off. Never heard from her again. Not to this day. As if all her relatives had died. She buried us, I tell you. She didn't bother to answer even when one of her brothers wrote asking for help to put up a marble tombstone for their mother."

I poured Arquímedes a glass of the foaming beer that the black woman in rollers had just brought, and I poured another for myself. Cuba, married in Paris: no doubt about it. Who else could it be? Now I started to tremble. I felt uneasy, as if some terrible revelation would emerge at any moment. I said, "Cheers, Arquímedes," and we both took a long drink. From where I was sitting I could see one of the old man's sneakers, full of holes, and a bony ankle, scabbed or dirty, where an ant was crawling that he didn't seem to feel. Was a coincidence like this possible? Yes, it was. I had no doubt about that now.

"I think I met her once," I said, pretending I was talking just to make conversation and had no personal interest. "Your daughter was on a scholarship to Cuba for a while, wasn't she? And then she married a French diplomat, right? A gentleman named Arnoux, if I'm not mistaken."

"I don't know if he was a diplomat or what, she never even sent a photograph," Arquímedes grumbled, brushing his nose. "But he was an important Frenchy and he earned good money, that's what they said. In a case like that, doesn't a daughter have obligations to her family? Especially if her family is poor and suffering hardships."

He took another sip of beer and was lost in thought for a long time. Some chicha-fueled music, off-key and monotonous, sung by Los Shapis, replaced the salsa. At the table to the side, the electricians were talking about Sunday's horse races and one of them swore: "Cleopatra's a sure thing in the third." Suddenly, remembering something, Arquímedes raised his head and stared at me with feverish eyes.

"You knew her?"

"I think so, vaguely."

"That guy, the Frenchy, he had a lot of money, didn't he?"

"I don't know. If we're talking about the same person, he was a functionary at UNESCO. A good position, no doubt about it. Your daughter, the times I saw her, was always very well dressed. She was a good-looking, elegant woman."

"Otilita always dreamed about what she didn't have, ever since she was little," Arquímedes said suddenly, sweetening his voice and breaking into an unexpected smile full of indulgence. "She was very lively, at school she won prizes. And she had delusions of grandeur from

341

the day she was born. She was never resigned to her fate."

I couldn't control my laughter, and the old man looked at me, disconcerted. Lily the Chilean girl, Comrade Arlette, Madame Robert Arnoux, Mrs. Richardson, Kuriko, and Madame Ricardo Somocurcio was, in reality, named Otilia. Otilita. How funny.

"I never would have imagined her name was Otilia," I explained. "I met her under another name, her husband's, Madame Robert Arnoux. That's what they do in France, when a woman marries she takes her husband's first and last names."

"People's ways are funny," remarked Arquímedes, smiling and shrugging. "Has it been a long time since you saw her?"

"A long time, yes. I don't even know if she still lives in Paris. If she's the same person, obviously. The Peruvian girl I'm telling you about had been in Cuba and got married there, in Havana, to a French diplomat. Then he took her to live in Paris, in the 1960s. That's where we saw each other the last time, it must be four or five years ago. I remember she talked a lot about Miraflores, she said she spent her childhood in that neighborhood."

The old man nodded. In his watery eyes, nostalgia had displaced fury. He held up the glass of beer and blew at the foam around the edge, slowly, evening it out.

"That's her," he declared, nodding several times as he brushed his nose. "Otilita lived in Miraflores when she was little because her mother worked as a cook for a family who lived there. The Arenas family."

"On Calle Esperanza?" I asked.

342

The old man nodded, staring at me in surprise. "You know that too? How come you know so many things about Otilita?"

I thought, How would he react if I said: Because she's my wife?

"Well, as I said. Your daughter always remembered Miraflores and the little house on Calle Esperanza. It's a neighborhood where I lived as a boy too."

Behind the counter, the black woman in rollers was following the dislocated beat of Los Shapis, moving her head from side to side. Arquímedes took a long drink and was left with a ring of foam around his sunken lips.

"Since she was this high, Otilita felt ashamed of us," he said, frowning again. "She wanted to be like the whites, the rich people. She was a smart-alecky kid, very crafty. Pretty smart, but always taking risks. Not everybody can move to another country without a cent, like she did. Once she won a contest, on Radio América. Imitating Mexicans, Chileans, Argentines. I don't think she could have been more than nine or ten years old. They gave her a pair of skates for a prize. She conquered the family where her mother worked as a cook. The Arenas family. She won them over, I tell you. They treated her like a member of the family. They let her be friends with their own daughter. They spoiled her. After that she was even more ashamed of being the daughter of her own mother and father. I mean, from the time she was little you could see how she'd turn her back on her family when she was grown."

Suddenly, at this point in the conversation, I began to feel a little sick. What was I doing here, sticking my nose into these sordid, intimate details? What else did you

343

want to know, Ricardito? What for? I began to look for an excuse to say goodbye, because without warning the Chim Pum Callao had turned into a prison cell. Arquímedes went on talking about his family. Everything he said made me sadder and more depressed. Apparently he had a slew of children, by three different women, "all of them recognized." Otilita was the oldest daughter of his first wife, now deceased. "Feeding twelve mouths can kill you," he repeated with a resigned expression. "It wore me out. I don't know how I still have the strength to earn my bread, caballero." In fact, he did look exhausted and frail. Only his eyes, lively and strong, showed a will to go on; the rest of his body seemed defeated and fearful.

It must have been two hours at least since we came into the Chim Pum Callao. All the tables were empty except ours. The owner turned off the radio, suggesting it was time to close. I asked for the check, paid it, and when we walked out, I asked Arquímedes to accept a gift of a hundred-dollar bill.

"If you ever run into Otilita again over there in Paris, tell her to remember her father and not be such a bad daughter, or in the next world they might punish her." The old man extended his hand.

He stood looking at the hundred-dollar bill as if it had fallen from the sky. He was so moved, I thought he was going to cry. He stammered, "A hundred dollars! God bless you, caballero." I thought, What if I told him: You're my father-in-law, Arquímedes, can you believe it?

I waited for a while on Plaza José Gálvez, and when a dilapidated taxi finally appeared and I signaled it to stop, a swarm of ragged children surrounded me, hands outstretched, asking for money. I told the driver to take me to Calle Esperanza, in Miraflores.

On the long ride in the clattering jalopy that was belching smoke, I regretted having instigated the conversation with Arquímedes. I felt sad down to the marrow of my bones when I thought about what Otilita's childhood must have been like in one of those Callao shantytowns. Knowing it was impossible for me to approach a reality so remote from the Miraflores life I had been lucky enough to experience, I imagined her as a little girl, in the crowding and grime of the hovels thrown up somehow on the banks of the Rímac—as we drove past them, the taxi filled with flies—where dwellings were intermingled with pyramids of garbage accumulating there for who knows how long, and I imagined each day's want, precariousness, insecurity, until, providential gift, the mother obtained a job as cook for a middle-class family in a residential neighborhood and managed to bring along her oldest daughter. I imagined the artfulness, the flattery, the charm used by Otilita, the girl endowed with an exceptionally well-developed instinct for survival and adaptation, until she had won over the lady and gentleman of the house. First they would have laughed at her, then been pleased by how vivacious the cook's little girl was. They would have given her the shoes and dresses that the real daughter of the house, Lucy, the other Chilean girl, had outgrown. This was how Arquímedes' little daughter had climbed up, achieving a place in the Arenas family. Until, finally, she won the right to play and go out as an equal, a friend, a sister, with the daughter of the house, though Lucy attended a private academy and she went to a state school. Now, after thirty years, it was clear why Lily, the Chilean girl of my childhood, didn't want to have a boyfriend and didn't invite anyone to her house on Calle Esperanza. And, above all, it was exceedingly clear why she had decided to stage that performance, to de-Peruvianize herself, to transubstantiate into a Chilean girl so she would be accepted in Miraflores. I felt moved to tears. I was mad with impatience to hold my wife in my arms, I wanted to caress her, stroke her, beg her pardon for the childhood she'd had, tickle her, tell her jokes, play the clown to hear her laugh, promise her that she never would suffer again.

Calle Esperanza hadn't changed very much. I walked up and down twice, back and forth from Avenida Larco to Zanjón. The Minerva Bookstore was still on the corner across from Parque Central, though the Italian woman with white hair, the widow of José Carlos Mariátegui, always so serious as she stood behind the counter and waited on customers, was not there now. Gambrinus, the German restaurant, no longer existed, and neither did the ribbon and button shop where I sometimes went with Aunt Alberta. But the three-story building where the Chilean girls lived was still there. Narrow, squeezed between a house and another building, faded, with little balconies that had wooden railings, it looked very poor and old-fashioned. In the apartment with its dark, narrow rooms, in the tiny hole of a maid's room where her mother would lay a pallet on the floor for her every night, Otilita would have been infinitely less unfortunate than in Arquímedes' house. And, perhaps, right here, when she was still very young, she already had made the rash decision to move forward and do whatever she had to do to no longer be Otilita, daughter of the cook and the builder of breakwaters, to flee forever the trap, the prison, the curse that Peru meant for her, and go far away and become rich—that above all: rich, very rich—though to accomplish this she would have to engage in the worst escapades, run the most awful risks, do anything at all until she became a cold, unloving, calculating, and cruel woman. She achieved this only for short periods of time and paid dearly for it, leaving pieces of her skin and her soul along the way. When I thought of her in the worst moments of her crises, sitting on the toilet, trembling with fear, clutching my hand, I had to make a great effort not to cry. Of course you were right, bad girl, to refuse to return to Peru, to despise the country that reminded you of all you had accepted, suffered, and done to escape. You did very well not to come with me on this trip, my love.

I took a long walk on the streets of Miraflores, following the itineraries of my youth: Parque Central, Avenida Larco, Parque Salazar, the seawalls. My chest was tight with the urgent need to see her, hear her voice. Naturally, I never would tell her I met her father. Naturally, I would never confess I knew her real name. Otilia, Otilita, how funny, it didn't suit her at all. Naturally, I would forget about Arquímedes and everything I had heard this morning.

When I reached his house, Uncle Ataúlfo was already in bed. Anastasia, the old servant, had left my supper on the table, under a napkin to keep it warm. I ate no more than a mouthful, and as soon as I got up from the table, I went into the living room and closed the door. I was

347

sorry to make an international call, because I knew Uncle Ataúlfo wouldn't allow me to pay for it, but I had such a great need to talk to the bad girl, hear her voice, tell her I missed her, that I decided to do it. Sitting in the armchair in the corner where Uncle Ataúlfo read his papers, next to the telephone table, with the room in darkness, I called her. The phone rang several times and nobody answered. The time difference, of course! It was four in the morning in Paris. But precisely for that reason, it was impossible for the Chilean girl—Otilia, Otilita, how funny—not to hear the phone. It was on the night table, next to her ear. And she slept very lightly. The only explanation was that Martine had sent her on one of those business trips. I went up to my room, dragging my feet, frustrated and dejected. Naturally, I couldn't close my eyes because each time I felt sleep coming on I awoke, startled and lucid, and saw the face of Arquímedes sketched in the darkness, looking at me mockingly and repeating the name of his oldest daughter: Otilita, Otilia. Was it possible? No, a stupid idea, an attack of jealousy, ridiculous in a fifty-year-old man. Another little game to keep you worried, Ricardito? Impossible. How could she have suspected that you would phone her now, at this time of night? The logical explanation was that she wasn't home because she had gone on business to Biarritz, Nice, Cannes, any of the beach resorts where they hold conventions, conferences, meetings, weddings, and other pretexts the French find for drinking and eating like gluttons.

I continued calling for the next three days, and she never answered the phone. Consumed by jealousy, I didn't see anything or anybody else; all I did was count the eternal days left until I could take the plane back to Europe. Uncle Ataúlfo noticed my nervous state, though I made exaggerated efforts to seem normal, and perhaps that was precisely the reason. He limited himself to asking me two or three times if I felt all right, because I hardly ate and turned down an invitation from the amiable Alberto Lamiel to go out to eat and then visit an unpretentious club to hear my favorite singer, Cecilia Barraza.

On the fourth day I left for Paris. Uncle Ataúlfo wrote to the bad girl in his own hand, apologizing for stealing her husband for the past two weeks but, he added, this visit by his nephew had been miraculous, helping him through a difficult time and assuring him a long life. I didn't sleep, I didn't eat for the nearly eighteen hours of the flight because of a very long layover of the Air France plane in Pointe-à-Pitre, to repair something that had broken down. What would be waiting for me this time when I opened the door of my apartment in École Militaire? Another note from the bad girl, telling me, with the coldness of the old days, that she had decided to leave because she was sick of the boring life of a petit bourgeois housewife, tired of preparing breakfasts and making beds? Could she go on with those tricks at her age?

No. When I opened the door to the apartment on Rue Joseph Granier—my hand was trembling and I couldn't fit the key into the lock—there she was, waiting for me. She opened her arms to me with a big smile.

"At last! I was getting tired of being alone and abandoned."

She looked as if she were going to a party, wearing a very low-cut dress that bared her shoulders. When I asked her why all the finery, she said, nibbling at my lips, "Because of you, idiot, what else? I've been waiting for you since early this morning, calling Air France over and over again. They said the plane had been delayed in Guadeloupe for several hours. Come on, let me see how they treated you in Lima. You're grayer, I think. From missing me so much, I suppose."

She seemed happy to see me, and I felt relieved and ashamed. She asked if I wanted anything to drink or to eat, and since she saw me yawning, she pushed me toward the bedroom. "Go on, get some sleep, I'll take care of your suitcase." I took off my shoes, trousers, and shirt, and pretending to sleep, I watched her through half-closed eyes. She unpacked slowly, in a very orderly way, concentrating on what she was doing. She separated the dirty clothes and put them in a bag she would take to the laundry afterward. The clean things she carefully arranged in the closet. Socks, handkerchiefs, suit, tie. Once in a while she would glance at the bed, and I thought her expression grew calmer when she saw me there. She was forty-eight years old, and no one seeing her model's figure would believe it. She looked very attractive in the light green dress that left her shoulders and part of her back bare, and with her face so beautifully made-up. She moved slowly, gracefully. Once I saw her approach—I closed my eyes completely and partially opened my mouth, pretending to sleep—and I felt her cover me with the quilt. Could it all be a farce? Absolutely not. But why not, at any moment life with her could turn into theater, into fiction. Should I ask why she hadn't answered the phone these past few days? Try to find out if she had been on a business trip? Or would it be better to forget all about it and sink into this tender lie of domestic happiness? I felt an infinite weariness. Later, when I was beginning to really fall asleep, I felt her lie down beside me. "What an idiot, I woke you." She turned toward me and with one hand rumpled my hair. "You have more and more gray hair, old man," she said with a laugh. She had taken off her dress and shoes, and the slip she wore was a light matte color, similar to her skin.

"I missed you," she said unexpectedly, becoming very serious. She fixed her honey-colored eyes on mine in a way that suddenly reminded me of the stare of the builder of breakwaters. "At night I couldn't sleep, thinking about you. I masturbated almost every night, imagining you were making me come with your mouth. One night I cried, thinking something might happen to you, a sickness, an accident. That you would call to say you had decided to stay in Lima with some Peruvian and I'd never see you again."

Our bodies didn't touch. She kept her hand on my head, but now she passed the tips of her fingers over my eyebrows, my mouth, as if to verify I was really there. Her eyes were still very serious. In their depths was a watery gleam, as if she were holding back a desire to cry.

"Once, so many years ago, in this very room, you asked me what I thought happiness was, do you remember, good boy? And I said it was money, finding a man who was powerful and very rich. I was wrong. Now I know that you're happiness for me."

And at that moment, when I was going to take her in my arms because her eyes had filled with tears, the telephone rang, startling both of us.

"Ah, at last!" the bad girl exclaimed, picking up the receiver. "The damn phone. They finally fixed it. *Oui, oui, monsieur. Ça marche très bien, maintenant! Merci.*"

Before she hung up I threw myself at her and put my arms around her, holding her as tight as I could, kissing her with fury and tenderness, telling her in a rush, "Do you know the nicest thing, the thing that's made me the happiest of all the things you've said to me, Chilean girl? *Oui, oui, monsieur. Ça marche très bien, maintenant.*"

She started to laugh and murmured that this was the least romantic cheap, sentimental thing I had said to her so far. While I undressed her and got undressed myself, I said into her ear, as I kept kissing her, "I called you four days in a row at all hours, at night, at dawn, and when you didn't answer I went mad with desperation. I didn't eat, I didn't live until I could see that you hadn't left, that you weren't with a lover. The life's come back to my body, bad girl." I heard her roll with laughter. When she used both hands to oblige me to move my face away so she could look into my eyes, her laughter kept her from speaking. "Were you really mad with jealousy? What good news, you're still head over heels in love with me, good boy." It was the first time we made love and didn't stop laughing.

Finally we fell asleep, entwined and content. In my sleep I opened my eyes from time to time to see her. I would never be as happy as I was now, I never would feel so fulfilled again. We awoke when it was dark, and after we showered and dressed, I took the bad girl to have supper at La Closerie des Lilas, where, like two lovers on their honeymoon, we spoke softly, looking into each other's eyes, holding hands, smiling, and kissing as we drank a bottle of champagne. "Tell me something nice," she would say from time to time.

When we left La Closerie des Lilas, on the small square where the statue of Marshal Ney menaces the stars with its sword, along Avenue de l'Observatoire, two clochards were sitting on a bench. The bad girl stopped and pointed at them.

"It's him, the one on the right, the clochard who saved your life that night on the Pont Mirabeau, isn't that right?"

"No, I don't think it was him."

"Yes, yes," she said, stamping her foot, angry and upset. "It's him, tell me it's him, Ricardo."

"Yes, yes, it was him, you're right."

"Give me all the money in your wallet," she ordered. "Bills and change both."

I did as she asked. Then, holding the money in her hand, she approached the two clochards. They looked at her as if she were an exotic animal, I imagine, since it was too dark to see their faces. She bent forward, and I saw her speak to him, hand him the money, and finally, what a surprise, kiss the clochard on both cheeks. Then she came toward me, smiling like a little girl who has just done a good deed. She took my arm and we began to walk along Boulevard Montparnasse. It was a good half hour to École Militaire. But it wasn't cold and it wasn't going to rain.

"That clochard must think he's had a dream, that his fairy godmother fell from the sky and appeared to him. What did you say to him?"

"Thank you, Monsieur Clochard, for saving the life of my happiness."

"You're becoming sentimental too, bad girl." I kissed her on the lips. "Tell me another, another cheap, sentimental thing, please."

7

Marcella in Lavapiés

Fifty years ago the Madrid neighborhood of Lavapiés, an old enclave of Jews and Moriscos, was still considered one of the most traditional neighborhoods in Madrid, where, like archaeological curiosities, the swaggering lower-class characters from the operettas called zarzuelas were preserved: flashy young men in waistcoats and caps, wearing handkerchiefs around their necks and tight trousers, and sassy young women in close-fitting polka-dotted dresses, with large earrings and parasols and handkerchiefs tied around hair gathered into sculptural chignons.

When I came to live in Lavapiés, the neighborhood had changed so much I sometimes wondered if in that Babel there was still some authentic Madrilenian left, or if all the residents were, like Marcella and me, imported. The Spaniards from the neighborhood came from every corner of the country, and with their accents and variety of physical types, they helped to give the admixture of races, languages, inflections, customs, attire, and nostalgia in Lavapiés the appearance of a microcosm. The human geography of the planet seemed to be represented in its few blocks.

When you left Calle Ave María, where we lived on

the third floor of a faded, ramshackle building, you found yourself in a Babylon of Chinese and Pakistani merchants, Indian laundries and stores, tiny Moroccan tea shops, bars filled with South Americans, Colombian drug traffickers, and Africans, and wherever you looked, forming groups in doorways and on street corners, a number of Romanians, Yugoslavs, Moldavians, Dominicans, Ecuadorians, Russians, and Asians. The Spanish families in the neighborhood resisted the changes with old habits like having get-togethers between balconies, hanging out clothes to dry on lines hung from eaves and windows, and, on Sundays, going in couples, the men wearing ties and the women dressed in black, to hear Mass at the Church of San Lorenzo, on the corner of Calle Doctor Piga and Calle Salitre.

Our apartment was smaller than the one I'd had on Rue Joseph Granier, or it seemed that way to me because of how crowded it was with the cardboard, paper, and balsa-wood models of Marcella's set designs, which, like Salomón Toledano's little toy soldiers, invaded the apartment's two small rooms, and even the kitchen and tiny bathroom. In spite of being so small and so full of books and records, it wasn't claustrophobic, thanks to the windows onto the street, through which the vivid white light of Castile, so different from Parisian light, streamed in, and because it had a small balcony where we could put a table at night and eat supper under the stars, which do exist in Madrid, though diffused by the reflection of the city's lights.

Marcella managed to work in the apartment, lying on the bed if she was drawing, or sitting on the Afghan rug in the living room if she was constructing her models with pieces of cardboard, bits of wood, glue, paste, coated cardboard, and colored pencils. I preferred to do the translations that the editor Mario Muchnik assigned to me in a nearby café, the Café Barbieri, where I would spend several hours a day translating, reading, and observing the fauna that frequented the café and never bored me, because it incarnated all the many colors of this nascent Noah's ark in the heart of old Madrid.

The Café Barbieri was right on Calle Ave María and seemed—this is what Marcella said the first time she took me there, and she knew about those things—like an expressionist set from 1920s Berlin or an engraving by Grosz or Otto Dix, with its cracked walls, dark corners, medallions of Roman ladies on the ceiling, and mysterious cubicles where it looked as if crimes could be committed without the patrons finding out, or demented sums wagered in poker games in which knives flashed, or Black Masses celebrated. It was enormous, angled, full of uneven floors, silvery cobwebs hanging from gloomy corners of the ceiling, feeble tables and crippled chairs, benches and ledges about to collapse from sheer exhaustion; it was dark, smoky, always filled with people who seemed to be in costume, a crowd of extras from a farcical play waiting in the wings to go onstage. I always tried to sit at a table in the back where a little more light filtered in, and, instead of hard chairs, there was a fairly comfortable armchair covered in velvet that once had been red but was disintegrating from the holes burned into it by cigarettes and the friction of so many rumps. One of my distractions, each time I entered the Café Barbieri, consisted of identifying the languages I heard between the door and the table in the rear, and sometimes I counted half a dozen in that brief passage of some thirty meters.

The waitresses and waiters also represented the diversity of the neighborhood: Swedes, Belgians, North Americans, Moroccans, Ecuadorians, Peruvians, and so forth. They changed all the time, because they must have been badly paid, and for the eight straight hours they worked, in two shifts, the patrons had them carrying and fetching beer, coffee, tea, hot chocolate, glasses of wine, and sandwiches. As soon as I was settled at my usual table, with my notebooks and pens and the book I was translating, they quickly brought me an espresso with a little milk and a bottle of still mineral water.

At the table I would look through the morning papers, and in the afternoon, when I was tired of translating, I would read, not for work now but for pleasure. The three books I had translated, by Doris Lessing, Paul Auster, and Michel Tournier, hadn't been too difficult, but I didn't have a very good time bringing them over into Spanish. Their authors were in fashion, but the novels I was given to translate weren't the best they had written. As I always suspected, literary translations were very poorly paid, the fees much lower than for commercial ones. But I was no longer in any condition to do them, because the mental fatigue that came over me when my effort at concentration was prolonged meant my progress was very slow. In any event, this meager income allowed me to help Marcella with household expenses and not feel like a kept man. My friend Muchnik tried to help me find some translation work from Russian—it was what I wanted most—and we almost convinced an editor to publish Turgenev's *Fathers and Sons* or the staggering *Requiem* by Anna Akhmatova, but it didn't work out because Russian fiction still didn't arouse much interest in Spanish and Latin American readers, and Russian poetry even less.

I couldn't tell if I liked Madrid or not. I didn't know the other neighborhoods of the city, where I barely had ventured on the occasions I went to a museum or accompanied Marcella to a show. But I felt comfortable in Lavapiés, even though I'd been mugged on its streets for the first time in my life by a couple of Arabs who stole my watch, a wallet with some change, and my Mont Blanc pen, my last luxury. The truth is I felt at home here, immersed in its ebullient life. Sometimes, in the afternoon, Marcella stopped by for me at the Barbieri and we would walk through the neighborhood, which I got to know like the back of my hand. I always discovered something curious or odd. For example, the shop and radio studio of the Bolivian Alcérreca, who learned Swahili to better serve his African customers. If they were showing something interesting, we'd go to the Filmoteca to see a classic film.

On these walks, Marcella talked without stopping and I listened. I intervened very occasionally to let her catch her breath, and, by means of a question or observation, encouraged her to go on telling me about the project she wanted to be involved in. Sometimes I didn't pay much attention to what she was saying because I focused so much on how she said it: with passion, conviction, hope, and joy. I never knew anyone who gave herself so totally—so fanatically, I'd say, if the word didn't have gloomy memories—to her vocation, who knew in so exclusionary a way what she wanted to do in life.

We had met years earlier in Paris, at a clinic in Passy where I was having some tests done and she was visiting a friend who had recently had surgery. During the half hour we shared the waiting room, she spoke with so much enthusiasm about a play of Molière's, *The Bourgeois Gentleman*, being shown at a small theater in Nanterre where she had done the set designs, that I went to see it. I ran into Marcella at the theater, and when the play was over I suggested having a drink at a *bistrot* near the Métro station.

We had lived together for two and a half years, the first year in Paris and after that, in Madrid. Marcella was Italian, twenty years younger than me. She had studied architecture in Rome to please her parents, both of whom were architects, and while still a student began to work as a theatrical set designer. Her never having practiced architecture offended her parents, and for some years they were estranged. They reconciled when her parents understood that what their daughter did was not a whim but a true vocation. Occasionally she would spend some time with her parents in Rome, and since she didn't have much money—she was the hardest-working person in the world, but the designs she was hired to do were of small account, in marginal theaters, and she was paid very little, and sometimes nothing at all—her parents, who were fairly well-off, sent her occasional money orders that allowed her to dedicate her time and energy to the theater. She hadn't triumphed, and it wasn't something she cared about very much, because she—and I as well—were absolutely certain that sooner or later theater people in Spain, in Italy, in all of Europe, would come to recognize her talent. Though she spoke a great deal, gesticulating like the caricature of an Italian, she never bored me. I was fascinated to hear her describe the ideas that whirled inside her head about revolutionizing the sets of *The Cherry Orchard*, *Waiting for Godot*, *Harlequin*, *Servant of Two Masters*, or *La Celestina*. She had been hired for the movies as an assistant decorator and could have made her way in that medium, but she liked the theater and was not prepared to sacrifice her vocation, even if it was more difficult to move ahead designing for the theater than for films or television. Thanks to Marcella, I learned to see shows with different eyes, to pay careful attention not only to plots and characters but also to places, the light in which they moved, the things that surrounded them.

She was small, with light hair, green eyes, extremely white smooth skin, and a joyful smile. She exuded energy. She dressed very carelessly, most of the time in sandals, jeans, and a worn sheepskin jacket, and she used glasses for reading and the movies, a pair of tiny rimless glasses that made her expression somewhat clownish. She was unselfish, uncalculating, generous, capable of devoting a good amount of time to insignificant jobs, like the single performance of a play by Lope de Vega put on by the students at an academy, with a set consisting of a few odds and ends and a couple of painted canvases to which she devoted herself with the perseverance of a designer working at the Paris Opéra for the first time. The satisfaction she felt more than compensated for the small or nonexistent monetary reward she brought home from that adventure. If anyone was described by the phrase "working for love of the art," it was Marcella.

Less than a tenth of the models that smothered our apartment had appeared onstage. Most had been frustrated by a lack of financing; they were ideas she'd had after reading a work she liked and for which she conceived a set that didn't go beyond a drawing and a maquette. She never discussed fees when she was hired, and could turn down an important contract if she thought the director or the producer was a pharisee, uninterested in esthetics and attentive only to the commercial side of things. On the other hand, when she accepted a contract—generally from avant-garde groups with no access to established theaters—she devoted herself to it body and soul. She not only had a great desire to do her work well but collaborated in everything else, helping her colleagues to find support, locate a theater, obtain donations and loans of furniture and costumes, and she worked shoulder to shoulder with carpenters and electricians and, if necessary, swept the stage, sold tickets, and seated the audience. It always amazed me to see her so involved in her work that I would have to remind her, during those feverish periods, that a human being doesn't live by theatrical sets alone but also by eating, sleeping, and showing a little interest in the other things in life.

I never understood why Marcella was with me, what I added to her life. In what interested her most in the world, her work, I could help her very little. Everything I knew about theatrical set design she taught me, and the opinions I could offer were superfluous, because like every authentic creator, she knew very well what she wanted to do without any need for advice. All I could be for her was an attentive ear if she needed to express aloud the rush of images, possibilities, alternatives, and doubts that would assail her when she began a project. I listened to her with envy for as long as I had to. I went with her to consult prints and books in the Biblioteca Nacional, to visit artisans and antiquarians, and on the never-failing Sunday excursion to the Rastro. I did this not only out of affection but because what she said was always novel, surprising, at times inspired. I learned something new with her each day. I never would have guessed, without knowing her, how a theatrical story can be influenced so decisively, though always subtly, by the set design, the lighting, the presence or absence of the most ordinary object, a broom or a simple vase.

The twenty-year difference in our ages didn't seem to trouble her. It did trouble me. I always told myself that our good relationship would diminish when I was in my sixties and she was still a young woman. Then she would fall in love with someone her own age. And leave. She was attractive in spite of how little time she spent on her appearance, and on the street men followed her with their eyes. One day when we were making love she asked, "Would you care if we had a baby?" No. If she wanted one, I'd be delighted. But then I was immediately attacked by distress. Why did I have that reaction? Perhaps because, in my fifties, and given my prolonged adventures and misadventures with the bad girl, it was impossible for me to believe in the longevity of any pairing that worked smoothly, including ours. Wasn't that doubt absurd? We got along so well that in our two and a half years together we hadn't had a single fight. At most, minor arguments and passing annoyances. But never anything that resembled a break. "I'm glad you don't care," Marcella said then. "I didn't ask so we could have a *bambino* now, but when we've done some important things." She spoke for herself, someone who undoubtedly would do things in the future worthy of that description. I'd be happy if, in the next few years, Mario Muchnik could get me a Russian book that would require a good deal of effort and enthusiasm to translate, something more creative than light novels that disappeared from memory at the same speed with which I rewrote them in Spanish.

No doubt she was with me because she loved me; she had no other reason. To some extent I was even an economic burden for her. How could she have fallen in love with me, since for her I was an old man, not at all good-looking, without a vocation, somewhat diminished in my intellectual faculties, whose only aim in life had been, since boyhood, to spend the rest of my days in Paris? When I told Marcella that this had been my only vocation, she began to laugh. "Well, *caro*, you achieved it. You must be happy, you've lived in Paris your whole life." She said this affectionately, but her words sounded somewhat sinister to me.

Marcella was more concerned about me than I was: I had to take my blood-pressure pills, walk every day for at least half an hour, and never have more than two or three glasses of wine a day. And she always said that when she got a good commission, we would spend the money on a trip to Peru. Before she saw Cuzco and Machu Picchu, she wanted to visit the Lima neighborhood of Miraflores I talked about so much. I went along with her, though deep down I knew we never would make that trip, because I'd take care to postpone it into eternity. I didn't intend to return to Peru. Since the death of Uncle Ataúlfo, my country had disappeared for me like mirages on sandy ground. I didn't have relatives or friends there, and even the memories of my youth were growing dim.

I learned of Uncle Ataúlfo's death several weeks after the fact, in a letter from Alberto Lamiel, when I had been living in Madrid for six months. Marcella brought it to me at the Barbieri, and though I knew it could happen at any moment, the news had a tremendous impact on me. I stopped working and went to walk, like a somnambulist, along the paths in the Retiro. Since my last trip to Peru, at the end of 1984, my uncle and I had written to each other every month, and in his trembling hand, which I had to decipher like a paleographer, I had followed, step by step, the economic disasters caused in Peru by Alan García's policies: inflation, nationalizations, the rupture with credit entities, control of prices and exchange rates, falling employment and standards of living. Uncle Ataúlfo's letters revealed the bitterness with which he awaited death. He passed in his sleep. Alberto Lamiel added that he was making arrangements to go to Boston, where, thanks to the parents of his North American wife, he had possibilities for work. He told me he had been an imbecile to believe in the promises of Alan García, for whom he voted in the 1985 elections, like so many other gullible professionals. Trusting in the president's word that he wouldn't touch them, Alberto had held on to the certificates in dollars where he kept all his savings. When the new leader decreed the forced conversion of foreign currency certificates into Peruvian soles, Alberto's patrimony vanished. It was only the beginning of a chain of reverses. The best he could do was "to follow your example, Uncle Ricardo, and leave to find better horizons, because in this country it's no longer possible to work if you're not employed by the government."

This was the last news I'd had of things in Peru. Then, since I saw practically no Peruvians in Madrid, I learned what was happening there only on the rare occasion when some report found its way into the Madrid newspapers, usually the birth of quintuplets, an earthquake, or a bus driving over a cliff in the Andes, with approximately thirty deaths.

I never told Uncle Ataúlfo my marriage had failed, and so in his letters, until the end, he would send regards to "my niece," and I, in mine, sent hers to him. I don't know why I hid it from my uncle. Perhaps because I would have to explain what had happened, and any explanation would have seemed absurd and incomprehensible to him, as it did to me.

Our separation occurred in an unexpected and brutal way, just as the bad girl's disappearances had always happened. Though this time it wasn't really a flight but an urbane separation, which we discussed. That was exactly why, unlike the other separations, I knew this one was definitive.

Our honeymoon after I returned to Paris from Lima, terrified she had left me because she hadn't answered the phone for three or four days, lasted a few months. In the beginning she was as affectionate as she had been on the afternoon she greeted me with displays of love. I obtained a monthlong contract at UNESCO, and when I came home she already had returned from her office and prepared supper. One night she waited for me with the living-room light turned off and the table lit by romantic candles. Then she had to make two trips for Martine, a few days each time, to the Côte d'Azur, and she called every night. What more could I desire? I had the impression that the bad girl had reached the age of reason, that our marriage had become unbreakable.

Then, at a moment my memory can't recall specifically, her mood and behavior began to change. It was a subtle change, one she tried to hide, perhaps because she still had doubts, and I became aware of it only after the fact. It didn't surprise me when the passionate attitude of the first few weeks slowly gave way to a more distant attitude because she always had been like that, and the unusual thing for her was to be effusive. I noticed she was distracted and became lost in thoughts that made her frown and seemed to take her beyond my reach. She would come back from these fugue states in alarm and give a start when I returned her to reality with a joke: "What troubles the fair princess with the mouth of berry red? Why is she so pensive? Can the princess be in love?" She would blush and respond with a forced little laugh.

One afternoon, when I returned from Señor Charnés's old office—he had retired to spend his old age in the south of Spain—where for the third or fourth time I was told they had no work for me at the moment, I opened the door to the apartment on Rue Joseph Granier and saw her sitting in the living room with the suitcase she always took on her trips, wearing her brown tailored suit, and I understood something serious was going on. She was ashen.

"What is it?"

She sighed, gathering her strength—she had blue circles under her eyes, which were shining—and without beating around the bush, she came out with the sentence she undoubtedly had prepared well in advance.

"I didn't want to go without talking to you, so you don't think I'm running away." She said it in one breath, in the icy voice she generally used for sentimental statements. "For the sake of what you love most, I beg you not to make a scene or threaten to kill yourself. Both of us are too old for that kind of thing. Forgive me for speaking so harshly, but I think it's for the best."

I dropped into the armchair, facing her. I felt infinitely weary. I had the feeling that I was hearing a record that kept repeating, each time with more distortion, the same musical phrase. She always was very pale, but now her expression was irritated, as if having to sit there giving me explanations filled her with resentment toward me.

"It must be obvious that I've tried to adapt to this kind of life, to please you, to repay you for helping me when I was sick." Her coldness now seemed to be boiling with rage. "I can't stand it anymore. This isn't the life for me. If I stay with you out of compassion, I'll end up hating you. I don't want to hate you. Try to understand, if you can."

She stopped speaking, waiting for me to say something, but I felt so tired I didn't have the energy or desire to tell her anything.

"I'm suffocating here," she added, looking around her. "These two little rooms are a prison and I can't bear them anymore. I know my limit. This routine, this mediocrity, is killing me. I don't want the rest of my life to be like this. You don't care, you're happy, better for you. But I'm not like you, I don't know how to be resigned. I've tried, you've seen that I've tried. I can't. I'm not going to spend the rest of my life with you out of compassion. Forgive me for speaking so frankly. It's better if you know and accept the truth, Ricardo."

"Who is he?" I asked when she fell silent again. "May I at least know who it is you're leaving with?"

"Are you going to make a jealous scene?" was her indignant response. And she reminded me, sarcastically: "I'm a free woman, Ricardito. Our marriage was only to obtain papers for me. So don't demand an accounting from me about anything."

She was challenging me, as enraged as a fighting cock. Now a feeling of being ridiculous was added to my exhaustion. She was right: we were too old for these scenes.

"I see you've decided everything and there's not much to say," I interrupted, getting to my feet. "I'm going to take a walk so you can pack your bags in peace."

"They're packed," she replied in the same exasperated tone.

I was sorry she hadn't gone the way she had other times, leaving me a few scrawled lines. As I walked to the door, I heard her say behind me in a thin voice, trying to be placating, "By the way, I won't ask for any of what I'm entitled to as your wife. Not a cent."

"You're very kind," I thought, closing the apartment door very slowly. "But the only thing you could get from me would be debts and the mortgage on this apartment,

369

which, at the rate we're going, will be foreclosed soon."
When I was outside, it began to rain. I hadn't brought an
umbrella, so I took refuge in the café on the corner,
where I sat a long time, sipping a cup of tea that grew
cold until it was tasteless. The truth was there was something in her impossible not to admire, for the reasons
that lead us to appreciate well-made works even when
they're perverse. She had made a conquest, and done it
with calculation, so she could again achieve the social
and economic status that would give her greater security
and take her out of the two confining little rooms on Rue
Joseph Granier. And now, without blinking, she had
made her move, tossing me into the trash. Who could
her lover be this time? Someone she had met through her
work with Martine, at one of those congresses, conferences, celebrations they organized. A good job of
seduction, no doubt. She looked very good, but after all,
she was over fifty. *Chapeau!* An old man, no doubt,
whom she might kill with pleasure to get his inheritance,
like the heroine in Balzac's *La Rabouilleuse*? When it
cleared, I took a walk around École Militaire, killing
time.

I got back about eleven and she had gone, leaving the
keys in the living room. She took all her clothes in the
two suitcases we had, and tossed into garbage bags what
was old or what she had too much of: slippers, slips, a
housecoat, stockings and blouses, and many jars of
creams and makeup. She hadn't touched the francs we
kept in a small strongbox in a closet in the living room.

Maybe someone she met at the gym on Avenue
Montaigne? It was an expensive place, prosperous old
men went there to reduce their bellies, men who could

guarantee her a more amusing and comfortable life. I knew the worst thing I could do was to keep shuffling through these kinds of hypotheses, and for the sake of my mental health I had to forget about her right away. Because this time the separation was definitive, the end of the love story. Could this farce more than thirty years old be called a love story, Ricardito?

I succeeded in not thinking too much about her in the days, weeks, and months that followed, when, feeling like a bag of soulless bones, skin, and muscles, I spent the whole day looking for work. It was urgent because I needed to confront my debts and daily expenses, and because I knew the best way to get through this period was to give myself over wholeheartedly to an obligation.

For a few months I had only badly paid translations. Finally, one day they called me to be a replacement at an international conference on authors' rights sponsored by UNESCO. For a few days I'd had constant attacks of neuralgia, which I attributed to low spirits and lack of sleep. I fought them with analgesics prescribed by the pharmacist on the corner. My replacing the UNESCO interpreter was a disaster. The attacks of neuralgia kept me from doing my work well, and after two days I had to give up and explain to the head interpreter what was happening to me. The doctor at Social Welfare diagnosed a case of otitis and sent me to a specialist. I had to wait hours at the Hôpital de la Salpêtrière and come back several times before I could enter the consulting room of Dr. Pennau, an ear, nose, and throat specialist. He confirmed I had a slight ear infection and cured me in a week. But when the attacks of neuralgia and dizziness didn't stop, I went to a new internist at the same hospital. After examining me, he had me take all kinds of tests, including an MRI. I have an ugly memory of the thirty or forty minutes I spent inside that metal tube, buried alive, as motionless as a mummy, my ears tormented by waves of stupefying noises.

The MRI established that I had suffered a slight stroke. That was the real reason for the neuralgia and dizziness. Nothing very serious; the danger had passed. From now on I had to take care of myself, exercise, have a balanced diet, control my blood pressure, drink very little alcohol, lead a quiet life. "A retired person's life," the doctor prescribed. My work might be reduced, and I could expect a diminution in concentration and memory.

Fortunately for me, the Gravoskis came to spend a month in Paris, this time with Yilal. He had grown a great deal and was a complete gringo in the way he spoke and dressed. When I told him the bad girl and I had separated, he put on a sorrowful face. "That's why she hasn't answered my letters for so long," he whispered.

The company of these friends was very opportune. Talking to them, joking, going out for supper and to the movies, brought back some of my joy in life. One night, when we were having a beer on the terrace of a *bistrot* on Boulevard Raspail, Elena suddenly said, "That madwoman was about to kill you, Ricardo. And I liked her so much even with all her madness. But this I won't forgive. I forbid you to be friends with her again."

"Never again," I promised. "I've learned my lesson. Besides, since I'm a human wreck now, there's no danger she'll come back into my life."

"So you think the sorrows of love cause cerebral hemorrhages?" said Simon. "Romanticism once again?"

"In this case yes, you heartless Belgian," Elena replied. "Ricardo isn't like you. He's a romantic, a sensitive man. She could have killed him with her last little pleasantry. I'll never forgive her, I swear. And I hope that you, Ricardo, won't be enough of a shithead to follow after like a dog when she calls you to get her out of some new entanglement."

"It's clear you love me more than the bad girl does, my friend." I kissed her hand. "As for the rest, 'shithead' is a word that suits me perfectly."

"We all agree about that," Simon declared.

"What's a shithead?" asked the little gringo.

On the urging of the Gravoskis I went to see a neurosurgeon at a private clinic in Passy. My friends insisted that, no matter how small it had been, a cerebral hemorrhage could have consequences and I ought to know what to expect. Without too much hope, I had asked my bank for another loan so I could face the interest payments on the mortgage and the two earlier loans, and to my surprise, they gave it to me. I put myself in the hands of Dr. Pierre Joudret, a charming man and, as far as I could judge, a competent professional. He subjected me again to all kinds of tests and prescribed a treatment to control my blood pressure and maintain good circulation. This was when I met Marcella one afternoon in his office.

That night, in Nanterre, after the performance of *The Bourgeois Gentleman*, when we went to have a glass of wine at a *bistrot*, the Italian designer seemed very amiable, and the passion and conviction with which she spoke about her work were fascinating. She told me about her life, the arguments and reconciliations with her parents, the stage sets she had designed for small theaters in Spain and Italy. The set in Nanterre was one of the first she had done in France. At a certain moment, among a thousand other things, she assured me that the best theatrical sets she had seen in Paris were not on stages but in the display windows of stores. Would I like to see them with her and lose the skeptical face I had as I listened to her?

We said goodbye at the Métro station with kisses on the cheeks and agreed to see each other the following Saturday. I enjoyed the excursion very much, not only because of the windows she took me to see but because of her explanations and interpretations. She showed me, for example, that the sandy ground and palm trees under white light at La Samaritaine would be marvelous for Beckett's *Oh les beaux jours!*, the canopy of flaming reds at an Arab restaurant in Montparnasse as the backdrop for *Orpheus in Hell*, and the window of a popular shoe-maker's shop near the Church of Saint Paul in Le Marais for Geppetto's house in a dramatic adaptation of *Pinocchio*. Everything she said was ingenious, unexpected, and her enthusiasm and joy kept me amused and happy. During supper at La Petite Périgourdine, a restaurant on Rue des Écoles, I said I liked her, and I kissed her. She confessed that ever since the day we spoke in the waiting room at the clinic in Passy she had known "something happened between us." She told me she had lived for two years with an actor and they recently broke up, though they were still good friends.

We went to the little apartment on Joseph Granier and made love. She had a slim body, with small, delicate breasts, and she was tender, ardent, and uncomplicated.

She examined my books and reprimanded me for having only poetry, novels, some essays, but not a single book on the theater. She would take care of helping me fill that void. "You've come right into my life, *caro*," she added. She had a broad smile that seemed to come not only from her eyes and mouth but also from her forehead, nose, and ears.

Marcella had to go back to Italy a few days later for a possible job in Milan, and I accompanied her to the station because she traveled by train (she was afraid of planes). We spoke several times on the phone, and when she returned to Paris she came to my house instead of going to the little hotel in the Latin Quarter where she had been living. She brought a bag with a few pairs of trousers, some blouses, sweaters, and wrinkled jackets, and a trunk that held books, magazines, figurines, and maquettes of her stage sets.

Marcella's entrance into my life was so rapid that I almost didn't have time to reflect, to ask myself if I wasn't being reckless. Wouldn't it have been more sensible to wait a little, get to know each other better, see if the relationship would work? After all, she was a kid and I could be her father. But the relationship did work, thanks to her way of being so adaptable, so simple in her tastes, so disposed to putting a good face on any setback. I couldn't have said I loved her, in any case not the way I had loved the bad girl, but I felt so good with her, and so grateful she was with me and even loved me. She rejuvenated me and helped me bury my memories.

From time to time Marcella came up with assignments for stage sets in neighborhood theaters subsidized by town councils. Then she would dedicate herself to her work with so much frenzy that she forgot about my existence. I had more and more difficulty obtaining translations. I had given up interpreting, I didn't feel capable of doing the work with my former certainty. Perhaps because word had gotten around the profession about my health problems, I was entrusted with fewer and fewer texts to translate. And those I did get—late, rarely, or never—took me a long time, because after an hour or an hour and a half of work, the dizziness and headaches returned. In the first few months of living with Marcella, my income was reduced to almost nothing, and I found myself very worried again about the mortgage and interest payments on the loans.

The branch manager at the Société Générale, to whom I explained the problem, said the solution was to sell the apartment. It had increased in value, and I could obtain a price that, after paying off the mortgage and the loans, would leave me with a sum that, managed prudently, would allow me to live in comfort for a long time. I talked it over with Marcella, and she also encouraged me to sell. To relieve my mind of the worry about the payments every month that kept me awake. "Don't worry about the future, *caro*. I'll have good commissions soon. If we're left without a cent, we'll go to my parents in Rome. We'll live in the attic where I put on conjuring and magic shows for my friends when I was little, and where I keep all kinds of odds and ends. You'll get on very well with my father, he's almost your age." What a prospect, Ricardito.

Selling the apartment took some time. It was true, its price had tripled, but the prospective buyers brought in by real estate agents found defects, asked for discounts or certain compromises, and matters stretched out for close to three months. Finally, I came to an agreement with a functionary from the Armed Forces Ministry, an elegant gentleman who wore a monocle. Then the tiresome transactions with notaries and lawyers began, as well as the sale of the furniture. On the day we signed the contract and made the transfer of property, as I left the notary's office at a cross street of Avenue de Suffren, a woman stopped short when she saw me and stood staring. I didn't recognize her but greeted her with a nod.

"I'm Martine," she said drily, not offering her hand. "Don't you remember me?"

"I was distracted," I said in apology. "Of course, I remember you very well. How are you doing, Martine?"

"Very badly, how would I be doing?" she replied. Anger soured her face. She didn't take her eyes off me. "But you should know I don't let people trample on me. I know very well how to defend myself. I assure you this matter doesn't end here."

She was a tall, very thin woman with gray hair. She wore a raincoat and scrutinized me as if she wanted to smash my head with the umbrella she was carrying.

"I don't know what you're talking about, Martine. Have you had problems with my wife? We separated some time ago, didn't she tell you?"

She fell silent and stared at me, disconcerted. Her eyes told me she thought I was a very strange beast.

"Then, you don't know anything?" she murmured. "Then, you live in the clouds? Who do you think that hypocrite ran off with? Don't you know it was with my husband?"

I didn't know what to say. I felt stupid, a really strange beast. Making an effort, I mumbled, "No, I didn't know. She only said she was leaving, and she left. I haven't heard from her since. I'm very sorry, Martine."

"I gave her everything, work, friendship, my trust, and I disregarded the question of her papers, which was never very clear. I opened my house to her. And this is how she repaid me, taking my husband from me. Not because she fell in love with him but because of greed. Pure selfishness. She didn't care about destroying an entire family."

I thought that if I didn't get away Martine would slap me, as if I were responsible for her family's misfortune. Her voice cracked with indignation.

"I warn you this doesn't end here," she repeated, shaking the umbrella a few centimeters from my face. "My children won't permit it. She only wants to wring him dry, because that's what she is, a fortune hunter. My children have begun legal action and she'll end up in prison. You'd be better off if you had watched over your wife a little more."

"I'm very sorry, I have to go, this conversation makes no sense," I said, moving away with long strides.

Instead of going back to pick up Marcella, who was putting into storage the household goods we hadn't sold, I went to sit in a café in École Militaire. I tried to put my mind in order. My blood pressure must have risen because I felt flushed and dazed. I didn't know Martine's husband but I had met one of her children, an adult whom I had seen in passing just one time. The bad girl's new conquest must be an old man, then, a doddering old man, I imagined. Of course she hadn't fallen in love with

378

him. She never had fallen in love with anybody except, perhaps, Fukuda. She had done it to escape the boredom and mediocrity of life in the little apartment in École Militaire, searching for the thing that had been her first priority ever since she was a little girl and discovered that the poor had a dog's life but the rich lived very well: the security only money could guarantee. Once again she had deceived herself with the mirage of a rich man; after hearing Martine say, in the accent of Greek tragedy, "My children have begun legal action," it was certain that this time too, things wouldn't go as she wished. I harbored rancor toward her but now, imagining her with that ridiculous old man, I felt a certain compassion too.

I found Marcella exhausted. She already had sent a small truck with what we couldn't sell, along with some cartons of books, to storage. Sitting on the floor of the living room, I examined the walls and empty space with nostalgia. We went to a little hotel on Rue du Cherche-Midi and lived there for a number of months until we left for Spain. We had a small, bright room, with a fairly large window overlooking the nearby roofs; pigeons came to the sill to eat the kernels of corn Marcella put there for them (it was my job to clean off the droppings). The room soon filled with books, records, and especially Marcella's drawings and maquettes. It had a long table that we shared, in theory, but in reality Marcella took up most of it. That year it was even more difficult for me to find translations, so the sale of the apartment turned out to be very advantageous. I put the remaining money into a fixed-term account, and the small monthly sum it paid required us to live very frugally. We had to cut out expensive restaurants, concerts, going to the movies more than once a week, and plays, except when Marcella obtained free tickets. But it was a relief to live without debts.

The idea of moving to Spain was born after an Italian modern dance company from Bari, with whom Marcella had worked previously, was invited to perform at a festival in Granada and asked her to be in charge of the lighting and sets. She traveled there with them and came back two weeks later, delighted. The performance had gone very well, she met theater people, and some possibilities had opened for her. In the months that followed she designed sets for two young companies, one in Madrid and the other in Barcelona, and after each trip she returned to Paris euphoric. She said there was an extraordinary cultural vitality in Spain, and the entire country was filled with festivals and directors, actors, dancers, and musicians yearning to make Spanish society current and to do new things. There was more space there for young people than in France, where the environment was supersaturated. Besides, in Madrid you could live much more cheaply than in Paris.

I wasn't sorry to leave the city that, ever since I was a boy, I had associated with the idea of paradise. During the years I spent in Paris I'd had marvelous experiences, the kind that seem to justify an entire life, but all of them were connected to the bad girl, who by then, I think, I remembered without bitterness, without hatred, even with a certain tenderness, knowing very well that my sentimental misfortunes were due more to me than to her, because I had loved her in a way she never could have reciprocated, though on some few occasions she had tried: these were my most glorious memories of

Paris. Now that the story was definitively over, my future life in this city would be a gradual decline exacerbated by not having work, an old age filled with austerities, and a very solitary one when *cara* Marcella realized she had better things to do than carry the burden of an old man whose head was weak and who could become senile—a polite way of saying imbecilic—if he had another stroke. Better for me to go and start over again somewhere else.

Marcella found the apartment in Lavapiés, and since it was rented furnished, I gave away to charitable organizations the rest of the furniture we had in storage as well as the books in my library. I took to Madrid only a handful of favorite titles, almost all of them Russian and French, and my grammar books and dictionaries.

After a year and a half of living in Madrid, I had a hunch that this time Marcella was going to make the great leap. One afternoon she burst into the Café Barbieri, very excited, to tell me she had met a fabulous dancer and choreographer and they were going to work together on a fantastic project: *Metamorphosis*, a modern ballet inspired by one of the texts gathered by Borges in his *Book of Imaginary Beings*: "The A Bao A Qu," a legend collected by one of the English translators of *The Thousand and One Nights*. The boy was from Alicante and trained in Germany, where he had worked professionally until very recently. He had formed a group of ten dancers, five women and five men, and created the choreography for *Metamorphosis*. The story in question, translated and perhaps enriched by Borges, told of a marvelous little animal that lived at the top of a tower in a state of lethargy and awoke to active life only when someone climbed the stairs. Endowed with the ability to alter shape, when someone walked up or down the stairs the little animal began to move, to light up, to change form and color. Víctor Almeda, the boy from Alicante, had conceived of a performance in which the dancers, emulating that marvel while going up and down the magic stairs Marcella would design, and thanks to the lighting effects she was also responsible for, would change their personalities, movements, expressions, until the stage was transformed into a small universe where each dancer would be many, each man and woman containing countless human beings. La Sala Olimpia, an old movie house converted into a theater on Plaza de Lavapiés, where the National Center for New Trends in Stagecraft was located, had accepted Víctor Almeda's proposal and would sponsor the performance.

I never saw Marcella work on a set as happily as on this one, or make so many sketches and maquettes. Each day she would recount with delight the torrent of ideas flooding her head and the progress the company was making. A few times I went with her to the ramshackle Olimpia, and one afternoon we had coffee on the plaza with Víctor Almeda, a very dark boy with long hair he wore pulled back in a ponytail, and an athletic body that revealed many hours of exercise and rehearsals. Unlike Marcella, he wasn't exuberant or extroverted but rather reserved, though he knew very well what he wanted to do in life. And what he wanted was for *Metamorphosis* to be a success. He was well read and passionate about Borges. For this show he had read and looked at more than a thousand items on the subject of metamorphosis, beginning with Ovid, and the truth is that although he spoke very little, what he said was intelligent and, for me, novel: I never had listened to a choreographer and dancer talk about his vocation. That night, at home, after telling Marcella of the good impression Víctor Almeda had made on me, I asked if he was gay. She was indignant. He wasn't. What a stupid prejudice to think all male dancers were gay. She was sure, for example, that in the professional association of interpreters and translators there was the same percentage of gays as among dancers. I apologized and assured her I didn't have any prejudices, that my question had been asked purely out of curiosity, with no hidden agenda.

The success of *Metamorphosis* was total and fully deserved. Víctor Almeda arranged a good deal of advance publicity, and on the night of the opening, the Olimpia was full to bursting; there were even people standing, and most of them were young. The stairs on which the five couples evolved metamorphosed just like the dancers, and, with the lights, were the real protagonists of the performance. There was no music. The rhythm was kept by the dancers themselves with their hands and feet, and by the sharp, guttural, hoarse, or sibilant sounds they made as their identities changed. The dancers took turns placing filters in front of the reflectors, which changed the intensity and color of the light and made the performers actually seem to become iridescent, to alter their skin. It was beautiful, surprising, imaginative, an hour-long performance during which the audience remained motionless, expectant, so still you could hear a pin drop. The troupe was supposed to give five performances and ended up giving ten. There were very positive articles in the press, and in all of them

Marcella's set design was praised. It was filmed for television, to be used as a segment of a program dedicated to the arts.

I went to see the piece three times. The house was always packed and the audience as enthusiastic as it had been the day it opened. The third time, when the performance was over and I was climbing the Olimpia's narrow, winding staircase to the dressing rooms to find Marcella, I almost ran into her in the arms of the good-looking, perspiring Víctor Almeda. They were kissing with a certain frenzy, and when they heard me approach they pulled apart in great embarrassment. I pretended not to have noticed anything strange and congratulated them, saying I had liked this performance even more than the two previous ones.

Later, on the way home, Marcella, who had been very uncomfortable, confronted me.

"Well, I suppose I owe you an explanation for what you saw."

"You don't owe me anything, Marcella. You're free and so am I. We live together and get along very well. But that shouldn't infringe in any way on our freedom. Let's not talk about it anymore."

"I only want you to know I'm very sorry," she said. "Even though appearances say something different, I assure you absolutely nothing has happened between Víctor and me. Tonight was just something stupid, without importance. And it won't happen again."

"I believe you," I said, taking her hand because it made me sad to see how awful she felt. "Let's forget it. And don't look like that, please. You're especially pretty when you smile."

And in fact, in the days that followed, we didn't speak about it again, and she made a great effort to be affectionate toward me. The truth is, it didn't disturb me very much to know that a romance had probably sprung up between Marcella and the choreographer from Alicante. I never had any great illusions about how long our relationship would last. And now I also knew that my love for her, if it was love, was a fairly superficial feeling. I didn't feel hurt or humiliated, only curious to know when I would have to move and live alone again. And from then on I began asking myself if I would stay in Madrid or go back to Paris. Two or three weeks later, Marcella announced that Víctor Almeda had been invited to present *Metamorphosis* in Frankfurt, at a modern dance festival. It was an important opportunity for her to have her work better known in Germany. What did I think?

"Magnificent," I told her. "I'm sure *Metamorphosis* will be as successful there as it has been in Madrid."

"Of course you'll come with me," she said quickly. "You can translate there and . . ."

But I caressed her and told her not to be silly and not to look so distressed. I wouldn't go to Germany, we didn't have the money for that. I'd stay in Madrid working on my translation. I had confidence in her. She ought to prepare for her trip and forget everything else, because it could be decisive for her career. She shed some tears when she embraced me and said into my ear, "I swear that stupidity won't ever be repeated, *caro*."

"Of course, of course, *bambina*," and I kissed her.

On the day Marcella left for Frankfurt by train—I went to see her off at Atocha Station—Víctor Almeda, who was to leave two days later by plane with the rest of the company, knocked on the door of the apartment on Calle Ave María. He looked very serious, as if he were consumed by profound questions. I assumed he had come to give me some explanation of the episode at the Olimpia, and I suggested we have coffee at the Barbieri.

In reality, he had come to tell me he and Marcella were in love and he considered it his moral obligation to let me know. Marcella didn't want to make me suffer and for that reason sacrificed herself by staying with me even though she loved him. The sacrifice, in addition to making her miserable, was going to damage her career.

I thanked him for his candor and asked if, by telling me all this, he hoped I would resolve the problem for them.

"Well"—he hesitated for a moment—"in a way, yes. If you don't take the initiative, she never will."

"And why would I take the initiative and break up with a girl I'm so fond of?"

"Out of generosity and altruism," he said immediately, with a solemnity so theatrical it made me want to laugh. "Because you're a gentleman. And because now you know she loves me."

At that moment I realized the choreographer had begun to use formal address with me. On previous occasions we always had used *tú* with each other. Was he trying in this way to remind me I was twenty years older than Marcella?

"You're not being frank with me, Víctor," I said. "Tell me all the truth. Did you and Marcella plan this visit of yours? Did she ask you to talk to me because she didn't have the courage?"

I saw him shift in his chair and shake his head no. But when he opened his mouth, he said yes.

"The two of us made the decision," he admitted. "She doesn't want you to suffer. She feels all kinds of remorse. But I convinced her that her first loyalty isn't to other people but to her own feelings."

I was about to tell him that what I had just heard was a cheap, sentimental thing, and explain the Peruvianism, but I didn't because I was sick of him and wanted him to go. And so I asked him to leave me alone to reflect on everything he had said. I'd make my decision soon. I wished him much success in Frankfurt and shook his hand. In reality I already had decided to leave Marcella with her dancer and return to Paris. Then, what had to happen happened.

Two days later, as I was working in the afternoon in my favorite spot at the back of the Café Barbieri, an elegant female form suddenly sat down at the table, facing me.

"I won't ask if you're still in love with me because I already know you're not," said the bad girl. "Cradle snatcher."

My surprise was so enormous that I somehow knocked the half-full bottle of mineral water to the floor, and it broke and spattered a boy with spiked hair and tattoos at the next table. While the Andalusian waitress hurried to pick up the pieces of glass, I examined the lady who, after three years, had abruptly been resurrected in the most unpredictable way at the most unexpected time and place in the world: the Café Barbieri in Lavapiés.

Though it was late May and warm, she wore a light

387

blue mid-weight jacket over an open white blouse, and a fine gold chain encircled her neck. The careful makeup couldn't hide her drawn face, the prominent cheekbones, the small bags under her eyes. Only three years had passed, but ten had fallen on her. She was old. While the Andalusian waitress cleaned the floor, she drummed on the table with one hand, the nails carefully tended and polished, as if she had just come from the manicurist. Her fingers seemed longer and thinner. She looked at me without blinking, without humor, and—absolutely the final straw!—she called me to account for my bad behavior:

"I never would have believed you'd live with a kid still wet behind the ears who could be your daughter," she repeated indignantly. "And a hippie besides, who surely never bathes. How low you've fallen, Ricardo Somocurcio."

I wanted to throttle her and laugh out loud. No, it wasn't a joke: she was making a jealous scene over me! She, over me!

"You're fifty-three or fifty-four now, aren't you?" she went on, still drumming on the table. "And how old is this Lolita? Twenty?"

"Thirty-three," I said. "She looks younger, it's true. Because she's a happy girl, and happiness makes people young. But you don't look very happy."

"Does she ever bathe?" she asked in exasperation. "Or has old age given you a taste for that, for dirt?"

"I learned from Yakuza Fukuda," I said. "I discovered that filth also has its charm in bed."

"In case you're interested, at this moment I hate you with all my heart and wish you were dead," she said in a muffled voice. She hadn't taken her eyes off me or blinked once.

"Someone who didn't know you might say you're jealous."

"In case you're interested, I am. But above all, I'm disappointed in you."

I grasped her hand and forced her to move a little closer to ask her, out of earshot of our spike-haired, tattooed neighbor: "What's the meaning of this farce? What are you doing here?"

She dug her nails into my hand before answering me. And lowered her voice, too.

"You don't know how sorry I am that I looked for you all this time. But now I know this hippie will make you suffer the torments of the damned, she'll put horns on you and throw you away like a dirty rag. And you don't know how happy that makes me."

"I have the perfect training for it, bad girl. In matters of horns and being abandoned, I know all there is to know and even a little more."

I released her hand, but as I did, she grasped mine again.

"I swore to myself I wouldn't say anything to you about the hippie," she said, softening her voice and expression. "But when I saw you, I couldn't control myself. I still feel like scratching you. Be a little more gallant and order me a cup of tea."

I called over the Andalusian waitress and tried to let go of the bad girl's hand, but she still clutched at mine.

"Do you love this disgusting hippie?" she asked. "Do you love her more than you loved me?"

"I don't think I ever loved you," I assured her. "You're for me what Fukuda was for you: a sickness. Now I'm cured, thanks to Marcella."

She scrutinized me for a while and, without releasing my hand, smiled ironically for the first time and said, "If you didn't love me you wouldn't have turned so pale and your voice wouldn't be breaking. Aren't you going to cry, Ricardito? Because you're something of a weeper, if I remember correctly."

"I promise you I won't. You have the damn habit of turning up suddenly, like a nightmare, at the most unexpected times. It doesn't amuse me anymore. The truth is, I never expected to see you again. What is it you want? What are you doing in Madrid?"

When they brought the cup of tea, I could examine her a little as she put in a lump of sugar, stirred the liquid, and examined the spoon, saucer, and cup, turning up her nose. She wore a white skirt and open white shoes that exposed her small feet, the toenails paintedwith transparent polish. Once again her ankles were two stalks of bamboo. Had she been sick? Only during the time of the clinic in Petit Clamart had I seen her so thin. She wore her hair pulled back on each side and held by clips at her ears, which, as always, looked elegant. It occurred to me that without the rinse to which it probably owed its black color, her hair must be gray by now, perhaps white, like mine.

"Everything looks dirty here," she said abruptly, looking around and exaggerating her expression of disgust. "The people, the place, cobwebs and dust everywhere. Even you look dirty."

"This morning I showered and soaped myself from top to bottom, word of honor."

"But you're dressed like a beggar," she said, grasping my hand again.

"And you, like a queen," I said. "Aren't you afraid they'll mug you and rob you in a place like this filled with starving people?"

"At this new stage in my life, I'm prepared to risk any danger for you," she said with a laugh. "Besides, you're a gentleman, you'd defend me to the death, wouldn't you? Or did you stop being a little Miraflores gentleman when you got together with the hippies?"

Her rage of a moment ago had passed and now, pressing my hand firmly, she was laughing. In her eyes was a distant reminiscence of that dark honey, a little gleam that lit her thin, aged face.

"How did you find me?"

"It was very hard. It took months. A thousand inquiries, everywhere. And a lot of money. I was scared to death, I even thought you had committed suicide. This time for real."

"That kind of absurdity you attempt only once, when love for some woman has made you feebleminded. Happily, that doesn't apply to me anymore."

"Trying to find you, I fought with the Gravoskis," she said suddenly, getting angry again. "Elena treated me very badly. She refused to give me your address or tell me anything about you. And she began to lecture me. That I made you miserable, that I almost killed you, that it was my fault you had a stroke, that I've been the tragedy of your life."

"Elena said the absolute truth. You have been the misfortune of my life."

"I told her to go to hell. I don't intend to speak to her or see her ever again. I'm sorry on account of Yilal, because I don't think I'll see him again either. Who did that idiot think she was to lecture me? I think she's in love with you herself."

She shifted in her chair, and I thought she suddenly turned pale.

"May I ask why you were looking for me?"

"I wanted to see you and talk to you," she said, smiling again. "I missed you. And you missed me too, just a little?"

"You always turn up and look for me between lovers," I said, trying to pull my hand away from hers. This time I succeeded. "Did Martine's husband throw you out? Did you come for an interlude in my arms until you catch another old man in your nets?"

"Not anymore," she interrupted, grasping my hand again and adopting her old, mocking tone. "I've decided to put an end to my madness. I'm going to spend my final years with my husband. And be a model wife."

I started to laugh and she laughed too. She scratched my hand with her fingers and I felt more and more like tearing her eyes out.

"You, you have a husband? May I ask who he is?"

"I'm still your wife and I can prove it, I have the certificate," she said, becoming serious. "You're my husband. Don't you remember we got married in the *mairie* of the fifth arrondissement?"

"It was a farce, to get you papers," I reminded her. "You've never really been my wife. You've been with me for periods of time, when you had problems, for as long as you couldn't get anything better. Are you going to tell me why you were looking for me? This time, if you're having problems, I couldn't help you even if I wanted to. But I don't want to. I don't have a cent and I'm living with a girl whom I love and who loves me."

"A grimy hippie who'll leave you just like that," she said, getting angry again. "Who doesn't care about you at all, judging by the way you walk around. But from now on, I'll take care of you. I'll worry about you twenty-four hours a day. Like a model wife. That's why I've come, and now you know."

She spoke with the old mocking expression, the ironic gleam in her eyes disproving the words she was saying to me. From time to time, she took a sip of tea. Her stupid little game succeeded in irritating me.

"Do you know something, bad girl?" I said, drawing her a little closer so I could speak to her in a very quiet voice, with all my accumulated rage. "Do you remember that night in the apartment, when I almost wrung your neck? I've regretted not doing it a thousand times."

"I still have the Arab dancer's costume," she whispered, with all the roguishness left in her. "I remember that night very well. You hit me and then we made delicious love. You told me some very pretty things. Today you haven't told me a single one. I'm ready to believe that it's true you don't love me anymore."

I wanted to slap her, kick her all the way out of the Café Barbieri, do all the physical and moral harm to her one human being can do to another, and at the same time, great imbecile that I am, I wanted to take her in my arms, ask her why she was so thin and worn, and caress and kiss her. My hair stood on end as I imagined she could read my thoughts.

"If you want me to admit I've behaved badly with you and been egotistical, I admit it," she whispered, bringing her face close to mine, but I moved back. "If you want me to spend the rest of my life telling you that Elena's right, that I've done you harm and haven't valued your love, and all that other nonsense, all right, I will. Is that what you want to stop being angry, Ricardito?"

"I want you to leave. Once and for all, forever and ever, to disappear from my life."

"Well, well, something cheap and sentimental. It was time, good boy."

"I don't believe a word you say. I know very well you looked for me because you thought I could help you out of one of your entanglements now that the poor old man has thrown you out."

"He didn't throw me out, I threw him out," she corrected me, very calmly. "Or rather, I turned him over safe and sound to his dear children, who missed their daddy so much. You should be grateful to me, good boy. If you knew the headaches and money I saved you by going away with him, you'd kiss my hands. You don't know how expensive this adventure has been for the poor man."

She gave a piercing, mocking little laugh, as wicked as it could be.

"They accused me of abducting him," she added, as if enjoying a good joke. "They presented false medical certificates to the judge, claiming their father had senile dementia and didn't know what he was doing when he ran off with me. The truth is, it wasn't worth wasting time fighting for him. I was delighted to give him back.

Let them and Martine wipe away his snot and take his blood pressure twice a day."

"You're the most perverse person I've ever known, bad girl. A monster of egotism and insensitivity. Capable of knifing with absolute coldness the people who have been kindest to you."

"Well, yes, maybe that's true," she agreed. "I've been stabbed a lot in my life too, I assure you. I don't regret anything I've done. Well, except having made you suffer. I've decided to change. That's why I'm here."

She sat looking at me with a hypocritical expression that I found even more irritating.

"Whoever doesn't know you can buy that. Do you actually think I'm going to take this repentant wife number seriously? You, bad girl?"

"Yes, me. I came looking for you because I love you. Because I need you. Because I can't live with anybody except you. Though you may think it's a little late, I know this now. That's why, from now on, even though I die of hunger and have to live like a hippie, I'm going to live with you. And no one else. Would you like me to become a hippie and stop bathing? Dress like a scarecrow, like the one you're with now? Whatever you want."

She had a coughing fit and her eyes reddened because of the spasm. She drank from my glass of water.

"Do you mind if we leave here?" she said, coughing again. "With this smoke and dust I can't breathe. Everybody smokes in Spain. It's one of the things I dislike about this country. Wherever you go, people are blowing mouthfuls of smoke at you."

I asked for the check, paid it, and we left. When we were on the street and I saw her in the light of day, I was shocked at how thin she was. When she was sitting down, I had noticed only how thin her face was. But now, when she was standing, and there were no shadows, she looked like a human ruin. Her body had bent slightly and her walk was uncertain, as if she were avoiding obstacles. Her breasts seemed to have shrunk until they almost had disappeared, and the bones in her shoulders jutted out sharply beneath her blouse. In addition to her handbag, she carried a bulging briefcase.

"If you think I've become very skinny, very ugly, and very old, please don't tell me. Where can we go?"

"Nowhere. Here, in Lavapiés, all the cafés are as old and dusty as this one. And all of them are full of smokers. So we'd better say goodbye here."

"I need to talk to you. It won't take very long, I promise."

She was holding my arm and her fingers, so thin, so bony, seemed like those of a little girl.

"Do you want to go to my house?" I said, regretting it the very moment I made the suggestion. "I live close by. But I warn you, it'll disgust you more than this café."

"Let's go wherever," she said. "But if that foul-smelling hippie shows up, I'll scratch her eyes out."

"She's in Germany, don't worry."

Going up the four flights was long and complicated. She climbed the stairs very slowly and stopped to rest at each landing. She never let go of my arm. When we reached the top floor, she had turned even paler and her forehead glittered with perspiration.

As soon as we walked in the apartment, she dropped onto the little armchair in the living room and took deep breaths. Then, without saying a word or getting up from the spot, she began to examine everything around her, her eyes very serious and her brows and forehead wrinkled in a frown: Marcella's models and drawings and rags scattered everywhere, magazines and books piled up in the corners and on the shelves, the general disorder. When she came to the unmade bed, I saw her face change suddenly. I went to the kitchen to bring her a bottle of mineral water. I found her in the same place, staring at the bed.

"You had a mania for order and cleanliness, Ricardito," she murmured. "I find it incredible that you live in such a pigsty."

I sat down beside her and was assailed by a great sadness. What she said was true. My apartment in École Militaire, small and modest, had always been impeccably clean and orderly. But this brothel reflected very clearly your irreversible decline, Ricardito.

"I need you to sign some papers," the bad girl said, pointing at the briefcase she had set on the floor.

"The only paper I'd sign for you would be the one for our divorce, if this marriage is still valid," I replied. "Knowing you, I wouldn't be surprised if you had me sign something fraudulent and I ended up in jail. I've known you for forty years, Chilean girl."

"You don't know me very well," she said serenely. "Maybe I could do some bad things to other people. But not to you."

"You've done the worst things to me that a woman can do to a man. You made me believe you loved me while you calmly seduced other men because they had more money, and you left me with no pangs of conscience. You haven't done it once but twice, three times.

397

Leaving me destroyed, confused, without the heart for anything. And then you still have the effrontery to tell me one more time, with the most brazen face, that you want us to live together again. The truth is, you ought to be on display in a circus."

"I'm sorry. I won't play any bad tricks on you again."

"You won't have the chance, because I'll never live with you again. Nobody's loved you like I have, nobody's done all that I . . . Well, I feel stupid saying this nonsense to you. What is it you want from me?"

"Two things," she said. "Leave the dirty hippie and come live with me. And sign these papers. There's no trick. I've transferred everything I have to you. A little house in the south of France, near Sète, and stocks in Electricity of France. Everything's been put in your name. But you have to sign these papers for the transfer to be valid. Read them, consult a lawyer. I'm not doing it for me but for you. I want to leave you everything I have."

"Thank you very much, but I can't accept this very generous gift from you. Because that little house and those stocks were probably stolen from mafiosi and I have no desire to be a dummy for you or the gangster of the day you're working for. Can it be the famous Fukuda again, I hope?"

Then, before I could stop her, she threw her arms around my neck and held on to me with all her strength.

"Stop scolding and saying bad things to me," she complained as she kissed me on the neck. "Tell me instead you're happy to see me. Tell me you missed me, that you love me and not the hippie you live with in this barnyard."

I didn't dare move her away, terrified of feeling the skeleton her body had become, a waist, back, arms in which all the muscles seemed to have disappeared, leaving only bones and skin. The frail, delicate person pressed against me gave off a fragrance that made me think of a garden filled with flowers. I couldn't pretend anymore.

"Why are you so thin?" I asked in her ear.

"Tell me first you love me. That you don't love this hippie, that you began to live with her only out of spite, because I left you. Since I found out you were with her, I've been dying slowly of jealousy."

Now I felt her little heart beating against mine. I searched for her mouth and gave her a long kiss. I felt her tongue entwined with mine, and I swallowed her saliva. When I slipped my hand under her blouse and caressed her back, I felt all her ribs and her spine as if they weren't separated from my fingers by even the slightest film of flesh. She had no breasts; her diminutive nipples were flat against her skin.

"Why are you so thin?" I asked again. "Have you been sick? What did you have?"

"I can't make love to you, don't touch me there. They operated on me, they took out everything. I don't want you to see me naked. My body's covered with scars. I don't want you to be disgusted by me."

She cried in despair and I couldn't calm her. Then I sat her on my knees and caressed her for a long time, the way I did in Paris when she had her attacks of fear. Her bottom too had melted away, and her thighs were as thin as her arms. She looked like one of those living corpses shown in photographs of concentration camps. I caressed her, kissed her, told her I loved her and would take care of her, and, at the same time, I felt an indescribable horror because I was absolutely certain she hadn't *been* gravely ill but was gravely ill now and would die soon. No one could be so thin and recover.

"You still haven't told me you love me more than the hippie, good boy."

"Of course I love you more than her and more than anybody, bad girl. You're the only woman in the world I ever loved, the only one I love now. And though you've done bad things to me, you've also given me wonderful happiness. Come, I want to have you naked in my arms and make love to you."

I carried her to the bed, lay her down, and undressed her. With her eyes closed, she let herself be undressed, turning to the side, showing me as little of her body as possible. But, caressing and kissing her, I made her straighten and open out. They hadn't operated on her, they had destroyed her. Her breasts had been removed and the nipples crudely replaced, leaving thick, circular scars like two red corollas. But the worst scar started at her vagina and meandered up to her navel, a crust between brown and pink that seemed recent. The impact it had on me was so huge that, without realizing what I was doing, I covered it with the sheet. And I knew I'd never be able to make love to her again.

"I didn't want you to see me like this and feel repelled by your wife," she said. "But—"

"But I love you and now I'll take care of you until you're completely healed. Why didn't you call me so I could be with you?"

"I couldn't find you anywhere. I've been looking for

you for months. It's what made me most desperate: dying without seeing you again."

They had operated on her the second time barely three weeks ago, in a hospital in Montpellier. The doctors had been very frank. The tumor in her vagina had been detected too late, and though they removed it, the postoperative examination indicated that metastasis had begun, and there was almost nothing they could do. Chemotherapy would only delay the inevitable, and in her extremely weakened condition, she probably wouldn't survive it. The operation on her breasts took place a year earlier, in Marseille. Because of her extreme weakness they hadn't been able to operate again to reconstruct her bosom. She and Martine's husband, when they ran away, had lived on the Mediterranean coast, in Frontignan, near Sète, where he owned property. He had behaved very well with her when they found the cancer. He had been generous and attentive, showering her with attentions, not letting her see, when they removed her breasts, the disappointment he felt. On the contrary, it was she who gradually convinced him that since her fate was decided, the best thing he could do was reconcile with Martine and end the lawsuit with his children, from which only the lawyers would benefit. The gentleman returned to his family, saying goodbye to the bad girl with generosity: he bought her the house in Sète that she now wanted to transfer to me, and in her name deposited in the bank the Electricity of France stocks that would allow her to live without financial worries for the rest of what remained to her of life. She had begun looking for me at least a year ago and finally found me in Madrid, thanks to a detective agency that "charged me an arm and a leg." When they gave her my address, she was having tests at the hospital in Montpellier. She'd had pains in her vagina since the days of Fukuda and hadn't paid much attention to them.

She told me all this in a long conversation that lasted the entire afternoon and a good part of the night, while we lay in bed, pressed together. She had dressed again. At times she stopped talking so I could kiss her and tell her I loved her. She told me the story—true? very embellished? totally false?—without dramatics, with apparent objectivity, without self-pity, but with relief, and happily, as if after telling it to me she could die in peace.

She lasted another thirty-seven days, during which time she behaved, just as she promised she would in the Café Barbieri, like a model wife. At least, when the terrible pain didn't keep her in bed, sedated with morphine. I went to live with her in an apartment hotel on Los Jerónimos, where she was staying, taking with me one suitcase with a few articles of clothing and some books, and I left Marcella a very hypocritical and dignified letter, telling her I had decided to leave, giving her back her freedom, because I didn't want to be an obstacle to a happiness that—I understood this very well—I couldn't offer her, given the difference in our ages and vocations, but only a young man of her own age, with a disposition akin to hers, like Víctor Almeda, could. After three days the bad girl and I took the train to her little house on the outskirts of Sète, at the top of a hill, from which you could see the beautiful sea sung about by Valéry in *Le Cimetière marin*. It was a small house, austere, pretty, nicely arranged, with a small garden. For two weeks she felt so well, so happy, that contrary to all reason I thought she might recover. One afternoon, when we were sitting in the garden at twilight, she said that if it ever occurred to me one day to write our love story, I shouldn't make her look too bad, because then her ghost would come and pull on my feet every night.

"And what made you think of that?"

"Because you always wanted to be a writer and didn't have the courage. Now that you'll be all alone, you can make good use of the time, and you won't miss me so much. At least admit I've given you the subject for a novel. Haven't I, good boy?"